W9-AHV-209

DATE DUE

FEB 2 8 1992			
MAR 1 4 1992			
MAR 2 1 1992			
APR 4 1992			
APR 1 8 1992			
MAY 2 1992			
MAY 9 1992			
MAY 16 1992			
JUN 1 3 1992			
MAY 1 5 1996			
OCT 3 2001			
AUG 5 2015			

DEMCO

A TOWN CALLED
JERICHO

A TOWN CALLED
JERICHO

A NOVEL BY

JOEL STONE

DONALD I. FINE, INC.
NEW YORK

Library of Congress Cataloging-in-Publication Data

Stone, Joel, 1931–
  A town called Jericho / by Joel Stone.
    p.   cm.
  ISBN 1-55611-319-6
  I. Title.
PS3569.T641295T6   1992   91-55192
813'.54—dc20   CIP

Manufactured in the United States of America

10 9 8 7 6 5 4 3 2 1

Designed by Irving Perkins Associates

*This book
is for Dorothy
whose faith and
talents of every description
permeate its pages*

PART ONE

CHAPTER 1

MOUNT RUSHMORE was the ultimate fantasy, the dewy mist of his imagination lifting to unveil a fifth bold mountain face—George Robinson.

The charm of the dream was the nowhere of the place, Dakota hills, Dakota hills all around. Against that big All-American sky, the stonefaced four seemed as ancient as the Sphinx, except the one with the eyeglasses, Teddy Roosevelt—Harvard on horseback—now, there was a political animal. TR, his cousin FDR, where the lion met the fox. Could there be a drop of Roosevelt in the Robinson blood? If he was the type of man to have a hero, it would be FDR, inventor of the braintrust—he breathed politics and lived life at the jaunty angle of his cigarette-holder. The Big Three at Yalta, Roosevelt with Churchill and Stalin, Babyface with a clenched cigar and Steely Joe and his amiable pipe. The twentieth century's drumroll of names, men who led nations and transformed the world. Gandhi, holy and wily, small and spindly, going around like a spider in diapers. Mao, the poet, his epic was Red China—with the stroke of a chopstick he abolished China's pianos. Hitler, the Führer, whose crazy signature like his Reich went straight up and down. And then there was Mussolini, poor pasta-faced Il Duce, who made his trains run on time but envied Hitler his people.

Politics and people. Wasn't that the reason, aspiration aside,

3

why he was finally making this race? People and politics, consent of the governed, the art of the possible, the hand and the glove. More politics, but less government, wasn't that the ideal? Think of politics breaking out all over the place, like happy little homesteads. It had a Jeffersonian ring to it: more politics, less government. It was an elusive idea. It was the type of concept you had to hold up to the light and focus slowly to appreciate. Rainey still couldn't grasp it, possibly because she lacked the interest. No matter; she would understand it all in due time. Besides— was he a practicing political animal or a philosopher?

Armstead was no pushover; far from it. He was a real force, if by accident. He kept getting reelected, usually unopposed, year after year, like a very small number that kept on being multiplied by itself, a mediocrity raised to the ninth or tenth power. But a power he had become: Robinson had no rosy illusions. If Armstead had been a pushover, they would have fed the nomination to a party hack or a crony of the state chairman, who was himself a hack and a crony of the governor, more or less, as one reckoned these things. So the nomination was hanging in the air and he grabbed at the chance, as at the flashing tail-light of his star. And the state committee had just called with its blessing—doubly important, he sensed, because it meant he would have the support of the governor in the race, a political ace of spades, possibly at his side; it was common knowledge, not to say common sense, that there was all sorts of bad blood between the governor and the obstreperous Dwayne Armstead. It was an uphill battle but Armstead could be beaten. Youth could do it, a fresh face, challenging ideas, the new generation rising. Brains would be an important factor in his favor, for those who noticed. Armstead reminded him of all those other politicians who described their constituents as the silent majority. A good description. The silent majority was the dead.

And why wouldn't he be a winner in the political game? He had good instincts, he grasped the system, had a way with people, a feel for power, could relish Machiavelli's *The Prince* while accepting its practical limits in American electoral life. He had political roots. Being mayor, of which he had grown frankly contemptuous, was still a significant plus. Almost a quarter of the electorate lived within his home base. Armstead would worry about that. All politics is local, went the maxim, and it was true. People voted their paychecks, their kids, their front porches and backyards. Politicians were no different. They all started from home. The great Senator So-and-so would recount how awed he was when he first went to Washington, and why? Because he shook hands with the famous Senator Such-and-such—who in his time was starstruck meeting some other celebrated man. All politics was local politics and all boys were local boys.

He was getting so excited that if Mrs. Prain was in the office this afternoon he would put his coat on and go home right now. But why not go anyway? Who could call him now who mattered? It was a lucky thing the phone hadn't rung before this and he got stuck with some tawdry lawsuit or one of his lonesome widows calling to gab about her estate. He got up, leaving his desk just as it was. He could be with Rainey the rest of the afternoon. If by a miracle the kids were elsewhere, maybe they could even sneak into bed. It was possible, though he wasn't hopeful. He would be happy with a log on the fire and cocktails on the sofa, Mr. and Mrs. George Robinson celebrating the future.

Throwing on his overcoat, he departed his law office, locking the door of the small one-story redstone building, and stepped onto Legion Avenue, main thoroughfare of Jericho. High snow-banks lay along the curbs, clogging the streetcorners, but he liked to walk. You never saw anyone else walking. They all drove. But he enjoyed the funny old avenue, the never-changing store win-dows, the hastily thrown up hundred-year-old storefront walls. His appetites thrived on the bright dry-ice air that seemed to keep New Year's day sparkling fresh all the rest of the winter. He felt glorious today. The flag flying in front of the Jericho City Hall looked redder, whiter and bluer. As mayor he had an office in there, but by custom no mayor ever used it. The Jericho Public Library's new coat of white paint caught his reformist eye. He would have the librarian order *The Prince* for the reference shelves—why should only mothers and children use the library? Besides, it tickled him to imagine Machiavelli coiled like a snake in the dimwitted high grass of Farmer's Almanacs and Jericho High School yearbooks.

Eager to get home to Rainey, he was walking but in his heart he was already running, the challenger, the fresh new face—past the three short blocks of downtown Jericho, beyond the farmers' grain elevator and Jericho water tower standing against the Great Plains sky—from here to other little towns like Grafton and Malden and back, the sky hanging like a bright blue tent over State Assembly District Five, George Robinson's first political baby.

CHAPTER 2

STEPHANIE ROBINSON descended the staircase in her dress of red velvet and red strapped shoes to match. Stephie clutched the bannister and took one careful step at a time. Still, she was hurrying. She wanted to cry, not to fall. She could hear the mothers talking in the living room, mothers on the sofa, mothers in easy chairs, mothers on chairs brought in from the kitchen. She could hear their voices, but she wasn't sure she could get her trembling chin and chestful of sobs to the bottom of the stairs in time.

"Look—here's Rainey."

"Don't tease her."

"I'm not. She looks more like Rainey every day. Come over here, come over to me, sweetheart. What did those bad boys do to you? Why is a little girl crying?"

"She gets herself so red in the face."

"Oh dear, she can't catch her breath."

"That's such an awful feeling."

"You don't think the boys would hit her, do you?"

"Oh no. She's so pretty. You're so pretty, Stephie!"

Several of the mothers raised their eyes to the ceiling.

"I don't like it when I hear furniture move. I don't mind them running. But when I start hearing furniture—"

"Isn't Margaret upstairs?"

"I saw Margaret go into the kitchen."

"Whatever is Rainey doing in there?"

"The last time I looked, she was starting to frost the cake."

"Frosting the cake? Why is she doing that now?"

"Well, dear, it just came out of the oven. That's why."

For a minute they had nothing to say and sipped their mild coffee from the demitasse cups with little saucers that to Stephie, catching her breath and nestling among them, looked very much like her doll dishes. Birthday cards stood on the mantle above the stone fireplace that took up most of one wall. Outside the big front window, as though badly wanting in, an ominous shape brushed against the foundations of the house; but it was only Big Red, the Robinsons' Irish setter, too big and sociable for his own good, so that he was being kept outside, nuzzling his cheek against the house, rolling over in the snow, sending up bouquets of snow from the bushes.

"This is why I bake in the morning. That way, whatever happens, I know my baking is done."

"I do my baking in the morning too."

"When I see something good in the Red Owl Store, that's when I do mine."

They all laughed, none harder than Stephie, who made sure they all saw her gaiety, which was certainly a more grown-up way than crying to capture their attention.

And then Rainey appeared, carrying a chocolate cake with a ring of blue candles, all lit. "Jamie! Boys! Birthday cake!"

"Don't run down the steps," warned one of the mothers, and a minute later they came thundering down the steps and crowded around the cake with angel faces, since they never knew when they were running. Rainey held the cake lower for them and beamed. It had fallen on one side and was a trifle lopsided. The tiny flames leaned and licked the frosting. "Careful. Don't blow the candles out," she told them, but there was a catch in her throat too. They looked like lighted candles themselves; an unkind look could blow them out. She smiled at Jamie, but she could have swept them all up and kissed them. She carried the cake into the dining room and set it down at the head of the table, the boys scrambling into the chairs and the mothers standing behind them.

Sitting in front of the cake, Jamie took a tremendous deep breath.

"Aren't you going to make a wish?" said Rainey. "Make a wish and it'll come true."

Jamie closed his eyes. "I wish—"

"To yourself."

"I wish, I wish," said someone else.

"Hush Stephie."

Then Jamie blew hard in all directions and snuffed out the candles, all nine, including the one for good luck that he got with an extra breath.

"I love you," said Rainey with her eyes.

And then everyone sang happy birthday, especially the boys did. They were all like comedians. All wore paper hats. All had teeth missing. All sang at the top of their lungs.

Now the party spread throughout the downstairs, the boys gobbling their cake and almost sitting still long enough to clean their plates. Games were organized by Rainey and Margaret, but the small players outspirited the rules; it was all the same game anyway, running and finding, running and doing, running and yelling. And Jamie was king—his paper gold crown tied by a string under his chin proved it. It was his cake, his birthday and his party. On a normal day, he was sensible, well-behaved, even quiet. But today he was seeing himself everywhere, practically running into himself, having a voice in everything. The joy of so much confusion made his eyes feel funny and his head spin—it was the pure delirium of scarlet fever without being afraid of burning up. Rainey sat down with her friends in the living room with a wedge of birthday cake, Stephie sat feeding on the sofa beside her, chocolate frosting adorning her face, swinging her legs at any boys who happened to pass, and the mothers sat back, taking their time over their cake and fresh cups of coffee, contented because it was still too early to think about collecting their children and going home.

Then Big Red bounded in—Big Red almost bowled over the umbrella stand in the hall in his attempt to avoid a morass of boots, skidded toward the wall, his wet winter coat resounding, and dashed into the living room. Big Red was in the house. With all the pains they took, how did it happen?

Robinson shut the door and stopped. Boots in the hall, cars on the street, cries and shrieks from within, dull recollections from the breakfast table—the birthday party. He had barely swallowed and digested this when Big Red, chased by his own surprise, came bolting out of the living room and leaped on Robinson, plush tongue palpitating for his face. He threw the dog off. Big Red galloped back into the crowded room. Rainey appeared—she saw Robinson and seemed speechless. He opened his arms wide to her and she told him to put Big Red out, to go and do it at once.

Small boys were running in circles, women stood brushing damp dirt and old leaves from themselves, a high-pitched babble filled the air; his living room was a state convention of mothers and children. Big Red by now was finishing a piece of birthday cake abandoned on the coffee table. Big Red's long jaw worked sideways across the plate; it looked like one thing on the plate eating another thing, like the chop devouring the potatoes, thought Robinson with a degree of pleasure. "Stand back, ladies," he said sternly, laughing to himself when they grabbed their urchins and stood behind the chairs. But it was easy. With a fist around the collar, a good grip, sweet talk and a little hauling, he dragged Big Red through the living room back through the boots in the hall and out the door and then nimbly let himself in. Throwing his coat over a chair, smoothing his hair in the mirror, he peered into the living room until he caught Rainey's eye and gestured with his head toward the kitchen.

Two small hockey players were sitting on the kitchen floor propelling an ice cube back and forth. Rainey filled fresh paper cups with lemonade for them and patted them on their way. Robinson pulled her to the little landing that led to the basement.

"When are they all going home?"

"I don't know. Before supper. Why?"

"Can't you make them go sooner? Come on, let's start cleaning up. They're bound to go then."

"George—can you hear what you're saying?"

"I want you to myself. That's all I'm saying."

"I'll cut you a piece of cake before you go."

She left him on the basement landing. There was a back door there, with a window that looked onto the yard. Against the pane hung icicles dripping in the sun. As a boy he had drunk thirstily, longingly, from icicles. Rainey! Come back! There's news to tell!

He leaned his gloom against the icebox, pondering what to do next. Jamie ran in bearing a slab of cake on a plate. "Thank you for the presents," Jamie cried. He left the plate on the table and ran out, his mouth wide open, breathless. Robinson stared after the little legs of the king of the party. On Jamie's heels Stephie came running in. Stephie—his little girl! He swung her up—they threw their arms around each other. He kissed her succulently and she laughed, pinching his neck, and though it stung astonishingly, Robinson laughed too. He watched her walk out of the room. So sweet! So pretty! She walked like a real little girl. He could never remember how old she was—five or four—he thought so, it seemed right, it was bound to be somewhere in there.

He hung around for a while longer, not knowing why he bothered. He went into the living room where he moved about, engaging in inane chatter with the mothers, taking revenge on Rainey with his carefree charm. But it was excruciating for him, like tax litigation, or a meatless meal. Mothers and children bored him to death. Still, had it been merely these lumpish women he found in his living room, he might have turned it to his advantage, made a public announcement of his candidacy, seized the occasion for a pretty little campaign speech, the first political speech of his life. But it was those little boys Robinson was wary of. He was afraid they would start running in circles, would whoop like Indians, wouldn't realize the importance of what he was saying, might break in with a disrespectful sound. "Vote for George Robinson—I'm running! Vote for me!" It was too soon out of the egg. It was still too featherless, too bare—he wasn't used to taking it among people yet. In his first test as a candidate he lost his nerve, and it was the fault of those little boys, all those damned little boys. So Robinson evaporated from his living room, put on his coat, buttoned up tight, and headed through the stinging cold back to his office.

The birthday party lasted too long. Soon it ceased being a joyful thing. Leftover pieces of cake were speared on forks or squeezed by smudgy thumbs like chocolate clay; hard candy was flung in the air, and so were feet-flattened paper cups; while on the dining room table sat the big lime-green gelatin mold that few tasted and that became a pastime for the boys to set aquiver with a forefinger as they passed. The abuse of the refreshments foretold the end. That last hour was filled with dissension, broken alliances, fighting and some tears. Windows reflected their faces as the winter dusk grew darker. There was a dispirited feeling in the air: the end of the party, resignation to coats and boots, their goodbyes, the shriveled car-ride home. The boys knew this moment was coming, the mothers knew it too; perhaps that was the reason the party endured for as long as it did. But in the end they all passed through the door and disappeared from the house, all except Margaret Hanson and her boy Jim, so Jamie took notice of Jimmy and they played, while Margaret helped Rainey through the worst of cleaning up.

"It was a beautiful party," said Margaret when they stood at the door with their coats on, a tall pleasant-faced woman with her arm around her boy. "We'll have to get busy on your party, Jim, to have one as nice as Jamie's."

"Thank you for helping," Rainey said.

"We'll have to bring this big fella over here more often. Jim shines on the ballfield, don't you Jim? Well then!" smiled Margaret and she shook Rainey's hand and Rainey hugged her.

"Out into the cold! Be seeing you. Wait up, Jim!"

Rainey returned to the living room, started to draw the drapes, changed her mind, glanced around her, yawned, switched the light off, fell into an armchair, kicked her shoes off and lay back her head.

A bath. She so longed for a bath that it must be a sign of her age when hot water in a tub had the allure of a date. But on the other hand, the bathroo was probably cold, filling the tub was a chore, climbing in an ordeal, feeling as lazy as she did, so she curled up in the chair with her feet tucked under her and bathed in laziness instead.

Jamie was upstairs in his room busy with his presents. Stephie was asleep in George's big wing chair, her cheeks sticky and shiny, her party dress ready for the wash, her breathing the only sounds to be heard. "Poor Stephie . . . Everything has to sleep sometime. . ." And there was something poignant about Rainey's affection for her child. She never thought, poor Jamie, who owned her heart; but it was poor Stephie who was fast asleep in George's chair, poor Stephie, George's little girl.

She wondered why George had walked in this afternoon. He

was always saying he was out-of-place at these parties. Funny man—he'd better be out-of-place! She could smile about the dog getting into the house—now she could. But that attitude of his wasn't as innocent or as funny. Pulling her toward the basement steps and wanting to send everyone home—was he really making advances in the middle of Jamie's birthday party? She should have advised him to mind his manners, that would have been the sophisticated thing to do—she should have told him to roll in the snow with his friend. She looked at her cool bare arm, her rounded bottom and slightly muscled leg tucked beneath her: under her paper-doll pregnancies was still the figure of a high school harvest queen. But nine years of marriage said that it wasn't romance that brought him home. He wasn't sick, he wasn't hungry. So what was on his mind? Whatever it was, she would hear about it without asking.

It might be nice to have a fire tonight, just the two of them, after she put the children to bed. As he lit the kindling he might start talking about how his father could never get a fire going— "It must have been the type of wood they sold him." He might talk about that. He frequently did. But she never minded, because expecting it, and then hearing it, made the fire cozier. She loved a fire with the wolfish dark night at bay all around them. She gazed at the fireplace, and at Jamie's parade of birthday cards on the mantle, and gradual tears came into Rainey's eyes in memory of her mother and father, Jamie's grandparents who never knew him. She clasped her knees and cried a little—she missed them still, both dead, both gone, out of luck. After a minute she wiped her eyes and the ache passed for now, since it was an old story and her tears like the ceremonial glass of wine, tasted only on special occasions.

And so she dried her eyes and reminisced about the party and the boys and how Jamie of course was the smartest and best. She thought about the cake and singing happy birthday and smiled some about the dog getting in. She thought about her friends and about their husbands, storekeeper, postmaster, Margaret's Bill who ran a filling station, and who all did nicely, but none like George Robinson, attorney-at-law, who had a building all his own on Legion Avenue and who was the handsomest and best.

And she thought: "I don't want life ever to be different from what it is. I don't ever want life to change. Why should things change? The world doesn't matter to me." And it felt deliciously satisfying to be able to say that. "The world doesn't matter to me."

She knew she should have gotten up and turned the lights on. She should have shaken herself, woken Stephie, put her in pajamas, started supper, made the house lively and warm. But she sat, gazing out, unwilling to move, like the ox on the prairie road. She felt at peace, at one with Stephie's breathing. She was serenely comfortable in this town where she was born, and uncompelled to see beyond its limits, as if there was no real county, no sprawling state, no borders, no countries, no America. She and hers were a tiny sparkle in space infinite. Whether it was the insular little town that explained her, or her parents snatched away when she was young, such was her apprehension of the great world beyond, and that sparkle was her answer to the darkness. So a small town wasn't too small for Rainey Robinson, who only asked to sparkle obscurely and be safe.

The only lights on were the light in the kitchen and the one upstairs in Jamie's room. Outside, where the glow from a rare streetlamp barely reached to the nimbus of the next, were the frozen front yards, the ruler-straight street crossing the avenues, the town's lone traffic light at the last corner—Legion Avenue— the city hall—the flagpole standing in front of it—the clanging of the chain against the flagpole at the raw blustery end of a winter's day. West passed it on purpose as he made his way home from work. It was the coldest sound in Jericho.

CHAPTER 3

THERE WAS a trampled path through the snow covering the green that surrounded the city hall and he cut through that empty expanse. He wore an old army coat, army boots, dark trousers, heavy gloves, and leaned his clenched teeth and slight build into the wind. One of these days he meant to get a cheap knitted hat, such as seamen wear—he really intended to. Day by day the stubborn wind blew at his head, whipping his black hair across his eyes.

Soon he reached his end of town, on one side of him the open fields, on the other, homes and yards that were sparser here on the outskirts. He supposed these people were his neighbors. He rarely saw any of them and had never exchanged a cup of sugar or a word with them. The house of gray shingle he rented had once been an old grainary that someone bought from a farmer and moved to town. A black stovepipe jutted from the roof. The one and only door was on the side, turned away from the road. His bicycle leaned up against the house under a piece of canvas. Out back was some patchy grass, bushes and a small shack. It seemed slightly absurd to West, like an infinitely shrinking universe, that a shack should have its own shack.

He unlocked the door and entered the larger of his two rooms, the kitchen. He kept his coat on and lighted the oil burner with a kitchen match from a box on a shelf. This room like the other had come with all its furnishings. In the center was a wooden table and two chairs. Over near the oil burner, source of the black stovepipe, sat an old farm rocker with a thin cushion nailed to the back. The kitchen stove came with a kettle; a few pans and some dishes were in the cupboards. Everything bore the stamp of a long-forgotten auction depositing someone's fraction of a house. When the sun came in, the faded walls gave it the feel of yesterday's sunlight. A big old-fashioned porcelain bathtub, set on graceful little feet, stood against the wall opposite the sink and stove. West bathed here. The bathroom was little more than a closet with a toilet and sink.

Cat had been asleep in the bathtub. When West took his coat off, Cat raised his head and sprang out. West held him and talked to him as he warmed Cat's food on the stove, then he watched Cat sniff and start to eat. Cat was a provisional name—his master was still in the process of settling down and deciding on a permanent one. West made a supper of thin fried ham and fried potatoes. He fried them together in the same pan, standing over it from beginning to end.

He chewed and ate methodically, staring straight ahead of him, as if he were eating at a lunch counter. Cat jumped up on the table and drank water from West's glass. West stroked him as he lapped: eyes shut, whiskers scattering drops of water when he took his jaws out of the glass. The weather was too cold for Cat to be out at night. In the fall, he had been too small and slow for the roving dogs outside; in the summer he had not been alive. He curled up on the floor in front of the oil burner, his front paws under his face, watching West. West sat in the rocker and read, taking his eyes from the page of his book from time to time, usually to rest on his only pieces of personal property in the room: he had nailed a calendar on the wall, and next to it a hand-drawn map of Jericho, with place names penciled in. On the counter was a round wind-up alarm clock from his army days. There was no telephone; who would call him? He simply showed up at work at the appointed times. Maybe one of these days he would get a phone. On the day he named Cat, he would have a phone installed, get a warm knitted hat, and take the beautiful Maid Marian to live with him in Sherwood Forest, all on the same day.

He closed his book and got up from the rocker. Cat, still curled up by the burner, began to purr. West wound the clock, brushed his teeth and went into the bedroom. There was no door, only a dark curtain over the doorway. It was a small room, with a narrow bed, a bureau, a chair. The wooden floor was cold to his bare feet; though he sometimes looked in, Cat never slept in here. Shivering, West got into pajamas and got in bed.

During the night he woke up suddenly. He felt stunned and for a second did not know where he was, or where in life, or what had cast him awake—and then he knew. He masturbated, fast, machinelike, wetting his hand on his mouth. He ejaculated with his eyes tight, his neck stretched, with a gasp; and then, deliberately, building a vision in front of him, he came again.

West got out of bed, brushed the curtain aside, pulled the string of the kitchen light. He fumbled a pencil from a drawer—he went to his map of Jericho on the wall. He found the place on the map he wanted but the pencil point was stubby; to write, he wet it on his lips.

West wrote in: "The Ice Palace."

ALAMAN WEST was his name—Alaman from the square-dance step Allemande left: his mother, taking her partner by the hand and starting to comply, felt the first pang of birth at that instant of the dance and the call of the square-dance caller rang with the blood in her ears.

Alaman was born that night, her only child. A waitress by day, nights she loved to dance, square-dancing, ballroom dancing, Latin dancing, whatever the craze was—she always knew the latest step. She was small, with a pretty, oval face; women she waited on noticed her fine hands and enviably dainty feet. Her name was Annie, from Annette. Her husband of less than a year, a ranch-hand, deserted her a few months before Alaman was born. She never married again and in her short lifetime raised Alaman by herself. With nothing to hold them to one place or another, they moved through that grain and cattle country, drifting eastward toward the heartland; and when he was ten the two of them landed in Jericho, where she waited tables in the dining room of the old Eagle Hotel, one of two hotels in Jericho then, the Violet and the once fancier, fading Eagle.

Alaman scanned the new town, was scarcely noticed, went to school, an apt pupil when he chose to be. Summer days he spent at the hotel, across from the train tracks and prairie, playing by himself under the sign with the painted eagle. He knew next to nothing about his father, his mother's sorest subject, only that he worked on ranches and had run off and abandoned them. If there were no pictures of his father, no possible memory of a face, Alaman saw the rest of him clearly, as a cowboy in full regalia, with cowboy hat, six-shooters, flaring chaps and boots; but an elusive sort of cowboy, stained by his mother's bitterness, a man of few words, a fugitive of sorts, like an outlaw.

Mother and son lived in a small apartment above the Red Owl Store, where Alaman had his own room and Annie made a bed out of the sofa in the living room. She had stopped dancing years before. Her legs grew veined and more tired, her prettiness chalky and dry. However unhappy she was, whenever she thought about leaving Jericho, she would say to herself that one town was like another town, just as each year that passed was like the other years. For Alaman's sake she joined a church, to better their lives and make new friends, but that too withered with weary Sunday mornings after working Saturday nights, until neither of them showed a face in their so much talked-about church. To Alaman, she never made good on anything she promised to do, and as he grew older, the son would sometimes think that his father must have had his good reasons for becoming a fugitive.

One morning when he was eighteen, still sleeping in the bedroom and she on the sofa, she couldn't get up to go to work, complaining about a stomach ache. When the ache got worse, not better, after she vomited, and she nearly fainted from the pain, Alaman ran to get Doc Sunderquist, who came, gave her a painkiller and aspirin for her fever, and within an hour her appendix burst and Annie died.

Alaman was taken in by the proprietor of the Eagle and given bed and board for the last months of high school. The church they had barely attended paid the burial expenses. The town was kind to him and to her memory. But mother and son had been together, been by themselves, for so long, that Alaman felt a paralyzing sense of disaster. He would wake up crying as if he'd never stop. He wept for past, present and future, his whole body weeping, like a hall filled with music. With his vast loss came a kind of shame, that his sole connection on earth was gone. And if he didn't see how he could ever forgive her for bringing him here and then leaving him all alone, he never forgave good old Doc Sunderquist or the town for what happened either. None of the women with husbands and families, houses and bank accounts would have been left with two aspirins to die.

He was out of high school, intelligent, able-bodied and free. He could have left Jericho behind him and for a long stretch of time he did, venturing to cities in the state that could be reached on the loop of the Great Northern Railroad line. In those small cities he usually found work in a hotel, as a porter, as a night clerk, often in the reassuring shadow of the railroad station. He considered these jobs marginal and never kept them long, though he never formed any clear idea of more suitable work. What he refused absolutely to do was wait on tables or work in kitchens—he would have nothing to do with that. He would sooner get on a train and try his luck in another city. Then, in the last stages of military conscription in the country, he was swept up and sent south to an army post for basic infantry training. After their training, nearly all of the men were shipped elsewhere, but West stayed on as a company clerk.

It was sheer luck—after the oppressiveness of soldiering with a gun he liked the self-contained world of the army post, the walk to post exchange or mess hall, the balmy air, the clean white rows of barracks in the sun. As a company clerk no one bothered him. He had his instructions; no one ever gave him a military order. He did his own work and had his own room. No officer inspected it, no one ever entered it. He came back on leave to Jericho once, in the fall. He felt much older. Not knowing what to expect, he walked the streets of the town. People remembered him and greeted him by name. A few oldtimers saluted. It was good to have a hometown. He had felt this when he got off the train, even as the train came chugging into the depot. Yet when he had walked his fill, and eaten an early supper at the American Legion Club, and again he strolled by the neat white-frame houses, now with the lights burning and glimpses of people inside (it was all so quiet that he imagined he heard their knives and forks as they ate), he still thought it was good to have a hometown, but he was less sure that he really had one.

While he didn't mind the army, even liked it, and had more independence than ever before, he never considered staying a soldier. He had been conscripted and this formed his attitude, which never changed. It was like remembering being born against his will: nothing that came afterward could quite make up for that.

He had his discharge and a thousand dollars from his army pay. He went home to Jericho. When he stepped off the train it was funny to see the same conductor who had boarded him in Chicago, where he made connections, standing on the little open platform in Jericho, like West's good angel. But the thousand-dollar bankroll was an illusion—its roundness fooled him. There was still nothing for him in the town, no work he could see himself doing. At his balmy southern post he had missed Jericho, because he always pined for something in his past; it gave him an important connection. Now walking the streets alone, boys speeding by him on bicycles, he missed the barracks and orderly room he had worked in, and his tending of the company's rosters and books, that brought a starch, a definition to his life.

He went to Chicago where he was familiar with the streets around the terminal. He rented a tiny hotel room and took a porter's job so as not to dip into his savings. But they seemed to flow away anyway. He had never had any money before, he spent it in minuscule ways that kept him almost ignorant of its passing, on greasy meals delivered to his room, on strings of movies, in late-night shooting galleries. He knew the money was running out. He felt as if he was running out of breath, there was a sense of urgency, speed and acquiescence. Then—just in time—he stopped dead, took his money and enrolled in a night-school bookkeeping course, something that had been in his mind from the beginning.

When he came back to Jericho for the last time, his attitude was somewhat changed. He was giving the town one more chance. But he was wary: he wouldn't be surprised if it failed. It was always so snug from a distance, snug and warm, like a scene on a Christmas card. But not when he got there—never then, or not for long, no matter how fast he traveled. He knew better now. There was no good angel. He would hammer himself in, like a nail. He would do it just to do it.

People were surprised he was back; they had forgotten his existence. It was the middle of July, dry, hot; the streets simmered with fresh wet tar. It didn't take him long to make his rounds. At first, the men he spoke to seemed uncomfortable when he presented himself as a bookkeeper. They had never thought of him in connection with anything, except when he showed up as a soldier. But some of them thought it over and decided they could use a bookkeeper for a few days a month. West had a certificate, seemed to know what he was doing, and he came cheap.

He never spoke to any one about his army service or his experiences in the city; never mentioned a thing he had done, a girl he had met, or a friend he had made. Bookkeeping suited his solitary nature. His reticence, his slight build, made it easy for him to work unnoticed in the back rooms and odd corners that people found for him. He was a bookkeeper. All that was missing were the eyeglasses and green eyeshade, but West did not require them. He had excellent eyes, tireless eyes. By the time winter came he was keeping the books of Amundson's lumber yard, the Legion Club, and several other enterprises in Jericho, enough work to keep him alive. His mother had been dead for six years. He was now twenty-four years old. On his return he found the Eagle Hotel sold to the grain elevator company and demolished to make room for a potato house. He felt a wrench, as if something he had been standing on had been knocked away, but when he felt for any damage to himself, he found he really didn't mind seeing the old hotel and its kitchen obliterated.

CHAPTER 4

AT TEN o'clock West left his house. He liked to set out in the morning even on days when there were no ledgers to do. In the fall he had bicycled to town; but now the wind strung ropes in his path, and often by daybreak the streets were covered with overnight snow or ice. The sun on it dazzled the eye, and only he was out walking.

His house and the road and fields were at the farthest corner of his map, but in ten minutes' time West was walking on Back Street, behind Legion Avenue. People were seldom seen on Back Street. Curley's Junkyard was here, with the old Dodge car under the elm tree. The Dodge had been at Curley's for as long as West remembered, parked there for life, with bare rims for wheels and empty sockets for headlights. Curley had sold West his bicycle, his last sale, possibly, before he retired and went to live with a sister in Malden; Curley was past eighty. Because he was retiring and nobody was taking over the business, he threw in a wire basket for nothing. West liked Back Street. It ran unnoticed, shadowed, often muddy. It was the only street in Jericho that made him think of Chicago, as if back streets everywhere were brothers.

On Legion Avenue he saw people for the first time. They were wives out shopping. Some faces he knew, some not. When he passed the grocery store and looked in, it was satisfying to see them. He felt curiously proud for them. Of them. They seemed completely self-contained, moving a cart down the aisle, thinking whatever they were thinking when they stopped and picked something up, some in haircurlers, their cheeks pink from the cold. They were in other stores too. Their kids were in school and their husbands were at work, at this hour of the day.

The few men he saw were farmers. Two came out of the hardware store, where their pickup trucks were parked, wearing wool jackets and rubber boots and overalls. When West passed them he looked the other way. Men like that—either they came out of the saloon or the hardware store. He didn't see what could ever pass between them and their wives. Farmers were the reason the town was there. But when West saw Jericho in his mind's eye, he never saw any farmers.

But up ahead was someone he always saw—Doc Death, getting out of his car. Doc had his office next to the bank—that was so his money bags wouldn't catch cold. As West came up to him, Doc hesitated and looked as if he was about to speak to West. That was because West hesitated as if he meant to speak to Doc. When he didn't, that left Doc standing there with mustard on his face. It was a game. Sometimes he did mumble something to Doc. But not always. That kept it going for the future. The hate in West was almost comfortable, like an old habit. He would see Doc and slip it over his face and neck like a sweater. Old Doc had fed his mother the smoothest painkiller of them all. He would like to get his teeth into Doc's books someday. Doctors were notorious for getting away with murder on their taxes. And why not, when they got away with murder?

He bought a newspaper in the drugstore and went next door into the café. The air inside was steamy from the grill and coffee urns behind the counter. He took a table near the window and leafed through the paper. Newspapers did not interest him particularly. But he liked the idea of sitting in the sunny warmth with his morning paper. He liked the idea of the waitress bringing his his coffee without his having to ask for it. He always sat down at a table. Storekeepers and farmers sat at the counter, which was crowded; the counterman too had been a farmer. West turned the pages of his paper. If he came here in the afternoon he would sometimes bring a book and read. Or a pad and pencil and write things down. Nobody bothered him. He always sat at the same table. He liked having a café to frequent. He liked having a café of his own. The Paris Café he called it. Why not? If he wanted to, why not? And as the Paris Café it had gone up on his wall map of Jericho.

The waitress brought his coffee. Ellie was her name. She wasn't pretty—a long way from it. But her homeliness didn't offend West. If anything, it put him greatly at ease.

The past summer he used to sit on a bench in the city hall park. Grass and trees surrounded the big brick building and set it back. There was a drinking fountain and a bench on either side. On through the fall no one else sat in the park. People came and went on the paths and up the steps of the city hall, the mayor and police chief, the town auditor and councilmen. And so on the map in his kitchen, the city hall was "Theirs." No one but himself sat in the green, beautiful park; and so that was "Mine."

HE STOPPED at the Jericho Public Library.

It stood at the end of Legion Avenue, a white-frame house with a wooden step and a porch.

He shut the front door behind him.

It was one big room, with bookshelves along the walls and a reading table with chairs; otherwise it was the plain old frontier house it had always been. The window shades were drawn so no sunlight got through; artificial light was all there was. It was nice. He liked that about the library. It was like himself, a world inside a world.

He was the only browser. This was often true. There might be mothers with their kids sometimes, but never men. He had never seen another adult male in the library. The place made him smile. Old worn books filled the shelves and each shelf was tidy and straight. Some, like the little row marked History, were never disturbed; there were gaps of centuries but the books were straight. And tight. West had to pull to pry one loose and then the others had all fallen out—it was a joke.

Behind her little desk sat the librarian, Alpha Davis, a postman's widow, widowed so many years that people were used to thinking of her as an old maid. Her hair was tinted blue. Her dresses were blue. From her silver-rimmed spectacles hung a fine chain that passed around her neck. She was bent over a small white card, going from line to line with her pencil. Alpha Davis's pencils were always new, always sharpened, with perfect points. If he ever felt like paying her a compliment, which he never would, he could drag that in about her pencils.

West dropped his chosen books on the reading table and went up to her desk.

"I don't see *Strange Stories* by Weird anywhere. It's my favorite book. I'd like to request a copy."

Alpha Davis put her work down and folded her hands under her chin.

"That's *Strange Stories* by Weird," West said. "Aren't you going to write it down?"

"What do you think?"

"Okay. Okay. What about *Weird Stories* by Strange? Can you get that one?"

"Goodbye, Mr. West."

"I'm willing to wait—I'm not in a hurry. Come on. I'll pay half. You choose which one."

He knew she always cringed when he came in. He hung at her desk, requesting his titles and grinning—he had fun with her. But the old widow was out of her chair and walking rapidly toward the back. There was a tiny room there with a wash basin and a hanger for her coat.

"Hey, what about my library books?" he called.

"Oh, goodbye, Mr. West, goodbye," and she disappeared.

He picked up a pencil and card and left her his titles, with his name. Let her throw it out. Whenever he asked for a real book, and she wrote it down herself, she threw that card out too. At least that was always the end of it. Nothing he ever asked for ever came in. She probably didn't like him—didn't like his looks. He wasn't her type. Any book he wanted must be a bad book. So why should he ask for real books? Why not have some fun with her? That was funny, though. About him not being her type. She must be seventy years old.

He left his books on the reading table. It didn't matter. He didn't always take a book out. He came here just to come here. Sometimes he took books to the table and sat and read. He liked the atmosphere. He liked the old books. Winter and summer the air was musty and the shades were always drawn. He supposed it was gloomy. Maybe that kept people away. But it didn't bother him. The library was a place of importance on his map.

West bundled up and put on his gloves and stepped out of "My Den" into the light of Jericho.

WEST'S ALMA mater, Jericho High School, was a rusted old building of red brick that stood beside a playing field on the edge of town. When winter came, a corner of the field was cleared of snow and hosed over, froze, and became the skating rink. Through the winter, banks of fresh snow and scraped ice accumulated on all four sides; the skaters simply stepped over it to get on the ice. The rink was empty during most of the day, but when school was over kids came to skate, small kids and older girls on figure skates and high school boys with racing skates and hockey sticks who swept and pummeled the ice until dark and beyond. This was late afternoon; the long rays of the sun slanted on the ice, without hope, without warmth. Though the wind was down, to stand still in the cold was to stand fractionally above pain. The only structure in the vicinity of the ice was an electrical generator surrounded by a chain link fence. Here West had taken up his position.

Nothing hid his presence from the skaters. No one cared that he stood and watched. But each time he came here, West stood by the fence, because it seemed important not to stand completely in the open; not to let them see that he was so willing to wait and so cold.

A little shack, a warming house, stood at the edge of the ice. This was stored away intact and brought out each winter. It had a small bench inside and a stove, and people would go in to put on their skates or to warm themselves. Nothing prevented West from crossing over and going in, except that he had no skates, had never been on skates, and most of those who skated here were kids. So West had never been inside the warming house. Whenever the door opened he strained to see inside but the door was too quickly closed. Puffs of smoke rose from a stovepipe on the roof. West's breath was vaporish-white in the icy air. He warmed his mouth against the inside of his coat collar and moved his gloved hands deep inside his pockets. There was a bend in the road as it wound past front yards and approached the high school. West kept his eye on that stretch of road and on the warming house door.

The door opened and two little boys came out on skates. One of them was Dixie's brother. West knew him; he came with his sister often and was unmistakable. Round little face, little pug-nose, light eyes, a small edition of Dixie. West felt tantalized and impatient. He stepped up and down in the holes that he had kicked in the snow to ward off frostbite. He thought he had been waiting here for fifteen or twenty minutes. Then he saw the warming house door again opening and Dixie skated onto the ice.

She wore a scarf that was wrapped around her mouth, the other end of it draped over her shoulder. She wore a jacket with a furry white border and furry collar and cuffs. Inside these cuffs peeped the cuffs of a sweater. There was a long warm skirt and tights and mittens and a knitted hat. Her brown hair was tucked under her hat. Short brown hair, brushed straight. A clear forehead, the slight pug-nose, the light-blue eyes. This was Dixie. She was sixteen or seventeen. Her father was the druggist who managed the drugstore. Though she was born in Jericho, West didn't remember ever seeing her until the day he passed by and saw her skating here, queenly and peach-colored against the ice and snow.

The frost of her breath, the white of her skates—he watched her pump up speed—her white-and-blue scarf flew. She coasted lifting one skate then the other and with a long gaze of self-satisfaction whose circle for a fraction of a second included West. She skated forward and then backward, and then, giving in to the hands crowding her, with her brother and his friend, holding the hand of each. The high school boys slammed the puck by them, hollering pep-talk to each other. They had positioned themselves on three sides of the ice and were firing practice passes danger-ously near. West heard the cracks, like gun-cracks, skull-cracks. Dixie pulled the kids to her and shouted at the hockey players, her furious shouts slapped down by their sticks and the crack of the puck.

Dixie skated to the bank, pushed off, came up behind one of them, slid by and made a grab for his hockey stick—he was astonished when someone jerked the stick out of his hands. Before he could catch her she threw the stick clear across the ice where it bounced and slid into a snowbank.

A shock of warmth, a thrill of justice, tingled through the cold in West. Dixie, her pug-nose in the air, a little red-faced, skated across the ice. The high school boy went after his stick. His friends were laughing, and one of them offered his stick to Dixie if she would come and take it from him.

But after that they played to one side of the ice and left Dixie alone; they made a game of slamming goals into the snowbank, one against two. Dixie circling all alone ignored them and they ignored her. West distrusted them as a different breed—because they were the same age she was, because they saw her in school every day, because they could see and ignore her.

The electrical generator and chainlink fence made a webbed shadow behind him—the sun was going down, a foreign red sun in contrast to snow and children skating. She skated over his soul. He never stopped looking at her. He thought she was blessed. She was pretty, though that was just a part of it. She excelled in skating and he had read in the *Jericho Pioneer* about other accomplishments and competitions and awards. She wasn't afraid to do things. She was a competitor. Her temper, he admired her temper. West sought ways to admire her. It didn't hurt him, wound him, knowing she was superior. Just the opposite; he wanted her to be. She was a girl—a young girl—almost like a sister.

His feeling for Dixie flushed his cold, numbed cheeks. The ache of it warmed him; was the warm meal he sat down to in the cold. He wet his lips that were cold and cracked.

He closed his eyes and held these lips to the inside of the collar of his coat.

He watched her skate to the warming house and trip inside. He supposed that she was alone. He knew she was. But he couldn't go in. It looked tiny all of a sudden, since he would be alone there with her and had never yet spoken to her. No, he couldn't go in; but he could wait outside. Her being inside it made the shack on the ice seem awesomely silent. He stood waiting for her to come out. He was like a boy waiting for a girl to come out and join him after the bell rang at school. It was very much like that.

But when she came out it was to go home, her ice-skates in the old brown knapsack that was her skate bag. She went over the top of the snowbank and came around it trudging through the snow; her brother shouted to her that he would be home soon and she nodded, waved back and pushed on with her trudge of the dreamer, a small aloof figure when she was all by herself, the brown knapsack weighing on her back, lifting her head every so often as if she were making a hill and not one of Jericho's flat roads.

West watched from the fence, watched her walk down the road and watched her come to the bend and disappear. Then he watched her vanishing point a minute more.

Then he walked home, going the way he had come, the road that wound past the high school being the same road that turned at the edge of town and ran past his house. It was snowing again, a light snow falling with its shadow. Old snow and ice between one driveway and the next crunched over the tops of his boots; the fields that began on the other side of the road were a continent of snow crossed by the icy dark fir trees of the windbreaks.

Like everyone else, he waited on—waited for spring and summer—he waited for the sun to warm the earth so that Dixie would start to take her clothes off. The scarf, the mittens, the knitted hat, her jacket and skirt and sweater, her tights, all would come off. Dixie with bare legs and brown shoulders. Dixie in the sun and Dixie in the shade. Dixie in her backyard, smiling, talking, leaning, whispering. Dixie his friend—Dixie kissing him.

He drank this in, this picture suffusing his mind, of Dixie's sunny face kissing him. He tried to make it persist for the rest of his walk home. How many months to summer? Five? Was it four?

Cat has hungry when West walked in the door. He matched steps with West across the room, rubbing against his legs, purring. Absorbed, West tolerated him. He lit the oil burner then heated Cat's supper and served it to him in front of the burner; as Cat ate, West fried his ham and potatoes. The smell made his mouth water, though when he sat down and began eating his lips bled, they were that badly cracked from standing in the cold at the Ice Palace. He daubed them as he ate and finished his plate. When his knife and fork ceased, in the lull following his hunger, his mind dwelt on Dixie and Dixie's brother. Strong family resemblances impressed West. They seemed mysterious to him, like a special force of nature. How did it feel to see your face in someone else's face? Did it feel funny? Did it make you closer to that person? Did the both of you feel that way?

His clock ticking drew West's gaze to the time. It was a few minutes to seven, a fact meaningless to him. He left Cat his dish but cleared the table, wiped it, and washed and dried the dishes.

He went into the bedroom. He kept his books on top of the bureau, lined up, two rows deep. Some in the front row were library books. His main sources for books were one, the library, and two, the rack of paperbacks in Haley's drugstore. West had never been a reader in school—that came later, on trains, in the hotel rooms he occupied when he lived in Chicago. He still had some of the time-killing westerns and thrillers of those days but now he kept them just to fill up space, to make a second row in his collection. He considered them things of the past and was replacing them gradually with books he could read and respect.

West liked biographies—men's lives. They seemed to become a part of him, all stored inside and ready to come to life. Charles Lindbergh, Sam Houston, Jack London, Tom Paine—each name was like a different explosive charge in his mind that was set off whenever he thought of that name. The library had a lot of good biographies. Most were children's versions but he didn't mind that, they were good books, better than some of the others. The author told you what you wanted to know, and in everyday language, without trying to show you up. It struck him that every hero had begun life as poor or sickly or considered ordinary. They were never the favorites but had come out of nowhere. They were all men from out of nowhere. There was a thrill to it like the thrill of justice, of revenge.

Cat slept as West read. He was curled up by the burner where the floor was warm and half-opened a yellow eye now and then at the creaking of the rocker. Sometime after nine West put down his book and got up to make some coffee. He set water to boil in the saucepan and took down a jar of instant coffee from the cupboard. Then he also got out some bread and jam. As the water boiled, he watched Cat sleep. It was a marvel to West that he could just decide and go over and pick him up and kill him. That he could do that. That he had that power over Cat. He loved Cat. He would never want to harm him. But the thought of Cat dead and dead by his hand sent the greenest, the tenderest feeling through West. He planted his terrible thought and tenderness sprang up. So Cat, who slept through it, was alive and never did West love him more than he did this minute.

He rocked and sipped his coffee and ate his bread and jam. On his map he lived in "The Castle." Simple enough. Not that he thought much of the house; he knew it was a shack that no legitimate family would live in. It was The Castle because is was all his. West gave careful thought to his map and was proud of it, though it would have embarrassed him if anyone saw it. When he first started it, he had almost been embarrassed himself. The pencil markings and names he gave to things made him feel queer to himself, like someone only half him, like his own half-brother. Sometimes he had the feeling that he was a branch growing out of himself, slowly growing beyond the reach of people, beyond his own reach. His map, this house, his loneliness all made it grow. His bookkeeping kept him connected by a thread. He was going to do things. Something. Was it good or bad?

At that point, he usually stopped thinking.

CHAPTER 5

FROM JERICHO'S traffic light at the corner where the city hall faces
Legion Avenue, it is a short walk to the Great Plains. Stretching
away to far horizons is that vast sea of dark earth and Jericho is
a tiny island in that sea. The trains of the Great Northern chug
to east and west, seemingly forever outward bound. The land is
flat; the sunsets are clear and red. The sky is Homeric. Even on
fleecy cloudy days it seems as if one patch of blue in that sky
could provide blue skies for a county. Here everything is terri-
tory-wide: the snow, the rains, the wind—the insulation. If you
stand at the edge of town where the grain elevator stands, or
around on the other side where JERICHO is painted across the
top of the water tower, and look out, no other island is visible
though they are all there to be found. Each has its water tower
and grain elevator. Each has its own life—each island is proud of
its sunset. Each is alone and each the center of Creation.

There are in Africa tiny tribes, numbering hardly more than a
trainload of people, who have, say, a river god, lord of a little
nearby river, and this god, to whom special language is spoken
and solemn sacrifices made, is none other than the high and
mighty King of the Universe, who has always lived in their river.

*　　*　　*

THIS MORNING'S *Herald* rolled up in his hand, Robinson strolled into Sam's barbershop.

Sam's shop was sunny, with the smell of hot towels and talcum in the air and just a sniff of witch hazel to tickle his perception: the aroma of a recent shave—Sam had been blessed with a customer. Sam worked alone. A couple of chairs, a mirror and a row of instruments on a towel, and Sam had a barbership that had stood here for twenty years and was so much of an institution that it took a comparative stranger to notice how pathetically plain it was.

He dropped his tweed jacket and cap on the bench. He passed up Sam's reading material, good reading that it was, since he didn't hunt, fish, or tinker with his car. He saw that he had neglected to wipe his feet on Sam's welcome mat. But what the hell, it was spring. There was fresh mud all over town.

Sam was asleep in one of his barber chairs. Robinson looked over the back at Sam's open mouth and slack cheek slumbering against his barber's coat. What was he dreaming about, Sam the barber? What did they find to dream about, the Sams of this world? A new barbershop? A shiny new car? Maybe a shiny New Deal? Sam the barber could use a shave. Sad somehow, sad and so typical. Who would shave Sam the barber? Part his hair for him, pat his cheek, shape his dreams, defend his interests? Who in this district possessed the heart for that, the brains, the wife, the office space?

All highly absorbing questions. However, Sam had a living to make.

Robinson glanced through the front window at the street. No one was passing.

He raised up his newspaper and whacked it across the back of Sam's chair.

Sam woke up with a dull cry and pushed himself out of the chair.

"My God, what a noise. Did you see anything? What was that?"

Robinson slipped behind him into the seat. "I didn't hear anything. You had a bad dream, Sam. I think the boss is working you too hard." Robinson unfurled his paper, read the headlines, saw nothing he liked, and tossed it onto the adjoining chair just as the laundered white robe floated down over him.

"Do me a favor and watch the small hairs, will you, Sam? They always go down the back of my neck."

"Face the mirror, George, I hear you."

"I always had that trouble. My mother used to say my hair was too fine. You wouldn't think so but she was a very critical woman. Talk about the human heart. I should start collecting stories about my youth. Did I ever tell you about my mother being the only woman in the world who knew how to cut a pie?"

"I'm listening, George."

"She cut it down the middle. In half. I'd eat one half for lunch and the other half for supper. That's why my mother was the only woman in the world who knew how to cut a pie. I didn't make that up about her—that's a true story."

"She still living?"

"Living? Certainly. She's living in Arizona with my father. They're as healthy and happy as kids. She grows tomatoes now. The pies were when I came home from school for the holidays, Christmas with the family and such, wonderful oldtime Christmases, but nothing fancy, church, a nice turkey, little gifts under the tree for everyone, you know what I mean, Sam."

"Just a minute."

"You come from a big family?"

"Four kids."

"Is that right? I never had that good fortune. There was just me. Which was just enough from what I understand. I was a holy terror. When I was six we had a visitor who thought I was twins. Anyway that was the legend that was handed down. Don't push my head, Sam. It might be helpful to you but not to me."

"I'm trying to cut your hair. Will you let me?"

"What's your point, Sam?"

"Don't fight me, George."

"You? I wouldn't dream of it."

"You turn this way, you turn that way, you turn your head around. I'll take a piece of your ear one of these days! I hate to see you come in. You're worse than the kids. Can't you just sit still?"

"I can do anything."

He sat wordless through the rest of the haircut, conscious of locks of hair falling, sitting like wax fruit compared to his former juices. "I hate to see you come in." Sam really had a way with a customer; it was lucky for him that the services he performed were so onerous.

Robinson stared moodily at the mirror. The fat chance, the pure fancy, that the face looking back at him might be free, alive, in competition with his own, and might make a sudden move, commanded his attention for several minutes. Which of them would blink first? It gave him a very funny feeling. You could see people on the street, in stores and offices all day long. But when you looked at your own face in a mirror, flesh really meant something. The desire came over him, not for a shave, which he never permitted a barber, but the steaming hot towel of the after-shave. His flesh felt a craving to this extent: if Sam had shaved him, and the razor slipped, he wouldn't have minded a cut or two, just for the added tingle.

Sam brushed, fine-combed, trimmed, and gave his scissors a little snip in the air.

"Okay, George, you've still got both your ears."

He whisked off the robe but Robinson grabbed a corner of it.

"No hot towel?"

And he watched Sam morosely go to fish out a hot towel. Sam lived by the philosophy that you didn't get a hot towel with a haircut. In order to get a hot towel you were supposed to have a shave. He came back with the towel and slapped it on. And Robinson pulled it down over his face and smiled and breathed. It felt delicious. It was the little extras in life that broke the other man's back. He stood up, put on his cap and jacket, and rolled up his newspaper. Sam stood by his chair, watching.

"No coat, George?"

"On a day like this?"

"You should wear a coat," Sam said.

"It's a spring day out there."

"No coat." Sam shook his head, "I think you're asking for trouble."

Robinson laughed. "So long, Sam, always nice to see you." He pointed to his head. "Swell haircut."

He jumped Sam's steps, waking up the barber pole with his

swinging paper. Sunshine warmed the thrilling breeze, birds followed chirping in his ears. Spring was in these ears. His maps were ready for his campaign. His wings itched, not hairs on his mortal neck. How sweet to be sweet on Rainey's hometown. He had married into more than a town! Here were grass roots and rooters, voters, a little world bubbling over with little human lives. He owned that he had a sweet tooth for people the way that campaigner of campaigners Roosevelt did. Legion Avenue was a marvelous avenue.

Sam the barber! And a few doors down was yet another friend and neighbor, Henry your corner grocer. Hello neighbor! Hello corner grocer! Hello Mary Ellen you corner grocer's wife! Hey, Joe, no day-dreaming, this isn't utopia you know, better get that broom moving, Joe you grocer's boy!

Legion Avenue! Your commerce—your bustling shops—your two-way traffic—your traffic light. Your square old city hall and shady park and sunny little library porch. Your far horizons—your east and west. Your sky, your latitude, your longitude. Jericho, you're beautiful! Gee, I'd be proud to represent a town like you. I see your name on the big water tower looking over the prairie (There she is—we're home, folks!). I see your tall important grain elevator, bursting with wheat and more wheat (Don't mind us, just admiring, Art and Ed!). And your humming railroad tracks and neat and spotless depot, and Roy, your lame but willing depot man (And let me tell you good people that if Roy here can drag his leg to the firehouse and vote, so can the rest of you folks!).

And there's Hank the town cop, riding with Pete the deputy cop. Hank's at the wheel—just look at them cruise! They're the law here, so respect them for it. Keep up the good work, boys!

And the Leader State Bank, most modern building in town, all new inside and out with one big plate-glass window. There's Elmo Peterson pleading for a loan. And that friendly Mr. Hodges and his wonderful gang, and the traditional tree and free pens at Christmastime. Makes you feel good just to walk in there!

And the big Dakota Store, justly famous for fashion and values. And Bob Miller's Coast-to-Coast Store, selling everything for the American home and yard, and the cleverly named New Sagebrush Café, serving one and all. Inside I see:

Old Johnson the steady postman.

Old John the steady saloonkeeper.

Young West the bookkeeper.

And Ellie the hard-working waitress, with a tray of dirty dishes. It's a dog's life—we're sorry, Ellie. But some dog has to do it.

And Haley's Drugstore. Gee, Haley's—the ice cream sodas they give you, the scoops of vanilla and chocolate they drop in! There's Mary Jo Sweeney putting cosmetics on the shelf; she was a Jericho High School majorette. But where's little Will the druggist? What's happened to little Will our druggist? Ah, there he is behind his apothecary jars. Careful you don't swallow yourself with a sip of water, Will.

And our fine American Legion Club down that street—I can always see the flag waving from this spot! (While I'm not a veteran, some of you may recall the free legal advice I gave after the mystery fire in the Buffalo Lounge.) I'll be speaking to you folks in the Legion hall come autumn! Thanks to the building fund, we've got over two hundred folding chairs!

There's John's Saloon. Nobody can walk past John's window without a grin. It's got the darnedest sign for a town with a sense of humor. It says "Come on in. We're open for repairs." That's what it says! I tell you, politics is people and people are just wonderful! Hey, what's that crowd in front of John's? Who are all those men?

Bill the wheat farmer, Bob the wheat farmer and Don the wheat farmer. Back view. Side view. Front view. Same thing! Hello, boys, been having a few beers? Don't forget to pee! Don't forget to vote!

Vote for me! I'm running!

Vote for Robinson!

RAINEY WAS sitting in his office sipping coffee when Robinson strode in. She jumped up, vivid and smiling in her red spring coat.

"You got a haircut! So that's what you wanted me to see today. Oh it's handsome. Turn around."

"Sure." Robinson headed for his desk; she caught his hand, kissed his cheek and kissed him on the ear.

"Hey!" said Robinson.

She squeezed his hands: "Hank and Pete are on their way over."

"Hank and Pete? What the hell for?"

"To arrest you for stopping traffic on Legion Avenue."

Robinson pushed her away and laughed. He went to his desk, pushed the buzzer and picked up the phone.

"Bring in the maps, Eleanor."

Small, soft, heavy-chested Eleanor Prain, wearing green pants and a jacket to match, her wheat-colored hair banked on top of her head, brought a large sheet of manila sideways through the door and carried it to Robinson's desk. "Thank you, Eleanor."

Mrs. Prain lingered. "I haven't finished the red lines yet. I've done all of the blue lines, plus the circles and the squares. But the stars, Mr. Robinson, shouldn't the stars be gold?"

Robinson smiled at Rainey. "Not all stars are gold stars, Eleanor. I think you'll find that out in politics. But thank you."

Mrs. Prain smiled at Rainey on her way out, "There's more coffee whenever you want. I think politics is going to be fun!"

Rainey sat again, loosened her coat, rearranged her white leather gloves beside her purse on the desk as Robinson perused his maps. "George, did you notice that today her shoes are green too? Where did she get the idea that everything she wears has to match?"

"Eleanor? I think she's done very well, when you consider the schooling she's had. I like her. She has an unquestioning sense of loyalty to me. But come and see the maps!"

Six maps covered the heavy sheet of paper. They were all square, bordered in black, and of equal size. They had red lines or blue lines, circles, squares and finely traced stars. "They're all maps of the same area basically, Jericho and the election district," said Robinson. "But look closely. This one on the left is really a road map of the territory, with the population centers circled, the towns, if you will. We'll use that for rallies, speeches, distribution of campaign literature and so forth. This one next to it is our financial map. Not useful really, but graphic. As these areas make their small contributions, their stars will be filled in with green, say a point at a time. You can see that Jericho has the biggest star by far, for obvious reasons. This is a ward map of Jericho only—I'll have copies of it for my ward captains. Knowing, holding, and getting out our voters here is the keystone of our campaign. Now down here the fun begins. On this map, the blue shadow lines show Armstead's main areas of strength, Grafton, his farmers, and so on. And over on this map, the red shadow lines, when they're all in, will show mine, Jericho and my farmers and so on. The last map is the whole show, map five superimposed on map four. His strength, my strength. His people. My people. The dark squares show the main areas in contention, where we lock horns so to speak. So!" He spread his hands over the maps and smiled. "What do you think?"

"I don't know what to say, George." She came back around the desk and sat down. She had been thinking how much she loved this office, the tall shelves of red-and-tan law books, the framed diplomas and scenes of the prairie on the redwood walls, the gold-framed family photographs on the constantly crowded desk. Though she had chosen much of the furnishings down to the potted plants, the room had a lasting aura for her. This was where some of the world's work was done. This was where she pictured him often and knew him least.

"I don't know what to say. That I'm impressed?"

Robinson laughed and got up.

"Don't be. This is all so much paper—I might decide to scrap it tomorrow for something else. It's the feel of it that I like. Eleanor Prain was right, in her small town, kindergarten way. Politics is going to be fun. It has a whole lot of what the law doesn't have for me and never will. Politics is people, Rainey. I felt that when I was walking on Legion Avenue just now—politics is people. How do you like that for a campaign slogan? Snappy enough? Armstead's never had a slogan in six campaigns—he probably can't think of one. He's still solving the problem of how to put on overalls." Robinson laughed and slapped his desk. "I like Armstead's style. He does law a little, he does real estate a little, he farms a little. There's something awfully horizontal about Armstead. He's never even tried for higher office—that should tell you something. By the way, did I mention that I'm asking the governor to campaign for me here in the fall?"

All of this whirred about her ears with an eggbeater's insistence and now he stopped, but only to sit himself down on his desk, sound the buzzer and lift the whole phone to him. "Get me the public library on the line. Don't go," he said to Rainey, "I just remembered something, the classic textbook on politics and power . . . Mrs. Davis? This is George Robinson. Mrs. Davis, I want you to order a book for the reference shelves of the library. Frankly, I think you could use a great book down there . . . No," said Robinson rolling his eyes, "but why should that create a problem? My wife has a card. Order it in her name if you like . . . Mrs. Davis . . . Mrs. Davis, to get to the point, I want you to order *The Prince* by Machiavelli for the reference room of the library . . . I know it's not actually a room. I was speaking metaphorically. Optimistically . . . It's a very small book, Mrs. Davis, in terms of size . . . Can you speak louder, Mrs. Davis? . . . It's a classic, why should it be difficult to obtain? . . . How do you know it won't be a popular book? Mrs. Davis, I don't propose to argue with you about a book. As town librarian you have obligations—to the mayor, to the council, to the taxpayers, if you understand me. Don't talk while I'm talking, Mrs. Davis! No one is indispensable! That's *The Prince* by Machiavelli. I expect to have it in my hands very soon!"

He slammed the phone down.

Rainey was on her feet. "I can't believe what I heard. You just threatened to fire Alpha Davis."

Robinson laughed lightly. "Did I do that?"

"You frightened a harmless old woman."

"A case of mistaken identity, forgive me. I thought I was talking to Alpha Davis."

Rainey snapped on her gloves.

"Rainey! Don't take everything I say seriously."

"I'm going, George. I'll see you tonight."

Robinson lifted his maps. "We're going to win this, Rainey, I know it. We're going to win!"

"You keep saying we. Who is we, George?"

"We is me."

She left. He stared at the maps. She had liked the maps. They were good maps! He was sure he could win this election; he had a good chance. He couldn't be so wrong about himself.

He punched the buzzer.

"Keep after Alpha Davis about a book I want. Keep calling her, week after week, month after month. *The Prince*—by Machiavelli. No, I don't feel like spelling it! I'll spell it for you in a memorandum."

ROUND SNOW-patched Cemetery Hill, a natural slope made for graves and kids' sleds, was the only high ground in the vicinity of Jericho. Once past it, all was level and almost bare to the horizon. A tree or two stood in the yard of the occasional farmhouse; between sections of land were the evergreen trees of the windbreaks, pine, spruce and fir, choice green sprigs in winter that became the drab wreaths of winter in the spring. Rainey drove her own little Ford, snub-nosed and blue in comparison to the lumbering black Olds that Robinson steered to the county courthouse and to homes of valued clients like his farmers' widows. Though she liked to drive, she seldom took to the road once winter began, so her parting glimpse of the fields was the dying sunflowers, a first snow often covering their shockingly meek, bowed heads. And now, in a wink, the ridged black soil was shining between pools of melting snow, the celebrated earth pushed up like a crop and unnamed roads again led somewhere. She had a native's attachment to the flat, unspectacular prairie, which had a beauty that needed to be defended and so felt more possessed. Here, winter was king, but summer was beautiful. This was the country; to Rainey, a town girl, it all sprang up each year like grass, the runaway mustard by the road, the light-brown stretches of barley, the new sunflowers, wheat, and flax, her favorite, blue flax, the most delicate color in the fields, its blueness fading as you gazed.

Her car was sunny and warm. When the tires struck a puddle, like Stephie in her galoshes, it brought a glee to the ride. She splashed over Robinson's maps—all six. Six maps he needed; don't want to leave anything out! Poor mapped land would be carved like a carcass before he was through with it. He had given a very fine example of himself this morning. Threatening an old woman was obviously not beyond the town's attorney-at-law. Because of a book—how important could it be? Of course, he couldn't fire her. She might be a touch senile, but the town would never stand for it. Rainey wasn't concerned about that. She just hoped that Alpha Davis never found out she was in his office when it happened.

What wounded her was hearing him belittle his law work. It was the same as belittling his life—including her. And she thought of the big desk and the gold-framed family. Here he was, one of the most respected men in town. Did Doc Sunderquist ever belittle being the doctor? She very much doubted it.

What wounded her also worried her. Dwayne Armstead was like a landmark in this area. Even Margaret seemed surprised that George was running. But one thing about him, he was the luckiest individual she had ever known. Suppose he won—where was George's luck going to take them? The trouble was, he never knew when to stop. That was the way he talked, that was the way he ate, that was the way he courted, that was the way he won.

If he won, he would be away from home at times when the Assembly was having a session. There might be days during the year when he had people in for dinner. So sometimes the house would be a little empty and sometimes a little full. And maybe that would be all there was to it. Still, it seemed like a good time to be a step ahead of him who was probably a step ahead of her.

Thirty-five miles west of Jericho, Grafton was the closest town to home that had decent shops and was as big. Clarke's Clothing Store was in Grafton; not that Clarke's was that different from their own Dakota Store, but she liked to see what they were showing, especially in the spring and fall. It was a large establishment, women's clothes on one side and men's on the other and shelves with fabrics, rugs and bedding along the walls. As she flipped through the skirts on the rack, warming to the process of really choosing, her eye ran over the clothes of other women who were shopping. Sometimes their glances met and they smiled at one another, though perfect strangers. None seemed unusual or strikingly dressed, but shopping beside them was pleasurable. It felt natural to compare herself with them in clothes, figure and face. Sometimes she felt drawn to know more about them than was showing, but seldom curious enough to imagine the particulars. She was twenty-eight years old and she couldn't remember the last time she saw the bare body of another female her age, probably back at girl scout camp and then by accident. It would be a shock to see a naked woman now, say one of her old friends. The fruity parts, the friend's face above— that would be awful, a lot more of a shock than seeing one of their husbands. She thought she could laugh about that.

On her way to a dressing room with some skirts over her arm, smoothing her hand over the covers of new fashion magazines, she wondered how she would like having one of those sleek women, elegantly dressed, as a friend, and she didn't think she would like that at all. But the ones on the Butterick's sewing pattern envelopes, the pretty faces that might spend months on the counter, and whose freshness and dustiness made them seem like your cousin, they could be her friend.

The skirts she tried on were a disappointment, soulless around her, or ill-fitting, or, a wound to the heart, prettier on the rack than on her. She spent most of the time in her stocking feet in a tiny cubicle with a mirror. She hummed to herself, considered each skirt, smoothed her thighs and hips, and stuck out her chest, and finally stuck out her tongue in her exasperation. She only leafed through the sweaters since she hadn't found a skirt. She was getting hungry. The new spring coats didn't look new at all, but that wasn't the problem. The problem was that she liked something expensive on occasion, almost self-righteously so, and this stuff could be for anybody. She felt let down. She hated to go home empty handed. Her maxim was, if you took the time to look, you could always find something at Clarke's.

She had lunch in the café, taking a booth in the sun near the window. It was a late lunch, a luxury. She ordered a milkshake and a chicken salad sandwich on toast. She almost always had that when she came to Grafton. Either that or a milkshake and an egg salad sandwich.

She never ordered the tomato surprise, though her eye would always pause there on the menu.

Almost did. But never did.

Neither did she know anyone who had ever ordered a tomato surprise in her presence.

She yawned with her hand barely getting to her mouth in time. There was a dull warning in the yawn, her sleepiness, her slow-revolving thoughts, as though their hum could hum her to death.

She knew times when her not-unhappy boredom became some-thing else, times when she had to watch herself, when as lovely, golden Lorraine she was a statue, impassive to everything, like the vision of a high school harvest queen high on a float that she once had been in the flesh. Times when she ought to rouse herself but would not, times like now, sitting here by herself in the town of Grafton in the sun, the sunlight so bright there was blackness in it, watching no one in particular come in and go out, her head leaning against the warm back of the booth, only her slow eyes moving in her small town beauty pageant face.

SHE MIGHT have taken a very different turn, married a farmer—some of her girlfriends did and thought it was romantic—that wholly removed yet snug existence in a farmhouse once looking like an answer to a prayer.

This was after her mother and father died, victims in a car collision on a bad curve near the town line. She was in a class in high school when it happened. A bright, well-behaved girl, never in trouble, she was brought down to the principal's office, where they were all waiting for her. She was like a Christian walking into the ring with lions, except that the lions were the principal, the school nurse, the police chief and Doc Sunderquist.

Her older sister flew in from the East. Family from around the region herded into the church for the double memorial service. In her fragile state, nothing chipped her more than the quick, vivid, well-organized married sister. As she sat, a deep well, un-responsive, they all discussed her future. Her aloneness and a little insurance money qualified her as an heiress in the town. Margaret's family warmly took her in—Margaret's mother con-sidered her almost a daughter. Margaret was her cherished class-mate, her best friend.

She was sixteen. All through her girlhood she had been a child of the light. She had thought herself to be the prettiest, the most popular, the best. She was the one girl who wouldn't stay in Jericho, who could do whatever she wanted. And not all of that vanished overnight; she still believed in most of the story. But now there was a dead little something that she carried with her, the cold mouse in the bottom of the hope chest.

She met George Robinson during the one year she ventured outside Jericho, when unlike Margaret and most girls in her class, in a brave act, she went two hundred miles downstate to the University. He was at a party she went to, two years out of law school, older than her date and most of the others, his looks and clothes more conservative, his presence keener and much more fun. She was engaged almost before she knew it. He was her first, her only love. She couldn't believe her happiness when he expressed a wish to live in Jericho after a visit there—he was tired of preparing briefs for senior members of a large law firm. It was an instance of his luck that the elderly lawyer in town was looking to retire, and soon after the wedding Robinson as the young partner began taking over the practice.

She loved Robinson—she liked being his wife—two different things but both were true. He had a city type of impatience and an only-child conceit, but he was loving and handsome. And very soon there was Jamie. To bejewel the other hand when they all marched out, three years later there was Stephie. Her life completely suited her. If her days all seemed much the same, it was the price she paid for her comfortable safe passage—a little monotony wasn't the worst thing in life! And if she gave the impression of being too appealing, too bright, and even too interesting for Jericho, it was a true impression, it didn't lie. She was a girl who could have left town, gone anywhere and done whatever she wanted. That was her standing in the town.

STEPHIE STOOD on the bathmat while she patted and wiped her with the towel.

"Did you have a nice lunch at Margaret's today? I had a chicken salad sandwich on toast. Then I sat for a while. I went shopping too. But I didn't see anything I wanted to buy. Wasn't that too bad?"

She wrapped the towel around her and gave the dampness a hug. Seeing the big brown eyes and bath-pink cheeks, she couldn't resist and gave her another squeeze.

"Go put your pajamas on, beautiful. And kiss your father goodnight."

Later she put Jamie to bed.

She sat down on the bed and brushed his hair. He was sitting up reading a book and she tilted her head to read as he read, her eyes going from the page to his face. His interests, his likes and dislikes, that he had them, excited her curiosity. As she brushed, she thought of Jimmy, Margaret's little boy. As girls she and Margaret swore they would give their first boy the same name, to start them out together. But as much as she loved Margaret, James Robinson and James Hanson would never be friends. It would never be—Jimmy didn't compare. He was a nice little boy, but just his name made him an echo, as if Jamie was the real little boy and Jimmy a copy of a boy.

She said: "Think you'd like to have Jimmy stay overnight sometime?"

Silence from under the hairbrush but Jamie's eyes were no longer reading.

"Don't you like playing with Jimmy? Isn't he nice to be with?"

"Jimmy Hanson?"

"Yes. Isn't he a nice little boy?"

"He's okay, I guess."

Rainey laughed. She bent down and kissed him. She didn't care about princes in books and especially not the one in George's stuffy book. "Good night, little prince," she said.

BIG RED ran toward the streetlamp way at the end of the street. Two of his friends nosed at the fringes of the light but it was the solitary light he always sped to. Robinson walked behind, holding an empty leash. He walked Big Red every night. Big Red roamed free all day, so there was no need to walk him, but Robinson enjoyed the late night air, the exercise and Big Red's company. There was no call for a leash either, but he liked the muscular feel of himself and Big Red contending as Big Red strained and swung his nose skyward and pulled from place to place, and then Robinson would grab Big Red, snap off the leash and let him run.

The whistle of a freight express—on its way in, on its way out—became the foil then the heart of the silence. He walked swinging the leash, the end of it floating above the town, the stars gleaming above the leash. It was a nice prairie town. There was good money to be made from a town like Jericho, the outlying farms, clients around the county. Over a lifetime the lawyer should end up a rich man. But maybe he made a mistake coming here, unless he could launch himself in politics and leave, though that might make Rainey less than happy. It was a shame he wasn't that interested in making money. It honestly surprised him that he wasn't a greedy man. It seemed like an inconsistency. He had the capacity to be greedy but he wasn't, and somehow that made his other excesses wonderful.

Sleep came not at all.

In bed, restless with plans for his campaign, he was still outside with the galaxies, his thoughts as crowded and scattered. Rainey was asleep beside him. Should he wake her up? It was tempting and convenient. Why? What for? The sake of a few sensations? For ten minutes of power—shaking the gasps of somebody else like fruit down from a tree? Pathetic power. Monster Earth was a bigger place than that. Sex wasn't serious; it was gasping and giggling, nagging and nibbling. This bunch of grapes is absurd. Yet I want to eat it, which is even more absurd. But since it seems I must, I will eat it in the most voracious way I know. I will bite off some from this side and some from that side, this side then that side and all around. I will devour every grape. I will do it time and again. And who knows, if I eat feverishly and with enough of an appetite, maybe one of these times it might decide to be something better, something less ridiculous, than a bunch of grapes.

He loved Rainey above all beings. In that election long since settled, she was his constituency of one. He built his practice and became the mayor, in part, to show her what her husband the newcomer was able to do. He loved to talk to her, because that meant, in the same breath, talking for her. When she was impressed, he glowed, and more words were born. He vowed that Machiavelli's *The Prince* would be in the public library, but he never forgot *The Adventures of Tom Sawyer* and Tom walking the picket fence to show off for Becky Thatcher. He never exactly thought about it, but it was in his mind, in his fibre, his favorite passage in all of books, if the truth were known. Tom daringly walked the fence for Becky and he, George, had leaped on for a lifetime of walking it for Rainey.

"This is important to me," he said to her sleeping side. "They're saying I don't stand much of a chance. But you know me better. I won't lose—I'm not a losing man. I say this is only the beginning. I'm going further. All men dream and I know it sounds foolish, saying it like this, in this room, here in bed . . . I can be governor someday."

CHAPTER 6

WEST WORKED with three ledgers, which were: the Combined Journal, the Accounts Payable, and Accounts Receivable, these three basic ledgers. At Amundson's lumber yard they were kept in the back office in that part of the yard that was a hardware store. The two men up front in blue company shirts were the same ones who helped outside with the lumber and were busy first thing in the morning uncrating and putting out stock. West walked in at nine. Jack Amundson stepped away from the cash register and kept up a conversation with a customer whose paint was churning in the mixer. West took yesterday's sales slips and charge slips from the machine next to the cash register, and the old used tape from the register, and took them into the office. He put his lunch bag on top of the open roll-top desk and hung his sweater on the clothes tree. There was a telephone—nothing of his concern—a file cabinet, and an old scratched swivel chair for the desk.

He took the three ledgers out of the top drawer of the desk. He took the charge slips, entered the charges in the proper accounts, and filed the slips. He posted the cash receipts in the Combined Journal, also the newly paid bills, which he then posted in Accounts Receivable. He thumbed through checkbook stubs showing disbursements and entered these in the Combined Journal and in Accounts Payable. Stubs, charge slips, checks, sales slips, bills, all were recorded and filed. Though he despised the work he was thorough, and felt physically cleaner when the desk was clean and had just the three ledgers on it. He opened Accounts Receivable and worked through it page by page. Once a month he did billing. Bills could accumulate for 120 days. After that, it was none of his concern; Amundson saw to the billing. As West turned the pages and wrote the bills, he sided with the people who owed. The longer they were carried from month to month, the more forgiven they were. Farmers, whom he mistrusted on sight, were flesh-and-blood when they owed in Accounts Receivable.

He had five bookkeeping jobs. A couple were sometime things like the quarterly tax report. At the Legion Club, where he was beginning to keep balances, he worked in a cubicle with the thud, roll and crack of bowling balls overhead as old men bowled in their cold-weather bowling league. He put in a few mornings a month in John's Saloon. There he worked sitting on a bar-stool, back room, card players and dark barroom behind him while he counted money and wrote checks. The lumber yard was his biggest job. He was here several mornings a week and into the afternoon when he did the billing. But wherever he was, he sat down with the moment in mind when the last entry was entered, the accounts balanced, the ledgers closed—he could forget them then. Still, once they were done, it gave him a pleasing sense of equilibrium. His work was neat, exact and uniform, more so than any of his predecessors. That was obvious, he thought. He always wrote in black ink; this had been left up to him. So in all of the ledgers he used the same pen, the same black ink.

He knew it was an uneducated man's work. It was menial work, even though it made use of paper and pen. Each time he came to the bottom of a page he had to sign it. He disliked his name, disliked seeing it—Alaman. The sound of it made him sink inside. Since he had no bank account, no mail or transactions, the only place he signed it was in the ledgers. The signature was for the audit. That was another reason for regretting it. They told him at school that he wouldn't enjoy the audit. But no one told him he would sweat. He had been audited twice so far, so it didn't happen often, but it lasted all day and into the evening and he always had to be present; not only that, he had to have supper with the auditor, that was the custom. They went to the Legion Club both times. It was the cat having supper with the mouse, West avenging his sweat by thinking: "Dope, you eat like a dope. You're still looking for my mistakes and I don't make mistakes. I will one day. But that'll be because I want to make mistakes." So both times it turned into the cat having supper with the cat.

As he worked through the billing the phone rang sometimes but they took it on the wall phone in the store. The door was open but no one bothered him. No one noticed him. He ate his lunch there, sitting at the roll-top desk, chewing his sandwich and staring into pigeonholes and space.

It was after three by the time he finished. He replaced the ledgers in the drawer, left the stamped, addressed bills in a stack on the desk, and told Amundson that he had done the work.

The damp morning brought a mild April day. When West stepped out through the side door to get on his bicycle he smelled the sultriness and lumber in the big barnlike space of the yard. The dampness and haze crept in like spring coming in the back door. He suddenly left the bicycle where it was. There was no one in the yard. It was open to the street at both ends, with skylights in the roof. There were bins of white bricks and sacks of cement. A saw was mounted on the wall. The boards, most cut from big evergreens, the taller ones standing on end, were up to twenty feet high. The height of the roof multiplied the silence.

West turned a corner and came walking back; as he did, looking through to the street, he saw the profile of Lorraine Spencer in the window of a slowly driven car. Not that he ever knew her enough to think about. She was far ahead of him in school, four years, four jumps ahead. If he still saw her face once she passed, it was because he couldn't remember the last time he had seen her. His struggle was with time. Lorraine Spencer, Rainey Spencer, Lorraine Robinson, a face out of the past. But not his, never his, what way his? They shared no past.

He came walking back, touching the boards with his hand, feeling the unfeelable grain. He knew the different names from sales slips and bills but not which kind of wood was which. He smelled just one raw wood smell. It made him remember the stacks of school supplies when school started each year, the new pencils and new notebooks—they always smelled different that first week, and never that way again. The new wood made him feel almost the same, sprang the same lock in him, sprang the same exaggerated hope. He looked at the lumber all down the row. He was enthused. The question was: what could he do with it, what could he make, what could he need?

A bookcase. He hit a board on the shoulder and laughed and then looked behind him to make sure nobody saw. Then he felt the board, surveyed it, did the same with boards next to it and boards in other bins; he spent more time choosing than when he had picked Cat out. Each time, his mind superimposed a bookcase.

It would be simple. Four pieces of wood for the frame, one piece across the middle, would give him three shelves. He could do it today. He had the time, the proper tools, a mind for exactness and detail. His mind sawed, hammered, sanded and saw a bookcase.

He went back into the store. He had them come out and cut five four-foot pieces of knotty pine, a pretty wood that was shelf-size and also cheap. It was the only wood he knew by sight, so he wouldn't have to ask them any questions, just have them saw it to size. He went out with the man and watched it being done. The first piece off the saw was longer than his conception of four feet which immediately altered his idea, but he watched silently, not wanting to go back on his instructions. He bought a box of nails and a packet of sandpaper. He half-expected them to throw these in for nothing because he did their books. He felt as if he had learned a lesson when they didn't. He carried his purchases out to his bicycle. Using his belt he strapped the boards to the rack over the back wheel. He put the sandpaper and nails into the wire basket in front. But it was hard going. The bicycle wobbled, the more so because he had to go slowly. It was an old bicycle, one-speed, with a foot brake. The boards stuck out like wings and West biked carefully.

The lumber yard was on a side street downtown and except to cross it he stayed off Legion Avenue. But at the corner, as a matter of course, like Cat looking in the very spot for yesterday's bird, he looked for Dixie through the window of Haley's Drugstore. He had seen her there twice when he went in, once talking to her father at the drug prescription counter, the other time getting a bottle of shampoo. A couple of days later he bought the same shampoo, kept it on the floor beside his bed and in his prize daydream smelled the short brown hair and kissed the crotch of the naked little goddess Dixie. Though he often biked past her house, those two times in the drugstore were the only times he had seen Dixie since the ice melted.

West rode the loaded bicycle down the short path to his door. He had seen an old handsaw in his one visit out to the shack. He went and dug it out. He unstrapped the boards, balanced saw, nails and sandpaper on top, and carried them inside.

The boards were too long; he saw that immediately looking toward the space. On one side was a cupboard, on the other a window. His wall map was there, and his rocker—the rest of the room was kitchen or the bathtub. So the three boards that were the shelves would have to be sawed down to fit, as he anticipated.

He spread newspapers on the floor. Then he lined the boards up evenly to make sure they were exactly the same size. He took a hammer out of a drawer and put it down next to the saw. It looked so easy. Step by step, in his head, it repeatedly took about four hours. In four hours he would have a bookcase. He made a quick early supper and ate it looking at the boards.

He cut a pencil to a strong dull point. For a tape measure he cut a piece of string nearly equal to the width of his space. He designed it as wide as possible, not only because it would hold more books, but because he wanted to keep all he could of his wood. Cat walked over the boards and sat down on the newspaper to watch. Before he measured, West picked his boards carefully. He chose the best ones for the sides since those would show more. He appreciated himself for this. He liked the idea of finding his own way to do things, like measuring with the string. Putting the two kitchen chairs close together he made a sawhorse.

The saw was dull—at its first screech Cat jumped up and ran off the newspaper. As a working saw it had the long use and disuse of the shack it came from. It caught and bent or else it bounced out and had to be edged back in. West worked grimly, holding it to his line. If he sawed too fast, little bruises appeared. His four hours began to look like a goal unattainable. When he should have been hammering nails he was still sawing the end off the second board. Then a knot popped out when he tried to grind through it; in disbelief he saw his shoe through the hole in the board. It was one of his shelves, which meant that the hole would be covered by books, be a hole invisible to him, and if he were closer to the end he might have been able to accept that. But not now—not so soon. He decided to do away with the hole by taking a little more off the board, even though it meant that when he finished these two he would have to go back and even up the first board.

He sawed and resented the extra sawing, which was his own fault, going back to his miscalculation in the lumber yard. But at the same time he could see its value, in that when the bookcase was all done it would be that much more his. He had been taught a lesson, not to saw through knots, and his new lines avoided them by a careful adjustment of the length. But when he went back and redid the first board the difference he left for himself was too fine and he split the corner of the shelf.

He threw down the saw. He pounded his thigh with the guilty hand. He spotted Cat and yelled at him for running. He laughed— his own fault again. Too fine. Too good. He knew it was going to happen. He knocked off the loose piece and threw it to one side. When he got some glue he could glue it back on. Anyway, it was better than a hole. And he was through with the sawing.

It felt good to pick up the hammer. He was eager to get on with it, nail boards together, see a shape; a shape would obliterate the details. Cat crept back to the edge of the newspaper and sat. Cat watched, tail swishing, ears laid back by the banging. West started with the frame. He had no knack, no skills. His carpentry was intelligent, careful, all thought out, but then exasperating when he did it. He could have used another pair of hands to hold the board steady, to keep the nail straight when he banged and held the board. He had the bookcase down on its side and knelt at it, tapping and pounding and peering. His poor skill, instead of making him more tolerant, made him less. He spaced his nails and kept the boards aligned. In each small thing his concern made him meticulous—which was beside the point, since nothing was turning out the way he envisioned it. He hated the knots. He couldn't hammer a nail through them. The nails were sharper than the saw but they couldn't go through either. Worse, some could but some couldn't, and then he had to pull the nail out and leave a hole or pound it into the wood doubled over. He drove one knot clean out with a blow of the hammer; another he pulled out like an olive, on the end of a nail. There were a million knots. Just where he wanted to put a nail there was always a knot there first.

Then, when he stood it up, and stood back, he saw that the middle shelf was crooked. It fit in, but slanted because it was slightly longer than it was supposed to be. His alternatives were to take the bookcase apart and saw the board down; go back to Amundson's for a new board sawed to size and then take the bookcase apart; or he could leave it.

He left it. It was beginning to be all one and the same. And it tottered. It was a defect easily nullified by putting something under the corner, or by the weight of the books themselves. But when he touched it, and it tottered, with its crooked shelf, its crooked look, its bent nails, holes, dents by the hammer, its knotty cheap-wood look, he suddenly saw where a couple of nails could go. Anyplace. So he drove them in. Then he sent in a couple more.

Then he broke the thing apart. It wouldn't stand so he destroyed in on its back, a back it didn't have. He used the hammerhead then the claw and when the side swung feebly loose the hammerhead again, fast, sending both halves flying. Pants, shirt clung to him, dark and light with sweat and sawdust. He crashed the hammer down on board after board, his anger past his control, his anger climbing up its own back to exact the next blow. But even as he brought the hammer down there was a part of him that whispered to him, it would have been all right, it would have been all right, it would have been all right. Why do you have to kill it? It wasn't so bad! Pity welled up in him, pity and shame for the thing that was so dead; that had been his for a minute.

He threw what was left of it into the shack. He wanted it out of his sight, out of his range. He had it all bundled inside the newspapers—the pieces of wood, the box of nails, the sandpaper, the small broken bits, the saw, the sawdust. When he came back into the kitchen there wasn't a trace of it left. It was a perfect ending. From saw-into-house to saw-back-to-shack had taken just under four hours. He had hit the time right on the nose. Except that he didn't sand it—he forgot that.

He punched his hand. He wasn't feeling so bad. He felt bad but good, ashamed and the opposite, filled with hopelessness and full of gaiety. He went and picked up Cat who had gone and hidden under the sink. West hugged Cat.

He carried Cat to the rocker and sat down with him. Cat struggled so West played a game of Cat trying to nip his hand with teeth or claws though he carried scratches from this game. He tempted Cat with the hand, but it was West who wanted to play, to have Cat stay there in his lap. He let go and Cat jumped down, trotted underneath the sink and started washing himself—he wouldn't come back. West rocked. He clasped his hands, knuckles white and open mouth wetting them. He looked at the clock because it ticked, not because the time meant anything.

Then he went and got his black bookkeeping pen and a writing pad and sat down in the rocker. He wanted that pen because he was going to do some bookkeeping. Some homework. He was in the mood. West had a trick he wanted to play on the town. Not one trick, a bag of tricks.

CHAPTER 7

WEST HAD always wanted to do something to the town. Even though he always came back here, after the army, after Chicago, still he wanted to do something to it. Just a little while back in town always made him see that. The streets, the people, their snug houses, just the smallness, invited him to do something— so maybe that was the hidden reason he came back. Some days, just on general principles, when he walked past the city hall, he felt like dropping in and asking them point-blank if they weren't worried that someone like him was living in their town. So he knew that someday he would try something. But until he got deeper into keeping their books he had no idea what.

West wrote down on the pad:

Bookkeeping Tricks
Trick 1. Mistakes in arithmetic trick.
Trick 2. The simple no entry trick. Charge slip filed, bill sent out, but no entry anywhere.
   3. Wrong page entry trick. Pick a charge slip. Debit the wrong person.
   4. The twist. Pick a check. Credit the wrong person.
   5. Right person, right amount, wrong column trick. Man's check comes in, add the amount to his balance.

6. The twist. Take man's charge slip and subtract the amount from his balance.
7. Mirror trick. Either way—any entry.
          $19
          $91
8. Special trick for Amundson's. The lost charge slip trick. Throw away charge slip. No charge slip, no charge. But bill the guy anyway.
9. Special trick for John's Saloon. The bank deposit trick. Make the bank deposit. Go home. Forget the entry.
10. The Great Tax Report Trick. Needs thinking. Long range. Brings state and federal agents into town.

It pleased him so much to see the tricks written out. It struck West that without these tricks the books weren't balanced. Whoever was to blame, they just didn't feel balanced without his hand in them. Something necessary was missing. But the tricks would help to balance them. Each time he wrote his plan down he would burn it in the sink as a precaution. They might get hold of it, it might fall out of his pocket; better to be safe. Yet he always expected to feel less safe when he burned it because his calculated destruction of it made the plan more real. Besides, making ashes of it meant that he could hatch it again, writing at his table in the Paris Café for instance, while Jack Amundson sat eating lunch at the counter, or Saloon John, or any of the other men, formulating his plan right in the midst of them.

Fix their books
Kill their books
Slay their books
That was the little tail he pinned on the end always.
Kill their books
Though he wondered if he didn't like the nice friendly one better.
Fix their books
He laughed and slapped his thigh. They were all good. Like the tricks. He had to move cautiously though. The tricks had to be buried, each one, and balances juggled, so that the false bills weren't sent out until near the end. He also wanted a few more

tricks. And then, he needed a few more jobs, more books to fix, more jobs, more people, that's what made it a trick on the town. He'd keep burying tricks until there were enough. The tricks would all hide there in the books, below the surface, in the dark. Then when the time came—air, daylight, chaos.

West knew that he would never do any of these tricks. He could write them down on his pad forever and all it would be was the biggest thing in the world in Alaman West's handwriting. He'd never work it out because he wouldn't survive the audit. Who else but him when the dope found all the mistakes? That was the sticking-point, the audit. He knew that he could bury two or three tricks on each job and survive. But there had to be a lot more than that or it wasn't any good, it wasn't an idea, it wouldn't be understood. But if he did more, it meant suicide in the audit. He was boxed in. It made him furious; he slammed the pad against his leg. The audit. It always came down to the audit—like his bookcase and the knots. His plans always had knots. His plans were no good—his and all no good.

Fix a man

His pen scrawled that. The pen was his pal.

Fix a man

The paper was heavy linen paper, letter-writing paper. The pen made a warm black scrawl.

Kill a man

It looked so real. It was equivalent to watching his tricks flame up. Scrawled, it was self-contained, powerful, explosive, like an infamous autograph.

He wrote:

Kill a man

Do it. Kill a man.

The loud clock ticked. The chair rocked. Chair and clock egged him on.

New plan

Kill a man

Who? West wrote:

Some man

Where? West wrote:

Out in the open

When? And West wrote:

On the Fourth of July
He laughed. He liked where his brain raced. He wrote now:
Assassination
He rested the pad in his lap. He wrote nothing more for now. Assassination was the pinnacle. Otherwise nothing had changed; it was a new plan but the same old idea, but stretched, from a height. He figured it would be understood. He could send a letter to make sure it was. The letter elated him. He started thinking about the letter, whether to send it before or after, and how to disguise his handwriting, and if he would cut and paste words together out of the newspaper. There was a lot to decide.

He went to his calendar on the wall and flipped the pages. July 4th. Three months from now. In three months a man would be assassinated. He took his pen and circled July 4th. He was going to assassinate a man. He was going to assassinate someone and that was the day.

The silence was enormous. He whistled at it. All of a sudden he wanted to make jokes. He said to his chair, "I'm off my rocker."

He was starving. He slapped a sandwich together and ate in big gulps walking around the kitchen. He eyed the calendar each time he passed.

Killing one of them was safer than killing their books.

No audit. He laughed—it struck him funny. No audit. No knots.

Some man.

Which man? He was curious himself. He'd go have a look around. He didn't want to start with a preference. *Some man* could be any of them, old, young, handsome, ugly, smart, stupid, big or small. He slipped on a sweater and went outside. *Some man* could be the first one he saw on the street.

Bike or walk? Bike; no telling how far he might have to rove at night with the downtown all shut up. But if he biked he'd go by his man too fast and miss that first real moment, since he couldn't so easily slow down on a bike and look back.

So West went walking.

Only Doc Death was safe. Doc was disqualified because West had a motive there. He hated Doc personally and always would and so Doc was safe. But nobody else.

A fine rain fell, a drizzle, a cloak, all around him before he noticed. A pickup truck sped past and was gone, but not so fast that he didn't see the face and recognize the truck. But that seemed unsatisfactory—not at all right. So to solve the problem, and be fair, West ruled that moving pickup trucks were safe.

Then a few minutes later he saw old Curley's nephew standing in his lighted garage. But he couldn't assassinate Curley's nephew because Curley sold him his bicycle, which was his trusty bike and part of himself. So Curley's nephew was safe.

Then who should he see getting into his car but Jack Amundson's kid brother who was one of the workers at the lumber yard. Wasn't there a lot of family on the street tonight! West felt indifferent to the brother but he really resented Jack Amundson, and that made it a blow at Amundson, a motivated thing, murder, so Amundson's brother was safe.

A car with a woman in it turned the corner and drove by him. Women were safe. Cars were safe.

So were men going into their houses and men sitting or standing in their houses.

They were safe.

All seemed safe.

But who was that coming down the street? Who and what?

Man and a dog. Man and a dog. Man and a dog.

HE WAS a bully. He was crude. He could be vicious. He ate too much. She would die before she ever again sat down at the table with him and a dish of butter and a plate of warm rolls. He was different from the man she married. He was always just like this. Rain rattled on the window panes and Rainey approved it, she blessed it. He was still out there in it. He better not come to bed soon. He had no business being a father because he was a baby himself. But Jamie was too fast for him. He swung and missed because Jamie ducked. Oh, pretty move, Jamie!

It was still beyond comprehension. She thought he was storming about something outside because he had hardly set foot in the house. She came in from the kitchen and he was swinging the newspaper. Jamie wouldn't give up the paper, Jamie wanted the comics, Jamie gave him a sour look. His picture was in the paper!

So he swung and Jamie ducked. He had his paper but he swung like a madman anyway! What if he hadn't missed? This was before supper. All of his buttering and roll crushing and roll eating was to come. He just stood there holding up his picture for her to see. She said to him: "You look like a fool."

No stars. Black night. Darkness between one streetlight and the next as though a brush dips into the same darkness as that surrounding the town.

Robinson walks swinging Big Red's leash. When he mulled it rationally, and in retrospect, it was fortunate that he had missed. If he connected, she would have said he was a lot worse than a fool. But not a fool—not a fool. There was very little that was all black and white.

Kids were pests, this was an immutable of life. They were permanent pests. They hung around when you were alive and they hung around after you were dead. Why should he have to fight to see his campaign story in the *Herald*? When you were on the trail of something momentous, what was less thrilling than to look up and see a kid?

He walks ahead, nearing home, Big Red lagging behind. A light breeze blows; a fine spring rain glistens on his forehead, drops replenishing drops. His face gets wetter but something like spite has kept him out walking. But not only spite. He welcomes the raindrops to his face. Here at thirty-six, at sixteen, at the age of six, night and wind and rain have always made him feel anointed, destined, a hero to himself. This is Robinson's consolation for being out in the rain tonight.

In front of the house, he stops. Big Red sees him stop, and when he does Big Red comes running. At the same time a man walks toward Robinson on the opposite side of the street. It is as though galloping dog and shadowy man have started together.

Robinson, ready for him, braces himself.

"Here Red! Come on Red!" Robinson yells.

It felt right—felt good. It fit right in. He had passed here at just the right time. Walking at a normal pace West crossed front yards across the street until he was well past the house, then he looked back. Robinson and the dog were gone, so he lingered. That was

Some man and that was his house. Downstairs a window was lit. Curtains covered it. That was where *Some man* had his easy chair. The upstairs was dark. That was where *Some man* slept. But he had been identified, he wasn't *Some man* anymore; he had an address, a house, a family, a dog, a yard, a yellow-lit lantern. He was George Robinson.

Lawyer Mayor George Robinson. What a surprise.

West knew he would have walked through the rain all week to get to George Robinson.

When he came home he was soaking wet. He stripped his clothes off, put on pajamas, and then threw on his army coat because his teeth were chattering. He even had to light the oil burner and move the rocker in front of it. It was a joke. He felt fine, marvelous, he had his plan, his hands were steady, his mind too, but his teeth were chattering as if they knew something he didn't. He drank hot coffee huddled in the coat. Then they clacked against the cup; it was scary. The teeth had a life of their own.

WEST HAD never set foot in Robinson's house just as he had never seen the inside of Robinson's law office. West as a kid had run through the city hall because it was in the park but that was long before Robinson probably even heard of Jericho. West had never bullshitted with, shot the breeze with, passed the time of day with Robinson. They had never been properly introduced. If the conditions were just right, if he was going in a door and Robinson was coming out, and there were just the two of them, and neither's eye was too distracted by bright sun, whipping wind, or falling snow, then they might have nodded their heads at one another a half-dozen times. West knew that Robinson was running for the State Assembly just as he assumed it was true that Robinson was mayor, because he had read it in the weekly *Pioneer*. That was the source of his news about the town. Names would appear that hadn't entered his head since he was a child. When he picked up the paper, people were dead or alive with equal suddenness. He didn't subscribe to the *Pioneer*, but would buy it on whim if he happened to be in the drugstore. But starting now he bought it each week the day it came out and took it into the Paris Café and turned the pages for news about Robinson, any news, a finger darting over the general news and Church News and Social News. He read that Robinson said this-or-that at a council meeting. That the So-and-so's had visited the George Robinsons last Friday and enjoyed an evening of bridge and a delightful supper. Trivial stuff but it was a question of feeling his way, getting into his subject, peeling back the skin, just finding a place to peel.

But April ended, May was here, and he had done nothing but circle the Fourth of July on his calendar and find Robinson's name every week in the *Jericho Pioneer*. Once or twice Robinson crossed his field of vision and West stopped and watched and felt suddenly scared, felt sluggish, felt unready, and shook off that sight as if it were a fly buzzing before it was time for flies. Whenever it felt real, he got scared; it was the inside story told by his chattering teeth. West took his eyes off the Fourth of July. It was more fun to sit in the Paris Café and look at the sports pages of the *Pioneer* at pictures of Dixie Carpenter in a track suit.

The *Pioneer* told its readers that track star Dixie Carpenter was planning to start practice for the national trials of the Olympic Games as soon as school was over. West studied a photograph of Dixie in track shorts and jutting jersey breaking the tape, jaw up, mouth open, mouth alive, a mouth of black newsprint like pain. The other pictures of her were hazy and uninteresting, but he cut out all three and kept them. He rode his bicycle past her house and around the rapidly warming little town, on the lookout for Dixie.

Then one morning he found Dixie's Olympic practice place, the kids' playground down a slope and not far from the town swimming pool. West was riding by when he spotted a girl in shorts running then in the air head over heels and when she stood up, sure enough it was Dixie. West straddled the bike and watched, surprised since he assumed that a track star would be training to run races. But whatever it was, Dixie couldn't have minded being seen. It was all in the open, no trees, no fence, just the grass where she practiced and nearby a swing, a slide and a bench. The next day, early in the morning, he rode straight down to the playground with a book in his basket. He had a pair of dark glasses from the drugstore, dark brown, the darkest he could find, not to disguise his face but his eyes, like blind man's glasses.

She showed up. He was overjoyed. Sitting on the bench, with his book, his dark glasses, he felt as good as invisible.

CHAPTER 8

SHE WAS there every morning. On days he was free he had only to ride down, open his book, and wait. Then along she would come, down the road she would ride, here she would come on her bike, looking like her pictures in the *Pioneer*, if not in her track uniform then in shorts and usually a jersey with JERICHO across the front and DIXIE across the back. She waved her hand the first day, on the third called "Hi!" On the fourth "Nice day!" That was how people greeted strangers. Which meant he was all right here. Which meant that he was free to sit and read his book. He studied her while she dismounted, kicked the kickstand on the bike, pulled off her shoes. It amused him that Mr. Carpenter was behind the counter when he picked out the dark glasses, Mr. Carpenter who was famous among boys and men as Mr. C. He had an older daughter named Sissie, married now and packed off to another town. All the boys in her class had a good time humping Sissie, who was small, small-eyed, low slung, with an expression that always looked smudged. So when West bought the dark glasses for Dixie, he couldn't help thinking about Sissie, he couldn't in spite of himself.

He never removed the dark glasses in the playground so Dixie was always browned, like the sky, like the grass. She worked in her bare feet on a stretch of grass and clover. He knew nothing about the sport she practiced; there were somersaults like small dives, flips in the air, cartwheels one-handed and no-handed with running starts. She ran and sprang and speed and motion were the light that let him see: the white soles of her feet and her trim legs and arched back, her whole neatly finished figure, her small chest under the jersey a little smack in his eyes. She stopped her practicing and rested sometimes. She would sit on the grass curled up with her arms about her knees, the track star curled up like a bookworm, the light-blue eyes at odds with the cute nose and cute round face, like blue mirrors, the eyes, like West's light-trapping dark glasses. Dixie the dreamer—Dixie the dream. He looked at her shoulders, her face, her bike, her discarded shoes.

He thought about it, thought about it, and finally called to her: "I read about your prizes."

A look his way—a smile—"I didn't hear you."

"I read about your prizes. The *Pioneer!*" West reached for his throat. It felt as if the vocal cords showed. "The *Pioneer* said you were practicing for the Olympic Games. They always call you the track star."

"You shouldn't believe everything you read in the *Pioneer*," Dixie called back.

West nodded his head. End of shouts. End of conversation. The next day Dixie threw herself into practicing her back-flip. This was her morning's Olympic practice. A spring and spin in the air, her hands touch the ground, she springs off them, lands, folds in half, stands up, arms up, and drops her hands. An hour went by; she was a small light machine, running on desire, seldom pausing for breath, resting by pacing, hands on hips and chest heaving at the sky, the imaginary starting line she walked back to, sprang from, about twenty yards from where West sat on the bench, some book across his lap, pale thriller hiding thrill. He wished he could smell her sweat. Patches sprang up under her arms and across her back, and when she stretched and the jersey lifted he saw drops running down her stomach. She was so remarkable. So wonderful. His adoration made him feel privileged. He longed to nestle his face against her damp jersey; to close his eyes and slide with the sweat drops down to oblivion and smell the Dixie smell between her legs. She collapsed when she couldn't do any more. She sprawled on the grass flat on her back and threw her arm over her eyes in the bright playground sun.

What if he sneaked up and kissed her? Could do it softly, like a ghost? He couldn't, but suppose he could. Who would see? Who would be the wiser? His ghost legs walked over as he sat stiff-cocked on the bench—he would give anything to kiss Dixie. He had no illusions that Mr. Carpenter would let her go out with him even if she was willing. He had no real place in the town, also he was too old for her, also he had no family, also he was Alaman West. And so he sat on the bench in full view hidden behind brown glasses. He had spent so much of his life on the outside looking in that it had become his assigned position. It felt natural. His official place was at the edge. To go to bed some night and wake up in the center would be like waking up in a strange bed. It would be the end of his few bearings. So he observed Dixie from the bench, intense and hidden. His method was a sniper's, his only range long-range.

"Hi!"

"Nice morning!"

"Nice day!"

"Yeah, nice day!"

He masturbated often, continually so it seemed to him. He would wait in the playground until she rode out of sight then swing on his bike and speed home to rub the abysmal wound. He was afraid he would contract gangrene and ignorant of the symptoms searched the abused cock for black, for green, because in the army he had heard stories about that happening to prisoners in the stockade. Each time the fear passed, he would feel sadness and remorse toward Dixie. He would think of her youngness, her sweetness, her seriousness. In the depths of his remorse, he would think she was like a sister.

He went down to the swimming pool once because she sometimes went there after practice. He stood outside the wire fence, fingers hooked in, feeling like an extinct form of life. Pool and pool-side were crowded with kids. His eye found her in the water with her brother. When she got out there it was, Dixie in a bathing suit. Only it was nothing to walk over for, no more than what he saw in the playground every day. And he didn't like her with a bathing cap, her face looked too round. And the place was too noisy and too crowded, and he didn't like the looks of the high school boys.

So he kept to the playground. He stayed with his book and dark glasses. There was a safety, a comfort, if regret, if embarrassment, about being alone with Dixie the sister. He usually accepted that now. Dixie was used to his presence. "What are you reading?" she called to him once as she sat on the grass leaning back on her hands. "I don't think you'd like it," he called back; and because this hinted at the truth, for the first time he felt deceitful. There was too much futility in the playground. It made Dixie herself seem futile. Dixie, the grass, the sky, all was uniformly wearisome through the brown lenses of the glasses. One day he didn't go back. He looked at her pictures one last time, then burned them in the sink. If something was supposed to rise out of the ashes, nothing did, just a lump in his throat, and it had nothing to do with Dixie. The lump was Robinson. The Fourth of July loomed, the big day, the day of days. He'd miss the deadline. He was able to stash it for a while, swallow it down, but there were no excuses left. What about Robinson?

He read in the paper that George Robinson would visit the state capital to meet with party leaders in connection with his campaign for the State Assembly. He was sitting in the Paris Café and leafing through the *Daily Herald* when he saw the item. The *Herald* was a real paper, printed in a nearby city and read all over the state. Seeing Robinson's name in it both intimidated and gnawed at West.

He drank up his coffee and cruised his bike past Robinson's office and rode home by way of Robinson's house, big, white and bright in the sunlight. There was the house, with a trimmed hedge, a flower bed blooming and a bicycle next to a car in the driveway. West turned back short of home. He rode back to town and sat in the city hall park and gazed at the Red Owl Store and their old apartment above it, as if the window could open and answer his question: What about Robinson?

He walked into the library. It was cool, the gloom bittersweet, time thick on the shelves. The old librarian sat bent over her little desk writing on a card, the can of sharpened yellow pencils in front of her. West sat down at the reading table. He coughed, drummed his fingers on the table; he made faces. Didn't she see him? Was she made out of wax? Was she crazy? He should shake her. The blue hair could be a blue wig. How would she look without hair? How would she look without hands? How would you look without anything, in a box? He walked out. So what about Robinson?

If the prairie was nowhere and the town was nothing then his house was on the border between nowhere and nothing. He was lucky to have such a simple address or he might not remember it. He might go somewhere else by mistake. West rocked and pictured himself on a train heading out, this time not coming back, going for good. His feeling against his mother for bringing them here in the first place, to the extent that it still embittered him, to that extent it brought his mother back. It was ever the same—it was like a blank wall stepping forward. She visited through despair.

West wiped his eyes. Maybe he would go ahead and commit suicide one of these days. He was getting that tired of living.

But that was good news for his plan. It meant he had nothing to lose. That meant he had nothing to fear. So Robinson wasn't safe yet.

Okay. But he was sick and tired of living with a rocker, a brain, a map and a cat. He was issuing a warning that it couldn't stay the same. He wanted something different, something new, like a friend.

PART TWO

CHAPTER 9

SHE REACHED down and opened the bottom desk drawer and from it took a small paper bag. She settled squarely in her chair, opened the bag, looked in, and removed a shiny flat package wrapped in tinfoil. Carefully, so as to use it again, so that it rustled between her fingers, she folded away the edges of the tinfoil. Inside were two cool slices of banana bread, cut from a loaf she had baked at the beginning of the week, sliced thin and buttered to the edges. This was Alpha Davis's lunch each day and she always waited till noon to eat it when no one came into the library. Chewing took her an unusual amount of time because while her upper plate fitted securely her bottom plate was wobbly again. These were her second set of false teeth; Mrs. Davis was going on seventy-four. The dentist, who always acted smart with her, called the first set of false teeth her baby teeth.

As she broke off bits of banana bread, and licked her fingers, with a special appetite for the crumbs, this was how she liked her library best, dim and quiet, the sun vainly knocking at the door, the shelves housewifely neat and clean. Her window shades were never raised. Sunlight exposed too much: in Alpha Davis's Book of Genesis, light created dust. Whether it was because she had always been a fastidious person, or because she had come to hope that by keeping the sun out she might keep people out, or whether it was that her once freckled, now Roquefort-blue skin shrank from ripening in the light—whatever the history of it was, it had only grown more personal with the years, Alpha Davis's war with the sun.

How she loved cloudy days. How she loved them! Clouds were the great feather-dusters, the great arrangers, the saviors of her day. There were never enough dark days in the year. Cold bright Easter sun and hot bright summer sun and still brighter Christmas sun dazzling on the snow, they all came around too soon for Alpha. When the door of the library was thrown open on days like these, chaos flooded the room. Not a book on a shelf moved, not a blue hair on her head. But chaos splashed over Alpha. Everything was better, was safer, when it was darker.

A book about the sun, called *The Sun*, a children's book, a yellow book, came in the mail one day because she ordered it. Much was uninteresting but one page stuck in Alpha's mind. The sun was several billion years old. It would die out in another several billion years. That took her by surprise. The sun had an age. It had a lifetime. The universe was so much older than the sun, and would go on for so much longer, that the life of the sun was nothing in comparison with the rest. The sun was like her. The sun would die too. Alpha couldn't repress a feeling of happiness. The sun would die too. "Everything dies" tied the whole thing together. The town had paid for that book, it was vandalism pure and simple, but since she was presently unprepared to make room for another book, Alpha took *The Sun* and dropped it into the wastebasket and covered the incident with trash.

As librarian she was one of a handful of people paid to serve the town. But her pay was so much the smallest, and her importance the least of the least, and she had been librarian for so many years, that the mothers who took books out of the library thought nothing of it if they felt they were entering a sanctuary, and mothers and children were the only ones who ordinarily came into the library. They all knew Alpha Davis, frail but stern, blue of hair, blue of dress, blue with age, and how she guarded her little budget and her books like drops of her blood. But they didn't guess how much like blood it was; how the minute they left she got up and followed their tracks and undid their browsing; how difficult it was for her to welcome a new book, except for the infrequent book about prairie life, or the occasional book someone gave in memory of someone, or the new high school year-book that she put on the shelf with the others when June came around. But beyond that, she would have liked for the shelves to remain just as they were, and no one to come in and disturb them, and herself to sit at her desk and gaze around her at the perfect order of her days.

There were children and grandchildren of Alpha's scattered over the county. One daughter's family lived near Jericho on a farm. She herself lived in the same little house she had shared with her husband Martin. Mr. Davis had been the postman for many years. They had been married for many years. And Mr. Davis had been dead for many years. So everything was many years. Because common sense told her that she must be close to the end of her life, she thought that at least she should be safe from human beings. To be ignored by them was the last thing she would ever ask of them; it was her living dying wish. People should leave her alone.

That West! Someone should slap his face for him. Someone should wring his neck. Who was West to come in and make faces, wasn't the one he had enough? Was it funny to ask for books that didn't exist? What ailed Mr. West? Who was he? He was a nobody, a browser, but maybe someone could do something about that. Maybe they had since he hadn't been in yet this week. Maybe he had lost his eyesight and wouldn't be back. She couldn't bear Mr. West! Then that other one had started coming in, the new man at the Red Owl Store. Types like that showed their faces in town sometimes but they usually just passed through. She wouldn't have thought he could read. Why was he so interested in the yearbooks? Was he looking for somebody? He might be a good worker in the grocery store but she didn't like his looks. How could she phrase it? He wasn't a type she would want to meet alone in a dark alley. That phrased it to her satisfaction.

That left the problem. Monday morning's phone call made eighteen phone calls in four months. Next Monday morning's call would start a new month. She knew very well who was the brains behind it, if there were any, but still each call was a strain. She had once not seriously minded Eleanor Prain. When she told Eleanor Prain that she was corresponding with the publisher about the book in question, Alpha had phrased that entirely to her satisfaction. From the list of publishers in the catalogue, she had decided on one in London and written a letter of inquiry as to whether the book was in print. That letter had recently been answered in the affirmative. Soon she would write another letter to ask if the book was in stock. After that, she was afraid she would have to order it. Eventually, it would come. As much as she detested him, she would have to say that it was here. Naturally, he would send Eleanor to fetch it for him. How could Eleanor stand him? He was so two-faced! And Rainey? She knew dear Rainey Spencer!

But she, Alpha Davis, could be just as stubborn as Mayor George Robinson. Bigwig. He was running for something else now. She wouldn't vote for him for dog, much less dog catcher. That one time he came on the phone he sent her blood pressure so far up she thought she would have a heart attack. He would kill her, that was the kind of mayor he was. He would see, he would see that he got much better results if he didn't push her so hard. If he just left her alone, he would see the results he got.

Her mind came back to West, not to compare the two of them, but in the sense that if you had two boils on the back of your neck you would know if one was worse. That was the difference between Robinson and West. West wasn't a menace. He wouldn't have her dismissed. He wouldn't do anything to her. Or gossip about her. That didn't mean she liked him, only a little bird told her she was comparatively safe with him; the little bird told her that she needn't feel afraid of what he thought because he was so strange and so crooked himself. But she was just as thankful she wasn't alone when he appeared in the flesh late this afternoon shortly before closing. Though she pretended to be busy writing she saw him shut the door behind him, stop, look around, suddenly sharp-eyed and tight-lipped for reasons best known to Mr. West. No other visitors had been in all afternoon, which made it seem even more uncomfortably strange that two people she had been thinking about were now in the library at the same time. Not George Robinson, who never set foot in here. West and Rainey Robinson.

Alpha visited the hairdresser every Friday afternoon. This was part of the pains she took to keep up her appearance as librarian.

At the hairdresser's she would sometimes meet Rainey. She and her husband had known Rainey's parents, and while it was years since they had really talked, she liked and admired Rainey. Whenever she saw her, she experienced something like freshness and hope for herself even a step from the grave. So when she saw Rainey Robinson stop for a minute to talk to Alaman West, and saw West look back as he left abruptly and empty-handed, as Rainey knelt with Jamie at the children's shelves, Alpha's intuition told her that she ought to say to Rainey, "I'd stay far away from him if I were you," in the same way she might tell a child she liked, "I would steer clear of me if I were you." But just because of that, because Alpha was ashamed to say that she was able to read things in West, there was no chance that what she read there would ever be said. "This should keep him out of trouble for a while," she said sternly as she stamped Jamie's books. Rainey smiled, "Tell *him* that." And because she did like Rainey, and never more than at the moment when she failed to do her a kindness, Alpha was ashamed of feeling relieved when Rainey was gone and she could restore the books they had browsed over and left on the table, and her tiny pocket on earth was dim and orderly and empty and hers again.

It hadn't always been this way. She had forgotten when it all began, the dust, the atrocious dust, the atrocious light, atrocious people. It was a war of deep habit now, the war with the sun, a war unto death, an unstoppable war. Hardest of all to bear, it was a secret war, and despondently waged, because there were lucid days, bright summer days, fresh fall days, many days, when she was ashamed of it, and sorry that it had ever begun.

CHAPTER 10

"This book," said Rainey to Jamie, turning the pages, "is even older than I am."

He knew that, Jamie said.

"The first time I read it I was just about your age. But after that I read it so many times."

He knew that too, and while his eyes were somewhere else, said so.

"That's because Mrs. Davis keeps these old books. I don't think she's thrown away a single book in all the years. And if they get really old she mends them. You and I might think it's a silly way to be, but it's a good thing for us there are people like that in the world."

Jamie had heard something like that before also. Running his fingers along the shelf as though it were a fence, and he was playing, not leaving, he went down the row to another part of the shelves.

"So do you want to read it?" she called a few minutes later. "It isn't a girl's book if that's what you're afraid of. No?"

No answer so the answer was no. Stephie could make her scream, but if ever she disliked Jamie it was when he made her into a nag. She was very sorry if she bored her son; she was sorry if she liked showing him her old books. The trouble was, as she always explained to herself, she was in the position of asking to be humored by an eight-year-old boy. And the sky would fall if that boy took home a book he might not like. That was one reason why the idea of going to the library with Jamie was often so much nicer than going to the library with Jamie. It took him so hellishly long to choose a book. The other reason was that he had to take home six books.

She pulled out, opened and stuffed back books with all of the interest of stuffing damp shirts back into the clothes dryer. Screaming and nagging were the little horror stories of her week. She had two children so she rode two broomsticks; but she had no present plans for a third. She thought she had better not assist him now, and she had felt embarrassed talking to Alpha Davis ever since George's vicious phone call about that book. But a new face in town was always interesting, particularly if the stranger had a family resemblance to people in the district whom she knew. So when she saw the stranger come round the corner bookshelves and stop to browse in the same row, and his face had that peculiarly positive-negative charge of a somehow familiar face, she glanced sideways at his profile and tried to make the connection. Suddenly she did. But it wasn't a family resemblance. He was himself—maybe not much older than the time she remembered him from, not by so many years, but not a high school boy any longer. Then she remembered all about him, that he moved here when he was a child, that his mother had been a waitress in the old Eagle Hotel, that she died, that now he came and went. "But what's his name?" Rainey said under her breath and finally called down the row:

"For heaven's sake, what are you doing back in town? Remember me, I'm Rainey Robinson, Rainey Spencer? That's my son Jamie. I said to myself that it must be you. How long have you been back?"

A startled look, a stare. A slight withdrawal?

"Eight, ten months."

"And no one's seen you in all that time? Where are you living?"

"West side of town. Over north. That corner."

"That's not far! Do you like it there?"

Smile.

"And you work in town now, you have a job?"

"Do books. Bookkeeping."

"My. That's serious work."

Smile.

"I could never do it with my arithmetic," Rainey said earnestly. "But I'll bet you're good at it." What's-his-name was shy; he had a pretty smile even if it appeared unexpectedly. Because she was being nice to him, because he was who he was, this shadowy boy she distantly remembered, it was like admiring herself in front of a mirror. She felt friendly, warm, charming and very kind.

"Isn't this a funny little library? It's so dark!" she whispered. "And the books are so tight! I think Mrs. Davis is going funny on us—I think she's turning like cream, people say she's been left here too long. But you won't repeat that to anyone. And this is Jamie. He's my eldest. I'm sure you've seen him riding his bicycle all over town."

"No."

"Why don't you come and see us sometime and have a cup of coffee? Then we can take our time. Do you know the house?"

Smile. Nod.

"It's been a real surprise seeing you again. I hope we'll see more of you. Goodbye. And please do stop by."

Of course the minute he was gone "Alaman West" popped into her head. That was the real name of What's-his-name. He wasn't so bad! Likely he had a not-too-awful girl somewhere ahead in his future. Temporarily, he had just needed someone warm and friendly and lovely and charming to show a little interest in him.

The first thing she did was to go over and kiss Jamie on the top of his head, and then she knelt down next to him and was his afresh and pulled forth book after book.

HE WAS amazed. It was the opposite of what he expected. He meant it was the opposite of no expectation at all since he had followed her inside to have a look at her as you might inspect a dead weight and the dead weight smiled, showed her pretty teeth and spoke to him. But he put a good clamp on himself. Surprised as he was, he got out without giving anything away to Robinson's wife.

It amazed him that she remembered him. Unless she was

lying. That was a possibility. If he went over her words word by word there was no real sign that she remembered him. So why would she lie about remembering him? Because this was such a friendly little town?

Number one, if she really remembered him she would also remember that she had never once spoken to him. So why talk to him now? She should have looked past him, or through him, instead. Number two, she was smart in school; she was out of the high school the year he got in but these things were known. She was smart, so it figured that she was smart in arithmetic. So why lie about that? Multiple choice; same answer as above. Because this was a nice friendly town.

He was shadowing Robinson and so why not take a good look at Robinson's wife? That was why he followed her in, just to satisfy himself, not as part of the plan. If not for Robinson she wouldn't be here. He thought this was obvious since out of all the girls of roughly his time she struck him as the last one who would want to stay in Jericho. She left for college but Robinson brought her back. Then she had his kids. If he saw her in town, which was seldom, he thought of her as someone who was here against her will, who stayed because the husband did, because his interests were here. He had another impression of her too, but this was old; old and shivery. He was a kid when her parents were killed, and while he heard about the accident when it happened he had no memorable feeling about it then. No. But when his mother died, he remembered Rainey Spencer, sixteen, the prettiest, most popular girl, whose mother and father were dead in a car crash. West remembered standing and thinking of that the day after his mother died, and suddenly appreciating the fact that unfortunate things could also happen to someone as fortunate as she was, feeling this so forcibly that it might have been happening to them both at the same time. By then she was married, living in her own house, and had a kid. But if he closed his eyes, that was a face he could still see, Rainey Spencer, sixteen, and all alone in the world.

So why did he lie to her and say he had never seen her kid? No reason. "No" just popped out. But it felt good. It was the only word he said to her he had any respect for. He started to stand up to her then. But go have coffee with her? It wasn't in the plan.

He didn't trust her. Triple that. Without bothering to ask why that question should ever come up, he said to himself that he didn't trust Lorraine Robinson.

Legion Avenue was dusty in the unused hours of summer light. The stores all looked empty. Robinson wouldn't be coming out of his office for another hour or more. Shadowing Robinson was a good start. But there was a limit as to how much time you could spend watching a man; but if he got tired of not watching, he could see the door of Robinson's office from the Paris Café.

West entered and took his table by the window. He took his pen from his shirt pocket and a little notebook from his back pocket. He tipped a hand to Ellie who was moving toward him and she retreated and brought him his cup of coffee.

He knew just a few things about Ellie. She was poor. She was ugly. She carted trays and wiped tables. He trusted her.

CHAPTER 11

THERE WAS that day toward the end of June when Robinson had a visit from Will Carpenter the druggist.

Mrs. Prain put her head in the doorway to announce Will; much surprised, Robinson made a face.

"Come in, why don't you," he said to Will who came bumping past a startled Mrs. Prain and then went back and shut the door in her face and came steaming up to the desk.

"Easy, Will. You don't have to knock people down."

Will slammed a sheet of paper down on the desk. Robinson raised an eye at him and took his time before finally picking it up. He read a note in pencil in big printing:

DIXIE GETS A PHYSICAL EDUCATION REAL SOON.
THE JOKE'S ON YOU MR. C.

"That came in the United States mail," spewed Will, pointing his finger. "That makes it a federal offense."

"What offense? Sit down, Will. Calm down. You need a drink, not an attorney. Why come to me with this?"

Will all but sneered. "I know what I need so don't start thinking about a fee. Unless you get a fee for being mayor."

Robinson said nothing. Will was Will. With his tightly buttoned druggist's tunic and his stiff little neck and mustache, he gave a passable imitation of a toothbrush.

"My God, don't you understand the letter?"

"Certainly I understand it, the context of it." Robinson picked it up again. "It's from a kid. Look at the printing and the paper. The paper has ruled lines. It looks like the kind of paper they hand out in school. Maybe it was written there. It's obviously just a letter from a kid."

Will cried, "I know it's a kid! Why the hell do you think I'm scared!"

"My windows are open—do me a favor, Will, pull yourself together. Have a chair. I'm listening. Have you gone to the police?"

"Sissie was a dirty joke to them. But not dirty enough. They told me that. Practically! Can you see me walking in there again?"

Robinson slowly and sadly shook his head. "No. I guess I can't, not with your memories," he said. And Will finally sat down.

"They're raping my daughters. They raped Sissie. And now they'll rape my Dixie."

"Rape is strong language, Will. Besides, Sissie's out of the picture now, so why dredge all that up? She's married and has a nice little family."

"They raped her! . . . They raped my Sissie so often."

Will Carpenter turned his face away and George Robinson said: "Now, now." They screwed her, they humped her, they banged her, they fucked her? To be fair to Will, out of that bouquet of roses, rape must have seemed the rosiest.

"This is not the town for us. I said that the first time. It's nice for others but not us. The day she was born I knew I had a prize. I sat by her crib to watch her sleep. I bathed her. She was so tiny and so pure. She was going to be wonderful."

"Sissie?"

"Sissie too! There wasn't any difference. They had their little dresses, their little toys, and they played. I still remember their toys. I knew every word they knew . . . Sugar and spice and everything nice, that's what little girls are made of." Will amazed Robinson by starting to pound the desk with his fist. "Snakes and snails and puppy dogs' tails, that's what boys are made of! I believe it! You can laugh yourself sick but I believe it."

"Maybe we all do," murmured Robinson.

"Their damned games. Their damned cars. And their damned fathers too."

"Boys have given you a tragic time, Will."

Will let out a honking sound to keep from crying; it was like the honking of an animal twice his size. Robinson reached across and put a hand on Will's arm but Will saved him the embarrassment by shaking it off. Poor Will didn't like him any more than he cared for Will.

"Have you talked to Dixie about this? Warned her?" Robinson asked.

Will shook his head.

"Can Molly sit down and have a talk with Dixie? Mother-to-daughter?"

"Don't concern yourself with my family. We take care of ourselves," Will snapped. "I showed you a letter. What I'm here to get from you is a curfew for the town of Jericho."

"A curfew? Thank you, Will. That's just what everyone wants."

"I don't claim to be popular. That's your specialty, not mine."

Will you incredible pill, Robinson thought, but said mildly, "All right, suppose we talk about it. Suppose a curfew is approved? Who's going to ride around with a flashlight all night and slap the kids on the shoulder? You and me? Hank and Pete? We'd need another cop, wouldn't we? Do you know how much a third cop would cost the town?"

Will snatched up the letter.

"This isn't dollars and cents. It's my flesh and blood!"

"Will, to tell the truth, it surprises me that I'm even talking about this. The council won't vote a curfew or a cop. If they did, the town wouldn't stand for it. My advice to you is go home, have a talk with Dixie, and forget about it."

"I showed you a letter and you said you understood! I call you a filthy hypocrite!"

"Don't insult me over a letter, Will. It's not worth it. Forget your stupid curfew. Do you think kids are only awake at night? Use your head . . . Use your past experience."

"Ahh," said Will. It was the gasp of acknowledgment as the pointy sword went through. But he bounced back up. He jumped to his feet and waved the letter.

"You'd like to think I'm the only one. That would be all right. Just Will! Lucky Mr. C.! But that's not the story this time." He struck the letter with his open hand. "There are others! I only speak for mine! You don't know what's going on in this place but you'll soon find out. It's going to blow up in your face this summer. They'll be calling this the town where children get letters and then get raped. And they'll see who the popular mayor is. That should get you a lot of votes! You're a dead man, Robinson!"

"Would you please calm down? Sit down, for God's sake. We're both on the same side in this."

Nobody wanted a curfew for the kids, and a third cop on the payroll was unthinkable. These were strictly town issues but he needed the whole town behind him just to begin to cut down Armstead. So far as he was concerned, except for Will, they weren't even issues.

"I can do this for you, Will, and I can't spend any more time on this. At the next council meeting I'll present your complaint myself on your behalf and we'll find out how the council feels about it."

"That won't be for weeks!"

"Two weeks, Will; less. You can wait. If the others can."

Will shot him a look of suspicion that Robinson absorbed with a very blank face. Will's white jacket set off the starched little man. In view of his home life Will probably washed it and ironed it himself. But the starch was all in the jacket; Will was mostly sad misfortune. In another life, had things been more equal, he and Will might have been enemies.

"How would you present my complaint?" Will asked gloomily.

"I'm not your enemy, Will. I'll be fair."

"You know I don't much like you, Robinson. You're slick. You're a bully. You're conceited. I don't like you."

"But you respect me."

Will turned without a word, strode to the door, opened it, banged it behind him and was gone.

Will was a pest. He was a crank. Will had strange notions of rape and sex in general. There were holes twice the size of Will in Will's story. There were no other sex letters. Will was bluffing.

Robinson phoned Hank at police headquarters across the street.

"Could you stop by the office for a minute?" he asked Hank.

"I could. But then I'd be getting all the exercise. Why don't we both stand up and come out for a cup of coffee?"

Hank was a friend. He respected Hank, not only for his physical presence, a professional presence, but for his attitude. He wasn't important and he wasn't unimportant, he was exactly what his wood-burned desk sign said he was, police chief in a small town. When Hank came to investigate a broken school window, or wrestled a drunk's bottle away from him, that fat stomach on a big frame was more than a fat stomach, it was Hank showing you his proper sphere in life, the comical and the grim, the fat and the muscle.

But Hank had his frailties. He thought the town needed another cop. Maybe he was getting a little bit lazy after eleven years as the chief. When he said "I'd just like somebody besides Pete to boss around" it was hard to say if it came from the fat side or the muscle side. Normally the third cop was a joke between him and Hank, but it was a joke that Hank cracked every chance he got. Robinson stepped out of his office and crossed Legion Avenue, his shirtsleeves flapping in the summery gust off the plains, sensing the total peace of the place, and thinking how funny it would be if there were real sex threats being sent around and Hank was quietly getting up support and leverage for a fling at a third cop this summer.

He saw Hank come out of the city hall and watched him come down the path in the park, ninety-nine percent ashamed of his suspicion. "I'm thinking about staging a big campaign event this fall, something unusual for the district," he told Hank when they were sitting in the café. "I thought I'd better warn you about it. Parade, barbecue picnic, firecrackers. The band. Something like the Fourth of July but in the fall."

"I was going to say it sounded familiar," said Hank.

"I'd like to use the park for the day. Legion Avenue too."

"You're the candidate from Jericho," Hank said.

"Any problems?"

"I hate to say this, but I think Pete and I can handle it."

They drank their coffee, sitting on round backless stools at the otherwise vacant counter. Robinson discussed his plan; they kidded one another. Provided he didn't get too much of him at one blow Hank was good company. Normally they were like two guys fishing together and having a heck of a good time even if they were after the same fish. "My invite," Hank said dropping change on the counter. Outside, Robinson leaned up against the warm café window, folded his arms and squinted upward, taking in the sun.

"Look like a quiet Fourth this year?"

"The usual mayhem," Hank said.

"Nothing funny in the air?"

"Nothing I know of. What did you have in mind?"

"Nothing in particular. Muggings, murders. Sex orgies. Rapes."

Hank thought a minute. "Pete got into both socks this morning. Mrs. Pete watched."

Robinson threw back his head and laughed. Robinson sprang off the window and punched Hank in the arm. "Don't hit me," cried Hank, "I'm an innocent man. You're the dumbbell who asked the question!"

He was satisfied. Hank wasn't hiding anything. That made it a dead issue, because if there had been other letters making the rounds those sensible people would have been to see Hank. As he knew all along, Will the Pill was full of shit, white shit, weak shit.

Once he felt safe, Robinson was livid at the thought that someone like Will could walk in with a crank's tale and throw a scare into him. It wasn't enough to mount his first campaign and do battle with a strong incumbent. At the same time, with the other hand, he had to swat at odd little interests, at people with funny quirks and queer designs, cranks like Will. And he had no doubts that there were others of them out there. Politics was people, but people could be a pain in the neck.

CHAPTER 12

HE WAS shadowing Robinson.

The Paris Café was the hangout. He reconnoitered on foot and by bike, slightly braking past the doomed house of Robinson by night, by day shadowing the office and points of interest between, Robinson buying suntan oil in the drugstore, standing at the men's shorts counter in the Dakota Store, trying out the lawn chairs lined up on the sidewalk outside the Coast-to-Coast Store.

West often wore the dark glasses he had bought to spy on Dixie. When he had them on he felt freer to enter places where he had to go; to perch on his bike and scan the street for the Robinson stride, the back of the head, the bullseye face. At his table in the café, on a bench in the city hall park, he wrote things down in Accounts Receivable, his nickname for his notebook. He recorded movements and the times of repeated movements taken from clocks around town. There was a page for habits such as the late-night dog walks and the usual time the upstairs light went out. There was another page on which West drew diagrams of streets and buildings, carefully marking fences, alleys and back exits. There was a blank page for *When and Where* and a page for *How,* also blank, except for an estimate of Robinson's height and weight.

It was a beginning.

It wasn't a beginning. It was a kid's game that just looked like a beginning. He wouldn't be finding it so easy if it was really a beginning.

Any way you looked at it, it was a beginning.

Shadowing was good practice. Shadowing prepared him for important things like timing, speed and concealment. It was serious work. When he shadowed he felt dangerous.

When he shadowed he felt safe. It told him he was the same old Alaman West, no matter what he thought was going to happen.

He was getting to know Robinson better. Soon there would have to be a real plan and shadowing could be a big help.

He was getting to know Robinson better—that was only fair. Maybe Robinson would turn out to be the wrong man. Maybe he'd start appreciating Robinson. Maybe Robinson would turn out to be his best friend.

The Fourth of July passed. Firecrackers popped a few days before and after, little puppy bombs exploded by little kids. He woke up to them at daybreak on the Fourth. He didn't go to the parade downtown. Robinson had to go because he was mayor. But he didn't have to go. To think this might have been the day.

He was back shadowing on the weekend—Saturday's weather was ideal. If he biked down the street adjoining Robinson's street, if he stopped to rest on his bike and sip a cold drink, and looked between a certain two houses, it was possible to see across the backyard and back alley into Robinson's yard. He had biked this way before, but it wouldn't do to waste a good stop and a good cover unless he saw Robinson in the yard.

But Robinson was there. He was alone, his wife wasn't to be seen and neither were the kids, but the dumb faithful dog was lying at his feet. He was at work writing something, paper, newspapers and books on the grass around him. He was in his new shorts from the Dakota Store and sitting in his new lawn chair from the Coast-to-Coast Store and his body was smeared with the suntan oil from Haley's Drugstore. Robinson sat there like a dummy that West had put together.

West looked at the unfinished job. He took a swig of his drink, eyes still looking. He felt at a disadvantage with men who had wives and kids and a house, who were on easy terms with big dogs, men with worries, with real burdens, men with a mortgage, a family to feed, an occupation—men who stood more firmly on the earth than he did. So West took a swig and smirked because Robinson looked so unsuspecting and dumb sitting there in yard. He looked so much like a cinch. West pitied Robinson's wife, even if she was almost as much to blame because she stood it, stood Robinson, stood Robinson's say, Robinson's force, Robinson's weight. West had no illusions about her but he pitied her as automatically as he mistrusted her. It was a slippery situation. When she was nowhere to be seen, he felt sorry for her. Then when he saw her face-to-face—downtown in daylight—the mistrust took over. Slippery. But it was a coincidence altogether, it was just an accident—if he was ever on the side of Robinson's wife it was because he was against Robinson.

When he got back home West wrote in Accounts Receivable: *Nice backyard, trees and flowers all around, big yard. But a big hole in the back. Clear view of his chair almost anywhere. Also, view of back screen door and kitchen window.*

He read through his pages and rocked with Cat in his lap, rocking thoughtfully, stroking Cat and making him purr.

"I have reasons," he told Cat. "Reasons, not motives. Only dopes have motives. Mine are reasons. That's why I can take my time making the plan."

He behaved in a special way. When he left the house each day and went downtown he felt the difference. He had a special way of walking, a special way of talking, a special way of standing. There was a secrecy about him. He stood wary, shoulders a little hunched, chest a little cage. He was watchful; his eyes dwelt on essentials as when they fished for information or when they stared at the approaching windshield then the backs of the heads of the cruising Jericho Police. There was an efficiency to him, a brevity, but armed. His talk was terse. At work he responded to questions with as few words as possible, with only one if he could. He invented this behavior for himself. It was original behavior; he thought that was obvious. Maybe other people took note of it and maybe they didn't—it wasn't for the benefit of other people. He was spinning a web. In it were him and Robinson. Robinson was the Fly.

The Fly goes into the bank. West happens to walk into the bank. West stands behind the Fly on line, reading the flyspecks in the Fly's bankbook, moving up when the Fly moves but vanishing when the Fly reaches the window.

The Fly eats a sandwich in his private office. His windows are wide open but there are screens to keep the smaller flies off his sandwich.

The Fly runs into Doc Death on the street and they chitchat. Doc Death and the Fly laugh—naturally they're friends. Doc sees West coming and quick gets in his car. But the Fly doesn't see him coming.

The Fly has regular habits. His fly-door opens at eight every morning. He kisses his wife on the cheek and goes, the Fly flies off the cake. At the same time, Who or What comes spinning around the corner?

The web meant hiding, seeing and moving. Each move he made had little legs on it and was a shift inside the web. He moved by inches sometimes, as in the bank, or scampered across town as when he guessed the Fly had left his office and he caught up with him, slowed down behind him, rode half a block behind him slowly. He controlled the Fly. He knew what the Fly would do and then the Fly looked dumb doing it. The web was important because it proved that the Fly was the Fly. Death to the Fly was inevitable but the web made it seem really possible.

By day there was the web. At night West came home to his four walls and insurrectionist's supper out of a can, to his plot stewing and Cat slinking and his rocker squeaking. Then it was back to the Fly and the web and his sinister special behavior. The life he led must have been playing tricks on West. Soon he began to think he was being followed.

Someone was shadowing him. Sure they were; he was almost positive they were. One minute West smiled at such an idea, the next he shrugged, the next it gave him the jitters. If he was being watched, the police were the obvious answer. But how could they know anything? They couldn't read his mind and Accounts Receivable was always with him, unless they were keeping an eye on him on general principles, because of who he was. He eased up on shadowing Robinson, just in case. Robinson was a suspect too, in that he might have spotted West, started wondering, and was paying to have West watched. That made sense, except that when West started looking over his shoulder the only one he saw wasn't the police and didn't look like somebody hired by Robinson. He was the bum who swept the floor in the Red Owl Store.

West carefully watched to see if there were others on his trail. But it was just the bum, strong-looking and chunky with peeping little eyes. The bum gave West the jitters even if he wasn't an agent of the police. The bum had a technique. He didn't so much follow in West's footsteps; he was already there or close by when West arrived.

There was the other table in the café near West's favorite table.

There was the side of the library where West browsed, and there was the side West had his back to.

There was the bench under the tree in the park and then there was the bench under a tree across from it.

There was Back Street, which was muddy and narrow and where no one but West ever walked.

West knew the bum's name was Joe, having heard Henry his boss at the Red Owl say Joe do this or do that, Joe sweep, Joe mop, Joe lick the floor. Joe was a good name for a bum. No reason; it just fit. When they named him Joe it gave him a real head start. Soon West was seeing him in places where he wouldn't logically be, like standing in the field across from West's house, and at night looking in his window. But he must have imagined that because there was no one around when he ran outside with the hammer in his hand. So it must have been a case of mistaken identity, like a dog looking in.

Then there was the case of true identity at the book-rack in Haley's Drugstore, when West stood looking over the new books. It was a revolving rack. When West gave it a turn a hand on the other side also turned it slightly. West gave it another nudge and the other side gave it a nudge. With a snarl West looked behind the rack. The bum's face was buried in a book; his little eyes flew from left to right and back. West spun the rack, just missing him, and delivered a vicious deferred kick to the kickstand of his bike parked out front.

He was furious at the bum, who nobody had asked to come here and whom he had never seen in town before the winter. It might not be a bad idea if some day soon the bookkeeper reported the bum to the police. Why was the bum following him? He was interfering with the plan; that was the result whether or not he purposely set out every day to cross paths with West. West still couldn't make up his mind about that. The bum had a job; he wasn't free to flit here and there all day, so he had to be in those places at those times on purpose. But why? West had never spoken one word to him or so much as looked his way. Why should he? This Joe was nobody. He was nothing. He was a menace too. He was spoiling West's haunts for him. If he wasn't following West it was almost as bad—if a bum like Joe liked all the same places he did.

Joe kept appearing but kept his distance. West swore that the bum was watching him. West couldn't figure it out. When he went into the Red Owl Store he ignored Joe totally, as much as ever. Only more so.

WEST WAS sitting at his table in the Paris Café.

Joe walked in and sat down at the table nearby. West was having a dish of strawberry ice cream.

Joe asked Ellie: "What flavor ice cream you got today?"

"Vanilla, chocolate and strawberry."

"Let me think," said Joe.

West stopped his spoon halfway to his mouth. West waited for Joe like Ellie waited.

"Strawberry!" Joe said. "My favorite flavor. But in a cone."

West stood up. He slammed some money down and went outside. Quickly he wheeled his bike around the corner and waited.

He'd settle the bum once and for all.

CHAPTER 13

HE CAME whistling down Legion Avenue, hands in the pockets of his short thick jacket and a black woolen knit hat above his little gray eyes. His wide blue pants had white paint stains across them but those stains were old and many times laundered and they made his appearance pleasant and somehow cleaner, like a baker wearing an apron dusted with flour. It was Joe on his way to work. This was back in winter when he had been in Jericho only a couple of months and had never heard of Alaman West.

Snow was on the ground and the town was colder than any place he had ever been, but Joe thought he had a lot to whistle about. He had a good warm room in the hotel where he had just eaten a hot breakfast, he had money to spare and a decent boss, and he knew that he could say the same things tomorrow. Joe wasn't looking for utopia. He had seen enough of the world to know that he just had an ordinary job in an ordinary town. But didn't that mean it was a good job in a good town?

Joe had only been here since the beginning of the year so he still didn't know many people. There were the two elderly sisters who ran the hotel, there was Henry his boss and Henry's wife Mary Ellen who tended the cash register. If the women who shopped at the Red Owl seldom spoke to him, Joe understood the reason. He was new and he looked different from the towns-people; not only that, different didn't mean tall, dark and handsome. Not only that, he had no wife and kids, so even if they wanted to talk what would they talk to him about? Joe carried their groceries out to their cars. He unpacked crates and filled Henry's freezers and shelves. Like Henry he wore a white apron, but because he was shorter it fit him longer, like a butcher's apron. He mopped the floor, pasted up the daily signs in the window, shoveled the snow off the sidewalk. In the back of the store he ground up the beef Henry sold from a white enameled tray, eating big red-and-white swaths of it from his thumb if Henry was up front near the cash register.

Joe had his eye on the big ground-beef sign that he changed every so often in the Red Owl window. Every morning he stuffed real chuck and odds and ends into the grinder. It was Henry's meat going in but when it came out it was JOE'S GROUND BEEF. Joe chuckled to himself when he imagined that sign in the window. But why not, he asked himself. It might be good for business. Also, people would see his name there—the town would get to know him faster. Joe bought supplies and started to practice his printing. And even though he laughed, it wasn't such a small thing to him either. It seemed to Joe that having ground the meat, if he could also make the sign about it, and put it in the window, and then go back and sell it to people, he would have a corner all his own in the store.

Joe had a room in the Violet Hotel which stood on the same street as a row of old railroad houses opposite the tracks and depot. The only hotel left in Jericho, and run by two widowed sisters, the Violet was a three-story handkerchief box of pale lavender stucco. It had a front porch, a little lobby with cane furniture, and the only fire escape in town, an iron ladder that ran down the stucco in back and stopped eight feet short of the ground. Joe thought the old place was funny—that fire escape with the drop was a riot when he saw the retired old farmers who were living there who had trouble just coming down the stairs. The Violet wasn't a crowded hotel. There were the handful of old men, the two old sisters who lived there, and Joe. His room was on the top floor. It was small and shabby rather than funny but no worse than he was used to and steam-heated all winter, so maybe there was an advantage in living with old people. Joe made himself useful by climbing a chair to replace light bulbs, shoveling snow off the walk, carrying in bundles for the sisters. He looked forward to going to work each day, though he was sorry it was the farmers' wives who shopped in the Red Owl and not the farmers. He admired farmers, whom he had never seen in person before; he thought he would love to be friends with a farmer and visit the farm. On a couple of Saturday nights, seeing they went there, he entered the saloon and sat at the bar, but they were all with their own farmer friends. More power to them. They had that right. He would be the same way!

Saturday being Henry's busiest day, Joe as his only helper had an afternoon off during the week. Joe, who had no car, would walk through town, taking one direction or another, and usually end up standing in front of the Red Owl Store, under the red-striped awning that was rolled down once winter was over. Joe's standing in front of the Red Owl on his time off and watching people go by was more reminiscent of big-city life than it was of a little town. Joe had always lived in big cities. He had worked as a day laborer, a housepainter, a deliveryman for a dry cleaner's; before coming to Henry he had been a helper to a thousand-and-one bosses. Joe wasn't being conceited when he thought that his life made him an expert on bosses. Not all were bad, but you couldn't be friends with a boss. Nothing was truer than that. If his life depended on it Joe would never try to make friends with a boss.

Why did Joe come to Jericho?

The one who happened to ask him that question was Henry as they were closing up the store one night. Henry was at the counter up front sorting out checks and charge slips and Joe was mopping in the center aisle. Mary Ellen always went home early to get supper ready so the two of them were alone, Henry and Joe.

"What made you come here, Joe?"

Joe paused in his mopping.

"You mean how it happened?" he asked.

Henry nodded his head and continued jotting down figures from the slips of paper; he was a good, conscientious grocer and all day long asked pleasant questions of people, with his mind on other things than the answers.

He came into town one day on a friend's truck, Joe said. He

was just along for the ride to keep him company. They were going further but when they came into Jericho his friend stopped for gas at the filling station and then went into the office. Joe waited out in the truck awhile then finally went into the office himself and it turned out that his friend was a friend of the filling station man.

"The filling station man," said Henry, who had finished his figuring of the charge slips and was starting on the cash in the cash register.

When he saw them each with a beer, Joe said, he knew it was going to be a while so he went down the street and went into the café for a cup of coffee. The cup of coffee was so good that he asked for another cup, but first he went out to buy a paper to drink it with. If that first cup of coffee hadn't been so good, he wouldn't have had any reason to buy a paper. Then he wouldn't have noticed—he took a little walk because the café was steamy and warm—what a nice street it was. He wouldn't have seen, when he bought the paper, what a nice drugstore they had, with hot roasted nuts, with a soda fountain, with kids. When he went back to the café and sat down (and the steaminess was nicer the second time too, since it was snowing and so cold outside) he wouldn't have had the town paper with him—that was all they had left. But the town paper was all right! It had pictures! It had news on every page! If he didn't have that paper, he couldn't have come to the last page where the Help Wanted was. He wouldn't have seen the ad for a helper in the Red Owl Store, the only Help Wanted that was there. He wouldn't have paid for his coffee and gone across the street to the Red Owl right away, because he had to hurry now, and then gone back to the filling station office to tell the truckdriver (and it was a lot different walking in there now) to get his suitcase out of the back of the truck because he was staying. He had a job here. He was going to stay. Joe laughed. So that was what happened—it was all because of a good cup of coffee that he came to be in Jericho. Joe laughed again and wiped his mouth with the back of his hand.

Mopping and talking, mopping nearer and nearer the cash register, he talked so much and so warmly that a little bubble of spit formed on his lower lip. Henry was mesmerized by that foamy little bubble; it kept reproducing itself like something unstoppable as Joe talked and laughed. That ad for a helper was the longest running Want Ad in the history of the *Pioneer*, so Henry was happy to have Joe. He didn't dislike Joe. But this was a different Joe from the one he saw every day, Joe suddenly very friendly, Joe eagerly talkative, who even when he finished that story of his wouldn't let it rest, but would laugh and wipe his mouth and swab with the mop and warm up for the third time this good part and that best part of how he landed in Jericho. When Henry thought Joe must be weary of that cup of coffee, and maybe now he could escape from Joe, Joe said with a look of surprise:

"Wait a minute. Was I talking about coffee? How about going for a cup of coffee after we close?"

"At six o'clock at night? I've got my supper waiting for me."

"Tomorrow?"

"I'm not much of a coffee drinker, Joe. Let's finish up."

Henry went on counting change slowly until out of the corner of his eye he saw Joe wring out the mop, take off his apron, roll down his sleeves, take his jacket and go; but just to be safe, he gave Joe a few minutes' head start before he came out of the store and locked up. After that night, when they were closing up, whenever Henry felt his grocer's itch to chatter, he would remember Joe's cup of coffee story and Joe's eagerness and the unstoppable bubble of spit on Joe's lip, and keep on counting to himself. Joe was a good worker, but he could make friends someplace else.

Joe's life in Jericho hadn't changed much when spring came and moved toward summer. He still enjoyed drinking a cup of coffee in the café while looking through the *Pioneer*. He liked going into the drugstore and poking around the shelves and walking out with a bag of roasted nuts. When the days got longer and warmer he spent time sitting on a bench in the park throwing the birds chunks of unbought bread from the Red Owl Store. He ate some of the bread himself. The birds were good company!

Then, if he got tired of that, or the weather wasn't too good, he might stroll across to the Jericho Public Library. Joe never took books out of the library, one reason being that he didn't read too well. The other reason was old Sourpuss at the desk. The way Sourpuss looked at him he was lucky she let him in.

Joe felt on strange ground in libraries anyhow, so he steered clear of her desk and then tiptoed around just in case his socks squeaked. He wasn't here to make trouble, Sourpuss!

Joe had a favorite shelf in the library. It was in the little section marked History, material Joe ordinarily ducked if he saw it at all. But it was here that he discovered the library's collection of Jericho High School yearbooks. They first attracted his eye because they were a separate row of books that matched in the way a set of encyclopedias did, but thin, black and unidentified on the shelf. When Joe took down one of these books and opened it he found that the town was inside. As he turned the pages he saw men and women he saw every day in the Red Owl Store, in other places of business, coming and going on the street. Joe was fascinated. He would come in and take one down and hunt for faces he knew. That's him! That can't be him! So this was how so-and-so looked as a kid! She was cute-looking then! Joe always read the little prophecies under the pictures. Some were funny and made him chuckle; others were serious and he respected their seriousness and wondered, did it come true? It made him stop and think about these people and what they were like now.

Alaman West.

That was a funny name. Alaman. Who gave a kid that name? His pop Percy West? Joe chuckled and read the lines under the picture.

Alaman is this boy's name
Algebra his road to fame.

He sounded smart. Joe looked at the picture again. It was him; Joe had seen him in the Red Owl sometimes and around town riding a bicycle, so it must be him, and Joe glanced in surprise at the cover of the yearbook again because he had assumed he was a lot younger, but he was out of school six years. That was interesting.

Joe paid attention to West the next time he came into the store. Then for the next week or so Joe stopped what he was doing when Alaman West came in. He didn't buy much food, Joe observed, enough for one person, things that were easy to fix like sliced ham or a can of stew. He didn't buy any extras, but he bought cat food. He didn't have a car but put his groceries in the basket of his bicycle. West was an interesting person. He was always buying for one, always silent, always alone.

That was wrong, thought Joe. That shouldn't be in a town like Jericho. In a friendly place like this people should get to know each other. It would be a very good thing for Alaman West too, mused Joe big-heartedly, watching West get on his bicycle outside the Red Owl and go on his lonely way.

But at night in his little room, with the freight trains hooting by, Joe only felt fooled by his long months of patience. He couldn't help it if he got mad and smacked his pillow. People should get to know each other. People who had no family and no one else and maybe not much money should have a friend to be with, not a cat!

Jericho wasn't big. West couldn't go far. Just find out the places where Alaman West went and be there, smiled Joe. He had all day Sunday and his afternoon off, he had his lunch hour and he could sneak a few minutes away from the store if he saw West downtown. He wasn't wrong; there were plenty of chances to make friends with somebody in Jericho!

But Joe would be careful. Joe knew from a lot of experience that sometimes other people weren't as friendly as he was. So maybe he wouldn't be so friendly himself! He wouldn't rush up and say, I'm Joe! How about going for three or four cups of coffee! He'd stay at a little distance. He'd be where West was by accident, a man just minding his own business whom Alaman West saw here, there and around the town. If West wanted to make friends, Joe was ready. Joe had faith in himself, but still he swore that he wouldn't be the one who made friends.

West would be the one.

CHAPTER 14

THE BUM came out of the café with his ice cream cone and stood looking up and down the street. Looking for someone, bum? said West around the corner under his breath, peering out as the bum peered elsewhere. It was a warm sunny day, so the bum stood licking the sides of the cone and blinking his eyes in the brightness of plate-glass windows and empty sidewalks. A bum with a sense of direction, he started walking in the opposite direction from West. Since it was Sunday afternoon the library was shut, the drugstore was shut, everything was shut, so the bum was going to do his looking in the park.

West jumped on his bike, swung it around and sped down a side street and through Back Street and up another side street and around the corner and then up the sidewalk where he rode it straight at the legs of the bum whose eyes popped and who yelled *"Stop"* the instant West stood straight up on his usually reliable brakes and yelled: "Still looking for me?"

"Are you crazy?" cried Joe, retreating. "I was eating my ice-cream!"

His bike rolled up to Joe and stopped short again, pointing. His mean ride and close miss exhilarated West.

"You were following me. If I was as dumb as you are I could still figure it out because you're always following me."

Joe looked at the dripping cone he had just crushed to pieces in his hand and dropped it and rolled it with the side of his shoe into the street.

"What would I follow you for? You my leader?"

West struck one finger after another: "The café just now. The library. The drugstore. Streets. The park. The café yesterday! You're someplace I am every day."

Joe shook his head. "Not me. It must be somebody else."

West shoved the bike by him, rode, then came charging back making Joe scramble out of the way. "My house! You were at my house!"

"Your house? I don't know where you live," said Joe astonished. "Or anything about you."

West laughed and came back and sideswiped him again. Joe was in the street. He could have stepped onto the sidewalk but he didn't even think of it. Instead, and as fast as he could without running, he followed after West down Legion Avenue. They passed the park and left downtown Jericho behind. West, when he didn't charge back with another accusation and a lunge with his front wheel, pedaled up ahead of Joe, not far, not fast, making half-turns to keep the bike steadily moving.

"There must be an explanation," Joe called. "The more I hear you talk, I don't think you would make it up. So what about this one? We both happen to like the same places?" West looked over his shoulder and laughed and Joe shook his head. "Then I don't understand it either."

Joe kept a wary eye on the bike. Once or twice West swooped back in his direction and Joe dodged but the rest of the time he walked without being too nervous. They didn't meet anyone. There was just the sunniness of the day, the Sunday-deserted streets, the peaceful sky over all. Joe never asked where they were going. When West arrived at a small house and turned in at a little path Joe just kept following.

"What a hot day!" Joe called up the path. "No wonder I'm thirsty!" As fast as he walked, the bike was already leaning up against the house. "Maybe you could give me a glass of water?" he called into the house. West didn't answer; there was no sign of West. *But the door was open.* So Joe walked in.

Cat jumped out of West's arms.

"Hey, you got a cat!" said Joe, remembering about the cat. "I'm surprised!" Cat backed away from the door, ears back, paws bunched together, tail quivering. West let out a laugh.

"Why is he pissing?" asked Joe.

"He's excited. He's telling you how much he likes you," West said.

"He pisses because he likes me?"

West laughed again and nodded his head.

"Okay. He pisses because he likes me," Joe said, glancing sharply at the cat and at West. "That's something. That's really something. That's a new one on me. Hey, wait a minute," he said, looking around him. "This is a nice place you got."

Joe went around the room. He didn't look into drawers or cupboards, or more than peek through the curtain of the other room, but he inspected everything he could. He liked the rocker because it looked so comfortable, the icebox because it looked big, the kitchen counters because they were there. He found something good in everything, the oil burner, the stove, the sink, the kitchen table, the two kitchen chairs. The bathtub tickled him when he noticed the little feet under it; he had never seen anything like that before, he said. He looked all around the tub, he did everything but get into it. And then he went to the window and looked out at the yard and the little wooden shack. "This all yours?" he turned and asked. "A whole house?"

West talked twice. The first time was when Joe asked, "What's this map on the wall?" and West jerked his head around because he had forgotten about his handdrawn map of Jericho. "It's a map of a place you never heard of," West said. Of course he didn't bother to answer at all when Joe asked, "Where? What place?" It was as if it hurt to talk. He decided that he was very, very tired and in a minute he would throw the bum out. He only answered Joe's question that he was a bookkeeper because sitting and not telling him was more tiring than telling him.

"You go to college for that?" Joe asked.

"To a school in Chicago."

"You were in Chicago? When did you come here?"

"Last year."

"What month?"

"Summer."

"I came in winter!"

"I was here for a long time before that," said West, hurting and unbearably tired. "I attended school here."

"You went to school here? Is that so? I'm very surprised."

Then Joe didn't speak and so nothing was said. West was sitting in the rocker, the door was wide open and Cat's puddle was still on the floor.

"What are we standing here talking for?" said Joe. "I came in for a glass of water. Should I get it myself?"

West got up and brought it to him and stood there as he drank and took the glass. "Thanks, that was good. I got to be running along now. You," he said, wagging his finger at Cat who crouched behind West's legs, "next time I come, don't get so excited, okay?" Joe laughed and finally headed for the door. "What a nice day. I'm lucky. My only time off is Sundays and Wednesday afternoons."

You were wonderful Cat, said West, looking out the window at the field's edge, the road and the bum walking and whistling. You were better than me. It was all my fault because I brought him here. But I didn't want him following me like he was. He was spoiling the plan. He might have followed me and found out about Robinson.

He saw my map. I forgot about my map. It's a good thing it was him and not someone else. I think I'd hate it to be anyone else alive. But Joe doesn't matter. Joe's piss. Joe's crap. Joe's nothing. He spits too. Except that he doesn't like to throw his spit away. So he saves it on his lip. Except that sometimes he wipes it off with his hand. The question is, which is better? Which did you like better, Cat?

Cat purred. He picked Cat up and hugged him. He was feeling very blue, very tired and very blue. He wasn't dumb enough to believe Joe's explanations for always being around but all that didn't seem to make any difference now. It was as if he forgot who he was when he let Joe come here. West had an awful premonition that Joe was going to be his friend. The bum would be what the world would call his friend.

Joe did visit again. He came knocking at West's door early one evening and spent the time describing life in the Violet Hotel and enthusing over West's house and how nice it was to have a whole house to yourself. Though Cat had curled up near the rocker he fixed an eye on Joe that unnerved him, so Joe laughed a lot to show West how comfortable he was here now. West let him visit because he came knocking, because he was a menial bum who soon came in handy, because nothing that ever entered West's life ever truly surprised him. Beyond that, West did nothing about him one way or the other. He knew he was always prepared to get rid of Joe, which he could do anytime he wanted. That meant West was still his old prime self. The way West figured it, as long as he despised Joe, Joe could stick around.

But it irritated him that Joe admired the bathtub. Aside from his rocker, the bathtub was the one thing in the house West respected, broad, curving and white, standing on its little graceful feet like something female in the house. Then West would remind himself that the bum admired everything in his house. So he could still feel private about the bathtub.

CHAPTER 15

HIS TRAIN pulled into Jericho. The blue Great Northern coaches slowed, each with its white crest, encircled, of a mountain goat on a mountain peak. Robinson sprang off with his suitcase. The only one to descend, he walked along the platform with a sense of quickening comradeship with the slowly departing train, and then he stopped altogether and watched it go out of sight, posed all alone on the little platform, profile minted against Great Plains and sky. Good-bye train—so long! All he was missing was a hat and a crowd to wave the hat at. Goodbye capital. Goodbye dome. Good-bye Miss Brown. I'll be seeing you!

The capital, the dome and Miss Brown. The cute, ambitious Miss Brown. The little Miss Brown. The deadly Miss Brown. Her ambition bowed to her cuteness and her cuteness curtsied back.

And who was Miss Brown? Not an easy question to answer. Possibly a needless question, except to determine whether or not he had been masterfully deceived. Officially she was a nobody, on the lowest rung of that tall shaky ladder under the dome, which meant, since he was mayor of a town and a candidate for the House, that she was a rung higher than he was. So he peeped up her skirt, as who would not, intragovernmentally speaking?

Miss Brown was the lieutenant governor's press aide. Miss Brown's little cubbyhole was in a suite of offices which had made up not even one of Robinson's thousand speculations as the train

carried him from Jericho to the capital and a private appointment
he had requested with the governor. Robinson was proud of his
appointment, even if he kicked himself for feeling proud. Rainey,
Mrs. Prain and others had seen the governor's handsigned letter,
even Jamie, who had read it in Rainey's hands. But it was still
crisp and clean when Robinson slipped it out of his breast pocket
and handed it to the governor's receptionist, who looked at this
piece of plain evidence, rose and went inside. An older woman
came out holding his letter in her hand. She was surprised, she
said to the letter, not to him, and he felt suddenly very uneasy,
absorbing the quietness of the empty reception room as if his
ticket to the big show was in the hand of the only person left in
the place, the old lady mopping up. She meant she was surprised
that he was here, she said, since the governor was away and all
of his appointments had been canceled. All but one, she smiled
sadly, and to have come all that distance too, one of their young
candidates, and how could they ever make amends. But wait. He
mustn't go; be assured, something would be done! And she disappeared, to find a body to save his face. It stung. He despised
his cheeks for turning red when he should have shrugged this off
or gotten angry; he was humiliated most by his humiliation. The
young receptionist returned and sat down lazily. The older
woman returned, all smiles, so that he detested her proposal
before she said a word. The lieutenant governor was waiting to
see him! Would be most happy to talk with him—wanted him
brought right in! Completely believable, thought Robinson,
since he probably had nothing to do. But Robinson trooped after
her down the corridor, down the State House ladder, for a talk
with the lieutenant governor.

He repeated all of the things which he had practiced for his
interview with the governor: the election, the issues, his candidacy, Armstead, party support and help. What he was really after,
and the only thing worth having, was an appearance by the governor in the district, a gubernatorial arm flung about his good
friend and great candidate from Jericho, and for that favor Robinson had nothing to plead except his personal force and enthusiasm, and to a governor who would sit there and perceive the
brilliant promise of George Robinson. But it wasn't quite the
governor he was trying to sell himself to. There was a minor

difference, a difference hardly worth mentioning, as between the sun and the moon. And the moon moreover was in a depressed half-moon state, there and not there, its chin cupped in its hands, strangely quiet and evasive for a moon who was so happy to see him. There were silences; there were times when the conversation would seem to breathe its last, then revive, live a few more minutes, before it finally expired and Robinson found himself back in the corridor.

There the lieutenant governor's secretary, or an aide, another of their hydra-headed staff, popped in front of him with still another face behind her. This is Miss Brown of our press department, said the first. Miss Brown would be so pleased to take him on a tour of the capitol building and answer any questions he might have about anything at all. Robinson looked at the further amends being offered to him and they were small, lithe and cute. There was no train back to Jericho until the morning, which left enough time to feel abandoned and unhappy, and so he, a candidate for the State Assembly in this very building, accepted the mockery of a guided tour. But he asked no questions of Miss Brown, or none that mattered, none that he might have dropped for sheer effect into the ear of a senior aide. He let her guide him up and down staircases and through lounges and dining rooms, over carpets, past portraits of old occupants, into corridors where Miss Brown's heels clicked past workaday offices and conference rooms, Robinson meeting himself occasionally in the memory of a tour he had been taken on long ago with his eighth-grade class. When they entered the empty House chamber, surmounted by the dome, and rimmed with galleries, he felt tears in his eyes. Why was that, he wondered? Because no matter what he did or how hard he tried he was going to lose? He walked over to one of the empty assembly chairs and sat down and looked up at the galleries. He felt humble; not intimidated or cowed, but truly humble, almost beseechingly, as if his humility could buy him the seat. No one looked down from the galleries and the members had all gone home to their districts. There was no old woman mopping up. Instead there was Miss Brown, placing a headstone on the emptiness with a last inventory of interesting facts and figures about the dome. He actually felt naive beside Miss Brown, not because she was smart, which she was, but because she was of this place, entered it and left it every day; he would have felt the same if she were merely one of their typists. Which demonstrated the condition he was in, what the State House expedition had done to him, how glad he was it was over and how much he needed a drink.

She led him outside onto the capitol steps.

"I have to tell you something," she said.

"Oh?"

"Don't expect much help from them," said Miss Brown raising her fine eyebrows at the State House. "Nothing that will be visible anyway."

"I don't understand," said Robinson.

"Dwayne Armstead is a big man in the House. And it's not a big House. They won't go out of their way to antagonize him."

"Then what's the use of running a candidate against him?"

"Oh, if you were to beat him, that would be different. You'd be the fair-haired boy. They couldn't do enough for you then."

He was so stunned that he barely noticed when she said goodbye to him and ran quickly back up the steps. Not give him any help? He wanted so much not to believe her. She could be lying just to impress him with what she knew, to show him how smart she was. But for the same reason she could be telling him the truth. The muddled appointment with the governor fit in. So did the lieutenant governor's evasiveness. And it struck him suddenly: not only wasn't she lying, she was supposed to tell him this. She had been delegated to do it. Who else could do it? It was only a theory. He was sure of nothing except that he believed Miss Brown, and that the domed building he had entered so expectantly looked far different to him now, looked cold, cynical, sinister and double-locked. So he went back up the steps, against a thin tide of workers who were exiting at the end of their day. Miss Brown drew him back, Miss Brown and her connections, Miss Brown who was certainly cute but without having to be. She was a little talisman of power, a tiny bit of the causes that produced effects, perhaps not even that, except for the feeling of being out in the cold which she produced in him. He went back to the lieutenant governor's office, asked to see her, was admitted and found her in her cubbyhole and though she hesitated, something made her say yes to his invitation for a drink.

He waited in a cocktail lounge on a street around in back of the State House. Miss Brown had directed him there. The moment she slipped into the booth she told him: "About what I said on the steps. I can't say any more about that." He knew better than to contradict her. There was nothing of the little tour guide about her now; her new surroundings, old, plush and a little dusty, suited Miss Brown very well. But he didn't like her any better. Rainey was prettier, was lovelier, was warmer. To compare them was sacrilege. Miss Brown, he decided after a drink or two, was probably unlikeable, which was part of her fascination. She made him think of cold contentious sex, bend-the-knee sex, an-eye-for-an-eye and a-tooth-for-a-tooth sex. Miss Brown seemed to know that her breath blew cold and not to care. She gave him her complete attention. Ordinary matters could wait; nothing was as important as giving a hand up the ladder to George Robinson. So were her bosses using Miss Brown? Was she here as a cute diversion? Was she here just to give him a terrific boost? So what if she was?

"I think you have a chance. You impress me. You're bright, you're attractive, you talk well, you look lucky. It could be your year."

"And if I were to mention the unmentionable, cite the uncitable, if it looked as though that could mean the difference?"

"That? If you ask me, politicians can't deliver votes to other politicians. All they can do is grab the credit."

"Which will be all mine when I win," he smiled drily.

She nodded her head.

He asked her for her advice.

"Get off to a solid start. Organize mightily if you haven't. Don't scatter your shot all over the place, you only need a few good debating points. Do you know Dwayne Armstead? Needle him. He won't like that. Remember, you're the challenger, so challenge. That's what I would do."

Words. He had sat in a chair in Jericho and generated the same words himself. But it wasn't the words—it just wasn't with Miss Brown. "So in spite of everything you really think I can win?" he asked her. And with her eyes she straightened his tie, patted his cheek, slapped his rump and sent him out into the world. "Definitely," she said.

He looked delighted. His spirits ballooned and the balloon was slightly tipsy. He said: "You impress me too. What's your goal anyway? Governor's press secretary? Bigger things? Something in Washington?"

"I never think about that. It's not an important concern of mine. I just do my job. Why are you smiling?" she smiled.

For a second he almost liked her, could have leaned across their table and kissed her, and done it with fondness. But Miss Brown with her feel for which way the wind was blowing, and perhaps to leave him at its balmiest, picked that moment to put a menu into his hands, recommend the prime ribs as first-rate, wish him all the luck in the world and say that she was leaving with a first-class impression of George Robinson. Or was it the other way around—the ribs first-class and George Robinson first-rate?

No, he couldn't say he liked her and he probably didn't trust her. When he remembered her afterward she was an oddly distended image, with her short haircut, her little hands and high stiletto heels. But she was so much a part of the State House and life under the dome that Robinson thought of her many times when he was back in Jericho. If he still believed in the possibility of victory, he could thank Miss Brown.

His HEART sank his first morning back in the office when he experienced Eleanor Prain, her cheerfulness, her dumpiness, her kindergarten world. His law files and campaign plans were her blocks and coloring books. Indulgent until now, sidelong he watched her plump hands doing this and doing that. Her chatty phone messages and big round handwriting got on Robinson's nerves.

"Have you been calling Mrs. Davis about my book?" he picked at her suddenly after having forgotten about *The Prince* for weeks.

"Mr. Robinson, I want to talk to you about that. You may not know it, but I see Alpha very often in the grocery store, in the drugstore, and at the hairdresser's. It seems like I'm always meeting Alpha. So I was wondering if I could ask her about your book when I see her instead of making a special phone call every week."

"Absolutely not. I want those phone calls made."

"Will you tell me why, Mr. Robinson?"

"Yes I will, Eleanor. If there is one thing about you that I value above all others it is your personal loyalty to me. I'm thinking of all these confidential files—I'm thinking of my election campaign. Your loyalty has been like pure gold to me, Eleanor, pure gold. Now, do I still have it, or don't I?"

"Oh, very well, Mr. Robinson."

She appalled him. Her grumbling was a minor sin compared to her cozy attitude, her mixing up his business with the grocer and the hairdresser. One taste of the capital and he couldn't abide Jericho. What little people they were here, a place where Eleanor Prain was the best imitation they had of a real secretary.

Then there was Hank.

Robinson walked into his inner office a couple of days later to find Hank waiting for him.

"Somebody swiped a rifle from us," said Hank.

"They broke into headquarters?"

"It was in the back of the car," said Hank with a sickly smile.

"Loaded?"

"Full. I had a call about a dog running wild out in the country but I never sighted him." Hank sighed, "I stopped for a cold drink on the way back. I parked on Back Street and I was gone ten minutes. I've done it a hundred times. But I forgot to lock the car this time."

"Who else knows about this?"

"Pete's the only one. I feel so dumb about it I wouldn't have told him either except he'd see it was missing. He's been helping me look for it."

Robinson burst out laughing. "You've been looking for it? How long ago did this happen?"

"A week ago. Don't sock me, George. I thought we could find it before I had to report it officially. A kid steals a gun, shoots some squirrels, plays around with it, then throws it in the dump or somewhere."

"That makes sense to me," said Robinson. He couldn't fault Hank for covering up because it was exactly what he would have done himself. He didn't feel much concern about one more rifle in a town full of hunting rifles. He thought that Hank was a primordial ass for having his gun stolen, though. "That makes sense to me," he said to Hank. "Besides, what more could be done than you're doing? You don't want a house-to-house search."

"Right," said Hank.

"Or a story in the *Pioneer*. Think of the hotheads reading it. Think of Will Carpenter. I think you're handling it in exactly the right way as a simple police matter."

"It was such a bonehead thing to do in the first place."

Robinson shrugged. Hank squeezed his arm, passing him on his way out. "Thanks, George—I'll keep looking."

Where, thought Robinson. In the back of the car?

His secretary and his police chief, a kindergarten and a farce. Here he was, back in Jericho, stuck in Jericho, with no visible help forthcoming, no help from the party, no visit by the governor, as if it had just penetrated his brain: the governor wasn't coming.

"The governor was called away unexpectedly but I had a very satisfying talk with the lieutenant governor. It couldn't have gone better. Of course, they're both behind me to the hilt," he told Rainey.

He told her, "They want Armstead taken worse than I thought. He's been a serious problem in the House. One of their key aides told me that. Admitted it.

"I felt surprisingly humble. Not intimidated but I think genuinely humble," he told her, describing his feelings in the domed House chamber for the second or third time. This time he followed her out into the backyard and stood over her while she pulled weeds out of the bed of pinks and pruned the wild roses.

But she didn't appreciate the difference, either that or she wasn't interested. She threw down the shears and said, "George, this is boring. It was boring the first time. Suppose I see a difference. What difference does it make?"

She disappointed him. He told her half-truths, possible truths and lies, not only to impress her but simply to seize her attention. His raw rebuff by the governor turned into an amusing little anecdote whose point was the red faces of the gubernatorial staff. Miss Brown became a key aide; it made for a much better story reporting her encouragement and advice. But the real Miss Brown wouldn't have asked him to stop talking and give her ears a rest. Miss Brown wouldn't have terminated a discussion of campaign coffee parties to go shopping downtown with the children. Did she know that she was giving him an appetite for Miss Brown? Her indifference to his campaign made him sardonic; made him belittle her. He told her: "The governor may come to Jericho this fall. He may bring a senator with him. Also the president if he happens to be in the state." This penetrated but not as he might have hoped. "Here?" she asked in horror. "To our house? How could you do that to me?" And he had to reassure her with the truth. "It's very very unlikely," he said to her with manifold bitterness.

Jamie got on his nerves. The both of them did but Stephie was little, was intriguing in small doses, and decorative. Once summer came, Jamie was omnipresent to Robinson. He was like a trick done with mirrors. There were always two or three of him, the one who was inside the house, the one who was out in the yard, and the one whose job was to stand at the back screen door and slam it constantly. Their house had never seemed so small to Robinson, a small cage that she made worse. She thought that Jamie should stay up with them later in the evening. George, you should go out in the yard after supper and play baseball with Jamie. You don't see enough of Jamie, she said!

He didn't think he was jealous in the ordinary sense of jealousy. It was the slight to himself that he resented, the little daily insult to his candidacy. He couldn't believe that it was about playing baseball with Jamie, so what was it about? She was not direct with him. He loved and gloried in her mystery but she was mysterious in unwelcome ways. There was the matter of the coffee parties, as an instance. If he calmly raised the subject of her hostessing a few stupid little coffee parties for him, she had to run downtown or downstairs to do the wash or upstairs to say good-night to Jamie.

But Jamie didn't go to bed with her. Jamie didn't slip off the little panties of her summer pajamas and push the top up around her neck. Jamie did not, like his Dad, suck the soft little spikes of her nipples.

"You're very warm," he murmured to her.

"The kitchen was warm tonight."

"No, no. You're lovely and warm, warm that way. No one is like you. I thought of it when I was gone, how pretty and warm you are.

I need you, Rainey. This way, but the other way too. Why won't you help me?"

"It's just not for me, George."

"But you'd be such a big help. I'm not flattering you. You have intelligence and charm, you know how to talk to these women. With a little help from you, people say I could neutralize Grafton."

"Get away from me."

"No, wait!" he cried. "Don't leave now—I'm aroused. Come back, Rainey! I promise not to mention the coffee parties!"

But she threw on her robe and she went. She went. How Robinson hated her iciness that minute. And her warmth, and her tasteless nipples and all her cloying flesh. A burning question was: "What makes you think you're so different from Eleanor Prain?"

GOVERNORS, SENATORS, congressmen, presidents meant nothing to Rainey. Her world got on very nicely without them. It was as though they were a pantheon she didn't believe in, and the truth was, she considered herself superior to those little gods who were always asking for her belief and her blessing. George being mayor was different because, for one thing, it merely crowned a fact that everyone knew, that he was the smartest man in town, and for another, no one had run against him in those elections. So he wasn't really a politician. He had never made a speech, never broken a promise, never made a promise so far as she knew. He wasn't one of those fickle, now-you-see-me, now-you-don't little gods. Being mayor was more like being chosen to head the family. If George looked down on their neighbors, which she knew and could be wounded by, when she wasn't secretly proud, he at least paid them the respect of making his home among them. But what if he won this election to the Assembly and he wasn't satisfied with that and went higher, and elsewhere, what then? She could never leave Jericho. It wasn't that she was afraid to, or acted selfishly. She couldn't imagine herself living anywhere else and being the same person she was, and if that was selfishness, it didn't feel that way at all to Rainey, but like love of a certain place on the earth. Packing all they owned into a truck would certainly get it moved, but like a burial, where all was still there, down to the last curl, except the spirit.

His politics seemed so insincere to her. It was like some obnoxious cologne that he slapped on his cheeks every morning so he could kiss the world. He had yet to make a speech, so he said, but he dragged her to distant potluck suppers where he collected little groups and talked about caring about you folks, and wanting to help you folks out, those words "you folks" never absent from his mouth as though they were a wad of chewing gum. She drove to a farm auction out near Grafton and what was the first thing she saw but George's Olds and then George's big smile among the other articles of brass. And once, at a wedding they went to, she overheard him say how much he respected The Farmer and she wondered how far she would have to go to find that unusual farmer. "But I'm running for public office, I have to do these things," he protested to her. She disagreed. To her, it was obvious that he enjoyed doing them and liked making fools of people. When she said to him, "And I don't see why you're always criticizing Dwayne Armstead," it contained both her innocence and the needle in her haystack of innocence.

She worried about Jamie. She saw that pursuit of the comparative stranger and avoidance of his own little son, and it was his perfidy brought to a boil. "You're changing," she told him. "Not me," said he, and probably he was right. He was never the father she thought he would be. She had had something different in mind when she visualized her children's father, that warm, affectionate, caring, unknown man. She supposed he wasn't even a friend to his children. His relationship with Stephie was that of a finger that furled up the frosting on top of a cake. Jamie he had to be pushed into knowing— into seeing. Not even a friend, George? A sad thought, that thought; but true. How much she saw when she saw. That, precious as he was, Jamie was not a perfect boy. That he outshone all others but there was an other-side-of-the-moon side to Jamie too, a side bookish and intensely sweet and sweet because it was not so sturdily formed, as if there was another boy curled up inside the visible boy. He was so much hers, so undeniably hers, that ordinarily all was sweetness and light to Rainey; but now she fumed with resentment toward Robinson.

"It's summer," she said to him when he had been back a week from the capital. "Why don't you take him fishing instead of running around the state? Fathers do things with their sons," she told him.

She said: "Take him camping. You two could drive up to Canada and camp out in the woods. You'll have fun if you give him a chance."

She came up to him and put her arms around his neck and hung there like a girl. "Do it, George. Be friends with him. It's important for him and besides I'd like you to. I'd be grateful."

He looked at her and said nothing and returned to the yard and his Sunday paper, but five minutes later he came back with a funny smile on his face.

"Are you blackmailing me?" he asked her.

She was shocked. His coffee parties—he was still thinking about his coffee parties—all that clinked in his head were asinine coffee parties! "How dare you," she said to him, "ask me for something in exchange for loving your son as if you were doing me a favor."

"Have I done that?" he cried. "I'm not even the one who started this conversation. There I was reading the Sunday paper. I don't know the first thing about camping or fishing!"

"Just don't follow me," she said to him.

In the back entry she grabbed her sunhat and sailed out into the yard. Her inclination was to cut up his lawn chair with her shears, but instead Rainey picked them up and brought thirty minutes of order to the world by pruning the rest of the wild roses.

She had these choices, Rainey figured. She could water the new shoot and help it grow, she could not water it and let it die, or she could snip it off. Watering it was out of the question because sooner or later it would grow into a dangerous tangle. But if she snipped, would that be the end of it? If it was a normal shoot that would have been the end of it, but since it wasn't that, but George's politics, it would bleed, it would holler, and it might be vindictive enough to grow anyway. So that was when Rainey decided that the only choice she had was not to water it, and help it die.

CHAPTER 16

HE HAD a gun—one of their own. One of their own made it much better. And he didn't plan it that way, it wasn't his fault; it was sitting in the back of the police car on Back Street and no one was around but him. He was so sure the car door was locked that when it wasn't his hand jumped like it had been bitten. He grabbed the rifle, threw it behind some packing cases, biked away, and then after midnight biked back, found it, rode home with it and put it under his bed. He could touch it without getting out of his bed. Joe was nosey but not so nosey that he would look under the bed.

Lifting a gun under their noses didn't seem like a crime; it was so much like his web, his special behavior and all the rest. The gun changed things though, making them heavier. Though it stayed on the floor under the bed, it lopped against West's mind as he crisscrossed the streets on his bike, as though a gun was too heavy for a web. Oh he was happy to have it, but in the beginning he felt a little silly and light, compared to his serious friend on the floor under the bed.

"ANYBODY IN favor of a third cop?" asked Robinson.

"Anybody in favor of a curfew for the kids? Is anybody interested in discussing either of these proposals? No discussion and no one in favor? Let the secretary so note and I ask the secretary to deliver a copy of these minutes to the *Jericho Pioneer*. Who moves to adjourn this meeting? Do I hear a second?"

Robinson tapped his gavel and slid it away from him on the table. "Council meeting adjourned."

He reached down to his briefcase and removed from it and placed before him a single sheet of paper. The six at the table formed his little circle of campaign workers. They seemed interested, they had some push in the town as town councilmen, and it was convenient to have a group that met regularly on its own even if he had no real use for them until the fall. They showed Robinson that he had an organization. They listened to him think; they were a reminder to the town that his campaign truly existed, and they kept him politically warm as he waded into the icy odds of the fight against Armstead. He showed them material like his campaign maps, which he described as confidential. He joked with them and flattered them and dubbed them his braintrust, while the little inside joke he reserved for himself was that as a braintrust they were strong on trust.

"It seems that my opponent has decided to sit and rock on his front porch all summer, boys. Well, that's his privilege. But it's a big opportunity for us. It means we have the campaign pretty much to ourselves until close to election time. So what we want is something to keep our momentum going at about the time Armstead makes his move, and the notion I've come up with is to get folks from around the district to spend a day here in Jericho in the fall. Make it a real event, a picnic lunch, a parade, bargains in the stores and sidewalk sales—give them something they can take home with them. I know you'll want to think about this, so let's save the other stuff for another time," he said, scrutinizing and folding up his sheet of paper. "But keep it quiet for the time being. Remember, the point is to get them here, have them meet the candidate, listen to a speech and go home happy. Think about it, boys, and give me some bright ideas."

Last to leave the council room, and letting the six walk ahead down the corridor, he listened to them estimating the number of people who would flock to Jericho for his event. That they were merchants and businessmen who would make some money out of a windfall of visitors didn't hurt their spirits any—he had given them something they could take home with them. He expected no bright ideas from them, least of all for an event that in essence, stripping away the politics, had a thousand cornball predecessors in towns like Jericho. The truth was, he didn't expect all that much to come out of the event itself. But it gave the braintrust something to think about. It showed them he would spend money to win and that he was optimistic in spite of the odds. Most of all, he hoped it would fire them up for that final month heading toward election day. Give them a big crowd, a little excitement and some business, and they wouldn't mind making phone calls and ringing door-bells, searching out his voters and making sure they voted, all of the drudgery that won elections. All this Robinson kept to himself, not merely out of common sense, but because secrecy satisfied him, the same way that walking behind the six men, all by himself, was to be the more emphatically central. When he came out onto the steps where they were dispersing, he saw it all in a legendary light, the obscure city hall, these oratory steps, his little band of followers, their humble end that was his humble beginning.

"Hold on a minute, boys!"

They stopped and looked at him.

"Boys, did I ever tell you that my mother is the only woman in the world who knew how to cut a pie? Listen to this. The way she cut a pie was in half. And when I was a hungry kid I'd put away half of that pie for lunch and the other half of it for supper. Boys, if we cut this pie right, if we take Jericho and I mean take it big, I promise you we'll be putting away half of Dwayne Armstead for lunch and the other half of Dwayne Armstead for supper. How do you like that, boys?"

There was a moment of silence. Then they cheered. They applauded him, all six; those who stood closest shook his hand or slapped him on the back. And he was elated. It was his first campaign speech. The speech was nonsensical and the audience his braintrust, figures he manipulated and laughed at, and yet he was elated. He grabbed his briefcase, ran down the steps, turned and raised his fist in the air.

"We're going to do it, boys! I promise you, we're going to win this thing!"

So the official campaign started, a miniature cannon firing off a miniature puff of smoke.

CHAPTER 17

SUMMER SET in, dry warm days, dry hot days. Dust blew in off the prairie to settle domestically around sunny kitchen windows. There was a feeling of yellow in the air like the sight of the wild mustard that spilled from fields to roadside. With grass fires and rubbish fires the firehouse whistle blasted more and sprang its sequence of wailing firetruck, men in cars, boys on bikes and barking dogs. Streets smelled of fresh-mown grass or else of freshly laid tar, a tar that patched each winter up, never dried all summer long, and clung to cars and bikes. Kids stuck to each other like the tar, best friends on front stoops, best friends in backyards, best friends biking to the pool. Few people went away in summer and semi-lost children came back home to visit. The town buzzed and dozed and seemed complete.

West sitting in the café behind a newspaper sees Dixie Carpenter's kid brother biking with George Robinson's boy, both of whom wave to Dixie coming out of the Dakota Store, who in a minute smiles hi to Alpha Davis who passes the Red Owl Store and out of the corner of her eye observes that browser-bruiser Joe who is rolling up the awning and whistling because he will soon be bringing a surprise lamb chop supper to the house of Alaman West, who will not be home because he is still sitting by the window in the Paris Café.

Chance meetings and near misses were a fact of life in Jericho.

In a world so small, with only one school to go to, few places to land a job and not too many streets on which to start up a home, one bank to keep the life savings in, one doctor, one minister of your faith, one funeral home and one last resting place on the town's lone pillow of a hill—in a world so small, coincidence was so sewn into the fabric of events as not to resemble a jumped stitch at all.

But still, West didn't know why he kept running into Rainey Robinson.

His haunts were not her places, the exception being the library where West hadn't set foot in weeks. In all the years since she was Rainey Spencer and high school harvest queen he hadn't seen her more than a scattering of times and then in the space of one week he seemed to see her everywhere, every day.

He saw her on Legion Avenue getting out of her car with her kids, crossing the street with the kids and entering a store with same.

He caught a glimpse of her in Robinson's private office through the usual open window and had to duck so as not to catch her eye.

He saw her coming out of Haley's Drugstore one morning and then in the afternoon coming out her front door.

She was in the Red Owl Store when he went in but since he was there legally to buy milk he didn't care that much if he caught her eye.

He rode past a yard sale and in the yard was Rainey Robinson.

Those were the meetings, part from his shadowing of Robinson, part by accident, and part from being on the lookout. At that, his back-from-the-dead cock surprised him when he rocked away the evening because he had never seen her in that light at all. He truly didn't have an urge for her. He mistrusted her. At most, he admired her. To feel an urge he would have to feel a way in, like a weakness, like an incidental hole besides the actual hole, and yet the true hole, like Dixie's youngness. It was all automatic. To West, he could walk around Rainey Robinson all day and see a woman without seeing a way in. She was beautiful, but she didn't interest him.

But it was interesting to rock and smooth Cat and mull over what difference it made to be turning over the extinction of Robinson in his mind and smiling hello to Robinson's wife on the street. So far as West could see, it wasn't going to make any difference at all.

So when he rode past Robinson's house and she was standing in the front door calling her kid, and she waved to him, and he stopped a minute on his bike, and she from the open front door said with the little lookalike girl in town, "How about that cup of coffee I promised you?" "Thanks," he said and went in.

Just like that. Except that his heart beat a little faster because he had never been in the house before. The little kid stuck with them, close to her mother but peering back at him, staring at him like Cat did, except that West knew he owned Cat. "Please sit down. I'll make a fresh pot of coffee," said Lorraine Rainey Robinson Spencer.

The sunny kitchen blotched his eyes and he fumbled a chair out from under the table, dopily awkward. The kid saw it. West made a face at her and she giggled but it didn't stop her from making cream-of-mush out of him with her eyes.

He sat with his hands in his lap. He couldn't come up with anything to say. He glanced around, but what would the kitchen give him to say? It was just sunny and nice; it had flimsy white curtains, crowded counters and stuff like spice racks and copper pots hanging on the wall. Rainey Robinson put two cups and saucers, a spoon for him, a bowl of sugar and a small pitcher of cream into the sunbeam on the table. "It's been a beautiful summer so far, hasn't it," she said to him. "Of course, we don't farm. Just between us, I can't sympathize with people who are always looking for rain." Rainey Robinson smiled at a dumb, a tongueless West and returned from the counter with plates, napkins and a plateful of cookies, saying: "Two for you to keep you quiet," plunking down two cookies in front of the kid. The coffee bubbled. The second she rose to get it the little kid asked him a question, but without any luck. Then Rainey Robinson sat down and poured for them and chatted to him, sipping her coffee black, West sipping his, slouched morosely behind the cup. Since they had a dog, she was maybe used to having dumb animals who couldn't talk in for coffee.

"I hope you'll be staying in Jericho now," Rainey Robinson said. "I think you would like it here. In a place like this, making a lot of money isn't important, or even having a lot of friends, if you don't care to. You'll find that people aren't exactly alike either. I think Jericho is a place where people can be themselves."

Another shovelful of silence fell on him, his own dirt; he provided the dirt, he did the shoveling and he was the one being buried. It was her, her or the house—he couldn't speak. Even a bum like Joe would find something to say.

"I like the kitchen," West got out, getting up. He poked around, feigning mild silence in a pit of silence. He asked a question about a pot on the counter, a picture on the wall, and she answered the deaf-ear question. He saw knives in a quarter-open drawer. He opened the drawer more because he felt like it, he took out a long blunt rounded thing for the same reason. "What's this for?" West said, taking it out and dangling it in front of him because he felt like it.

"Melon balls," said Rainey Robinson. She walked over to the counter. "Haven't you ever seen them? I take these ends and scoop them into a melon, and I can make big balls or small balls, whichever size balls I want."

Then Rainey Robinson stopped talking, glanced at West, blushed, looked the other way and started laughing. "I don't know why I'm laughing," said Rainey Robinson. "There's nothing funny about them. I put them into a salad, or I chill them in wine, or I can freeze them if I want to," she said, and burst out laughing. "Excuse me," Rainey Robinson said. "Dear oh dear," she said, clearing her throat, placing her hand on her throat, staring into space and immediately bursting out laughing. "Why am I laughing?" she gasped.

West laughed too. At that, Rainey Robinson gave a groan, threw back her head and laughed harder, West watching her, emitting his funny bark of a laugh and watching with cautious eyes. West laughed because she laughed. He saw teary eyes, raw lip, unladylike pink of gums, and he laughed in the face of confusion and aversion because he had never seen a reality like Rainey Robinson's sunny, breathless and distortedly beautiful face.

She caught his arm. "I'll stop," she panted. "I shouldn't laugh. It isn't funny. Those poor—those poor frozen little balls."

And she howled. So did Stephie who ran dodging and screaming around the table. So did West.

West could scarcely stand in one place. His laughing came in gulps; when he stopped, out of breath, or out of spirit, he had only to stand, prime himself and see her laughing for it to start up all over again. A pair of balls hung between them and West roared in their shadow. And he didn't give the game away either, anymore than she did. Why should he? He was having too good a time. It went on for minutes. The completely ignored little kid just made it a madhouse.

That was the visit. He got on his bike once he got his strength back over another cup of coffee and rode away, luckily just as her other kid came biking up the street and into their driveway. She had told him to come back. Sure; he'd probably oblige. It might be interesting being in the house. It might be useful seeing the life of the other quarter, which was the other half of the other half. He named a page after her in Accounts Receivable. He forgot about being dumbstruck and remembered himself watching her prettiness like a cat. When she laughed, she meant real balls. She was beautiful but mice ran around inside her head.

This was how he saw her from the beginning: he felt pity for her for Robinson's say over her but face-to-face he mistrusted her. She was almost as much to blame as Robinson because she stood it, stood Robinson. It was all an accident—if he was on her side it was because he was against Robinson. So except for finding out that he liked her, nothing that vital had changed.

Yet the next time he saw Robinson after being in the house with her, which was the following afternoon downtown, such was the danger he felt, and panic, that he fled on his bike and dashed into his house and hid like a loony until Joe came. He wished he had never set foot in their house for even a couple of minutes. Being Alaman West, he was going to pay for liking Rainey Robinson. When he felt pain shooting through his mouth a day later, he was sure it was swift revenge if not by Robinson then in the name of Robinson.

Pain was banging the laugh out of his mouth. The mouth of the laugh spouted pain. And the pain was Robinson's laugh— Robinson's laugh and his pain were one and the same.

It was a deep dull inaccessible ache, down in his jaw, in the back, and soon spreading into his neck, a toothache, and not vengeance and a warning, even if something whispered to him that he had never had a toothache before. Maybe the pain would hit the roof and drop like a fever. Perhaps if he endured his pain, and sat quietly and let it stretch, it would stretch to its utmost and break. They had a dentist over in Malden, Malden or Grafton, someplace out there. But he hated doctors and dentists, except for the military ones he had seen on the base down south, the ones who got their paycheck from the army. Doc Sunderquist who would go anywhere and do anything, Doc Death would also take care of your teeth. But Doc had been waiting for a long time to do a good deed for the West kid and the West kid would sooner die than go ask Doc for help.

He went to work on foot, mistrusting the bike, fearful of jarring bumps in the road; without pain or with pain he looked silent, intact, the same, so his morning at Amundson's passed and he bore himself home. It wasn't only the pain; it was being sick and tired of the pain. But even if he was willing to go to the dentist, who would drive him there, who would take him, who would sit with him, Rainey Robinson? And silently West laughed himself silly; but he possessed that wild idea.

Joe came in the evening and peeped through the bedroom curtain at West sitting up in bed with an icebag to his jaw. Joe saw the same scene as he had the day before, only now the icebag was huge like a moronic second head. "Why don't you go to a dentist?" Joe asked.

"I'll kill myself first."

"Okay, the doctor then."

"He killed my mother," West screamed hammering his fist on the wall.

Joe didn't have an answer for that. It was the first time West had ever spoken of his mother or anything personal, but Joe wished his friend had picked a better time to do it. So he turned away quietly and unwrapped the sandwiches he had brought and sat down to eat at the kitchen table. West banged on the wall from time to time but Joe knew that blind pain was the reason and though he chewed almost rhythmically and itched to go in, he stayed put until the banging and slamming got bad enough that he stuck his head into the room.

"I could fix it for you," Joe said.

West clutched the icebag to his jaw. The fingers of the slamming hand boned out trembling against the wall.

"I could fix it. I could yank the tooth. I once did it on a ship."

"When were you on a ship?"

"On the docks then."

West lay back and said nothing. "So?" asked Joe and got no answer. "You got pliers?" asked Joe and West shook his head. "I'll be right back with pliers," Joe cried and ran out.

He ran to Legion Avenue but it was late and the Coast-to-Coast Store was dark. So was Amundson's lumber yard when he chugged around the corner. Joe ran to the Violet Hotel and got the pliers out of the toolbox behind the deserted front desk. He walked and ran along Legion Avenue and saw the open saloon and got a bottle of whisky.

He dashed into West's house. West was up and roaming around the kitchen. Joe got towels out of a drawer, washed his hands and started boiling the pliers. "Just do it!" yelled West. Joe poured whisky over the pliers and rushed over with half a glass for West who waited on a kitchen chair. "You better," said Joe, so West took some and Joe swallowed the rest.

The pliers, Joe's thumb, Joe's taste almost made West gag. His pain, even West's pain died of that taste and that mouthful. But that was before he screamed. "That's the one!" cried Joe from behind the chair, holding the pliers near the tooth and peering in. "Okay, I'm all ready—we're starting."

West held onto the seat of the chair with both hands, his head all the way back, locked there just in case by the addition of Joe's arm under his jaw while Joe worked to get a good grip on the tooth with the pliers. Joe started to sweat because the tooth was in the back where if he got set to grip it he couldn't exactly see it. Not only that, at the same time as he worked the pliers around he had to keep pushing West's head back in place with his other hand. Not only that, even if West held still, and Joe got a good grip on the tooth, when he squeezed the pliers they kept slipping off and batting the roof of West's mouth or his other teeth.

West grabbed Joe's arm. His mouth felt in shreds. He longed to faint; he was feeble, he had no voice. Joe gave him more whisky and he poured the conflagration down over torn gums with a fresh and delicious pain. Then pliers, Joe's fingers, Joe's sweat and Joe's face all were back again because the world consisted of Joe, Joe and pain. West gripped the seat of the chair, clenched his eyes and tried to sail into darkness and instead dragged the chair inch by inch along the floor. "Don't move," Joe pleaded, a plea that to West was so infuriating and so insane that he tried to grab Joe's upsidedown face by the hair.

Joe suggested the floor. He pleaded and he insisted, and much to his surprise the floor felt dear to West; he longed to curl up and surrender, give up and die, but this bum wouldn't let him, this bum was his friend. Joe clamped a knee on West to keep him on his back and cupped his free hand under West's chin. He had his best view and best leverage yet. West moved less, the pliers gripped better, and he had West's head practically between his knees, but still Joe needed all his strength and maybe more. Joe pulled. He twisted the pliers left and right. That was very good because he thought he felt and even heard things break, not the tooth but hidden things, little bits of things underneath it. Blood trickled over the pliers and Joe didn't know if that was good or bad, but he kept twisting the pliers back and forth, West's frozen face incapable of expression but his legs eerily like the pair of pliers, parting and closing in agony.

There was a crack. Both heard it. Both felt it. To Joe, it was like jumping from rock into slush. "I got it!" he cried to the eye-bulging West.

But not yet, even though West passed out and Joe had to finish alone. The tooth was loose but Joe needed to work the pliers more and break a few more ends before he gave one good yank to the side and it all came out. Joe looked at the slumping West and then at his tooth, embarrassed a little by the tooth and the bits of gum and bone clinging to it. But it was a perfectly whole tooth and Joe beamed at it as if he had made it, not pulled it.

West came to his senses and sobbed. Joe put his arm around him as West fought for breath and cried and slowly helped him to sit up. "It's okay, it's okay, cry," Joe said. West opened his mouth and spit out blood. Joe was alarmed but said brightly, "I got the tooth out, so it don't hurt anymore, so it must be okay, right?" West nodded his head. Joe suddenly tore a piece off a towel, wadded it and put it over the socket in West's mouth.

Then he helped West get to his feet and walked him a few steps but West looked back and spotted the tooth on the table. "Get rid of it," he gasped. "Now." And he stood watching while Joe threw it into the garbage pail, and the next Joe saw, West was passing through the curtain into the bedroom.

Joe went home. When he woke up the next day he was still afraid that he must have done something wrong. But the second he saw West's face in West's house after hurrying there that evening, Joe let out a yell and clapped his hands.

"The operation is a success!"

Joe had been afraid because it was the first time in his life that he had ever pulled a tooth, although he could never tell West that because he had lied about it. So when he stopped applauding and laughing Joe said: "It's the first time in my life I ever did that." Joe added apprehensively when West didn't speak, "You ain't mad?" And West shook his head. "You ain't mad but you ain't surprised," said Joe roaring again.

Joe couldn't get enough out of the tooth-pulling. He talked about it all evening. He didn't expect West to talk because he could see for himself that it must hurt him to talk. But Joe talked until his lips bubbled. "That was some tough tooth," he said. "You're lucky to be rid of that tooth." And every five or ten minutes all evening long: "Tell the truth, how does it feel? Does it really feel okay?"

IMMENSITIES SEEMED to detach West from the world, the immensities of sleep and peace and not least that soft gap that he would sometimes touch with his tongue, that was like a tiny bed, past pain. He woke it seemed a dozen times that day and basked in nothingness inside and out. He scarcely noticed where he lived, what space he moved through, all was touchable but all seemed made of air.

This lasted a couple of days before things shrank to their proper size as West came back to life. The gap in his mouth became a part of him and peace itself shrank away. In a couple of days the only reminders were nothing better and nothing worse than a little soreness and Joe. For a get-well present Joe brought him a coffee pot from the housewares section of the Coast-to-Coast

Store. "Now you can make a real cup of coffee," he told West. As Joe unwrapped the coffee pot he felt contented and even a little smug, but he set his gift on the counter and left it there. It was West's coffee pot to enjoy all by himself, Joe said. "By yourself or with your other friends." Joe felt that he could say that to West. He knew there were no other friends.

It was barely midsummer and West, who had been through fright, through pain, even through bliss, West had his old will back, maybe stronger. So there must have been a weakening or poison in his system before the tooth began to ache because he wasn't afraid of Robinson or the house of Robinson any longer. He still blamed himself for screaming in front of Joe, but only because the scream told Joe about his mother, but he didn't care that he had cried in front of him. Joe had taken care of the tooth, but he could never forget that Joe was ordinary, ordinary was to put it mildly, so ordinary that it tugged West's heart to see him in the house sometimes, sitting in the same room with him. It tugged at West's heart at suppertime to know that Joe was likely to walk in any minute and he, West, wouldn't mind it all that much when he did. And it tugged his heart like Joe's pliers had the roots of his tooth to think that maybe he wasn't scared by the Robinsons because he had Joe.

Who was strong? Joe. Who was loyal? Joe. Who followed him around? Who could he trust? Who did the dishes? The punchline was always Joe.

Joe was the punchline—Joe was the butt of all jokes who even followed West like his butt. Because Joe was just a helper. That was what he did all his life long and all week long and what he did in West's house, help. But there was nothing wrong about having a helper, a good lesson West learned before he smashed his bookcase, when he could have used a helper to hold the boards for him while he aimed and drove the nails in.

No different now. Joe could be his helper. It might be a wise idea. For one thing, it was practical, because he couldn't very well tell the bum he was going to do it and then not do it. Also, Joe could help out with the plan. Also, Joe was happy and liked him. The bum deserved to know.

So West smiled to himself and looked at it in this light, and the more he did, decrying the years of aloneness, his immense innate darkness, and focusing on what he deemed the light, the light of it, like Joe doing the dishes, the better idea it seemed to tell Joe about his plan to get Robinson and pull him into it too.

Before that night of the tooth-pulling, whenever Joe saw the cat in West's house, he was thankful if it didn't take any notice of him, much less piss on the floor. But after that night, Joe liked to say to West that the cat didn't treat him like a visitor anymore but more like a new member of the family. The truth was, Cat slept and slunk about and scratched at the door to get out and scratched to get back in every bit the same as when Joe had never been. But Joe wasn't pretending; he felt much safer at West's after what he had done for him. He didn't expect any thanks, first because it was West, and second because thanks were splashed all over West's doorstep and open door, there to be savored by Joe almost every day. It seemed like a long time ago that he had stood in front of the Red Owl Store on his afternoons off watching people go by. Joe didn't pine for that streetcorner, the bench in the park or the hungry Jericho birds either; those days at the beginning, those days were over.

So Joe was making the coffee at West's on his first free afternoon since the tooth-pulling and talking to West about city life and things he didn't miss, such as his old boss at the dry cleaners who kept promising to teach him the business. Joe hoped that West, who sat rocking as usual in the rocker, might start talking about his own city experiences in Chicago, which West would never talk about after the first visit. West didn't talk about his family life either, with the exception of that scream about the doctor killing his mother, a subject that Joe didn't think he had the nerve to bring up. But he was always curious about West, ever since he saw the face in the photograph in the yearbook and then met West in the flesh. He had that abiding itch to know all about West that West never would scratch. So Joe that afternoon offered up bits about himself and his life, bubbling on along with the new coffee pot, and West said to him:

"There's a man here. I don't know him, I don't want to. There's a man here I see often," West closed his eyes, "often, and this man can't go on living."

"He's so sick?" asked Joe looking concerned.

"No, Joe, I'm going to kill him."

It was out of the bag—out of his brain, out of the rocker and in the open where it was suddenly short and crazy, something with its head cut off. Joe said dazedly, "You what?" So West smiled, got up from the rocker and put the head back on. "I've thought about it for a long time, made my mind up, and I want you to help me, Joe."

Joe only gaped, still stalled on the killing line. "Help you to what? What did you say? Maybe I didn't hear it."

"I'm going to kill this man, Joe."

"Stop, I didn't hear it!" cried Joe. "Stop talking! That's crazy!"

"This man I don't know. It won't be hard," said West. "It looks hard but it won't be. He thinks too much of himself, like the town. I can kill him though. And you can help."

"I'm not hearing!" Joe cried, clapping his hands over his ears.

West paced and stroked a twitch at the corner of his mouth. He felt good, nervous but good, his tension rising like cream. He paced up and down in front of Joe and stopped.

"I kill him. You help."

Joe shut his eyes.

West shrugged his shoulders and resumed his walking. "I'm making you a partner and you're not interested." And Joe shot him a look that was filled with disgust and with misery. A partner. A partner to kill somebody. Joe didn't know what to believe, what part was pure talk, what was pure West, what was another West. Joe did know that he wasn't running away from the craziness by asking a question about it, yet he asked gruffly of West, "Who's this man?"

"It's George Robinson. I have reasons."

Then Joe couldn't do anything except shake his head, which he would have done at the unbelievability of anyone named by West, and so to make it easy for Joe, West said, though it was the opposite of what was precious in his mind: "It's like this. I have a grudge against him."

"You don't know him and you got a grudge against him?"

"That's right."

"You got very easy grudges," Joe said, "I better watch my step." But Joe breathed a little easier. This thing with West was getting more far-fetched and unbelievable each time West opened his mouth. It was becoming so unbelievable to Joe that he asked almost scornfully, "What's the grudge you got against Robinson? Because he's got money? Because he's got a pretty wife? Because he's the mayor?"

"That's private," West said.

Joe nodded his head. "Okay, you got a grudge. What do you need me for? You want to go kill Robinson, only you don't know him, so you need me along for company? Doesn't it sound crazy to you?" asked Joe.

"I don't need you for anything. I don't need you for anything. Is Joe the name? Joe I need you for nothing."

And West stood with his arms about himself, glowering out the window, and Joe was scared suddenly. Talk like that frightened him more than all the talk about killing did, because West could kid himself about killing a man but not about something believable like opening the door and throwing Joe out. "Okay," Joe said cautiously, "I'm listening," since it didn't make sense to get West angry over a subject that was nothing but a subject of conversation. "You got a grudge and let's say you got me. How would you do a thing like this?"

"Rifle."

The immediate answer shook Joe's nerve a little. "You ever shoot a rifle?" he asked warily.

"Many times."

Joe thought, "You got a rifle?" but he didn't ask. He decided that now was a good time to stop asking questions. So West disappeared into the bedroom and came back carrying a rifle and put it down on the kitchen table. At the sight of it Joe felt light-headed and leaden in the stomach. "Where'd you get that?" he asked backing away.

"I've always had it. It's part of me."

"Don't joke," Joe said, going over to a corner, as far from the kitchen table as he could get without going out the door. "And don't say anything else for a while, okay?" To make sure, Joe turned his back, or practically, and in a minute saw West pick up the gun and take it back into his bedroom, and this little sequence of Joe turning his back and the rifle disappearing made an impression on Joe. Okay, Joe thought to himself, he has the gun, he has the grudge and he has me. But that doesn't mean he'll do it. He'll never do it. When West said, the doctor killed my mother, he didn't mean that the doctor killed his mother because that couldn't be. That was just the way West talked, killing didn't mean killing. So it must mean something ordinary. So it must be the same about Robinson. Joe poured himself a mug of coffee and sat down at the table; his logic didn't rub everything away, but it made Joe feel much better. The doctor didn't kill West's mother. A rifle on the table didn't poison the table when it wasn't there anymore. With West, killing didn't mean killing.

After sliding the rifle back under the bed West went into the bathroom and sponged under his arms and washed his face and shaved himself and brushed his hair. He looked at the face looking back at him and rubbed the healed jaw and tested the laugh, a short laugh, then a medium laugh, then a big laugh. Nothing hurt; nothing showed. It was the same old original laugh even if laughing was almost at the bottom of his list of things to do. His preparations took West some little time. He emerged from the bathroom fresh-faced, slick-haired, exalted and silent, put on a clean white shirt and strolled past Joe at the table and out the door.

Joe followed him out, alarmed, having heard West laughing in the bathroom.

"Where are you going?" Joe cried.

Go back in dope, it's not today, not yet, it's not for a while, West muttered, and nosed his bike into the long nowhere of a road that looped the prairie and pedaled off to the house of Robinson.

CHAPTER 18

THERE WAS this to be said for Will Carpenter. A proud man, head of an unfortunate family, slapped in the face by heaven and earth, he fought back as hard as he could.

Will had a wife who took little white pills that transformed her into a teaspoon of sugar stirring listlessly in a bathrobe all day. He had a daughter, Dixie's older sister, now living in another town, who was the best example of a bad example that Jericho's young girls ever had. Then Will had an unfortunate personality. He was a cranky little man, a scrappy little man, and a vindictive little man. People would flee the only drugstore in town to get away from the druggist's temper, but no one was truly afraid of Will, just as no one was completely sorry for him. Whether he strutted or raged before them or suffered, people's feelings were touched with a smile. There was something perilously light and like a toy about Will.

But Will held his unfortunate little world together, made sure it got up each morning, the part of it able to at least, and was tucked safely into bed each night. With Molly in her sweet trance so much of the time, Will had to be father and mother to Dixie and the little brother. Of course it was Will who supplied Molly with the pills she ritually got down on her knees and begged him for. Coming soon after Sissie's escapades, the bitterness of Molly's sweetness was almost too much for Will to swallow. At

Haley's, whitecoated and in the light of day, he dispensed the drugs and condoms that privately wrecked his life. Sissie they saw infrequently now and usually in her adopted town. Though she was over twenty-one and had a family of her own, Will could never forget. He could never forget the gray of Sissie's face some mornings and the smell of boys on her breath. All in the past, all water under the bridge, only there was a point at which the water under the bridge topped the bridge, at which one swam in tears and spilt milk.

Swimmer to the end, Will hated Jericho. The town so nice for others wasn't a good town for them. If one daughter was gone, the high school boys remained, the old batch, who made a varsity sport of Sissie, and the new batch, coming of age with Dixie. Will had hates, but the high school boys were his rage. Mammoth brats, baby Gullivers, were always stepping on Will, grossly as with Sissie, unintentionally just by living and breathing, mischievously as on hell night when they paid Halloween visits to other homes too but got the most fun out of celebrating with Mr. C. Then Will would experience a hell night beyond their hopes, thinking that these same kid numbskulls who emptied his gas tank and threw eggs at his house and dumped garbage on his porch and ignited dog crap on his doormat so they could watch him stamp it out, that these same numbskull kids got a man's thrill out of Sissie. Will never forgave. Yearbooks changed, classes graduated, but not for Will; old batch or new batch they were all brothers in blood to the ones who raped his Sissie. He pictured their deaths by smash-ups, mangling farm machines, football crunches, rampant disease. He wished he had a gun and could shoot and kill or knew a tall stranger who would. He wished he was the stranger. He wished he had a nickel for every time he wished. He hated their cars, their music, their pricks and their lives. Send them to war. That was his supreme prescription. Send them to war. Coming home dead would be the best medicine they ever had.

As well as he knew them, the sex note about Dixie was a jolt to Will—he thought because Dixie was so admired and so precious they would have to leave her alone. "Dixie gets her physical education real soon." When he opened the envelope and unfolded the smudged paper and read that, Will was petrified.

Dixie like Sissie? Even the father of Sissie cried objection—girls
like Dixie were too fine, too modest, too smart to let that happen.
But the high school boys were the soul of Jericho to Will, which
was perhaps why he hated them so much. They were the heart-
lessness of their mothers and fathers, the heavy boot and big
block jaw that he saw when he looked up, a giant with a giant
appetite for the Will Carpenters. This giant, a little town, was
eating up him and Molly, it had gobbled up Sissie, and now it
was starting on the sweetest meat of all, his Dixie.

So rose Will's cry for a third cop for Jericho and a curfew for
the young. And Will kept on crying for it long after his talk with
George Robinson and after the vote of George Robinson's council, Will vowing that he would never speak to that snob, that
fake, that bastard Robinson ever again. Because he knew the high
school boys so well, Will was smart enough not to write letters
to the *Pioneer*, just as he shrank from going before the council
personally and hoisting Dixie's name over Jericho. He lacked a
reason or the words or the heart to ask Dixie herself about the
note, but he talked to Molly about it endlessly, simply because
he couldn't be silent, knowing that little he ever said ever added
a tear or took one away from that sad, sitting form. He talked to
the handful of friends they had, to the female clerk in the drugstore, and to Doc Sunderquist who was a kind of friend, but he
was so shrill about the high school boys and a nonsensical one-
line letter that they all concluded he was ranting. There was a
little bottle of venom in Will's head that he shook furiously and
took with meals, between meals and when he opened his eyes
in the morning, and that he wanted the whole town to take in
order to be cured of their young. He wanted a cop and a curfew
to help save Dixie; that was uppermost, that was for the present.
But for the past and all time to come, he wanted to see the high
school boys kept in, kept down, buckled, strapped and broken.

He swore that nothing would happen to Dixie. Dixie was the
hope of the family. She was precious. She had ability—he went
to track meets, he had seen her run and jump. She was an athlete
who had her heart set on winning medals, not on common
things. When she wasn't competing she was practicing, when
she wasn't doing either she wasn't happy. She wasn't only different from Sissie, she was different from all the other girls in

Jericho. And she had just one more year to go in high school and then she'd go away to college. Just one year more and Dixie would be safe.

Early one midsummer morning, when Will came out of his house to leave for work and started toward his car, there overhead, tied to the aerial on a string, shining in the sun and swaying in the breeze, was a long balloon with DIXIE painted across it— ON DIXIE!—like a cheer at a track meet, speculated Will, coming nearer, looking up and blinking, blinking all the way to his heart, because the pale balloon was a condom blown up into a balloon, and the word on the other side of DIXIE wasn't ON, it was SOON.

SOON DIXIE
DIXIE SOON

Just a patch of blue sky away, her shade pulled down, his little athlete slept so as to be fresh for Olympic practice, slept and dreamt so as to be all fresh and rosy when the boys herded in to feast on the little sister of Sissie. Fathers shouldn't see their daughters this way, begged Will. Fathers shouldn't have to have these pictures of their daughters!

Will grabbed the string. Frantically he hauled the condom in, battling its height, arm over arm, and then when he had it, wringing the skin of their skin in his hands, goring their pricks with his nails.

THERE WAS even a breeze from outside to flutter hearts and the little flag on its pedestal as the President led the club members, their friends and their guest through the pledge of allegiance and the Treasurer read an appropriate passage from *Isaiah*, glanced meaningfully at the audience and closed the sacred text. People and Politics was the topic for the day at a rare summer gathering of the Jericho Tuesday Club.

The President replaced the Treasurer at the small table that held the flag, her gavel and her purse, and with modesty introduced their guest. It was not often that the Tuesday Club heard a speaker from outside, self-improvement and self-expression being hallmarks of the club, even if the guest who sat facing them, whose fine hair stirred in the same breeze that stirred the flag, was no stranger to them but none other than the husband of their President, Jericho's own mayor and State House candidate, George Robinson.

The speaker rose, the President again demonstrating her restraint by quickly seating herself in the audience as the others applauded. The speaker thanked her for her words and thanked all present for their welcome and for giving him their time. The speaker said that as he looked around him he could think of no audience so perfectly qualified to hear a maiden address—no, not even that other club that naturally sprang to mind, the Jericho Lions Club, and the speaker coughed lightly, and sadly shook his head, and smiled, and his audience smiled back.

The speaker glanced at the President seated before him, then thoughtfully at his little sheaf of notes, and starting with the words, "My friends, this is no ordinary election because there is no longer a place for the ordinary in our legislature," delivered the first formal adddress of his campaign, that speech slaved over in backyard and back office, polished on nightly dog-walks and to a sheen before his bedroom mirror, and delivered now into the soft bosoms and safe laps of the Jericho Tuesday Club. Sensitive to his solitariness in the political world, kicked in the pants by party and governor, the speaker made everything of his youth, fresh face and independence as a candidate. Longstanding local concerns were set forth, and counties-wide mismanagement, and statewide disappointment. Dwayne Armstead was skewered, not as picturesquely as he might be before the Lions Club, or as harshly as he would be later on, but sufficiently to surprise the little audience. The issues were addressed, the state agency reform issue, the nagging sales tax issue, the water-for-the-west issue—"that goldarn dam issue"—and issues of tomorrow or sooner that were waiting down the pike. Finally, the people were borne in, "you and I," because "politics is people, my friends, politics is people whether the politicians like it or not. Unless"—and he seemed uncertain, vulnerable suddenly—"Politics *are* people. Because to tell you the truth, though I know all of you ladies so very well, I have had the strange feeling all this while of speaking in front of my schoolteachers. Thank you very much."

They rose to their feet and applauded him. He smiled and asked if there were questions and there were none so they applauded him again. They faced and applauded the President when she stepped forward and tried to conclude the meeting.

Refreshments were served, coffee and cake, the hostess of the house and her co-hostesses serving on a white tablecloth laid with birch leaves, white china and silver spoons and cake forks. Robinson, rather looking like a tall fork himself, stood beaming in a wedge of Tuesday Club ladies and smiled across the room at Rainey a smile of helplessness.

"I thought he was terrific," Margaret Hanson told her. "And if you think I'm fibbing, I've got the goosebumps to prove it."

"You and I are prejudiced," Rainey said, ice water in her heart, but putting some sunniness into her face when her friends came by to sing the praises of George. She felt they had been used, her own Tuesday club, and she felt ashamed for them, and of them, and a little disappointed in her moonstruck Jericho sisters. He had gone behind her back and asked them for this, and what could be better proof of the kind of treachery she could expect from George's politics?

Since she had already brought him cake and kissed his cheek, she now only waited for him to go, and at last he did, like the family cherub leaving home, waving and smiling at the door, waving goodbye again as he came past the big picture window.

"He's a winner," said Margaret Hanson, she of the shiny eye and the goosebumps. "I like his words. 'My friends, my friends, this is no ordinary election.' Friend I may be, Lorraine, but it wouldn't surprise me if you whipped Dwayne Armstead."

Alone among the many it seemed, and not a soul could be trusted to know that she wanted Dwayne Armstead to win. Rainey felt tired; a headache was knocking at the door. With Margaret her follower at her side, and pretty and tanned in a navy blouse and white suit, a rather gloryish red rose in the lapel, she drifted over to the refreshment table, took up coffee and cake and walked from her hostess's living room to the pleasant emptier kitchen, where outside bloomed depth-of-summer flowers, balmy air and the season's first tomatoes. Unless, she thought, conjuring up the mayonnaise eyes of the Tuesday Club, George Robinson was the season's first tomato.

"Stop dreaming and answer my question," pushed Margaret pushing her elbow. "Why don't you think George can win?"

"Maybe I was wrong." The President smiled and passed her hand across her forehead and through her hair, the hand pressing in against the aching temple and reemerging in the light to fluff up her sunbleached, honeycolored hair. The President picked up her fork and lopsidedly smiled at her old best friend.

"What luck. Now I won't have to bake for his birthday."

HIS EXPERIENCE at the Tuesday Club affair marked the birth of Robinson the challenger, or was anyhow the latest of his several leaps into political life. Whether it was Rainey's incubation he sought on that winter afternoon months ago, or Miss Brown delivering him from innocence in the capital, or the good wives of the Tuesday Club holding out their arms in adoration, it was no surprise to Robinson that women should be present at each birth. He acknowledged no political fathers; the governor and his crowd were as inimical to him as Armstead, who was a relic and ripe to fall. He was new, Armstead was old, he was quick, Armstead was slow, he was smart and Armstead was Dwayne. Robinson embraced the terms that set him out in the cold: he was his own ticket; his sole asset was himself.

He took to the road in his big black Olds, letting prairie dust accumulate on its handsome face just as he himself rolled in the dusty interests of the district, stopping at a filling station here, a farmhouse there, and cafés of towns littler than Jericho. There was the first afternoon coffee party, given by the wife of a member of the braintrust, and the first of his "Evenings with the candidate" at the house of a client farmer in Grafton, where the candidate, uncomfortable in a roomful of heavy-sitting farmers in Armstead's hometown, dropped his pretense of brotherliness, spoke feelingly of his differences but his willingness to learn and in the end drew a nice burst of applause.

As doubt dwindled and self-assurance grew, he wondered what Miss Brown would think of him, she as a political intelligence, as a smart woman, and as a pretty girl. He saw now that his humiliation by the powers in the capital had bruised not some peachskin conceit but his hard pit as a man. But now he was pitted against Armstead, a man the capital was afraid to attack, a fact Robinson never forgot. Never as in his politicking had he been so conscious of his maleness, the sound of the voice, the choice of the words, the entrance, the exit, the look, the hand-shake, the hand wave, the hand.

He challenged Armstead to debate, in Grafton or in Jericho, anywhere and anytime, knowing that the strategical response of the incumbent would be no response at all. "Mr. Armstead seems unable to believe that an election can be held in his district," he declaimed to the telephoning *Herald* reporter. "With the help of the voters of this district I am about to change his mind." Before a group in Malden, having completed his formal remarks, he introduced an empty chair as "my opponent, Dwayne Armstead" and proceeded to ask questions of the chair, saying to his audi-ence at the end: "I hope you were listening closely, my friends, because that was as good an answer to our questions as we are likely to get from Mr. Armstead."

He made the empty chair a feature of his campaign. The brain-trust loved it; individuals he met for the first time spoke of it. To Robinson it was little more than a tactical exercise, like firing shots at a sitting target, but the hanging questions and the chair's heavy silence seemed to characterize Dwayne Armstead. Noth-ing discouraged the challenger, not the fact that his audiences were small, or that to an unusual degree they were the old and the odd, or that despite the capital he made of it he was still running against an empty chair. He knew that all would trans-form itself by fall, and some of the oddity he deeply cherished like donations of moral gold. In one town, a man with a stump for a hand came up to him and said: "I voted for Dwayne for years, how do you think I wore out my hand?" A worn little stump of a smile—the sense of humor of a human being. "But today," the man growled, extending his good hand, "I'm with you." Robinson felt touched. There was something quintessen-tial, something that was wholly trusting about a one-handed man's handshake. He drove home that night solitary and happy, never so conscious of the earthy reality of State Assembly District Five, stretching away in the darkness on every side of him.

They were gaudy days for the challenger, on the go, his politician's blood pumping, his gifts as natural and his tricks as nimble as Tom Sawyer catching the eye of Becky Thatcher. Tom was walking the political picket fence. Tom was doing it, but Becky Thatcher wasn't watching.

Rainey bewildered him. Strangers opened their homes for him, gave their time, made parties, but she didn't even make promises. Sadly he knew that she was cold to politics, but more was at stake than his feelings. Women voters wanted to meet the wife. If that was too much, they wanted to see the wife. If only they could, they would want to feel the wife.

He shamed her into appearing on a platform with him, her husband, her mainstay, the candidate of her friends; but he paid the price for it in that same currency of shame. She said he was a hypocrite. She said: "Do you really care whether they build that dam or not? You know you don't. How do you think I feel sitting up there and hearing my husband tell lies? Don't you think it hurts me a little?" she asked him, her mortification enlarging her eyes.

He looked into himself and she was right. Yet wrong. He didn't feel like a hypocrite; he didn't disbelieve what he said, what words he spoke. It was the decibel that was a little off. He disbelieved the sheer volume, the loudness, the intensity—he did disbelieve that, he granted her—but what could you do about it when you were standing in a hall making a speech and trying to win an election?

They argued over money, for the first time in their married lives. It wounded him, considering the amount of money she had at her disposal, that she resented every dime he spent on his campaign. He didn't manufacture these expenses. There were the letterheads and hall rentals and the socials to be paid for; soon to come were the front yard stakes, the portrait posters, the ads, the leaflets and other socials and he hadn't even discussed with her yet his all-day event in the fall. "Money means votes," was his reasonable plea—"Money has been called the mother's milk of politics."

"Not by me. Not by this mother."

The debater of the empty chair threw up his hands. "Is a mere figure of speech really the issue?" And he stomped out of the room, or escaped, fearing the return of the father issue and another of her harangues about Jamie.

He tried to paint for her a human picture of politics. He described his farmhouse visits and the one-handed man's handshake, but she warped that simple story by forcing him to acknowledge that he normally shrank from the crippled and saying that he only tolerated people when he could use them. "I use people when I ask them to vote for me?" he asked in wonderment. "This is politics. You might as well say a fish uses the water he swims in." She agreed with him. "Yes, you might as well."

He grew weary of trying to share his excitement with her. It struck him that despite his sense of his brilliance she was cooler to him sexually rather than warmer, less indulgent rather than more, which confounded his notions of women and men, if not of elemental punishment and reward. He felt not so much angry at her as he felt perplexed, disappointed and cheated. There was the father issue, the hypocrite issue, the money issue and the sex issue. He finally asked her outright:

"Don't you want me to win?"

"It's all in your mind, George, you're the one who cares about winning and losing. Win or lose, you're my husband."

Then Will Carpenter offered to fill his treasury, Will the Pill of all people offered him a bribe; frantic Will Carpenter came into his private office the way a carpenter ant comes into a room, anticipating being stepped on, going in three directions at once. Will took a condom out of his pocket and flung it on the desk, forcing Robinson to say, "I hope it's a fresh one," forcing Will to say, "The man's making jokes!" forcing Robinson to say, "No I'm not, I eat lunch here."

"You know why I'm here," Will cried, "I wouldn't be here for any other reason. I want a curfew and a cop."

"You know the council turned those down. I'm shocked to see this, and I understand your concern, but I can't go back and try to alter a unanimous vote by the council."

"You think I'm nobody. You think I'm completely insignifi-

cant," said Will, and Robinson saw that Will was deaf to everything and would speak the piece he had come prepared to speak.

"But I don't care what you think, I happen to think you're the
scum of the earth, I think you belong in that bag."

"You don't have to say all this," sighed Robinson closing his
eyes.

"You're a politician. You want to be one—you are one. If you
help me, I am ready to contribute five hundred dollars to your
political campaign. I said five hundred, and don't think you'll
see it all at once."

Robinson opened an eye, astounded, first by the offer of a bribe,
then by the folly of the amount. It could never buy what he
wanted but five hundred dollars was a lot of money for Will.

"Thanks, if thanks are in order. I don't know who you think I
am, but you've made a bad mistake about me."

"Five hundred cash dollars," said Will.

"Go home. Save your fortune for your family."

"Isn't five hundred enough for you?" sneered and sniveled Will
Carpenter, and Robinson, beginning to appreciate what it must
be like to be Will all day long, said not unkindly: "Go home,
Will."

"You want her raped. Then you'll do something. Maybe!"

"I will not accept insults, I will not pursue this matter, and I
will not have this discussion again."

"And this?" cried Will, snatching up the condom.

"That you can take with you."

"Robinson," shouted Will from the doorway, raising his fist in
the air: "Hear me. There can be other crimes than rape in this
town!"

The fouling of his office by the monkey and his business pro-
pelled Robinson to take a long walk. On the outskirts of Jericho,
ducking the sun, he sat down amid the trunks of giant pines, and
not blind to their perspective mused on Will Carpenter's attempted bribe and pathetic threat, if it was a threat. Will was
not sane. He was a man being driven crazy by kids, other kids
and his own kids, whom he still pictured as little girls, a delusion
that suited Will. What kind of man built his life around his kids?
In the first place, kids were boring, in the second and third place
too. They were more a subject for science: kids were a phase.

They were full of missing things, like missing teeth, missing words and missing the point. Kids were the opposite of glory. They kicked your shins with their little clay feet and pulled you down by the hand. Oh you could love a kid; but they were the enemy of romance. Kids cut off your dreams at the knees.

There was another little twist to the Will Carpenter business, though, as Robinson discovered when he got back to his office and returned a phone call from the police chief.

"Why didn't you tell me about Will Carpenter's rape letter?" Hank asked him.

"He's been there?"

"This time he has. He says you double-crossed him, which I don't believe, but I don't know why he went to you in the first place."

"That letter was a kid's joke, Hank, not a threat of rape. I honestly didn't feel it was worth bothering you about."

"I'm thinking about our rifle."

"The stolen gun? You think there's a connection?"

Hank put the matter this way, and then put it the other way, and ended by saying that while he would investigate as if there might be a connection, there very likely wasn't. But a wheel turning was a wheel turning, and Robinson was slightly shaken. "You didn't have to scare me," he muttered to the hung-up phone. There was no connection with the rifle because there was no rape letter, and the only crime that threatened Dixie Carpenter was having her father for a father.

Will's was a sorry house. There was an aura of cunt over Will's house; there was a definite female glow. Will went around pulling down the shades and locking the doors and windows, but being what it was it seeped out anyway, between its sister cracks. Whatever the cause was, Molly's sickness, Sissie's reputation, his own ineffectiveness, the boys in town kept on seeing that starry-bright cunt over Will's.

CHAPTER 19

JOHN'S CASHBOX in John's Saloon. It sat in a bolt of sunlight on the bar, glinting at West, strong and cheap, cheap and strong, like Joe taking the sun. West sat perched on a bar stool by the window, back of him the bar, barroom, tables and pool table stalled in their tunnel of Monday morning darkness.

John's cashbox was open. Take some or not? Dip in or not? John dragging empty boxes out the back door would never know. West dipped in and felt the bundle, the dampish bundle offending him the same way the barroom did, with that inimitable feel of stag Saturday nights. Money was unique stuff. A number he posted in the ledger wasn't at all the same as the bankroll, the bundle, the wad. Even when he had his own bundle, his army discharge pay, he spent it almost just to spend it—lightening himself of it gave him a bowelly satisfaction like a crap.

Dip in, take some. He could easily cover his tracks. He could use the money to cover his expenses. Steal the gun, steal the money for the shots. He played with temptation but temptation never had a chance. Stealing the rifle was different, it was part of the point. But stealing money was cheap. It was ordinary. It stank, like the air in John's Saloon. A man with a motive might steal money, John's bartender would steal money and probably he had, but not a man with reasons.

He dumped the money out on the bar, counted it, posted the

amount in the ledger and was starting on the bills, his real morning's work, when in the left-hand corner of the window Robinson came walking down Legion Avenue, crossed the street, passed by and out of the picture on his way to his law office. West bent to his work, drumming on the bar, humming to himself, writing checks and killing time, curling his tongue around a mint. John read and signed the checks. West slipped them into envelopes, licked the flaps, licked the stamps, eyed the street, graced the street, biked to the post office, mailed the checks and was free for coffee at Rainey Robinson's.

"Come back anytime," said she. She never stopped to think about the middle of the night. It was an open invitation in the sense of being closed. The evening, the weekend, the friend's car parked out front, the neighbors' eyes, they all warned him off. He went cautiously: not only the sunny streets were paved with sticky tar. He went unnoticed and humming, like the high-tension wires above his head strung from pole to pole.

It was easy to visit because she liked him—maybe. Did she? Did she like him? Really dumb question except that if she liked him she couldn't be that Rainey Spencer of old, of snub, of snot. Something funny must have happened to her in the meantime if Rainey Robinson liked him. Two kids had happened in the meantime, and West knew what that meant: maybe she thought she was getting old; maybe she thought she was losing her glow. The glow needed dusting off and shining up like the lamps from time to time. Maybe, but West doubted it, having seen her with the son home the last time. "How's the swimming?" he asked the son who came through in a wet bathing suit and the son looked down and shivered "Cold," whereupon his mother laughed and hugged him and glowed. The son made West feel invisible, though West opened up his mouth and laughed also, without it being audible, of course. She smiled and asked the visitor please to stay. Dixie Carpenter's kid brother, the son's best friend, was there and they all sat down and had pie, except for West who had pie and an extra helping of another dimension. He left in a fog when Dixie's brother did. When he climbed on his bike, he felt he had been smuggled into the house in a crowd of bicycles. The mood carried into evening, West sitting in his rocker and thinking about his mother and Rainey Robinson, the one then the other, as if they were the earth's two hemispheres.

The house came into view again, neat and white, dangerous and not, only the little girl out front on the walk, she and the dog, unless she was the dog, a watchdog, disguised. With her mother's face pinned to her from ear to ear he couldn't say just what she was; since she was always around, she might be a picket fence. West crossed the lawn, mounted the steps and pushed the bell, looking everywhere around him but at the front walk as he hummed. "Want to see me skip?" asked the voice from the walk. "Sure," he answered, so she danced down the street as her mother opened the door and West ducked inside as quickly as he could while she skipped and sailed away. He felt a little ashamed of himself fooling a little kid, who stood in the kitchen doorway, breathing fast from dashing home a couple of minutes later, yet he relished it, he enjoyed the mixed-up breathlessness of the girl with the mother's face.

So, there was the mother, the daughter, the dog and somebody who was always missing. Who could that be who always seemed to be missing? Rainey Robinson put a fresh pot of coffee on to brew and washed and dried the breakfast dishes and put a giant coffee cup that drew West's eye back into the cupboard. He screwed down a jouncing nerve and waited for her to talk about him, spring his name, brag about him being the mayor, the law-yer, the future senator, governor and president, but she never did, to West's surprise. Instead she gossiped about people in the town. He learned that this one's business was failing, and that one's health, and that one's marriage after a dozen bumpy years. So-and-so was drinking as much as his brother ever had. So-and-so's children must have paved the way for his untimely heart attack. She poured the steaming coffee into mugs at the counter and carried them to the table and sat down with him. Will Car-penter's name came up: Will's Dixie was in trouble, well not in *trouble* trouble, not a jewel like Dixie, but did he remember the boy trouble of the older sister Sissie? Molly's misfortune started then, though it was all Will's fault as everyone knew, or didn't he know the truth about Molly Carpenter?

As gossip it was mild stuff, even Sissie's exploits scrubbed up for the ears of the little kid who sat with them. But West was in a land where nothing was ordinary to him. Her gossip was like music incidental to a dance. To the accompaniment of other people's secrets floated and fell the veils of the secret of being Rainey Robinson, daughter of the town. It was a living secret, made of flesh and blood. No words told it, her intimacy said it; to him she was the town. She confided to him things not commonly known. She pinked his cheeks and burned his bookkeeper's ears, though not with the fires of gossip. She made him feel welcome in the world. She made friendship possible, and damped the fires not one bit by breathing: "Don't breathe a word of all this."

She invited him to have iced tea in the backyard. This was an afternoon a week later, the day he spotted the little kid going somewhere in a carload of kids downtown and sped to the house.

It was that day. She was finishing the laundry down in the basement. "Go on out in the yard," she said, "I'll just be a few minutes. Go on."

He paused in the back entry where she had turned and gone down the steps, paused before her sunhat and garden shears hung up on the wall over a pair of crusty shoes. Sunhat, shears and shoes configured a ghost of a woman, ghost of attention, ghost of care, ghost of all he ever wanted.

That was why it was such a ghost. He flipped open the screen door and stepped out into the yard where he had seen Robinson that day sitting in his shorts in a lawn chair. Lawn, trees, flowers and chairs seemed asleep in that other frame of time. West looked out beyond the yard and neighboring houses to the spot where he had stood looking in and his eyes opened to the flowering strangeness of being here. He was all alone with his design to kill Robinson. He had never been here alone with it before—she was always with him. Robinson's chair looked at him with gravity: it was a serious business if it was serious. So when he finally caught sight of her through the kitchen window when she was finished downstairs why shouldn't he start to breathe easier as though she was his friend on the premises? He missed her. That was what it amounted to. He was almost ready to hug her by the time she opened the screen door and came out carrying a tray with a pitcher of iced tea and two tall glasses.

Flies buzzed, the sun glittered down, wisps of cottonseed blew. Mourning doves sang crisscrossed songs from the unnoticed high-tension wires.

"Mr. Whitehead was nice," mused Rainey Robinson, sitting on the freshly mown grass with her legs tucked under her, sitting in the shade in her own backyard and remembering way back when. "Mr. Whitehead was nice, but there was also something peculiar about him. But that may have been the algebra," she said to West with a smile.

West sat crosslegged, looking down, poking a twig at the ground. "He still there, Whitehead?"

"Oh yes. Same room. Same man. Same blue suit. I think he was born in that suit."

And West stopped his poking and gave a smile: "Mr. Whitehead born?"

She smiled back at him, smiling back through time in appreciation of that, in appreciation of him who said it. "Why did you leave Jericho so soon after high school?" she asked him a moment later, taking up her glass, looking at West, sipping her tea.

Because the doc graduated my mother, was the A-plus answer to that, but since he didn't think he could say it and stay for tea, he made up a story that he had gone away to join the army and see something of the world. "Did you like being in the army?" she asked him. "What did you do in the army?"

"What did you do in Chicago?"

"Did you like Chicago?"

"Did you like bookkeeping school?"

"Why did you decide to come back?"

"Were you lonesome?"

West sat back and played a part. He played the part of an innocent kid, all alone in the world, poor, poor but smart, an unusual kid, an unusual man, full of unusual ideas, who was living in Jericho biding his time and planning the future of his life. He didn't mind her asking the questions; they fell in his lap, it happened to be a part in which he shone. The queerness, the physical queerness, the queasiness, was her having the questions, her thinking them, Rainey Robinson mixing Alaman West in with the cells of her mind.

Did he have any family, she wanted to know.

West shook his head.

Friends, did he have friends here?

"No. No friends. You."

If she didn't open her arms and take him in, this living bundle on her doorstep, she didn't close the door in his face either. She spoke to him about her own sad experiences in life, spoke, reflected, smiled and touched blades of grass as though they were the unhappiness she was talking about. She herself had an older sister, maybe he remembered her, married and living in the East, she said, a couple of thousand miles away. "But we're really not as close as that," she said with another sad smile. "And of course my parents died when I was young. So I think I know what it means to feel alone in the world."

She said, "I do remember your mother and when she died," so unexpectedly that the impact of woman and woman made West flinch. "She was a kind person. I'm sure many people still miss her," said Rainey Robinson, and West almost believed her, those condolence words off a condolence card. "Yours too. Yours too," he mumbled, formal as death.

"Were you with her when it happened?" she asked him.

"Yeah. I called the doc."

"Mine were in a car crash. I was in school. I was sixteen years old," she said.

"I was eighteen," said West.

Little clouds of gnats, little bodies like a soul, floated from shade to light. West sat embracing his knees, profoundly still, and listened as Rainey Robinson remembered her parents' fatal accident, their crash, her news, two parents dead, in school in the principal's office. Then West, her grave attention his, told his mother's painful story, though being ever so soft on Doc Death. Small details were remembered. They grimaced for each other, sighed and shook their heads. Sorrow egged on sorrow, smile supported pale smile, the wondrous wheels of intimacy oiling themselves as they turned.

"Were you very scared?" she asked him.

"Not much. Sure I was."

"Were you angry?"

He slammed his fist into his hand.

"Didn't talk," she said. "Didn't eat. Didn't go out of the house.

I was ashamed to. I thought the sun would look down and say, there goes the girl whose parents are dead. I also—" her eyes brushed West's, "I also didn't bathe for a long time. I don't know why, I just let it go. So I started to smell. I could smell myself. The odor made me weepy. I smelled to high heaven. I was rank."

A tear rolled down her cheek; fresh ones welled in her eyes, tears of recollection, tears of frustration, tears aplenty, he fathomed about the past. "I always cry so wet," she groaned, her face a pretty mess of smiling, crying and wiping away of tears. She was human like him—he had never guessed half the truth about her. That frightened girl was her; that ashamed, weeping girl he never pictured, was her also. But he didn't believe for a second that she could ever smell that bad, not her. That was the reason she could say it: he wasn't fooled. He wasn't far from heaven either. He absolutely forgot that she was married, that she had children, that this was her family's house and yard. For a minute she was all alone in the world, like him. As though nothing had been settled, as though all still hung in the balance, "What happened then?" he asked.

"Then? Then I woke up one day and I had to go back to school. So I took a long hot bath." She picked up her glass, shook the bits of ice around, and laughed. "Bathing confessions of a Jericho housewife. I'm sure you really find this interesting. You better say no."

"I think you're wonderful," West said.

"What was that?" she said laughing and cupping her hand to her ear, "What did you say? Tell me again. I'm a little hard of hearing."

He couldn't just sip the tea, he drank in gulps like a thirsty man, as if he could rethink, refill and drink in everything, the words, the peace, the sun, the shade. Neither could he leave the place, not until his hostess stood up with the tray of tea things and started slowly back to the house. As she opened the screen door she glanced up at the sky: "What a beautiful afternoon—thank you for coming by. To think there are people who are blind to the happiness they could have here."

West followed, passing by and rapping his knuckles against the chair that stood for Robinson.

*   *   *

HUMAN LIKE him. She had a few things of her own up her sleeve (that little cup of shadow up her sleeve), the warm flesh part of the beautiful ghost in the entry. She invited him into her back-yard where she flirted with him; she made up a story about know-ing his mother, which was a lie. She probably fought with her own sister. Bang, hit by death, she hid away scared from the world. He must have been looking at it the wrong way around. She wasn't so different she wasn't burnt by things that happened to her. It was just that they didn't stick with her, they didn't last, not the way they did with him. Burnt, so she cast off the old skin; hurt, so she healed—she took a bath and death washed off. West laughed. He was back where he started. She wasn't the least like him.

Suppose he loved her, would he kill Robinson to have Rainey Robinson?

World's best motive. But he had reasons, he never started with a motive. Killing for love was the same as killing for gain.

But suppose he loved her, and for his reasons got Robinson out of the way, *at the same time knowing it was the only way to have her*—how would it be if he took up with her after the deed was done?

West sat down with pencil and paper and fooled with the prob-lem of love and his reasons, and at first they seemed like two separate lines that never touched, like two different things that ran their course, but then all of a sudden they seemed to cross, lock and be inseparable. It was nowhere on the paper in front of him; it was something he felt far back in his mind, like a chord struck, like a grunt, love and the reasons coming together. He sat a long while, pencil to his lips, sometimes letting the lines be, coming back always to the woman under the tree with him, their circle of shade, the smell of paradise that was the backyard grass just cut.

Joe came in the evening and cooked supper. West ate nothing; Joe asked him, "You feeling sick?" and when West left the table and went and sat in his rocker Joe ate conspicuously from both plates, grumbling, "What did I make us such a good supper for?" Joe cleared the table, clattering the dishes into the sink for West to wash, clattering them some more when he did them himself later in the evening because West never answered, spoke or stirred from his chair. "Beans tomorrow," Joe said darkly, and left him, almost banging the door.

West took a bath. The bathtub with its curved sides and delicate feet was the body of Rainey Robinson. He lapped in it, he played in it—his hands were hers. From the arch of his head thrown back he watched the spearhead of the ejaculation.

"I love her," he wrote on her page in Accounts Receivable, knowing he did, basking in it, not worrying too much about the separate lines crossing because he could never piece it out and it might come to the same thing anyway. Good old Mr. Whitehead helped him out: it could be like those parallel lines in math, that looked as though they could never meet. They met, but only in infinity.

CHAPTER 20

"WE DO it before the election," West told Joe.

Joe froze in the doorway with his bundle of Red Owl groceries, but then he came in and shut the door fast. "Why before?"

"Suppose he loses, Joe. Do we assassinate the loser?"

Joe carried the bundle over to the counter past West's grinning face, bitterly swept West's dirty lunch plate out of the way and put the bundle down. But West was brimming over tonight and not only with scary jokes. He had the new *Pioneer* on the kitchen table, the one with George Robinson's picture on the front page. Joe had seen and skipped that article; he read the *Pioneer* every week in the store but never anything in it breathing Robinson's name. He didn't think about the killing, he didn't think about Robinson, he didn't know about any election. So far as Joe was concerned, "Why before?" meant why after, why ever?

"Listen to this, Joe. 'State Assembly candidate George Robinson has unveiled plans to hold a major campaign event in Jericho on Saturday, October 5th, one month prior to election day. Hundreds of visitors from the district are expected to flock to Jericho for the unusual event, which will begin with a parade down Legion Avenue in the morning and continue throughout the day. Special attractions in the city hall park,' " scanned West for Joe's motionless back, "Speech of welcome by Robinson from the city hall steps . . . fireworks and firecrackers . . . free turkey barbecue . . . the Jericho High School band . . . 'Mayor Robinson's first venture into state politics has drawn enthusiastic support from the entire Jericho community, which has pledged to make October 5th a day to remember. Mr. Robinson, who is seeking the Assembly seat long occupied by Mr. Dwayne Armstead, told the *Pioneer*: "I invite and urge everyone who is interested in better government and his family's welfare to join with us in Jericho on Saturday, October 5th." ' "

West stopped reading. Joe started unloading groceries. "I think I'll skip it. I never go to things like that. Too much noise." Joe held his breath. "You thinking of going?"

"You know I'm going, Joe. You are too. That's the day we do it."

Joe put his hand in the bag and took out more groceries. Act normal, he told himself. Not that he was scared worse than in the beginning, and not that he believed any more seriously that it was really going to happen. But be normal, Joe, because West has just named the day.

"Why pick on that day with so many people around? What do you want such a crowd for?" Joe asked in a normal and reasonable way.

"The more crowded the better."

"It's safer?"

"No, it's just better. It goes with my reasons. It fits the assassination. The election—the crowd—it's ideal. I shoot then, I assassinate Robinson."

"For what? Is he the president?" cried Joe, who could be normal no more, so pent up, so fed up, that he flew at West, his spit on his bottom lip boiling.

"You never said anything about assassinate. You didn't tell me about elections. You said you had a grudge against him—that's what you told me, a grudge," Joe yelled as though he had slippery West backed into a corner.

"Yes I did, Joe, you're right . . . I have that too."

Joe opened his mouth to speak, but shut it tight; his eyes followed West as West folded up the *Pioneer*, put it under his arm and disappeared into the bedroom. "You got that too. You got things all over the place," Joe muttered, staring after him. "The hell with you."

Joe heard a lot about assassination in the next couple of days. Assassinate was the new killing word. Maybe to understand it better he should ask West sometime why the doc assassinated his mother. Because Joe didn't hide his feelings and stayed so quiet and looked so glum, West tried to explain. He said you didn't necessarily have to assassinate a president. He said it could be a governor or a senator. Or a state senator, or not even that, a state house member, and not even that either, only a candidate for it, a candidate like Robinson, running in his first election, since being mayor of a town like Jericho didn't count. There was something fair about cutting down a man like Robinson right at the beginning, West said. West smiled: "We'll nip him in the bud."

The *Pioneer* article had been torn from the page and he carried it around in his pocket, Joe saw, folded up inside a little notebook. Joe didn't notice these things on purpose and what he saw he tried to forget, like the rifle that was hidden in the bedroom. But West kept taking the notebook out of his pocket and the article out of the notebook, unfolding it on the table, smoothing it down with his hands, speaking to it with his eyes. "The speech from the city hall steps," West said finally. "That's the one time we know where he'll be. That's the time, that's the place. His speech—right at the start. We'll nip everything in the bud."

Joe started to feel panic. Maybe it was West's eyes, or something in West's voice, but what if this assassinate was worth risking his life to West—what if assassinate made the killing more possible than the grudge did? For the first time, Joe could picture the killing in his mind: he passed the city hall and those steps every day, they were right across the street from the Red Owl Store. "You forgetting something?" Joe asked wildly.

"Like what?"

"Like the police? They got their office in the city hall. The police!"

West only grinned. "Hank and Pete?"

"So you know their names. So you can say their names. They still got guns! They're still the police!"

"Yeah. Only they got one less gun than they used to. They lost a gun somewhere. That's why I'm so worried about Hank and Pete."

"They lost a gun?" Joe sat down at the kitchen table next to West and pressed his head between his hands. A new surprise. A big new headache. "That's their gun in there? You telling me that?"

West smiled and started folding up the article along the well-worn lines and when it was the small economy size he slipped it into the notebook and slipped the notebook into his pocket, all the while looking over and smiling broadly at Joe.

"So smart, so smart," Joe sneered to himself with curled, ugly lips when he sat alone on his bed in his tiny hotel room that night. West astonished him, frightened him, made him want to run and made him want to come back. Joe and West—they were partners, if only Joe forgot to remember what they were partners about. But even if he remembered, he didn't hate West for it. West was only being West, he was unusual, not like the people Joe tried to be friends with ordinarily. No. He was proud when he thought about West, not only not so lonesome.

But the gun scared Joe more than ever if it was stolen from the police. If it was stolen, one crime had already been committed and by not going to the police he was guilty too. And why would West lie about the gun? To brag? West wasn't like that. It needed all of Joe's optimism about the future to get him through his day at the store and then to pack some supper into a bag and take the long walk back to West's. No more surprises, he silently pleaded when he walked in, no more headaches please. But West was in a happy mood; better than that, he was in a nice mood, smacking his lips over the supper Joe made, making jokes and pitching in with the dishes, all of this lasting until he sat down at the table and took the little notebook out of his pocket and unfolded the torn-out article. Since Joe was so worried about the police, he had started worrying too, West said, because Joe was his partner and his partner could be right. Then West read a sentence from the article out loud: " 'Like the Fourth of July, firecrackers will be allowed the night before and all during the event, to add to the festive atmosphere.' That solves our problem. We use the sound of firecrackers to hide the sound of the shots. It gives us more time. It means they won't hear the shots and know where they're coming from."

"Where's that," Joe asked bleakly. "Where they coming from."

West unfolded another piece of paper, a drawing he had made of the location, with the city hall ("Those are the steps"), the city hall park ("There's the crowd"), the street ("More people sitting in parked cars"), and the buildings on the opposite side of the street. "One of these. That's where the shots will be coming from."

The four buildings were there, neatly marked in black with his bookkeeping pen; all were attached, several with apartments on an upper story: the barbershop, the Feed and Seed, an insurance office and the Red Owl Store. Joe digested it all, West's drawing, the four buildings, the firecrackers, and tried to put the new surprise into perspective. It didn't seem so bad. It only confirmed what Joe had spent the afternoon telling himself: now that he was used to the word, maybe assassination didn't make the killing more possible, maybe assassination *made it more impossible.*

"That's all for today?" he said to West. "Firecrackers?"

"That's all for today," said West.

That's all until I tell you you're picked to light the firecrackers, thought West, eyeing Joe through mild eyes. How do I know anybody will be lighting firecrackers when I'm shooting? If I miss I shoot again and suppose I keep on missing? I'm a pretty sight up there, I'm spotted, I'm dead. I'm doing it the way I should but I can't afford those chances. There's more coming, Joe.

But a few minutes later Joe walked back to the table with a foolish smile on his face. "Was that on a Saturday?" he asked, smiling because his question struck him funny, "Was that on a Saturday? I just remembered. I usually work on Saturday."

West looked up, mild and serene, absent and dreamy.

"You can get off work. It'll only take a few minutes."

"Oh, sure, sure . . . in that case," murmured Joe, nodding his head and moving noiselessly away.

Out in the open, from a height—just the way he always saw it. He saw the height as a window. He saw the window in his mind. He saw Robinson opening his mouth, when a blast out of nowhere—

October the fifth—first thing in the morning. Jericho City Hall steps.

CHAPTER 21

WHEN HE mailed the announcement of his October event to the *Jericho Pioneer*, the *Grafton Gazette* and the other little weeklies of the district, Robinson hoped to fill a late summer lull in his campaign. He saw the towns falling asleep all around him and such was his anxiety to wake them up, lest their sleep prove fatal to his dreams, that he leapfrogged his timetable and pushed the announcement up by several weeks. October, never mind November, seemed too far off. He itched for fall, clear fall, crisp fall, downfall, when he would walk over Dwayne Armstead's career as though it was a pile of dead leaves.

What if he won? What if George Robinson beat Dwayne Armstead, amazed the capital, stunned the governor, started heads turning, became the man to watch? What if he won?

He wouldn't win. He'd never win. His aloneness would break him. His fresh face would beat him before he ever got started on the road to the governorship. How did he ever imagine he could win? As soon as hope rose, doubt would slither into place, doubt of winning and his innate dread of losing. He had too much time on his hands, that was the trouble, too much time in which to think. With his political battle in the August doldrums, the struggle moved into the shade within himself.

"A turkey barbecue for all those people?" was the only comment she could make the day he carried home his announcement in the *Pioneer*—"A free turkey barbecue?"

"Don't be so negative," he grumbled. "My campaign contributions will cover most of it."

"Most of what? The wishbone?"

What a wonderful partner she could have been, with her sense of humor, her intelligence, her charm, her women friends. Instead she became the partner of his doubts. Not that he ever admitted doubts to her—on the contrary, he radiated self-assurance and declared himself happy to see her go her own way. Still, when she told him she had made a friend of the bookkeeper, he was more than casually suspicious. Why pick a nonentity like the bookkeeper for a friend? Was this another slap at his candidacy somehow? It wasn't hard to see the bookkeeper's side of it, she was the best-looking woman in town, but what was he? Lonely, she said—unfortunate. Her compassion unrolled like a nurse's bandage in Robinson's mind. If he was a little bit jealous, he was only jealous in the abstract, as of something that occupied her attention while he fidgeted, like a magazine she was reading or a sock she was darning. A sock she was darning was a very good description of the bookkeeper. A stray sock without a mate, an odd, a very odd sock.

"How's the bookkeeper?" he inquires at supper, merely to be annoying. "I haven't seen him keeping the books lately."

"That's unkind. He isn't just a bookkeeper."

"I beg your pardon. The cyclist."

So Jamie pipes up, "His name is Alaman."

"So?"

"He's not just a bookkeeper."

"What is this, a gang?" laughs Robinson, looking at their faces and laughing without much pleasure.

She was like a weight across his hopes, she who was once of the lightest of touches. He truthfully disliked her at times; she made him feel so selfish about his plans. It was evident to him that should he ask, "Would you be happy if I lost?" she would say "Yes," so he could never bring himself to touch that throbbing question. Restless all day, he carried his tension to the marriage bed: he rode her as though she were not so much a wife, a delight, as a feat, a test of will. He rode for the hell of it, with his grievance as his spurs. Seldom a tender lover, none too thoughtful, he sought softness all the way in—all the way up—not physical, but spirit softness. His question was: how did you know, with a wife, when she surrendered? It was her surrender he pressed for, unconditional surrender, to see her breasts' softness in her face perhaps—it was this Robinson wanted and couldn't win.

August pressed on. His widows came to play whist one evening, his widows being two septuagenarian ladies whose money and property he had managed since their farmer husbands died. Having them over for dinner and whist once a year was a neighborly touch by George and Rainey Robinson.

Dinner done with, the widows flush with the glamor of their attorney running for the State House, the foursome adjourned to the card table, nickels and dimes in little stacks in front of them, little snacks in a bowl, Rainey partners with Widow A and Robinson with Widow B. His talk of his campaign bobbed up again, kept surfacing like a card she tried to bury, talk of October's event, Armstead's strength, mounting costs, dwindling contributions. "Maybe we can help," said Widow B—"Is there something we can do?" asked Widow A—the evening fanning out into an interesting little hand, Robinson playing whist and playing widows, Rainey playing on in disbelief, too conscious of their fabled marriage to speak against him, but nudging him under the table with her foot when she wasn't nudging him furiously with her eyes.

"How could you? How could you? They came here as our guests. How could you ask them for money?"

"Very hard thing to do. Not easy. But you seemed so worried about the money for the turkey barbecue, I wanted to relieve your mind."

"I'm to blame? It's my fault? I'm the one who's charging those two old women for sixty turkeys? You're supposed to be their attorney—their financial adviser—their friend."

"So what are friends for? They can well afford it. I've earned a lot more than that for them."

"And from them! And from them! Do you know what their

families are going to say? You're lucky their husbands aren't alive. You are evil, George. You prey on widows. You did the same thing to Alpha Davis."

"I asked Alpha Davis for a campaign contribution?"

"Do you expect me to even answer that?"

"Rainey, that was months ago. That was about a stupid little library book. This is about the State House."

"The State House? Don't talk to me about the State House— I'm sick of hearing about the State House. We live in this house!"

RAINEY'S UNHAPPINESS was Rainey's greatest shame. As she told Alaman West, remembering her grief of long ago, when she was afraid the sun would look down and say there goes the girl whose parents are dead, so now she was afraid the sun would look and say, here comes the woman whose marriage is bad.

At odds with Robinson, distrustful of his State House pursuit and where it led, unhelpful, ashamed of it yet determined, she entertained her friends, presided over her club, cared for her children and kept her unhappiness to herself. His story in the *Pioneer*—Robinson to Host Major Event in October—chilled her like early frost, as she pictured his one face for the multitude and his different face for his little family at home. The only person in the world she might have confided in was Margaret Hanson, but a wifely loyalty, or was it vanity, silenced Rainey's tongue. How could she tell Margaret about his behavior as a husband when she couldn't find the voice to say that he was a hypocrite in politics and she hoped he lost the election. Even to Margaret Hanson, to worshipful Margaret especially, she couldn't admit, it couldn't all come out, that Rainey Robinson's marriage wasn't wonderful.

He hurts me in bed, not my feelings, not just my feelings, he hurts my flesh. Tell Margaret Hanson that? As well shout it out while he was up on a platform making a speech: Don't vote for this man, he hurts my insides, people!

Her pain, like their money, would have been uncomplainingly spent, had she only liked him more these days and prized what he was doing. But she couldn't change her nature, and she couldn't slip her feelings off with her clothes, so she also blamed herself for his resentment in bed. Quiet, curled up and distant as she made herself to be, that was how predictably he pounced, finding her hand, finding her mouth, finding her breast, not forgetting her breast, opening her up like a can. Her submission cleared her conscience. A breeze of pleasure almost blew submission away, but not for long, not with bullying, not beneath his strength. As usual, the wrong one moaned. It was her honeymoon all over again, her tolerance of him and her wonder at herself. This is me, I'm making love, was never distant from her thoughts. Here lies me became the headstone of her connubial life—making modesty a faith, darkness the rule, and afterward a treasure.

She loved him, of course. Her thoughts all revolved around him, so of course she loved him. Sex wasn't love, thank heaven. When she said to Alaman West, "To think there are people who are blind to the happiness they could have here," she meant Robinson. When she poured coffee for West, with a smile like cream, she had Robinson in her mind. Her mind was a bed of trouble. West grew there because of Robinson.

What was her attitude to West? How exactly did she feel about him? He didn't infuriate her; she didn't fight with West. He wasn't the unadoring father of her children. She didn't nag him, disappoint him or pray for his defeat behind his back. Her attitude to him was simple and natural, being just what it seemed to be. She was the hostess and he was the guest, the stranger, and if she was the good hostess, he was the perfect stranger in every sense of the word: quiet, nice-looking, lonely, and she thought, interesting. With home baking and concern for him plus the spice of a little gossip, she entertained him in the nicest, old-fashioned sense. When Alaman West sat down, they were her own little coffee parties, things of hospitality and sincerity, not excuses for money-grabbing and hand-grabbing and votes.

He was a troubled young man. He was very unfortunate—she wasn't exaggerating; he was downtrodden and unfortunate and poor. He was slightly not white. She didn't know how else to put it. Could he in fact have Indian blood in his veins? He had the dark hair and a suspicion of the cheekbones and the dark, dark eyes. He gave that impression, not so easy to see as to feel, of someone to whom misfortune comes more easily, more naturally, as less of a surprise, than to people she ordinarily knew. He wasn't full of conceit. He was more like a victim of the world than like someone who wanted to manipulate the world. She congratulated herself on her unselfishness when she opened her home to Alaman West.

Could she be trying to punish Robinson for his misdeeds by forming this friendship with a nice-looking, younger, lonely single man? She didn't think so, although the idea made her smile. Even in Jericho, tiny homespun Jericho, it wasn't completely unheard of, the married woman and the other man. But for Rainey Robinson, proper wife, girl-most-popular, harvest queen for life, a different interest finds its way into a corner of her heart, simpler than another man, sweeter, and more appealing to her instincts. Call it the other boy.

This boy is not as handsome as the one she makes her hero, not as forceful or confident, far from it. He is shy and hesitant and without much knowledge of the world (and he will never have it) and without fine friends (and he will never have them) and while quick to anger when he is stung, fundamentally submerged and afraid. With this boy she speaks of things that she would never talk about with her hero, not that this gains him much, since her hero is a hero for being above these sensitive things. She flirts with the darksome notion of this other boy. He is the sort of boy who makes her feel, not proud of being seen with him, but proud that she keeps him company all by herself. She lavishes her quality on him, glows with her warm generosity, with good humor lifts his spirits, with sadness wipes his tears if the world is too hard for him, and of course, supremely, she is that world that is too hard for him. She will never love him and she will never have to. He is her luxury, a gracious part of herself that, if it should go tomorrow, will never be missed. She would leave him and run to her hero at the first congenial sound of his voice. But in the meantime, since there is this other boy who has come all this way on his bicycle, and who (her mother calls to her) is waiting outside and wants to ask her a question, why not go out into the backyard and speak to him?

For Rainey, this other boy, this not quite other man, was Alaman West.

CHAPTER 22

FLIGHTS OF birds flew over the tops of the trees of the windbreak where West lay, nameless birds, early birds like him. Maybe hunters knew their names. They would have to know, to know what bird was what, to be able to tell their buddies: I almost shot an Alaman bird this morning, he was out early looking for his worm and I almost got him but he flew away. But there weren't any hunters out this morning and the farmer whose fields he trespassed on was maybe busy plowing Mrs. Farmer back in bed. His bicycle down out of sight, and stretched out on his stomach, his eyes addressing the sky, West felt something like a hunter, a pair of eyes wedded to potency, but more he felt like the birds, very much like the birds, a brother to anything with wings.

His worm appeared, the sun, the very morning, the sunrise. It warmed West like a kiss, a kiss to savor, with warm arms, warm cheeks, a true-love kiss, a kiss that didn't know why to stop, his Rainey kiss, a kiss with a smile in it that tingled and blessed him and rolled him over on his back with sappy pleasure. So he stayed a while exactly as he was, stayed and dreamed of a life so rosy, before he picked himself up and biked through the empty daylight back to Jericho.

His days weren't long enough, they couldn't start early enough. It seemed to him that he had never been so busy, had never felt so alive, planning for the Day, riding off to see Rainey, rushing back to stay clear of Robinson and be ready to whistle for Joe. His bookkeeping flew by like something that did itself, did so under his nose, beneath his notice. He never went to the café anymore or to the library or sat on a bench in the city hall park, unless it was to sit there and ponder the plan; he never sat in his rocker and read a book. He was much too busy. Besides, what book should he read? He was better than a book.

He had an audit—same dope as the other times. He enjoyed it very much. They had supper at the Legion Club where the dope talked about his greatest audits and then they went back to finish off West's books. It was most enjoyable. One, he knew he hadn't made any mistakes, two, he didn't give a damn if he had, and three, he was plotting assassination and the dope was looking for errors in arithmetic.

And love struck everywhere. When he felt a breeze, saw a sunrise, combed his hair, love struck. When he started his hello to Doc Death on the street, suckering him into believing and then suddenly not seeing Doc, it was because he thought he saw the back of her head in the reflection of the glass of Haley's window, and love struck again. Love struck in the street, at work, in the chipped enamel arms of the bathtub. It struck wildly outside her windows late at night. It struck in ways pleasant and not so pleasant. It could strike him in the throat and in the eyes seeing her stretch up to reach for something in a cupboard so that her breast bulged for an instant, love hit like bullets, like hail, like locusts that he tried to wrap himself against and battle off. When he was alone, love could tug him out to sea and dump him there without a prayer of ever coming back.

She was lush to him, like summer, like no summer West had ever known, like no island paradise he ever dreamed of; hers was a prairie lushness, like the browning grain, the color-me-yellow sunflowers, a lushness of homegrown things. He found warmth in the commonest subjects she talked to him about. Her voice put a special stamp on words, her voice was so whole, so positive—he was also in love with her voice. He saw Jericho High School in her face. He wasn't scared by her prettiness anymore. He knew that she was a conventional woman, a good mother, a small-town wife. He didn't see a great mystery when he looked at her. Now that he loved her, she wasn't strange to him at all.

He could even see himself as her son—Why not? He was only imagining. He happened to like the real son very much and Rainey loved the son dearly, so it wasn't a difficult dream. Lying in bed musing in the shadowy dusk made the proposition solemn: husband, lover or son, what was best?

Now West always felt a little embarrassed when he saw Dixie Carpenter around town. Though they never spoke, and she knew nothing about his daydreaming over her, he felt almost sorry for Dixie, as if he owed her an explanation for his unfaithfulness. Dixie was just a kid, small and pale beside Rainey. She and her kid sweat and the bottle of shampoo belonged to a youthful time. West saw it as an emblem of his growth that he loved a woman as finished and as lush as Rainey Robinson.

He didn't mind so much her being married. Except for it being Robinson. The only fly in the ointment was the Fly. And yet when he dreamed up other husbands for her he couldn't picture her married to anyone except Robinson. It was like a riddle: What was right and wrong—hot and cold—sweet but bitter? Rainey married to Robinson. Married nine, ten years, nine, ten years of marriedness. Her womanliness shot up the mercury in his cock and sent it to a watery grave. West would lie there and see it slumped over, his face slumped over too, two sad pals, two deserving friends. How would it be, how would she feel, how would she look? Did she moan? What did she taste like? An orange? Like mint? She would do him a favor to let him taste her. What would it cost her, that favor?

He brought her a bag of cinnamon redhots—candy, the sweetheart gift. They caught his eye in Haley's Drugstore. They clicked off a plan, not a big plan, a little plan. Also he liked the name, it expressed him, it captured his cock: redhots.

He set the bag on the kitchen table when her back was turned. When she saw it she laughed, laid her hand on her chest, widened her eyes and popped a redhot in her mouth, rolled it around her tongue a couple of seconds then popped it out. "Thank you for the thought," she said to West. The plan was working—he couldn't believe it. "Hot stuff, Stephie, no dear, you'll burn your tongue," taking the bag out of the reach of the demon little kid. "Jamie will thank you," she smiled at West. "Redhots are still for the young I'm afraid to say." Now came a big break. She was putting the bag up in the cupboard when the washing machine in the basement stopped washing and so she went downstairs to throw the clothes into the dryer.

The little moist redhot was on the table where she forgot it, the little moist redhot shiny from Rainey's mouth, achingly sweet from inside Rainey. West's hand itched to put that piece of Rainey in his mouth, to taste her tongue, taste her taste.

Trouble was, the little kid was watching the table too. The little kid craved the candy too, the funny red candy that was okay for Jamie but not for her. "Hey," West said when she stuck out her paw and it was lucky she obeyed because he didn't feel he could touch her. So they stood eyeing the piece of candy and each other, each wishing the other one would go away, West fidgety with impatience for solitude, the precious candy and Rainey's lingering taste.

"Do you like my mommy?" the little kid asked suddenly, truly scaring West, but then the smart kid said: "If you like my mommy, you would go downstairs with her."

He almost warmed to her for a second, not warmed, appreciated, respected. She wasn't the family favorite, not in her mother's eyes, so she took what she could for herself. If he couldn't really like her, maybe it was because she was always scratching for his attention even though she didn't seem to like him much either. She would have him if her mother's back was turned; she'd be happy to have the spit-out redhot from her brother's bag of redhots, would the poor kid with Rainey's face. So he did her a favor, he left her to burn her mouth and went downstairs to the basement just in time to catch the wet slap in the face of Robinson's shirts and Robinson's underwear dropping from Rainey's fingers into the dryer.

He wasn't in daily search of Robinson. The days of the web were long over; the Fly had a different meaning now, as in the Fly opening his fly. This was the cruel part, the bitter and cold of her being married: Robinson. Where West pressed a doorbell and had a cup of coffee, Robinson had breakfast every morning, or came and got an apple from the icebox, or smelled his dinner cooking on the stove. Robinson's car stood in the driveway, his umbrella stood in the hallway; Robinson's being stood in the way. West was mortified by the existence of Robinson. There was a realm shared by Robinson and Rainey, a high place, a deep kiss, that he would never succeed to. In his fears he always fell short, as though try as he might, he could never fill Robinson's shoes, his shirts, his void. The Fly with the fly hurt enough, just jealousy burned him enough, but shame crisped up his jealousy with a flame second only to love. He longed for Rainey and he dodged Robinson—why would he want to meet Robinson in the flesh before the Day?

But Robinson came home one afternoon and found West there. They were in the kitchen, West and Rainey. The sound of the door, the tread of the shoe, the sum total of Robinson in the room and West half-stood and wet his pants.

He dragged himself through the act of standing up, which became an act of inadvertent nonchalance, his hand draped in front of him to cover up the stain, wet drops like lit matches running down his leg. Rainey introduced them to each other: "I'm sure you both have seen one another around the town?" Robinson nodded and narrowed his gaze. West sat down again. Seconds thundered by. What had been scalding now was cold, the disgrace of an instant set in wet cement. Robinson leaned down, kissed her cheek, noticed the table, flung his briefcase down and hauled up a chair.

"I'll have a cup of coffee too. Or is it a tea party?"

Robinson smiled and slowly smoothed the side of his face with his hand—it was the written version of the same language of sarcasm. "We're all having coffee," Rainey said cheerfully, rising and going to the counter.

West died for her presence though she was barely a step away. Without her, only a slouching indifference sat between him and Robinson. His eyes flitted, avoiding Robinson's, which stared, as Rainey made soprano sounds with cup and saucer and spoon. Pissed-in pants put him at a slight social disadvantage. Pissed-in pants clung to him like a born disadvantage in the presence of Robinson. Maybe he would wake up in a minute and discover he was dreaming. It had the slow-motion of dreams, the slippery plot, the iron-clanging dread, the sense that he was doing all the thinking and all the feeling while others went about free. Had

Robinson seen? Rainey, did she see? He thought he covered it up in time but had one of them seen first, did one of them notice, and would the one who had seen tell the other?

"I noticed your bicycle out front," said Robinson. "I don't ride a bike, myself. My little boy rides a bike. My little girl rides a helluva bike—one more wheel than yours."

"You're in a very strange mood today, George," laughed Rainey as she carried his cup and saucer to the table. "You're quite embarrassing me."

"Me, my dear? Well, well."

Rainey sat down at the table with them. West was afraid to look at her: he thought Robinson was sure to see the love gushing out. He hunched over the table, hooded his eyes and brought his coffee to his lips at the same moment as his fingers were feeling his fly.

"You must have a lot of leisure time," Robinson said to him. "I only wish I had the time you have. What a life you must lead! Of course we can't all be footloose part-time bookkeepers the way you are, not to mention the fascination of the work. Not to intrude on your privacy, but I'm always puzzled by the question, What do you do all day?"

West's head snapped back. "I use the time. Don't worry. I keep busy."

"Alaman reads a great deal," said Rainey looking at him and smiling.

"Does he? I wonder what."

You wonder what, your death, I read your death, thought West. He took another polite sip of coffee; his mute smile was like a tight top on a bottle, a bottle that fizzed with his justice, his reasons, his jealousy, his love. Except for the wet pants it was the way he had always predicted. He always felt, if he ever met Robinson, he would sit like a time bomb, saying little, foreknowing all, a time bomb ticking away. So it was exactly the way he predicted except for his wet pants—if only he could have begun without the dumb numbing shame of piss in his pants.

"More coffee?" Robinson said to him.

"One more cup?" asked Rainey.

"No," West said aloud, convinced they were trying to get rid of him, but half-afraid they were trying to fill him up again for fun, making him a dope either way. "No," he muttered, sitting back, rocking and shambling to his feet behind the privy of his hands:

"Please excuse me—thank you for the coffee. I have some work to do."

"Sounds important," Robinson said, smoothing the side of his face slowly with his hand.

"Goodbye," said Rainey in the entry with a quick smile, closing the door on West.

Ten times worse than Joe—worse than Cat who pissed on the floor. He pissed all over himself. If there was a being West hated more than Robinson it was West. He didn't piss the stain—he was the stain. He didn't even dare look down at the stain until he was a mile from their house. That was how much of a stain he was.

Did she see? The great unanswered question. He strangely mightn't have minded her seeing. "*See?*" He could picture himself saying that to her, baring his cock, the wetness, everything—jumping right into the teeth of the living dream, being eaten alive by shame.

But Robinson seeing. That was unforgivable, because Robinson would think he had done it to him. Robinson walks in and West pisses in his pants, West disgraces himself, sits in wet pants, makes weak excuses, is driven off. And Robinson sits there laughing.

It was lucky time was so short. Robinson could be laughing all his life at what he had done to West.

CHAPTER 23

THE BULLETS were the first step in the plan.

He had thought it all out. The rifle was fully loaded because Hank and Pete always loaded their guns in case they lost them, but he needed many more bullets than that for practice alone. It was a Browning semiautomatic, four rounds in the clip, one in the chamber, five chances in all. It was very much like the rifle he fired in basic infantry training; having it was like a reunion with an old army buddy, and in nicer circumstances, a buddy he didn't have to dismember and clean everynight or march with in the rain.

He couldn't buy the bullets in Jericho—that would tell them that he owned a gun. He couldn't steal them here either, because in the Coast-to-Coast Store, the only place that sold them, bullets were kept in a locked case behind the cash register counter. That left some other town nearby where no one knew him, so he walked down to the depot one morning and took a train to Malden. He told Joe in advance why he was going; Joe was small on surprises and there was still a big one coming, the one that had Joe lighting the firecrackers. Thanks to Joe bringing in food all the time he had a nice little wad in his pocket, also the empty rifle clip and one sample bullet, for speedy reference.

So he took the morning train to Malden to start the plan, but even before he got on the train, while he was standing on the open platform at the depot, the fun fled down the tracks and the rails started singing in West's stomach. He was alone on the platform except for the depot man. The depot man was sweeping, starting from the opposite end. He was lame and dragged a foot, dragged West's nerves as he swept, bent to his broom and coming nearer, sweep of broom, sweep of broom, and the foot. The train pulled in and West got on. He took a window seat and affixed his dark glasses. It was three-quarters of an hour's ride to Malden. Field, house and field flew by, flew yet hugged the window. Not halfway there, all of a sudden West remembered: he knew someone in Malden, someone who could spot him there. Who the hell could that be—who and why? The trepidation passed, only to meet him in Malden when the train pulled in and he saw a pile of scrap near the depot: Curley of Curley's Junkyard, former home of West's bicycle; Curley had retired to Malden. West left the train and walked toward Main Street, all ready to duck Curley, trusting his dark glasses and quick step to get him through the three blocks of downtown Malden.

The hardware and sporting goods store had a man standing up front behind the counter and a woman feather-dusting in the back. Curley was nowhere on the premises; the place was empty. Behind his affronting deadpan and dark glasses West felt more drawn to the woman dusting, but he pushed against that swell and walked up to the counter with the man, the man and the bullets, boxes of them sitting in a display case back of the counter, getting to his shopping list fast because he figured that a hunter coming in for rifle bullets wouldn't stop to browse.

"I'd like two boxes of shells for a Browning semiautomatic, thirty-zero-six calibre, please."

"Nice gun," said the man—Nice gun or Nice day—West didn't care which, his eye on the glass case the man was opening and then on the two boxes that came sliding toward him, the price and number of bullets to a box finally close enough for West to see. He casually opened the lid of one, calculating and palpitating: long tapering brass bullets, fitted in neat red slots, handsome things, like cuff links and tie clasps, things to be sparing with, not waste. "Make that four boxes," West said huskily, "I may not be back here soon. Also—" he reached in his pocket and pulled out the rifle clip, "could you match this for me, please?"

Holding his brown paper bag by a fist, a little dazed by his riches, a little shaky in his knees, West walked out of the store with eighty rifle bullets and a fast-for-reloading extra clip. Curley wasn't on the street, or standing in any doorway; he wasn't in the clothing and drygoods store when West went in and bought a pair of too-small tight kid gloves, neither was he in the café where West sat with his back to the street and ate a ham and cheese sandwich, chewing it slowly, chewing up the time, because his train back to Jericho didn't leave for two more hours. The old junkman Curley wasn't anywhere, though West kept looking for him as if Curley put a little tic in his neck, a little hitch in his walk, fear of bumping into Curley and being tied to Malden, the hardware store and the bullets. Then there was Malden itself to throw his world off-balance, Malden with its grain elevator and tarry streets and plain old age and thrown-up wooden storefronts, a town enough like Jericho and enough unlike to make it seem like Jericho askew. The hardware store where he bought the bullets was a Coast-to-Coast Store. There was a Red Owl Store here too. But not the real Coast-to-Coast, not the real Red Owl, not the real people either, their collective faces told West, as if he was the only one here who was as he should be, the only one who truly existed. His train pulled out exactly on time—he had spent his last hour in Malden watching out for Curley at the depot. He never did bump into old Curley despite all his worrying, but it wasn't entirely a waste. The fear he nursed all day was good experience. When his feet finally touched ground, he couldn't believe how safe he felt to be back in Jericho.

Eighty bullets meant that he had enough for practice, the assassination, and a reserve for escape in case he needed it. The extra clip meant that he would have a full clip at his side ready for immediate delivery. Wearing gloves meant that he could wipe everything clean of fingerprints beforehand and leave gun and all behind him up in the roost. West relaxed for the next few hours. He felt the plan almost planning itself, all it needed was a little shove from him in the right direction. "Who you going to shoot, everybody?" Joe said gloomily when West brought out the four boxes of bullets after supper and lined them up on the kitchen table.

"Some are for practice, some are for him, and some are for afterward," explained West.

"Afterward? What afterward?"

"A reserve, in case they come after me, if it's not too late by then. I'm sitting up there all alone. Suppose they see where I'm shooting from? It's goodbye West, Joe."

Joe came walking back slowly, staring at West's face as West fiddled with an open box of bullets. "Don't I remember something? Didn't you talk about firecrackers hiding where you are?"

West laughed out loud. "How can I light firecrackers down in the street when I'm upstairs shooting a rifle? I'm only a human being."

"No, not you, other people, kids."

West laughed again, only louder. "Other people do West a favor and light firecrackers just when he wants to shoot Robinson."

"So what's the answer?" said Joe.

"Don't you see, Joe, don't you see, partner, why I need you to light the firecrackers?"

"Oh no, not me," cried Joe, jumping back, "not me! I resign from partners. You're a snake, West. Friends, sure, but partners are dissolved. Did you see what you had me doing, West? You had me thinking about it just like you!"

"I told you I work Saturdays," Joe said coldly the second time West brought up the subject of Joe lighting the firecrackers.

"You said you could get off for a few minutes."

"Maybe I wasn't telling the truth. Maybe I lied for a change."

"Why would you lie to me, Joe? To hurt me? Or was it to help me? I think I know the answer. I think you were trying to help. I need you to light the firecrackers for me, Joe."

"I never lit a firecracker in my life. I could blow my hand off!"

"Little kids light them all the time."

"You get a little kid to do it then. And don't ask me about it again tomorrow, West. You hope I'll be sorry and say yes, so I'm telling you that my promise will be no."

"No, no, no, no, no! How many was that? You need a couple more?"

"Just say yes once, Joe. That's all I want. Then I won't bother you again."

"Maybe I'll do that. That would solve my problem. Say yes and never do it."

"No, I'd trust you. You wouldn't let me down. Not when I'm alone up there."

"If I won't light the firecrackers you won't go up?"

"I didn't say that. I said if you didn't light them I'd be alone. All alone and dead."

"Dead. Sure, dead. Dead is easy to say. You don't look too worried to me."

"I'm not worried. I'll be alone but I'll be dead. I might be hanging from a window but not because I'm lonesome. I might be all shot up but not," West made a tragic face, "needing a friend. Won't you miss me, Joe? Say yes. Do us both a favor. Say yes about lighting the firecrackers."

"Not yes," groaned Joe. "Yes is for my tooth hurts, can you help me, or did you bring home strawberries today—that's what yes is for. Not help me shoot somebody or I'll go up anyway and get killed!"

"I stand there and light firecrackers while he's making a speech? I'll look stupid. I would if I was dumb enough to do it," said Joe to West in their last installment of Joe lighting the firecrackers.

"Just a handful. Just one or two. Maybe none, if other people do it."

"You're not as crazy as you think," said Joe. "You got the rifle, you got your grudge, you're up in the window—I can believe that—but you never really shoot. You say you'll shoot, you think you'll shoot, but always something stops you. It's like a little voice inside. You never pull the trigger."

"Believe whatever you want," said West.

"Why should I light firecrackers when you're not going to shoot?"

"Stop talking and make up your mind, Joe!"

Joe shook his head. "Saturday morning . . . it's the busiest time in the store."

"Dammit Joe! I'm sitting up there with a smoking gun. If you don't do it I'm gone—I'm dead!"

*   *   *

"You got me in the book too?" Joe asked softly as West flipped to a new page in Accounts Receivable and wrote down about Joe lighting the firecrackers.

"Only the once," said West.

He HAD been many times to that fateful corner on Legion Avenue to choose the window for his roost. All the years past when he saw the same corner, coming home from school, coming home from the army, coming toward it most of his life, all those old times seemed prophetic to West now that he saw the corner with a purpose. He inspected it in different ways, from different angles, approaching it slowly on his bike, sitting on a bench in the park across the street, taking a stroll around to the back alley. The four buildings together made a picture postcard in his mind. He sent himself the same postcard every day: Sam's barbershop, the Feed and Seed, the insurance office and the Red Owl Store. He looked at their second stories, he studied their upper windows, and always he felt in back of him the stone-studded eyes of Robinson's city hall steps. He saw Hank sometimes, and Pete, and daydreamed Hank's fat stomach on Pete's long legs, the united Jericho Police Department falling on its face. He saw where Joe would stand and light his firecrackers, and it made him laugh because Joe was right, lighting firecrackers while a man made a speech was stupid. But necessary, argued West, to hide the sound of the shots. Necessary, argued a secret voice inside, to hide Joe being there as Joe. It was buried deep in the plan by now, that he couldn't get by without Joe.

He had his image of Robinson, Joe, the police, the crowd—he saw everything plainly except where he would be. As many trips as West made downtown, he couldn't will his face into any of those windows. As many heights as he climbed, there was always a misstep at the top of his resolve that plunged him down again. Sam's barbershop had an empty room on top but with the entrance to it right on Legion Avenue; the Feed and Seed had a little loft with a window but an open, spiny staircase down the back that ran in full view of people in other buildings; the insurance office had top floor space that might be good but the entry and stairs were an eyeful to the man in the office. The best roost of all was the apartment above the Red Owl Store, the place where he lived with his mother and where she died. It was too bad people were living there, thought West about their old two-room apartment: he might still be able to find his way around. His old bedroom was in back, a dark closet of a room, facing the closet that was the kitchen. Her room, the living room, where she bedded and bled and died, looked out over Legion Avenue to the steps of the city hall. It was a pity there were curtains on the windows and he had seen lights there at night, thought West smugly to himself. The Red Owl Store apartment had inside stairs, an entrance in back and was on the corner, making escape from above confidential and escape down the sidestreet easy. What a shame people lived there, sighed West to himself, petting his aversion like a pet, playing with his dread of ever climbing the stairs to that old apartment again.

"There's a loft above the Feed and Seed," he told Joe at last, because telling Joe clinched the deciding. "It could be a store-room but no one goes up there. There isn't any lock on the door. I shoot from that loft," West said, touching his pen to the little box-window on his drawing.

"That's no good," said Joe. "You got your stairs on the outside. They could see you coming and going, especially going when it's busy downtown. Don't worry," Joe blushed at his sudden concern over the plan, "you're not going to shoot anybody. But you still got the rifle and you still got no business being wherever you are, so it's best nobody sees. And what about me? If I'm in it acting like a dope I got to protect myself too. So I took a walk around. The only place for you is the place over the store."

"Take your time, Joe. There's someone living there."

"No, no one. It's empty."

West froze. "I saw lights."

"Maybe, but it's empty. I should know, don't I work over there," said Joe to a dumbstruck West.

And Joe didn't stop at that. All day at home alone West seethed at Joe's mistake, but as soon as Joe came in he told West: "I went up there today. Don't scream—nobody saw. The door was open. There's no furniture, nothing."

"But the curtains—"

West went out alone on successive nights: no light in the win-

dow; no life. Joe was right—dark and empty. The light he had
seen that once was a fluke. So as Joe said, the Red Owl Store
apartment was the best place for him, and not only for escape.
Even the curtains made it a better roost—better than a bare loft
window. I don't want to go up there, don't make it always come
out there, West pleaded with himself. He felt he would be par-
alyzed in that room. He went from a man to a man without arms,
in a wink—it was as if he had been flying and been shot down.
The Old Red Owl Store apartment was still alive in West; he
could still smell the doom on the stairs, wafting up around the
door like a cooking smell, surrounding mother and son, going in
with them with the bedding when they came to town, settling
down with them and sharing their little home, doom sweet doom
for Annie West and Alaman her boy.

But escape from there was so easy, escape from the Red Owl
Store apartment was a breeze—if he shot from the Feed and Seed.

West let the foregone conclusion rest for a day, giving it time
to sink in, seem like thought, seem like resolution, sticking with
the Feed and Seed loft as his roost. Why should a little flight of
stairs be that important? What did it matter if a window was
bare if he only used a little corner of it? But he had to decide
what to tell Joe. It wouldn't be the story of his life, whether that
meant his first word, his first step, or the Red Owl Store apartment. When the day came, he could invent a reason for switching
places, but in the meantime he had only to picture Joe's dumb,
sad, stubborn face and he knew all right what to tell him.

"Okay, Joe. I shoot from the Red Owl Store apartment, if that's
what it takes to keep my partner happy."

This was the plan:
West has normal day on the Thursday, Joe at work at the store;
Joe buys firecrackers, gets okay from Henry to hear Robinson's
speech, at night brings firecrackers (and matches) to West's for
West to check; last meeting before the Day—supper and final
review. The Friday: Joe at work in the store. West brings bike
into house, straps on rifle, packs bullets and extra clip into basket, lays out clothes, rests up. Saturday Oct. 5, the Day: West
with gloves wheels out bike at 4AM and bikes downtown; re-

moves gun, etc., parks bike in back alley, climbs up into roost. At daybreak loads rifle and extra clip. At 8 Joe comes to work with firecrackers (in a paper bag), reminds Henry about hearing Robinson's speech, acts excited. 9:00, parade starts, West starts sighting city hall steps. 9:15, Joe leaves store with firecrackers and goes to his spot at edge of city hall park. Joe watches city hall steps, not West's window—Joe NEVER EVER looks up at West's window. Band plays music. At 9:45 band stops playing. Robinson in place on steps. Joe lights first string of firecrackers. West rests gun barrel on sill and sights Robinson. Robinson starts speech. Joe lights next string of firecrackers (unless others being lit). Instant West hears string start he shoots. Joe quick lights third string THEN looks at steps. If Robinson still standing lights more. Keeps looking and lighting firecrackers, if no one else does. West is shooting—reloading or shooting. Robinson falls. All confusion. Joe drops firecrackers and goes with people near him, goes where they go. West leaves rifle, etc., behind, leaves roost by back stairs, walks back to bicycle, rides away. Joe ends up in store, West at home. Joe comes around for breakfast on Sunday morning.

That was the plan.

CHAPTER 24

HE FELT like a serious man, a man with a serious purpose. He had known from the beginning it would be so, but he never dreamed, could not have guessed, the transforming gravity of it. His old way of behaving, his web, his spying, belonged to a different time, to a different West, almost. He was awed by the way he felt. He saw himself moving toward a chiseled end, much like an athlete preparing. Taking action, he felt grown, older, taller. Important weight was added to his height. Taking trips downtown he rode his bicycle less. Now he walked. Walking was more suitable. He ought to let people go by him more slowly, he ought to go by them more slowly, so they could take his measure more.

He took a cool view of Robinson, a typical tyrant, a husband and father, an arrogant son-of-a-bitch. Having Robinson for a father was maybe what kept West from hating him for having Rainey for a mother. Robinson always won. There he was with Rainey, there he was with money, there he was the mayor of the town. If it wasn't for West he could go on winning far into the future; he was a very fortunate man, all except for the fact that West was part of his luck. Everyone would be better off without Robinson. There were stories West had heard concerning him, tales, rumors, hisses—West wished he had paid more attention. Robinson had threatened a man, a man had been cheated by Robinson, this man, that man and that. The stories had to do with cruelty, injustice and taking unfair advantage. West was positive he had heard them. They originated in the town and now they circulated with his blood.

The town deserved Robinson and Robinson deserved the town. That seemed self-evident, a point that proved itself. Jericho disappointed West so much it was a joke. The town slapped him and winked at him, killed his mother and welcomed him back—home was a humorous hometown. Removing Robinson from Jericho was a thing of inspired balance. It was a blow to the town and yet he was doing the town a favor. It was a forked thing, the one idea confounding the other idea, but they both marched together to the end of the road, the fatal blow and the favor, hand in hand. The ending looked bright to West. He had come a long way from his bookkeeping tricks on the town, little deceptions that took place all in his mind. His serious purpose felt almost physical to him. When he thought, Teach them a lesson, his throat opened like a floodgate, like a prophet's. When he thought, Do justice, his heart leaped. Right a balance, and his being braced, his spine was satisfied.

Rainey of course would be his. With Robinson out of the way she would turn to him. The accident of her meeting Robinson in the first place would be canceled by a more recent event. He worried some about hurting her but he had faith in her resilience, her sunniness. She could get over anything, she had proved that to the world when her parents died. His faith in her made removing Robinson a whole lot easier to do. He dismissed as silly the idea that with Robinson gone she might marry some storekeeper or farmer, stay a widow or abandon Jericho. She was as much his as his star, as fixed here as her picture in her high school yearbook. Her being here was guaranteed. Afterward, when she was alone, who else could she turn to but him?

Summer was ending, autumn was ripening, like a pumpkin in its own mellow light. Rainey's roses still bloomed, fields of sunflowers still held up their heads—it was the season holding its breath. He rode out to Cemetery Hill one morning because he overheard her tell her friend over the phone that she was driving out there to plant bulbs at her parents' graves. He acted in secret, to surprise her. Cemetery Hill was out on the prairie, far enough from the edge of town; no Joe around to see he knew her, no

Robinson to guard himself against, maybe she wouldn't even bring the little kid to a scary graveyard, West prayed as he biked past wheat fields toward the silent, solitary hill. Shady trees grew there, and grass, and things eternal, like this summer past. Their talk about their buried parents lured him on. Expressions like Our loss and Our sorrow and We Two, those words from her backyard, whispered in his ear. From up on Cemetery Hill, a promise beckoned West.

He left his bike at the bottom of the hill outside the gate. There was no fence, no wall, only an iron gate, which stood wide open. All are welcome, said the gate, meaning West. The shady trees addressed him too, with rustling leaves. But the stone spoke not. Good listeners, good bunch, West praised them with a smile, stepping lightly past their heavy brows midway up the hill. Since he saw at a glance that no one else was here, he made a small excursion of climbing toward the top, keeping an eye out for her car as he browsed through names on stone. In time he found her parents' graves, a grassy plot with a family stone marked Spencer and withering white blossoms on a single plant, her touching handiwork. A little uneasy, feeling like a suitor, he stood before the two white graves, Rainey's mother and father. Himself, he had no father. He took it matter-of-factly: no dad. No mother either, for that matter—there's just me. Nice meeting you, Mr. and Mrs. Spencer.

Leaves rustled, a bird twittered on high—the Spencers in their peaceful backyard waited for their precious daughter. West moved on, beginning to miss her too, a softness, a roseate sadness, on his face. She wasn't late because she hadn't set a time, just morning. That was cemetery time: I'll be there on the dot of morning. Like a ruminating kid walking home from school, stopping and starting, in quest of really nothing, he drifted back across the slope, lightening himself by reciting names on graves in different voices as he came around the quiet hillside, round and small like the earth. He came to her grave, Annie West. That was the reason for the walk: Annie West. "Annie West," West said in the falsest voice of all. There was no family stone, no family plant, not a flower to brighten up the place. The pretty little woman, the little dark apartment, the little plain grave— all in a nutshell. West gave Annie a smile, a smile that twisted in, like a rose with thorns. Rainey Robinson is better than you, Annie West. Much better. She's prettier too. West said it out loud to punish himself for thinking it, his punishment coming from feeling so bad, so sorry, so bleak about his own poor flesh-and-blood. Poor Annie West—poor little woman. She danced till dawn, the dawn of Alaman. She danced till Alaman cut in. Always so tired, it wasn't her fault she lay down to rest and the rest of her seeped away. Annie so quiet, it shouldn't have surprised him to find that he was suddenly all alone. He'd always feel sorry about Annie, just as he would always feel rage. The rage was mixed up with the pity like a soup, rage-and-pity soup, and it was served up on her dying day the same as every other day, no different, the same soup, only that day it was served up piping hot.

Trees whispered—birds beat their wings—the box in the ground edged closer. A dispiritedness crept over West, even after he left the spot, a weariness, a small lesson in earthly gravity. Defeat in everything was what it said, the quiet message from the grave. He wished that Rainey would hurry up and come. Rainey! He pressured the heavens by calling her name. He needed her here—he wouldn't even complain if she brought the little kid.

He retraced his steps around the hill of graves, looking down at his bike, the gate and the road, as far up the road as he could, whistling up her car. By and by he found his way back to her parents' graves and planted himself there, by Mom and Pop Spencer, as if they were the appointed place to be, the hub of a thronging town. By and by he abandoned them too and walked the silent hillside or stood and gazed for minutes at the Jericho road. Morning must have long since died because West felt hungry.

Make me a sandwich, he told Greta Nordstrom, sixty years dead. Make me a cold sandwich, he told Greta with a twisted grin. Better make the bed, Greta, he said wearily sometime later, patting Greta on the shoulder. Greta kept him company. It was a good thing he had Greta because otherwise he might cry. But Greta said: There, there. Don't cry.

Only an ache kept him here finally, an ache he was too much pals with to leave behind. It was the same hill that Annie West had brought him to. Here he was again. Same hill, same view, same nowhere. Same twittering birds. West wiped an eye. Standing waiting for the one—crying burying the other—today he had a foot in either day. He felt so blue his swollen eyes played tricks on him: the world shrank and he grew, swollen, vast and blue, though not like the sky. Nowhere all around him. Alone then and all alone now. No-faced Annie West. No Rainey Robinson.

West kicked the ground, kicking Cemetery Hill, he didn't know whether for the woman who was here or the woman who was never coming.

He biked home, looking for nothing on that road, feeling a hate for the road to Jericho now that he was fleeing homeward on it.

Home. And still nowhere. The old grainary shack that had once held wheat sat perched on the edge of the world. His kitchen felt ominous and cold; it had an ugly, repellent, accustomed look to it, being the same coloration as himself. He sat in gloom, a gloom so total it weakened his limbs. He knew he was hungry so he threw that in the pot too, along with his chills, his tearfulness. He was nothing and mattered to no one. He was cold, he lived in a shack. He had no money, no luck, no starry future. He was hungry, poor and alone and living in the last place on earth anyone would look expecting to find anything.

That was West one minute. But in the next, as in a bathing light, with a tantrum joy, cold, poor, hungry and alone, like an infant in a rage, West was the center of the universe.

He tore off his clothes. Still tearful, he invited the cold, the aloneness, to trumpet his nakedness. He ran and threw the door open—chill dusk air made it worse but the worse the better. West spread his arms; the exaltation made him radiant. He could feel a light shining from his skin. Cold, poor, hungry and alone—the center of the universe.

And Joe spoiled it all, dumb Joe, workaday Joe—West had forgotten he existed. "Hey West! I'm here," Joe came up the front step calling. "I brought us pork chops for supper."

And West grabbed up his clothes and made a dash for the bedroom.

A surprised Joe stood in the doorway, decidedly red-faced, but through his embarrassment beaming and laughing. "What's the matter? Hey, what are you hiding for? I'm a man. What you got I got too!"

CHAPTER 25

WEST WASN'T a killer, the doctor never killed West's mother—
with West killing didn't mean killing.

Joe would often repeat that to himself. It was like a little rhyme
he knew, like a hum that hummed almost wordlessly in Joe's
head and whose melody always made him feel better. The doctor
never killed West's mother—with West, killing didn't mean killing.

Joe knew there was plenty to be scared about, like the plan,
the gun and West's grudge; like his name in West's little book.
Joe had a darting fear of the little things in the plan, the details,
such as the exact times West wrote down, and breakfast on Sunday morning, because they were creepy and real to him, like bugs.
But being at West's side day after day helped Joe see things in a
softer, soothing light. West wasn't the type to harm anyone. West
was the friend whose aching tooth he had pulled. He was that
almost skinny man Joe had just glimpsed, whose skin without
any clothes was boyish white. Even West's killing plan had the
benefit of this softer candlelight of Joe's, once he was over the
shock of his own part with the firecrackers. What kind of plan
could be serious that had bicycles and firecrackers? Kids made
up plans like that, not men who were killers. If West ever carried
the gun up to that window, he'd be too smart to pull the trigger.
If he pushed himself into going up, when he saw his mistake and

wanted to escape, West could do it, thanks to Joe who had discovered the empty Red Owl Store apartment. As he grew to see
things better, Joe felt safer. Robinson was going to live a long
life, Joe certified. If he didn't contradict when West would talk
about assassinating Robinson, it was because he wasn't that
scared of it happening that it was worth a fight. He didn't even
pay attention most of the time. West going over his plan seemed
like normal life to Joe.

Sometimes, just to make sure, he thought of getting the rifle
from wherever it was in West's bedroom and finally getting rid
of it, since he was sometimes alone in the house or awake in the
kitchen at night while West was sleeping. But how could he go
into West's private room and move a rifle out; and even supposing he did, when West went to see about the rifle, and it was
missing, who else would he look at but his partner Joe?

IT WAS the happiest summer of Joe's life.

Except for sleeping there, he spent little time in his room in
the Violet Hotel. The old proprietor sisters and their old men
guests would be gone from the porch and lobby by the time he
walked across the town from West's. As he walked through those
streets, the little town dark and asleep, Joe could have whistled
if he wasn't afraid of waking his neighbors up. A place like Jericho
was like the streetlight up ahead, the bright light at the end of
the road, except that Joe knew he was already there. He was
happy to get up each morning and go to work in the Red Owl
Store. He practically lived at West's—he and West had meals
together. Joe often brought cake and day-old bread and other bargains from the store, plenty of ground beef too. Joe did the cooking and then Joe would do the dishes; the coffee pot, Joe's gift,
was always on. They would spend the evening there in West's
kitchen, West sitting in his rocker occupied with the plan or
with his little notebook, Joe at the kitchen table, leafing through
a magazine or the *Pioneer* while he might be dipping into a dish
of roasted nuts from Haley's. Late in the summer, he bought a
lawn chair at the Coast-to-Coast Store and sat out in the back
in the sun near the rickety tool shack. Once, scraping carrots in
the sink, he turned his head around and said to West: "You

should have a garden. You got the space in back. Maybe next year."

It wasn't such a terrible partnership that he had with West, this close and constant partnership heading nowhere. He had West's friendship and West's house to share, he was more at home in the house than West's cat, a delicious pleasure to Joe who had never grown fond of the eating, sleeping, bothersome cat. When it got tired of roaming and came inside, the cat would sit and stare at West, or circle West's chair, or else it ran, growled, jumped in the tub, jumped in West's lap. Joe didn't interfere when West took the cat, carried it to the door and tossed it out of the house. The cat scratching at the door to get back in would bring a satisfied smile to Joe's nicely sunbrowned face. It didn't even have a name, the cat, just Cat. It was mad because West didn't talk to it or pet it the way he used to. West was outgrowing the cat—a healthy thing, celebrated Joe. West shouldn't waste his time on an animal, he should spend it on a human being—it was better for West himself. It would be better still if he didn't spend so much time sitting and dreaming or with his nose in his little book. But Joe made allowances: that was normal for West. When West saw him downtown, for instance, Joe would wave hello but West never stopped or even looked at him. Normal for West. He wasn't like other people exactly. You didn't expect the same things from him. He was more interesting, more fascinating. Just not a killer.

What was inside West? What made him different? What did he think, dream, smile or look so glum about? What was the grudge he had against Robinson? What were his secrets that he hid from the rest of the world? His partner Joe was deeply concerned, concerned and tantalized. Now leaning over his mop in the Red Owl Store, now brooding over his friend in his own tiny room, Joe would wonder about West; but Joe wondered in the bright clear light of West's kitchen too. There in his own house West sat and rocked like a question mark. His little book lay open in his lap. There was an invisible rope all around him. He was like someone Joe could see but never approach. That moment he saw West naked, his tanned face and arms he showed to the world and the whiteness of the rest of him, it wasn't a surprise but it was still a small shock, West's skin—so personal. It didn't answer Joe's questions, West naked. It gave him a new and bashful glimpse of the unknown, as if skin and beneath-the-skin belonged to the same West mystery.

Should he take a peek in West's little book? That might tell him something. Joe brushed the shameful thought away. Joe brushed it away a second time but again it buzzed quite near him, this buzzing end-of-summer mosquito thought. Just a quick little peek at a couple of pages? Joe brushed the thought away once and for all. West trusted him as a friend, he couldn't read West's book. If he had a little book he would consider it private and what was private for him was Private First Class for West. No, Joe slapped away the pesky thing again, it was wrong to read such a private book, even though it was a mistake to think that West would have to find out.

But maybe West was too private, said the little mosquito thought. After all, he Joe was in the book too, if only once. Didn't he have a right to see his own name? If he went looking for his name and he saw something else, it wouldn't be his fault, it would be an accident. West's secrets couldn't be so bad that he should be ashamed of them, admonished Joe. Besides, Joe wasn't an enemy, he was a friend. He could even be doing West a favor by reading his book. It would be good for West himself to have someone who understood him better. By now the bug thought was biting him all over and Joe was itching and burning: to know West better, to know West's thoughts, the mystery inside West.

Joe crept up while West was sleeping. Not on slumbering West—his room, his dresser-top, his chair, his pants on it, his pocket. Joe didn't hesitate. His fingers in West's back pocket lifted out the surprised little book. Joe was only borrowing it for a while—he'd have it back in the pocket before West ever woke up.

But Joe stood all jitters beside the kitchen table, not daring to sit down, not deserving to, overcome by what he was, a thief in his best friend's house. As Joe anguished and grew in guilt the little book grew in innocence, plucked like a flower from Alaman West's life. Loose petals, loose papers, fell out of it suddenly. Joe's contortions reached to his core as he grabbed and scooped them up. They were the *Pioneer* article about Robinson and West's drawing of the assassination scene. Joe already knew those, so he could stop before he saw anything new.

Joe opened the book.

Accounts Receivable greeted him just inside, a beginning typical of West, a mystery introducing a mystery. Almost shyly at first, Joe began to read, swimming eerily through West's eyes and into pools beyond, little dark pools of black-inked words where West spoke alone to West, and yet as Joe read on, West's words themselves seemed less and less an answer to any mystery. He turned the pages over one by one, wondering why he had felt ashamed of himself, looking for West's grudge or even West's mother and instead reading about Robinson's street and yard, the doings of the Fly (what fly?), R's—must be Robinson's—kitchen, plus a page of arithmetic about bullets. Joe turned the pages faster, just looking for his name, when another name popped out at him, a name Joe knew, at the top of a nearly empty page. Joe's eyes took in the name and page all at once:

Rainey Robinson—I love her.

Joe blinked his eyes—blinked and looked—*I love her* stared back at him in West's exact, neat hand. He loves her. He loves Mrs. Robinson! This still-being-digested lump of news made Joe sit down. West loves Mrs. Robinson. Joe felt numb all over, except for a place inside his stomach that was turning sick. He loves Rainey Robinson. It was the answer to every question, if Joe could any longer stand to ask those questions. There were no more questions! Rainey Robinson, I love her.

How much of his night he passed alone in West's kitchen, West asleep beyond the curtain to his room, Joe was neither conscious of nor cared. His fears made the time pass anyhow, fresh fears scarier than the old, fear that West might kill for Rainey Robinson as he never would for his Assassinate; still worse fear, colder, sober fear that sure nobody would kill but Robinson would find out about West and his wife and West would be run out of Jericho. And Joe would end up where? With what? Not with West, Joe reckoned. Joe knew: West would pack up alone. And all because of her. Because of Rainey Robinson. Because she was pretty.

Joe's unhappiness skirted and swirled so thickly about the person of Rainey Robinson that he scarcely perceived an able and willing West. She should know better, Joe scolded. She was a married woman with kids. She had Robinson, what did she want with West? Joe, who only wanted everything to stay the same, sat into the night as if West's kitchen was a rocking, moving train and when the night lifted and he looked outside he would find that he was in a strange and fruitless country.

But before daybreak came West emerged from his bedroom, pushing aside the divider curtain, eyes heavy-lidded with sleep, in his pajamas and bare feet, and Joe, who was ready for him, flung his book in his face, the loose papers flying out of it and Joe's words flying after them:

"I know your grudge! And her name is Rainey Robinson!"

As West gaped, Joe sneered, "I love her," bottom lip quivering, boil of spit and all.

West, still astonished, still somnambulant, stooped to pick up his book and papers, mumbling almost to himself, "You stole my book." He seemed not to see the smoldering presence of Joe, who crouched by the table a couple of steps away.

"You're crazy, West! He'll find you out. You'll lose everything you got. He'll run you out of town!"

"You just stole my book."

"You'd kill him for his wife? That's the best reason you got? Because of her?"

"Bum, you stole my book!"

"I never stole it! You left it in the kitchen"—Joe slammed the tabletop—"Right here!"

"What's it to you who I love?" screamed West. "I'll love whoever I want. I'll love the table if I want—the toilet, I'll love the toilet, but not this." West grabbed Joe's coffee pot and threw it at Joe's head. Joe ducked and the pot flew apart and crashed against the wall. To West, it hadn't traveled far enough. He pounced and jammed in the parts, flung the door open and hurled it into the night, sending the disassembling coffee pot sailing up into smithereens of stars.

"Okay . . . now we're even," said a subdued, swallowing-hard, ready-to-talk-about-it Joe.

"Out," said West. "This is the end of everything."

CHAPTER 26

JUST AS the pain and then peace too subsided when Joe pulled his tooth for him, so West, when his rage over his notebook cooled down, when icy zero coldness itself was gone, West entered a new realm of feeling about Joe. He was still stunned by it: Joe had read his book. Here he had trusted him and the bum had taken it, read it, opened him up. The bum lied about it too. He didn't believe for one minute that he had left it on the kitchen table: it always traveled in his pocket with him, near him. Joe had taken it and knew. The bum knew about Rainey—bum fingers had turned the pages and bum eyes had seen the light. Joe had read it and knew.

So he could never trust Joe. An emptiness, a scorn and hate but an emptiness, settled down through West . . . Don't trust Joe.

Don't trust Joe meant that Joe had his own private wishes. It meant that Joe had thoughts, incurious as West might be about them. Don't trust Joe meant that Joe wasn't completely controllable. But in that wary, cautious Don't trust Joe lurked an assumption that West as yet only dimly appreciated. It might not be the same as it was, but it wasn't the end of everything.

So turned the thoughts in his mind the day after the fight with Joe; so spun the stalled wheels as West sat rocking toward evening, when a letter came sliding under the door. He had heard nothing: the floorboard was bare one minute and a letter was

196

there the next. West seized it and opened the door fast, thinking implausibly, Rainey, but no jewel face was there in the twilight, no small-heeled step was heard, and the letter was a note from the bum.

I'M SORRY I MADE A BIG MISTAK
LETS BE FRIENDS OK?

"West?"

He stood in the doorway holding the letter and heard Joe calling "West?"

Joe stepped out from behind the tool shack, met West's eyes, hesitated, and started nearer, wading through weeds and West's gaze, contrite as his letter, slow and shambling as his printing.

"What do you say, West? Are we still friends? Is it okay?"

So Joe was taken back; was let in wordlessly, a sparing of words that said one thing in the beginning but quite another as West's silence became the air Joe breathed. Never again was he left alone in the house for long, or loose in the kitchen after West had gone to bed. West watched his partner Joe, watched Joe's broad back piercingly and Joe's face out of the corner of his eye; watched with the intentness of a horseman keeping tabs on the nag that was carrying him, slow-witted and ponderous afoot, a nag of the cheapest pedigree, thick-chested, sweaty and mangy, none too beautiful either, a whimpering nag, a nag he would leap off and kick to oblivion the minute he reached his goal, but that for the little journey ahead would serve the purpose.

He watched Joe just guilefully enough that Joe might catch him at it, and so Joe eyed him back, meeting suspicion with a friendliness that kept trying to make amends. Joe went out back and scoured the yard for the far-flung coffee pot, and when he couldn't find all the pieces he bought another coffee pot and carried it back to West's. "Good as new," said Joe to West about the bubbling new coffee pot. Joe tried not to think about Rainey Robinson. When he did, picturing in his mind the pretty woman shopping with the little girl, he found ways to cheer himself up . . . It wouldn't last, this thing with Mrs. Robinson . . . Maybe he loved her but did she love him? . . . Robinson would never find out. The husband never guessed ... With West, it probably wasn't love.

And all the while, hidden from Joe, West held on to Joe's letter. When he was alone he would set it before him and tinker with the letter in his mind. The handful of words meant nothing anymore; Joe's printing spoke to West, hit a nerve, lit a fuse, Joe's big block printing that was stuck in the second grade.

What if Robinson got a letter printed by Joe? What if Joe printed a kind of a warning to Robinson? What if? So went the late-night tinkering in West's mind as he looked at Joe's big-lettered, big-headed, moron printing.

A letter by Joe would be a life insurance policy for West. Joe would be so bound to the plan, in it so deep, he would stop being the partner West was afraid to trust.

A letter by Joe would scare the wits out of Robinson. Robinson's head would crack from the split of a death threat with words by West put down in that moron print.

A letter would be dangerous because Robinson would run to the police. Not as dangerous as if it carried West's handwriting, on display in ledgers held around Jericho. Dangerous in that they would be ready for him now, Robinson, Hank and Pete, the town.

But how would they know why Robinson fell without a letter? How could they see without a letter to open their eyes, thought West, the light tinkering becoming serious hammering now, words for a letter building as he rocked with Joe's clearly arrested, Joe's dumb and explosive printing there in his lap.

Joe didn't fight him this time. "You want me to write a letter, I'll write a letter. I got paper, I got a pencil—I'll do it. I'm lighting firecrackers while you shoot him, I might as well sit down and write him a letter."

Joe laughed sarcastically, making himself say and do whatever was asked because that was the free and happy way with West. He wasn't pleased but neither was he panicked by the letter, because Joe had crossed into the kind of world where nothing was serious anymore. Things were too far gone; Joe felt numb and giddy. Everything seemed like a joke to him now.

"So what do I say in the letter, anything in particular?" he asked when he sat down at the table with the sheet of paper and stubby-pointed pencil West had put there.

"Not yet." West had on his tight kid gloves and he had a glove for Joe, a large yellow work glove to wear on the other hand as he wrote so as not to leave his fingerprints on the letter.

"I'm okay now?" asked Joe, looking at himself and trying not to laugh when he had on the yellow glove and held the stubby pencil in the other hand.

"Death to tyrants," said West. "That's the first line. D-E-A-T-H. Death."

Joe printed. West stood over him and spelled, leading him letter by letter, flexing a gloved hand to ease some little nerve, ranging about the room to release other ones as Joe and the pencil caught up, coming quickly back to read the big printing over Joe's shoulder. "Good, good," West said patting the shoulder. "Now the second line. The assassin is here."

Joe chuckled without meaning to. He wiped his grin with the back of the glove and tried to keep from laughing.

"Assassin," said West. "A-S-S-"

"A . . . S . . . S . . . Okay."

"A-S-S-"

"Two times? The same thing?"

"That's right."

"Hey, West—" Joe laughed—"Do you see what it says? That's really how it starts?"

"Correct."

"Ass Ass?"

"Keep your mind on your printing, Joe."

Joe tried to print what West spelled out, but when he looked at the word he started laughing again. Then he tried to print without noticing ASS ASS. But the thought of ASS ASS sitting there expecting him to look was just too much and he had to laugh or choke. Joe struggled to print, West leaning sternly by his elbow, but each time he touched the pencil to the paper Joe started laughing. West got angry and Joe got worse, got hoarse, his eyes teary. Then a drop of spit from Joe's poor mouth fell onto the letter. Joe stared at it, dumbfounded. "That's not, that's not my fingerprints," he gasped. "No dirty fingerprints on Ass Ass!" Joe cried, and West lunged and grabbed away the letter. West ripped it in two—and two again—"See your letter?"

"I see it! I see it!" roared Joe.

"Okay we do it again—take all day—no difference to me," West asserted, his venom in his shrug. "Rest your hand, take a walk, and when you come back, if you come back, we'll do the letter again."

"I made a change," West said when Joe walked in the door fifteen minutes later after walking to a spot that kept him out of range of West's house. "I made a change, it's slightly different. Not because of you. It's just improved."

Joe sat down, sober after his time outside, all drained of laughter. The giddiness was gone, leaving him spent and glum as he sat down to the stubby-pointed pencil and a fresh sheet of paper and slowly put on the glove. The work went easily this time, allowing for Joe's ponderous block printing, West standing behind him, bent and eager, until Joe dropped the pencil and stretched his fingers and West with his gloved hand snatched up the letter to Robinson:

> DEATH TO TYRANTS
> AN EAGLE IS IN THE WINGS
> THIS IS HIS WARNING FROM NOWHERE

"Next the envelope," West said to Joe. And that went smoothly too:

> CANDIDATE GEORGE ROBINSON
> LEGION AVENUE
> JERICHO

"No return address. The Nowhere takes care of it," smiled West. He licked the flap of the envelope, sealed it, licked and pressed on the stamp. All licks were enclosed free of charge. Joe was still sitting at the table and staring at the sink when West hurried out the door.

The only letterbox in Jericho stood outside the post office—across town—past the city hall—across Legion Avenue—up a sidestreet. The fat, safe, red-white-and-blue letterbox stood all alone in the hazy Sunday morning light when West with his kid-gloved hands on the handlebars and his letter in his shirt pocket came pedaling up to it and stopped, not dismounting, sitting perched on the seat, one leg braced for balance, his letter in his hand, holding it and slowly fanning himself.

Finally to do something—after months of thinking—finally a day. But to do something without really doing anything, not the main thing, not anything unstoppable, a letter wasn't a blast in the chest.

Do and don't do. Act and pretend—delay—always work up to it, stroke it, coax it. Scare Robinson. Scare himself? Oh sure. From doing it?

West ceased his fanning, here on the brink, he and the letter he held. Its wait in a dark box and passage through neutral hands might as well not be. All his sightings of Robinson, Robinson's sight of him, might as well not be. The letter canceled all. It was contact with Robinson, first contact. Contact one.

He opened the slot of the letterbox and let it go.

CHAPTER 27

MONDAY MORNING being the cold awakening it is—the splash in the eye, the toe in the icy pool—Monday morning on Legion Avenue had that same baptismal chill of Monday mornings everywhere.

The Red Owl Store awning comes noisily rolling down, cranked by cranky Henry or by Joe. A whole lot livelier than Sam, the red of Sam's barber pole begins to chase itself around. In the Sagebrush Café, from table to grill and back, Ellie's clean white apron starts life in America anew; and druggist Will Carpenter stabs a key into a keyhole and opens another week in the town he eases headaches for and hates. Up and down, east and west, the three small blocks gradually come to life, if more yawningly than on the other days. But common acts come to save the day—acts of dull routine are the army, navy and marines of Monday morning. So it was with Mrs. Prain and the coffee-making, and Mrs. Prain and the watering of the plants, and Mrs. Prain and the opening of the mail.

Mondays, like all days, she collected the mail at the post office on her way to work, dialing the lock of Robinson's business box, a thing apart from the Robinson family box, and carrying her bundle to the redstone building where Robinson would already be at work. Some mornings he might want her to fish out a piece of correspondence he was impatient for, but ordinarily she set the bundle of mail, bound by a heavy rubber band, on her wholesomely cluttered little desk. Then she filled and started up the coffee pot, then she made the rounds of the plants with her watering can, and then, if she wasn't summoned to dictation or some other task, then she sat down and opened the mail.

As she opened the envelopes, unfolding and smoothing their contents for Robinson, and just starting to perk like the coffee, the phone might ring and she might be asked to buzz him or to take a message, another small moment she enjoyed, but for this quiet span of time her attention and affection were for the mail. She liked opening each different envelope. She had a filigreed ivory letter-opener whose delicacy as she wielded it still would please her eye. She knew each missive when she slipped it out would be much like something in last week's mail and other weeks before, but she loved slitting the envelope and unfolding the crispy paper, just for itself, just as she cherished Robinson's assembly campaign for its colored maps and posters and brochures. There never was a great deal of mail for his campaign; most of the letters were for George Robinson the attorney and sometimes for George Robinson the mayor. So when the envelope addressed to Candidate George Robinson reached the top of the pile, with its obviously forgotten return address and its somehow, to Eleanor Prain, sympathetic printing, when she saw it, she purposely saved it for last, the way she might save the maraschino cherry served on top of a creamy dessert. And so, with one thing and another, and Monday's mail being the heaviest of the week, it was the middle of the morning and starting that slow bend toward lunchtime, when she finally took up the long white envelope with the childishly appealing printing, opened it, took out and unfolded the sheet of paper, and turned it right side up.

Mrs. Prain was a creature of decorum. She didn't scream; her cry lodged in her chest like a bad pot-luck pie. Groping at her desk, her face drained to her upswept wheat-colored hair, she found her legs with difficulty, but once standing she ran with the letter extended toward Robinson's door.

The letter hit Robinson's eyes like a spray of buckshot: DEATH ... EAGLE ... WINGS ... NOWHERE ... "What is this?" he said half-angrily. And when Eleanor Prain helplessly shook her head, Robinson whispered: "It came in the mail?" He rose quickly to put an arm around her and walk her back to her desk. "Sit down. Don't do anything. Don't answer the phone. Don't worry . . . Just sit. It's a hoax."

He closed his office door behind him and dialed the chief of police. As he spilled his news to Hank, who sat at headquarters two blocks away, a dread crept over Robinson.

"Hank—don't bring the car. Walk over. Look unconcerned."

Rainey was the reason: she might be downtown shopping. He didn't want Rainey passing by and seeing the patrol car parked out front. Minimize—contain. Stay in control. As he sat and watched the door, waiting for Hank to come, he remembered that the last time Hank crossed his threshold it was to tell him that a loaded rifle had been stolen, more than likely by a kid. Next, his thoughts latched onto the only other threatening letter to have appeared in Jericho, Dixie Carpenter's printed sex note. By the time Hank was seated and scanning the letter, Robinson had produced a theory about a prankster kid who stole a rifle and dreamed up sex notes and death threats just to frighten people. "Not a young kid. An older kid," he urged on Hank, whose quietness grew as he looked at the printed letter and the face of the envelope, lying side by side on the desk.

"I think it was a kid who took the rifle. And I damn well know it was a kid who wrote Dixie's note. But no kid wrote this letter. Don't kid yourself, George. This is a threat of assassination."

"Assassination?"

"Look at this guy. He's got a grudge against the world. He see tyrants. He knows you're an influential man, he reads you're running for the State House, he writes to 'Candidate George Robinson.' "

"Oh God. I knew it was that. Rainey—she mustn't know!"

Hank grabbed him by the arm and anchored him down. "Sit down, George. Sit. Nobody's scaring Rainey. I'm not even saying that this is anything more than a harmless letter from a very demented guy."

Hank picked up the letter by a corner, looked at the reverse side and let it drop, the same with the long white envelope. "Postmark Jericho; this morning. That means it was mailed between noon Saturday when the post office closed and very early today. Dropped in the mail by somebody living here or somebody driving through. It's unusual printing, very crude. Have you ever seen this printing before?"

Robinson shook his head.

" 'Death to Tyrants, an eagle is in the wings, this is his warning from nowhere.' " Hank's hand strayed and stopped, just short of touching the letter. "Very neat words, almost pretty. I read the words and I see the printing and I get a very funny feeling. It bothers me. This is not an easy guy."

Still pondering the letter, Hank drew a notepad out of his back pocket, and a pen from a row in his shirt pocket, and only then encountered Robinson's sagging, staring face. "This is dumb of me," Hank said, shoving back his chair. "Nothing says we have to do this now. I'll do some thinking and come back later."

"Stay—stay, let's get it over with. To tell the truth, I could use the company. No. I don't have any mortal enemies, to answer question number one. Except for this guy, evidently."

"Take your time . . . Think about it a while. Don't rule anything out."

Hank was giving him all the time in the world to answer the question of who might want him dead. But Robinson couldn't focus his mind, things kept skimming across his mind as over ice. Faces skidded by, clients, acquaintances, adversaries, cranks, the petty aggrieved. Will Carpenter's face appeared. Will the Pill skidded by, and old book-bitch Alpha Davis on her old hickory stick legs. Puny Will Carpenter was out to assassinate him? Old Alpha Davis had mailed him a death threat?

"Tyrant," Hank said after some minutes passed. "Anyone ever call you that?" Hank stared into space as more time slipped away. "Eagle? Does that suggest anything?"

"Will Carpenter," Robinson blurted, "I had a run-in with Will Carpenter a few months back, over those sex threats to his kid. We had an argument. Will got sore at me."

"Threatened you?"

"I don't remember. Possibly. Probably."

Hank made notes as Robinson described the scene, and Robinson, watching him do it, felt more solid ground slide away. It wasn't Will's handwriting and it wasn't Will's hate. To please Hank he threw him Will Carpenter because he was too embarrassed to throw him Alpha Davis, and neither of them had anything to do with the letter. Who was the eagle in the wings? Where was No-where? Even Rainey's rare pal, the cyclist, the bookkeeper, came into Robinson's head, but Robinson swept it away with the rest out of sheer self-preservation. He was almost getting more sick of this than he was scared, stomach-sick, queasy-ill.

"As long as we're talking about odd guys," Hank said slowly, "I never really met the guy . . . but that helper who works over at the Red Owl Store—Joe Something?—he's not from anyplace around here and he's pretty different looking for a grocer's helper. I could never figure out why he came here in the first place. Ever have any business with him?"

"Never. Nothing."

"He seems to be a pal of that West who does the bookkeeping, who knows your wife I think? I've driven by and seen him com-ing out of West's house once or twice. But he's different—he's no bookkeeper. I think I'll stop by the Red Owl after hours and pose a couple of questions."

Hank made a note of it, then picked the letter up gingerly. "I'll take this with me now. The state police will want a look. They'll check it out for fingerprints and whatever else they can find. We might be lucky." He let the letter fall into its fold, slipped it back into its envelope, put away his notepad, and clipped his pen into his pocket. All actions were stamped official. "I'll make inquiries around the town. I'll nose around and be around. Pete will help out too; we'll give you all the protection we can. This guy may write again . . . We can't say anything for certain, we're up against the unpredictable. Until we know differently, we act as if the threat is real. Stick close to home. Don't go out alone at night. Avoid lonely places. Stay out of crowds. Be careful."

"You want me to stay out of crowds in an election campaign?"

"Act within reason. Be sensible. I understand the election an-gle and Pete and I will do our best, but remember we're only two men. If the slightest odd thing happens, pick up the phone and call me—day or night. You don't keep anything at home, ah, in the way of self-defense?"

"No guns! That's all I need to explain to Rainey. God, a gun."

"Rainey, right. No gun. Easy does it; no weapon. We'll manage, we'll come up with something. We'll talk about it later."

"I think I'd like to go home," said Robinson.

"Sure you would."

Hank's gruff-grave voice was followed by Hank's big hand proffered across the desk, and Robinson seized it and held onto it.

"Mr. Mayor, let me drive you home. I can have my car here in five minutes."

The invitation lulled, Hank's car looming as plush as Hank's hand; but Robinson in the end let go of both. "Thanks, friend. There's enough of a problem waiting for me there. I'd just as soon not have to lie about why the police chief brought me home."

He watched Hank go out with the letter in his hand, heard the outer door close as Hank and the death threat moved to the swept sidewalks and housewives' traffic of downtown Jericho. Poor Eleanor Prain who was taking phone messages for him should be allowed to go home, but Robinson for a minute couldn't get out of his chair or even project a voice. What kind of lunatic fanatic would assassinate a longshot candidate, a novice, a beginner? If Rainey ever found out—Rainey who always opposed his candidacy and up to now for no good reason. She'd make him quit—not quit, don't say quit!—but rein in his whole campaign, and just when the great fall push was supposed to begin. And that time of challenge was almost here. He would really have to stay out of crowds and stick close to home if Rainey ever knew.

He had one fear too many, the death threat and Rainey knowing. The one fear rubbed up against and skinned away the other. It was such a small town. Where could he ever hide except at home with Rainey? Where would Hank and Pete hide their police protection? The state police Hank was sending the letter to, where would they hide if they came to town, so as not to let Rainey know?

Hank was smart. Hank said he understood the angles. What else was it Hank just said, said about him and Pete? *We're only two men. But we'll come up with something.* A third cop! A third cop was the angle Hank best understood. Seize the letter, scare the mayor, maybe get a brand new cop to follow the mayor around. A third cop was being born behind Hank's back in Hank's other big hand.

Fear of the letter and fear of Rainey knowing, he had these two fears and they bled like dyes, one across the other. Imagining the one brought on bleeding in the other. It was such a bloody tiny town. Hank questions Will Carpenter who talks to Rainey . . . Hank questions Joe Something who talks to pal bookkeeper who talks to Rainey . . . Robinson shot out of his chair and ran past Mrs. Prain and out onto Legion Avenue in pursuit of Hank. The police chief and the letter were crossing the city hall park on the way back to police headquarters when Hank turned at the clatter of steps and a breathless Robinson ran him down.

He made Hank give him back the letter. It took some doing; Hank refused then argued and then pleaded with Robinson, warning him of a danger that could even reach to the members of his family. "Don't fight me, Hank. Call it a political decision."

"It's an ass of a decision."

"Forget there ever was a letter. No extra protection—no third cop!"

"I never suggested it."

"And don't question anybody. Not Will Carpenter, not Joe Something, not anybody—I personally vouch for everybody."

"Pete will have to know. I won't keep it from my deputy."

"Only Pete. No state police. Nobody else!"

"This is foolhardy, George."

Robinson hurried, letter in hand, back down Legion Avenue and straight into his private office, where he shut his door, moved quickly and locked the letter in his safe. Then he asked himself: Why did I do that? Suppose there was some unlikely need for the letter, suppose there were other unlikely letters, suppose there was an actual unlikely attempt—there were good, sound reasons why he couldn't tear the letter up and throw it away. Adrenalin was flowing. Instinct was showing the way. Eleanor! He found her still at her desk with her hand on the telephone as if ready to snatch it up just to hush its ringing. He sat himself on the edge of her desk and told her, first, that the letter was definitely a hoax, second, that good news though that was, she mustn't breathe a word of the letter to anyone, not to Mrs. Robinson, not to her own husband, because the police chief believed that telling other people would only invite more letters from the mischievous perpetrator of the hoax. Then he patted her on the back, sent her to lunch and told her to take the rest of the day off.

So Mrs. Prain was silenced. Hank was silenced. The letter was in the safe. All of that had been accomplished. So why was his heart pounding as he put on his jacket and prepared to show his face in the street?

Looking to right and left, seeing the whole of the little downtown, from the Jericho depot and a continent to the corner grocer and the sky, unable to believe that he had come out running just minutes before, Robinson moved from the step of his law office building and onto Legion Avenue. Street and sidewalk were calm and clear; it was getting on toward noon, a time of day when the pulse had dropped again. Robinson's eyes flitted as he walked, like carnivore flies, lighting on every door and window. As he passed by John's Saloon and looked in, who should he see sitting at the bar doing his bookkeeping but the bookkeeper. The fact of just having had the bookkeeper in this thoughts, and now seeing him in the window, startled Robinson, as nervous as he was. What right did the bookkeeper have to sit near the window like that? Why was the bookkeeper sitting on a barstool? Why was he working? Why was he alive?

The streets guided Robinson home, the shady trees, the white front porches, the washline-draped backyards. Nothing overcame the quiet. Soon it changed complexion like the scuttling leaves. The very calm was undependable. Death to tyrants, wrote the eagle in the wings. Robinson's steps hastened as he came up the path to home. Home brought relief, release and a kind of light-seeking fear that came rushing toward the surface. Rainey was on her way out to have lunch at Margaret's. She accepted it of course, his excuse for coming home, his invention of a terrible headache that was not so invented anymore. When she took the time to bring him aspirin, water and a hot washcloth for his head, he was so touched by it, so shamed by his own deceit, so shattered by his love, he almost reached out to touch her precious cheek.

Someone's out to assassinate me.

Honey they're out to get me.

I might die.

The instant she left the house he dumped the water, got the whisky out of the cabinet, splashed it into the glass and gulped a few fingers down. He carried the glass upstairs and swallowed the rest sitting on the bed. Then he pulled off his shoes and fell back on it exactly as he was, dressed, gaunt, sweating, waxlike, the damp washrag, a token of Rainey, spread across his forehead. The whisky was working—Robinson's head was going around and around. Would someone really try to kill him? Why did they want to assassinate him? Who was calling him a tyrant? Why?

You were swimming by yourself in a sunny pleasant pool. All of a sudden there was a little splash next to you, and circles moving in the water, round and round, getting bigger and bigger, the way they would if someone had tossed a rock in the water. You looked around but no one was there. All you saw were those circles moving in the water, but you knew that something had been thrown, and you knew that somebody out there had thrown it, and that whoever it was must have first decided to throw it. The warning from nowhere was the rock thrown in the pool. But it wasn't only the throwing, it was the deciding, the mulling it over, the thinking and thinking about it, the festering thinking, that cast of mind, that pot of stew, that crowded Robinson's being, as though he shared place and time, this planet, this minute, with this unseen being.

Nowhere was out there somewhere.

CHAPTER 28

MEANWHILE, AWAY from Robinson and West, beyond the help of
Hank and Pete, the fall of the year was closing in on the short
hair and pug nose, the small face and tidy body of that unmo-
lested privacy of space that was Dixie Carpenter.

The Dixie of *Dixie gets a physical education real soon* and
Soon Dixie—the Olympian-to-be—Jericho's star—was like a
baby Eve being torn from Eden, in the view of her frantic father.
Will knew there would be no protection by the town, no added
cop, no curfew. All summer long, visions of rape paraded through
his mind, Dixie's rape by the high school boys. Which boys had
sent the sex threats? Were there many more than one? What
would they do to his child? His parade of boys tormented Will.
Days dawned when the father was afraid of his own thoughts.
But then he looked at Dixie and remembered the boys and he
couldn't stop the trampling parade.

Will never told Dixie about the threats that had come to their
house. He couldn't put a warning into words that would warn
and yet not soil her. But Will begged her to work hard at her
Olympic practice. He let fall heavy words about the roughneck
high school boys. He invented reasons she should stay home at
night, ways she could help more with housework, why she
should watch her little brother. She was the only one in Jericho
with an added cop and a curfew. The rest of the town lived open

and free but theirs was a house besieged, a troubled house, haunted and occasionally dusted by Molly, its sweet and drowsy ghost. Will could never blame Dixie for arousing thoughts of rape—Dixie wasn't Sissie, the father of both children knew. But blame of his own kind burned in Will's house like the burning shit of hellnight on his doorstep, blame of Sissie for being Sissie, Molly for being useless, blame for the little brother because he had a boy's form but was fatally small, like Will.

The little brother, a virtual watchdog on his sister, a little son almost, usually followed Dixie to her Olympic practice grounds and then over to the town swimming pool, a place awash in sunlight, crowded with kids, a loud wet bubble on flat dry land under the baking sun. The little brother accompanied her here because he wanted to play and be with her, as ever. But the scarved and bundled sister of the winter seemed a warmer being to him than the pensive Dixie of the pool. She played less with the little brother, endured him less; when he nagged at her, she even fought him less, as if there were a hollow ring to Dixie's temper. Swimming slow laps or sunbathing on the bank, she was as good as dead mackerel to the restive little brother. He had a best friend, Jamie Robinson, who was usually there, but he missed his oldtime older sister, and besides, her resistance in front of his friend wounded and embarrassed him. In revenge, and because he was less afraid of her now, he would happen to splash her as she floated on her back, and accidentally splash her while she sunbathed, imitating the drollery of the high school boys, who seemed like unexpected allies to the discontented little brother. He splashed her and he sulked by the edge of the pool, his the same round face as hers, the same pug nose, entrenched in an expression that was like a sullen claim.

The high school boys were brazen but they were also cautious in their attitude to Dixie. She was not like other girls, they agreed among themselves, and it wasn't only that she was the daughter of their favorite enemy, Mr. C. She was the star of track and gym, with talent, determination, and a temper, and the girls' world record for chilly distance. It was a novelty to see Dixie Carpenter supine and sleeping instead of cartwheeling or dashing toward a finish line. Dixie was different from other girls, went their watchful speculation. Some wondered if she had an actual cunt,

since no one had ever seen it. Dixie had a cunt, her defenders
said, and she inherited it from her father: "Mr. C." They con-
trived to jump and splash quite close to where she sunbathed on
the bank. Their splashing showered Dixie and when she sat up
straight and screamed at them they hung their heads and
laughed. Then Dixie would peer around her and go back to sunbathing in her very modest bathing suit, modest except that she
dropped the shoulder straps when she sunbathed and forgot to
hold on to them when she suddenly sat up. The soft white sight,
the dumpling skin, was something the high school boys could
feel in their adam's apples. It drew their eyes, kept them splashing and set their minds to working. They all knew Dixie Carpenter the aloof Olympian-to-be; they had heard from their older
brothers about sister Sissie's escapades. Blood is blood—Sissie
and Dixie—day by day they waded in their thoughts, as though
wading from the shallows of the pool to the enthralling deep.

The lazy smell of suntan oil, the constant bleating of radios
turned up, the boy and girl lifeguards on their perch—as she lay
there and listened, stretched out in the sun, it was a vast and
clouded question to Dixie Carpenter as to why she trudged here
and why she stayed each solitary day after her Olympic practice.
Dixie only knew that she was tired, tired of the game she was
playing with the town.

She was the girl who was going to the Olympics, that was the
flag she flew. It wasn't hard to keep it flying over flat, smug
Jericho. Dixie the runner was routinely first in trackmeets with
other towns. In the summer, by herself, she worked at her gym-
nastic somersaults, her back-flips and cartwheels. The town believed, and why wouldn't they? She seemed a wonderful enough
athlete to them. She was quick, fast, stubborn, a winner, and she
was forever practicing. Dixie alone on earth knew that she was
practicing for the never-to-be. When she sprawled on the grass
of her practice grounds, when she sat and hugged her knees, it
was about her whole unhappy life that Dixie was thinking. She
wished the town would stop talking—the paper would stop writing—her father would stay home and stop rooting for her. There
was this picture the world had of Dixie Carpenter always sticking out her heart to be first across the finish line. If only she
could just be average, daydreamed Dixie to her grass-skinned

knees. If only she came in second a little more, stumbled once or twice—if she could try a little less.

She was tired of trying to be first. The breath of that girl had expired. Even if she might be as good as people thought, even supposing the impossible was true, she couldn't try anymore, so either way something was missing. This summer, more and more, Dixie started to hurt herself in practice. When it wasn't her back it was a twisted knee, if it wasn't that it was a hand she jammed. Sometimes Dixie felt like throwing her body away with the garbage. All of her practice all year long, plus things at home and her brother to look after—schoolwork and school sports—housework and homework. She was so tired of trying.

There was a part of Dixie growing very old while the rest of Dixie bloomed, a deathly part, just budding. She carried it, this fetal weariness, this baby death, inside her all the time; carried it down track runways, over the hurdles, over the parallel bars; she tucked it under her desk at school and into bed with her at night. Dixie was so tired of trying.

Dixie cried sometimes—about her mother, not a normal mother—about her father too. Be different from Sissie, her father asked, and Dixie wished for that also; she knew she had to be. There were times when she hated Sissie, the town tramp Sissie of old, who turned a little sister into that most infamous child of all, the good example. If she had no friends, and trouble at home, if she had something less than a mother, Dixie had fathers to spare, eager fathers, anxious fathers, a jack-in-the-box father whose head popped up everywhere: be good—be better—be different from Sissie. She had gone miles past being different from Sissie. She was different from the whole town. What was the good of being different, Dixie raged as she wept. Her wish was to be like everyone else, no better.

So Dixie left her practice earlier and earlier, her practice for the never-to-be, and started coming back all those lonesome miles by trudging the narrow distance to the town swimming pool. She started going to the pool, not to sit there but to swim, not to swim but just dip in, not that either but to sunbathe, not to sunbathe but to stay.

Laziness and yards of skin, skin for arm rests, skin for head rests, constant music and the ever-blessing sun—all of it drew

Dixie to the pool. The high school boys collected at the diving end, sunned with girls, sprang off the board, roughhoused and amused themselves, big-boned and unfinished, big and browned, like so many summer gods. These gods of ordinariness kept up their slouching, sidelong interest in Dixie. Something good peeped at them from Dixie's bathing suit, but they were still uncertain what to do with her, still approaching in their rough-house, cautious way as they splashed and gaped to see the melted snow and former ice of Dixie Carpenter's breasts.

And Dixie sunbathed, dove and floated on her back. Floating lightened her, like a fresh new faith, her arms outstretched, her legs apart, her body resting, not running, her spirit floating, not trying. As she floated, the water lapped to Dixie's thighs and up around her bust, framing a picture of her that Dixie was not unconscious of, even though her eyes were closed. As she sun-bathed, boys splashed her and she screamed, and her scream con-tained as undulant a plea as did her unstrapped bathing suit. Dixie sunbathed and floated for the gods of ordinariness whom she had known and thwarted all her life, floated and sunbathed as though she were Sissie, almost imagining herself in Sissie's skin to give herself the heart. She wanted to come back the final mile to the town. She wanted fun, pleasures, friends and not to be different. She was so tired of being Dixie Carpenter, the book-worm of the locker room and gym.

Dixie ignored her little brother when he tugged on her to join him in the pool. She stopped wearing her bathing cap because with her hair tucked in she thought she looked exactly like her brother. She felt she was appealing, when she studied other girls. With her eyes closed, her straps down, a knee alluringly raised, Dixie lay in the sun, feeling brown on the outside and pink in-side, like a roast that might soon be done.

What if she got pregnant, was one of Dixie's stumbling dreads. She had others. Being felt and feeling, being seen and seeing, all were on her list of private dreads. But pregnant—Sissie herself had never been through that. What would her father say? What would he think? How could she go on practicing? How could she compete? What if she got pregnant, was one of Dixie's sinking, floating thoughts as she lay by the pool in the sun.

Two friends, two college boys, home for the summer, had begun to separate themselves from the younger gods of ordinariness at the pool. Two friends, one rangy, one husky, both tall, emerged from the noise and the spray like quiet bronzes condensing themselves. Always stationed in the same place, always together, the two worked odd hours for the local moving and storage company, whose warehouse stood within easy loping distance of the swimming pool.

These friends, the two tall movers, would rest on their side and an elbow and scan the scene around the pool and not infrequently come to rest their eyes on Dixie. After some minutes passed, every day, they would roll off their backs and rise to their feet and take a little stroll around the pool. It wasn't these two who sent the sex threats about Dixie to her father; that was the handiwork of younger slighter gods, not out of high school. But like everyone at the pool they knew about those jokes on Mr. C, just as they knew the lore of the town about Sissie. They would rise together and take their stroll, and there was a little song they sang as they parted around the towel where Dixie sunbathed.

> *I wish I was in Dixie*
> *Hooray*
> *Hooray*
> *I wish I was in Dixie*
> *Hooray—*

From her towel Dixie watched them approach her and come past through the narrow sun-slits of her eyes. If she jerked her head away and made an angry face, it wasn't that Dixie fathomed the meaning of the song—it was the constant scary recognition of her name. She had never spoken a word to either of the two, who were several years and social light years ahead of her in school. "Don't say my name, you don't know me," was not a speech that Dixie felt inclined to say. She was drawn, alerted and afraid. She squinted at the two of them with her sun-slit eyes and they looked back with their far-seeing ones from the opposite side of the pool. When she dove into the water, so would they, to rise unnervingly near her at either hand; they hummed the song to her as she floated, and they wove underwater around Dixie. Though she was as oblivious to the message of their song as to the sex threats about her to her father, Dixie sent the important message back, the annoyance, the temper, the indolence, the sunbathing, the something the sharp eye, the boundless floating on her back. Her fear carried her to the place where indifference had carried Sissie: she couldn't have been approached by one alone. She floated between and clashed with the movers in the pool. They followed her ashore, behind her back. They grabbed and threw her in the water, then jumped in after her and tossed her back and forth. As one stood making peace, a hand on her shoulder, the other swam between her legs, like a whale upending her. She was angry, gasping, bewildered and open for more. They each ran off the end of the diving board, carrying Dixie kicking. They lay beside her on a towel, taking turns, Dixie's and a bronzed leg touching, a radio playing music into two ears.

The little brother was no match for the tall, intriguing, bruising movers. His sister's two new friends kept him away by merely being there with her. He watched the three of them from down in the water when they were sunbathing, and sat wrapped in his towel while they cavorted in the pool, blue-lipped and chilled, wrapped up in hurt, watching unfold with unknowing eyes the very thing that was dreaded by Will.

Around behind the warehouse of the moving and storage company, cornered by one of the movers at last, Dixie Carpenter, who had poured a summer of her life into the back-flip and one-handed and no-handed cartwheels, sat pushed up against the back seat of a parked car, her bare legs out from under her, her bare feet pigeon-toed—a husky shoulder driving under her face and her face trying to be brave.

Dixie did get pregnant. And Will did find out of course and rant and call it rape. But that discovery lay tucked away and hidden in the future. It was many weeks before the practice stopped, the trying stopped, and snow had fallen, before Dixie was delivered of her weariness, her baby death.

CHAPTER 29

THE OLD place stood about a mile outside of town, set back a little distance from its leaning, nameless mailbox.

It could all be seen from the road, the deserted farm buildings and weedy yard, the boarded-up house, the sheds, the unhinged grainary, the barn. It was all visible from the road, but not the backs of things, the tiny ghost town around in back whose men and women and kids were the birds, and West was at rifle practice.

His bicycle was down in the overgrown grass behind the barn, a sun-dappled place that was ringed by shady trees. Behind the barn was the ghost town center of things, where West held his methodical practices, portioning out his bullets with skinflint care so as to stretch the mornings out. Each day when he finished he carried the rifle, shell casings and other traces of himself up to the loft of the barn and hid them under the years-old hay that was still there. He had biked everything out late one night and when he had practiced to the full he would bring it back home the same way.

Not many cars came by along the gravel road that the old buildings faced, not many thrill or curiosity seekers rode by. He had the day pretty much all to himself. It was always peaceful back of the barn except for the crack of the shots and the thwack of a bullet through and around the target, a brown paper bag with rough circles and a bull's-eye that he thumbtacked to the wall of the barn. The red crayon bull's-eye danced on and off the sights and the rifle stock kicked and antagonized before West had tamed it to his person through memory, grimness and desire. In the army he had been an average marksman firing the rifle in basic training without much like or dislike. But after his army days ended, when he drifted alone in Chicago, he was drawn to shooting galleries in cavernous all-night arcades. He went back to one gallery over and over, eating up his discharge pay. The gallery man said he had "the knack" and West distrusted him and disliked him and believed him.

The shredded bag wore a human look in the end, a flight of tattered mouths and gaping eyes. The oil smell of the rifle of the Jericho Police Department yielded to a smell of burnt powder, a wisp, a whiff, of the unknown. West brought out fresh targets to demolish, big beef tomatoes and also pumpkins, which were just coming into season, good, soft targets that reacted, in a way. He set them on a distant mound of dirt or arranged them fruitlike on the boughs of trees. He practiced quick reloading, and just once, not to expend his bullets more, filled the extra clip and put it to the side, fast fired the loaded gun, fast replaced the empty clip with the full one and then practically had to sit on himself to keep from blasting away with those rounds too. Whenever he practiced, he wore the tight kid gloves. He tried to make everything the same as it would be, as far as possible. He had paid a night visit to the Feed and Seed loft, throwing the light of a flashlight around, disturbing the sleep of old sacks of meal and such, and kneeling down at the window to look across at the city hall steps. Now he climbed up to the loft of the barn and fired at his targets from an opening in order to practice firing from a height. The shots kissed the pumpkin—kissed the beef tomato. Devotion to the plan and his purist nature kept him kneeling there and firing down until by midday the loft was almost unbreathably hot.

He would climb down when he was finished and sit in the shade back of the barn. He watched clouds, the sky, birds flying. A mourning dove was always there. After his firing stopped, it always came back—he listened for it. When he was about the age of ten, when he was new in Jericho, the father of a boy in his class kept promising to take the both of them hunting. They would all get up before dawn, take guns and drive to the woods somewhere and the boys would learn to hunt. Or so the boy always said his father said.

He brought a sandwich along with him to eat when he felt hungry. He liked to eat his lonely lunch and then stretch out there behind the barn. From time to time his hand felt the rifle. He enjoyed shooting it, merely as a sport. He liked handling it. The solid feel and machine smell of it interested him. From the treetops the bird sang to him like the mourning doves in Rainey's backyard. Sometimes he closed his eyes and slept and dreamt all sorts of things. Guns made him think of fathers.

PART THREE

CHAPTER 30

THE JERICHO High School marching band—it arrives with fall the same as newborn school supplies, the firemen's pancake supper and swirling leaves. Each afternoon the varsity football team will scrimmage on its practice field and every day the marching band rehearses through the streets of town, preparing for its season in the sun between the halves. The Jericho High School marching band sports no uniforms when they rehearse. Wearing light shirts and shorts one day and warm sweaters and bluejeans almost overnight, they come marching through the streets as the leaves are turning—day in and day out—coming around the same streetcorners playing the same marching songs time and time again. A lone schoolgirl leads with a baton, on either side strut the would-be pom-pom girls, and everywhere at once is the band-master, a teacher with a whistle to his lips, scampering both to see and hear his ragtag bunch whose trombones, trumpets, drums and cymbals send thrilling music into Jericho's kitchens and backyards.

Fall never lasts too long in Jericho—fall is the short-winded season of the year, a far cry from those brilliant autumns in the wooded East where the leaves take their good time dying, which is what so pleases the eye. Here, for what huddled trees there are, the end is quick, a comparative beheading. The first snow falls before the drooping sunflowers do and Alpha Davis's old

223

enemy the sun soon grows too feeble for the marrows of everyone else; by the time the jack o' lanterns are flickering through cut-out eyes, the season will be running out of breath. The town digs in against all this with all the busy, threadbare make-do of the pioneers. Dozing social clubs reawaken, church groups recircle in their basements, the winter bowling league resumes. If there is an election going on, the hometown name appears on stakes in many front yards, testaments to the straight and narrow loyalty of the dwellers within. The old crew returns to the card table in the back of John's Saloon. In a land of empty vistas and few real firesides, there are a hundred variations of the hearth. Some dark nights, in a perfect spirit of brotherhood, the Jericho volunteer fire department speeds to a bonfire sighted glowing near the limits of the town, someone burning leaves there on the edge.

THIS WAS the shape of Robinson's fall campaign as it passed through the mind of the candidate as he lay in bed at night restive and sleepless . . .

There would be speeches in all the towns. There would be informal evenings with the candidate in shirtsleeves in certain selected homes, and afternoon coffees in suit and tie tailored for the women voters. An open house with free food and drink would take place in the candidate's happy home. Up to a thousand and more people would flock to the big, climactic Event even now in the works. Special mailings, phone calls, handshaking and doorbell ringing would all chime in down to the very end.

These were the campaign issues as the candidate from Jericho saw them: the old shopworn agency reform issue, the bore-them-to-death perennial sales tax issue, the bore-them-and-drown-them water-for-the-west issue. "The only real issue," as every pronouncement written and spoken would say, "is Dwayne Armstead and his dreary record of so-called public service."

The already being delivered advertising included: front yard stakes bearing the candidate's name, gumbacked posters with his photograph ("Elect George Robinson"), attractive leaflets ("This is George Robinson"), and timely one-page handouts ("Come and Meet George Robinson"). Regular ads would appear in the local papers and pasteboard signs with his name and *Politics is People* be placed beside selected roadside mailboxes.

The feverish-to-start challenger's strategy was: Challenge—attack. Ignite the crowd. Smoke Armstead out. Make a real campaign of it. Draw Armstead into debate or make the most of his squirming out—the Empty Chair. Win with the smart vote, the young vote and the women's vote; youth and brains versus age and Same Dwayne Armstead.

The youthful candidate's campaign treasury would include: contributions from local businessmen, starting with his braintrust of town councilmen; funds from sundry other individuals; the take from personal appeals and coffee party collections. All contributions welcome. Financing was still largely self.

The trim campaign staff consisted of: Mrs. Prain on clerical; the braintrust to place the signs and posters, make the phone calls and ring the doorbells; paid high school boys to deliver the leaflets and handouts.

Consultants to the campaign were: Miss Brown on tactics via occasional long-distance telephone call. Hank on routine matters of traffic and safety for the open house and the Event. The braintrust on likely names and homes for campaigning purposes and all manner of such detail except those calling for brains or serious trust.

There were special problems connected with the campaign: An unwilling wife who said she hated politics. A source of pain and a political misfortune; but winning would help change her mind.

A death threat, sender unknown, existence known to only a very few. Police protection refused. Fear of the threat: sufficient; but with no palpable effect on the young candidate's campaign.

Chief aide, adviser and confidant to the candidate: None.

He would be his own campaign manager from the beginning to the end.

CHAPTER 31

A CROWD of nine attended a speech the challenger exploded in a veterans' hall in Malden. Fourteen people gathered in their town green and listened to the bombshell speech on folding chairs with folded hands. Two hundred printed handouts released by a fast-cycling high school boy produced a group of eight at a Come-and-Meet-George-Robinson evening with the candidate.

The marching band drummed its way through empty streets and now Robinson's true campaign began, an uphill struggle at the very best, a lonely race without a visible opponent and mostly playing out against deaf ears, from the little tree-lined towns and tiny depot stops to the house-and-barn horizons of the district. Sometimes a member of the braintrust rode beside him on these drives; more often he piled in alone with his speechi-fying lips to keep him company.

Former journeys and his raft of maps ill-prepared the candidate for what he found. Space stared back at Robinson everywhere he went, wearying space between the habitats he sped to, and nearly empty space when he arrived, in the dreary meeting rooms where he installed his poster and a flag—in cold old Legion halls with their rented atmosphere of bingo nights and bandstands.

Dwayne Armstead was an opponent who was scarcely to be seen, as if the old part-time farmer had plowed himself under for the season. He was observed at a church breakfast and then upstairs where he unveiled a stained glass window; he was seen pouring afternoon coffee for his elders at a county nursing home. The Chairman of the Public Power and Rates Committee handed out Eagle Scout badges at the annual banquet, and when he was made an honorary Eagle Scout himself, he called it "the proudest moment of my life." Confident or lazy, lazy or crafty, he made no partisan speeches, mentioned no opponent, he never acknowledged an election. Only once did the new Eagle Scout change his lofty attitude, when he broke ground for a new emergency power system for a local clinic, and recalled for those who were present, "the long years of service that I hope to continue on behalf of the people of this district."

None of this was any great surprise to Robinson, who had foreseen that classic strategy by the incumbent, and whose challenger's axe would chase Armstead's goose all across September. But being armed and poised was one thing and executing quite another. The fast start he counted on was slipping by him every day. The women and young voters he had to bring forth still failed to show themselves. The promising interest he had seen in the spring was proving an ephemeral bloom, the first flush of novelty produced by the man who was running against Dwayne Armstead.

The usual small disasters befell the fledgling candidate. The predictable trail dogged the steps of the man who acted as his own campaign manager. His Grafton-for-Robinson signs ended up in another town and for weeks stood unplanted. A hall that had been rented for the evening was found occupied by a lively social-and-dance, whose host amiably invited Robinson's people in. The candidate hurried to an evening with himself to discover that no one was expecting him at that address. Phone calls to the braintrust availed him nothing. He never knew where it was that a group of people had waited for him, who they were, or if there had ever been any such people at all.

But not all of his scurrying led to nothing—not every cupboard in the district was bare. His widows gave a coffee party for him. The two patrons of the turkey barbecue fluffed their wings and created a table and a prospect for him that put his own wife to shame. For one golden afternoon he basked in the glow of promises exchanged with a procession of dear old ladies. He had a very successful Evening with the Candidate at the home of the man with a stump for a hand. That faithful follower assembled a living room full of friends from other battles, some being avowed dissenters, some being unusual persons like himself, and Robinson spent an evening that took him down unfamiliar paths into concerns and problems that he never dreamed existed, an evening of rapt faces all tilted to him, that left him shaken with the solemn truth of his own slogan, the truth that politics was people. But only a few nights passed on the campaign trail when Robinson looked out at his fervent group of loyalists sitting in the small crowd he had drawn. There was the man with the stump for a hand, there was the lank-haired old farmer-weaver, there was the almost too holy girl and the rest of that little band of slighted oddities, people with causes, a few people with grudges, people with time on their hands. "Who am I?" cried Robinson to himself, diverting his eyes. "Am I the candidate of the pitiful, the unfortunate, the unhappy?" With chagrin, he saw himself going down those strange paths with those unfortunate people, and he knew he wouldn't have minded, except that there weren't enough of them. There weren't enough unfortunate people to elect him to the State Assembly. "Why aren't there more of them?" the desperate candidate and his campaign manager wanted to know.

He sat down and rethought his strategy. No new idea, no credible promise, nothing handy sprang to mind. As far behind as he must be, and falling further, and with the sleeping-pill issues there were, he could see no alternative to taunting and swinging at Armstead. Maybe October would be better, prayed the debater of the Empty Chair. He issued a thousand handouts of "Man Wanted—Reward" for anyone who could produce Dwayne Armstead. Miss Brown over long-distance suggested that he ask the interesting question of whether it was proper for the chairman of the Power and Rates Committee to broker a private real estate deal for the chairman of the state's leading utility. Armed with this charge and fresh energy, Robinson went on the attack, but Armstead would not be smoked out, even though Robinson demanded an accounting and called for an honest answer from "my invisible and tongue-tied opponent." Clear-eyed, with an aching heart, he abandoned the Empty Chair because it was too much like the empty seats in his audience. There was a kind of tacit union between them. The empty seats all favored the Empty Chair.

Hope, enthusiasm, disillusion, weariness, dejection—they were like a musical scale that Robinson tripped up and down. His moods controlled his day and made it a torture to sit down to his law practice, the minimal time that he gave to that chained routine. He was always hurrying somewhere, hoping for something, and returning without it. The death threat stood apart. It had no solid shape to it, no face, but cast a shadowy presence that he had come to recognize. Because of Rainey, or through some mingling of his fears, the premonition was always strongest close to home. But he still had to walk out the door each morning and come home after dark each night—he still had to leave home again to walk Big Red to keep Rainey from being suspicious. Some nights he was sure that Hank exaggerated the threat, and then there were the other nights, alone with his street, his dog and the warning from nowhere, when he turned up the collar of his coat and just kept walking.

His name in windows, his face on telephone poles, now mortified the failing candidate. The multiplication of George Robinson everywhere only made him more alone and more absurd. An election campaign, a lucid, reasonable, accepted, public process, had opened up a strange new district for Robinson, one that was dimly lit and solitary, and steadily more cruel, that every day disapproved of him, at every turn knocked his chances down. He had no words for dealing with this district. There were no angry speeches, no long-distance telephone calls that he could make. He had no experience of it either, that might have mapped for him the human outskirts where he was lost.

He developed a physical aversion to the bookkeeper. It went far beyond the contempt of earlier days. Now in one place, now another, he would see that marginal figure standing nearly off the page, and each time he saw him, the skin would crawl on Robinson and a tautness rise to his ears. And a little tale would unfold in Robinson's mind, a tale in which he approaches the men in town who employ the bookkeeper. He informs these men that the bookkeeper is a liar and a thief. He only asks that Rainey who likes and trusts the bug must never know. The grateful men act fast. A thief in their cashboxes, a lying bookkeeper? They all fire the bookkeeper. Nothing avails him. He can't get reasons, he can't get work, he flees the town.

One day soon he would do it, Robinson promised himself. Why not? It would be a public service to erase the bookkeeper. True, he faulted the worm for his wormy access to Rainey, but there were other reasons too why the bookkeeper should be squashed. He was insignificant, weak, a loner, a flop—his reasons for despising the bookkeeper seemed wholly appropriate to Robinson. The truth was, he hated the bookkeeper as an infectious human example, a loathsome carrier of woe. The creature sense by which he would have shrunk from beggars and from a leper made his skin crawl when he saw the bookkeeper. The loner lived as a germ inside himself. The flop lived and breathed inside the slapped-down candidate.

Who could he bring his unhappiness home to but Rainey, although he carried it in secret, since his botched campaign was a secret, the death threat was an absolute secret, and his humiliation by Armstead was a secret in that he never spoke of it in words. Of everything that he felt was missing in his campaign, the floral centerpiece was Rainey. When he spoke to Miss Brown, clever but so far away, he wished for Rainey; as he watched Mrs. Prain, playmate of the gumbacked posters and bright gold stars, he sighed for Rainey, with her natural common sense and hometown touch. Why wouldn't she help him? What difference did it make if she hated politics? The worse it went for him, the more he resented her removal of her person from his campaign. The unrealized women's vote, the empty halls, the cold farmhouse evenings and tepid coffee parties were all her fault. The President of the Tuesday Club had no time to spare for any lesser office.

He actually said this to her to her face, or approximately did, speaking sidelong from the table in the kitchen as she made his breakfast, and watched her sizzle, or was it slowly boil.

"I have my own life," was her very low reply.

"You'll be surprised when I win," George Robinson said.

They lived parallel lives that seldom turned and met. At breakfast they met, and at supper sometimes, and in bed. Their meetings in bed were the apotheosis of Robinson's day. He clutched at straws. He rolled toward her like a man rolling downhill and expecting her to break his slide. Bodily warmth was all he sought, or bodily compassion, or one brief spasm's worth of life—he could never have told his pawed, offended, frightened partner what it was he really wanted. It was the same thing he wanted when he came home and hugged his little daughter so tight she gave a cry. It was what he wanted when for no good reason he lost his temper and swung at Jamie with a vicious open hand and this time didn't miss. "I want to win. I want to win. Why can't I win?"

Wild unreality framed his question, as if asking it alone could move the stars. It was the question of a man with a noose around his neck, a bullet in his brain and a dagger through his heart—"Why can't I live?"

CHAPTER 32

ONE VERY wet September day, Rainey and her friend Margaret Hanson were in the basement of the Hanson house where Margaret was in the midst of doing her family wash.

Rain ran down the panes of the high little basement windows; a smell of rain and laundry mixed a kind of springtime into the warm and musty basement air. Rainey was very quiet. She watched her friend piling up sheets and towels, shirts and socks in that monotonous and reassuring work, and her eyes shone elsewhere. "What's the matter?" Margaret asked her, and came over to where she was and put an arm around her. "What's wrong, Lorraine?"

"Oh, just my namesake, just a rainy day. Nothing to talk about."

"The kids all right?"

"Kids are fine."

"Is it something with George?"

And Rainey nodded her head.

"If it's George it can't be very serious," her best friend said to her, at which Rainey detached herself and answered: "Why do I always see such a mountain of dirty laundry whenever I come down here?"

"Do I hear someone changing the subject?" Margaret Hanson smiled and said.

When the washing machine was loaded with wash, the two of them sat down on the basement steps, the way they always did without thinking about it. Sitting there together on the steps brought back the easy, impromptu feeling of much younger days.

And Margaret told Rainey about the washday advice her mother had given her before her wedding day.

"Mother was doing her laundry and I went down to the basement to pack some things of mine. 'Come over here, Margaret,' she called to me and I walked over. 'Yes mother?'

" 'I might as well tell you this while I think of it,' said mother, keeping her back to me. 'Just remember. When you do your bedsheets, whatever you see, it all comes out in the wash.'

" 'What comes out, mother?' I asked.

" 'Oh, something. You'll know what it is when you see it.'

" 'Oh mother, you don't mean blood again, do you?'

" 'No I don't mean blood,' she said crossly. 'This is something that is not the woman's and is not blood.'

" 'Not the woman's and not blood. Let me see . . . Can I have a hint?' I knew of course, but I was teasing mother.

" 'No, I'm not giving you any hint!' cried mother, never looking at me. 'Upstairs with you!' She was almost laughing now herself. 'Get upstairs before I spank you!'

"So that was mother's advice to me before my wedding day. I didn't have to worry about anything that happened because it would all come out in the wash."

Rainey smiled at her friend's story and its happy little washday moral; smiled wistfully. She took and squeezed Margaret's hand, touched and a little teary-eyed with talk of a wedding and a mother, here in the musty, imitation springtime air.

Neither of them spoke. In their silence they listened to the whirring and the whirring of the machine.

"We were always thinking about blood, weren't we," Rainey said. "If it wasn't blood because of one thing, it was blood because of the other thing."

"All the boys ever had were bloody noses."

"Lucky boys," said Rainey.

"Bloody noses!"

And Margaret Hanson threw back her head and laughed.

"That's the trouble with husbands," Rainey said, with a sudden curling of her lips that bared her teeth. "They just don't bleed often enough."

CHAPTER 33

HER ANGER moved through Rainey. In strength, in wheel of purpose, it felt inexorably male to her, like a muscle, like a machine, like Rainey's fierce, majestic king of seasons, winter.

It lay in bed with her. It gripped her belly and sent its curling tongue of fire ever inward. It made her cry and when she knew this hard and heartless rage to be her own, the deliciousness of it made her want to laugh.

It protected her, spoke to her—stroked her. It was more of a mate to her than George was. Rainey's anger. In what it might make her do, she flirted with it more dangerously than she ever had with Alaman West.

Never would she forgive him for striking Jamie in the face. How could normal-seeming women bring forth and shape such men? It was worse than his mistreatment of her in bed; it was the same man, the same meat paw, but mean and worse, a thousand blotches worse. Her little boy ran screaming to her, clutching his cheek with the little petals of his fingers that she peeled away to show the whip-red welt. At the sight of that extra lip she shrieked, lost all her self-control and ran into the living room pulling Jamie with her. "How could you do it, how could you hit him!" she cried, pummeling him with screams that landed on the back of his neck. His arms flapped out in a kind of helplessness or shrug—she didn't take the time to fathom him. She shooed Stephie out of sight and moved with Jamie leg to leg back into the kitchen and there held him to her while he sobbed, his every convulsion a storm against her heart, and then she moved with him upstairs with a towel full of ice cubes, lay him in his bed and sat with him and cooled the burning cheek and thanked all heaven for sparing the eye. She heard the murderer go out. It was evening, after supper, and the murderer was going out to pet his dog.

What could be said? That she loathed the thought of him? Her constant anger and fits of shame kept her secluded all next day; she was afraid to show her face downtown as though her husband's abuses, like the business of newlyweds, would send a signal that all the world could see. And what of him, the cause of all their pain? He brought home presents for Jamie and extravagantly petted Stephie, but he had not a word of contrition for her, but tiptoed around her anger like a spectator around a fire, never goading her—not tossing on more blaze—but content to let the fire keep on burning. She didn't understand him. His ways were not hers. The love, the money he poured on his politics, for nothing it seemed, for losing—up to now she had kept quiet about that and mostly bit her lip. She parted with the money the same as she parted her legs: to have it over with. A wonderful time in her life was to have just begun, Jamie a little man, Stephie starting kindergarten, her mornings all to herself. And what did the days bring her but a heart full of anger, a husband who frightened her, and now a scar for her child's face.

Her public shame rode with her a few days later when with Jamie back in school, armed with a story about a bicycle fall, she drove through Jericho on the way to the road to Grafton. Those signs of his were all over town, ROBINSON in yards, ROBINSON on fences, ROBINSON defacing the beautiful trees. If only people knew him the way she did, Rainey smiled. If people could see the inventor of Politics is People the way he was at home. She smiled at the signs, dreaming of justice done, but all too surely her misery returned. Their name was their marriage. Their name was them.

As she left Jericho and its farms behind, gradually his signs lessened. As she approached Grafton, the Armstead signs began to thicken, silent soldiers in the field. She was in the enemy camp, with Armstead's people. Because of George and the election, and despite herself, Grafton felt different as she came through town, the air smelled different, a familiar dish with an odd new tang, Grafton, after all these years. These folks would never know but she and they were on the same side—these were the people who were going to beat George. But she parked the car and walked their street selfconsciously, wife of the candidate from Jericho, a foreigner from a foreign land thirty-five miles down the pike.

She went into Clarke's Clothing Store to look at the new fall dresses, looking for something to wear to his free-food-for-your-vote affair that he called his Open House, announced weeks in advance in the *Pioneer* and now suddenly looming this week. Once upon a time it was to be her grand concession to his fall campaign. Now, come pain, come scar, come bitterness, come fall, she couldn't humiliate herself and uninvite the town. But whether her tastes were too fine, or her feelings too raw, or she could visualize that souvenir hanging in her closet for eternity, she didn't buy a new dress for Robinson's Open House, but spent her time picking out a frilly dress for Stephie to celebrate kindergarten and then walked through the center aisle of Clarke's Clothing Store and across the human divide, her heart in her shopping, she supposed, until she picked up a little boy's shirt, held it up and melted. The little shirt was so small and complete. The little shirt cried out for love. His clothes without Jamie were like Jamie without his clothes. Disintegrating and in a state all over again, she left Stephie's unbought dress there in the store and made her way to the café, taking a booth in the corner in the back. The waitress found her and hovered near. To make the bumblebee go away, and maybe feel less teary, she ordered her usual milkshake and a sandwich. No tomato surprise for Rainey Robinson, not today, maybe never. She wasn't sure she could stand the shock of a tomato surprise.

And she ate around the edges of her sandwich, and nibbled around the awful question of whether she should leave him.

Not for long—only temporarily. And not until they had the Open House; she couldn't disappear from town before that night. But soon after that, for a few short weeks, until the election was over. He would live alone, learn his lesson, and then she and the children would come back. Where was the harm in that?

No harm, beyond the stab in the back. She didn't know anything about politics, but she knew her neighbors, and they would as soon eat their garbage as vote for a man whose wife and children had left him. Moving out would sure do it, she smiled with her teeth around her sandwich. That would take a nice bite out of him, thought Rainey with a laugh.

He was going to lose anyway. What difference did it make if he lost by one vote or an avalanche, and this way he would learn a very fine lesson that would also bury his politics forever.

But how could she do that to him? Wishing was one thing, but treachery was another. She probably still loved him, and she still wanted to stay married, given the end of politics and a few other home repairs. Did she want an avalanche on her conscience? And what about living with him afterward? He would blame her for everything. He would say: "I would have won if not for you." Oh yes.

If she moved out, where would they go? Not to her sister in the East; there wasn't the room and they weren't that good friends. She couldn't take her unhappiness to George's parents in Arizona; that would be a welcome mat immediately worn thin. And if she was looking for some other home to go to, there was no such address on the map.

Yet how could she stay with him either? How could she know that he wouldn't go after Jamie one day when her back was turned? How would she fend him off in bed without punishing him so entirely that he struck her too—or worse? And what had her own state come to if she could even frame such a picture and believe it of the husband she knew?

She didn't want to leave her home. She dreaded the four walls if she stayed. She had to protect her child and she cringed for herself, mind and body. What should she do, where could she go? What was the answer?

A tear rolled down her cheek, one clouded crystal tear and then another. She hated this woman she was, who hugged life, was even a woman, only by marriage. She was not anything by herself. She was not earthy, not motherly, not truly, not of the land, not out in the world, not this, not that, but half a thing, leaning, precarious. She lived in a house with a yard, in a town, on the edge. This woman who was sitting here crying, she wouldn't know the answer to anything. And between crying and wiping tears and turning her head so no one saw, she kept busy until the check came and she left the café and all of the town of Grafton behind her.

Out on the road going back, the peaceful sky, the patient fields, the enormous hush, her common sense—they told her: Don't worry about packing your bags. You'll never have to go. Just wait for the election to be over. Have the Open House, face the rest of it, and see. Be the patient wife. Watch his every move. Keep the threat to leave, but in the pantry; in reserve. Losing the election would settle him down. Father Time would take care of everything the way he always did. Where signs for Armstead and Robinson stood, fields of wheat and flax had come and gone. Out in the farmers' windbreaks the trees were turning brown and bare. Soon would come the day of the evergreens. There they were, arm in arm, waiting to step to the forefront.

Father Time was on the side of the family Robinson. All that was left of the fall were the sunblackened sunflowers, longest lasting things in the fields, poor things, their drooping heads waiting for the axe and Farmer Jones to put them out of their misery.

CHAPTER 34

ALAMAN WEST gazed out on harvest time too, from the window of his shades-of-nowhere grainary home.

Across the road, a farmer on a tractor pulling a windrower was haying his field. Round and round went the yellow and green paddles of the windrower. Round and round went the contraption, the tractor and the farmer, moving in ever-narrowing circles toward the center of the field, leaving swaths of fresh-cut hay behind. West never saw the face of the farmer. A peaked white cap sat up on the tractor, atop a light-blue shirt. Man and wheels would disappear behind a clump of trees, a building, alone with their busy tractor-hum, and reappear, paddlewheel turning, the whole device moving in that ever-winding circle toward the center, sometimes a toy, sometimes a farm machine, sometimes a riverboat paddling through the hours, through the muddy waters of none too distant time.

West would turn from the window to his yellowed kitchen walls, circumnavigate the room and then go out, bike past Robinson's office, swing by the Eagle's roost above the Feed and Seed, biking breathlessly but never far. Rifle practice was over. The real event was one short hop away. It was the hour before the dawn and the peace before the storm neatly rolled into one. Time had moved in with West. Time was his new boarder, a constant eater, a great talker, a loud snorer who could wake him up from any dream with a snap. New frost gleamed at West when dawn smiled outside his window. Fresh winds blew almost through his walls, applecheeked winds, pumpkin-cheeked, bringing in October.

Joe knew what time it was but he made believe he didn't. Joe acted as if nothing was brewing but the pot of coffee on the stove. So West reminded him in thoughtful little ways, such as passing Joe and whispering in his ear: "A week, a week from Saturday." Or West should whack the table with the newspaper and yell out, "There goes your first firecracker, Joe!" He liked to see Joe dropping things, Joe going around the room holding his hands over his ears—Joe running out the door. Except that Joe was too far in ever to run out now and only escaped into the yard for air before he crept back in.

West's own palpitations made him relish Joe's fear. He didn't mind being jittery. His nerves testified to his nerve: if he was that jumpy about it, the plan was definitely alive. He bought the *Daily Herald* every day looking for news of a threatening letter to Robinson. There was nothing. Nothing in the *Jericho Pioneer*, no clue between the school news, church news and household hints. Why no news about the letter? Why no police around Robinson? The police must know. From John's Saloon that morning he had seen Hank hurry by, going toward Robinson's office. A little later Hank came walking back, holding what looked like the letter. A minute later, Robinson ran past in the same direction and soon came back holding what looked like same letter. Conclusion? Robinson got the letter—called the police—gave them the letter—then took it back. For good or temporarily? And why? To show to someone? Who? Rainey? Did Rainey know about the letter?

Nerves that jumped and frightened Joe went to call on Rainey. West waited on her streetcorner, shifting feet in the biting morning air. It was tantalizing to think she knew. Not a sex hole, not that sex was missing, there was a peephole of fear he wanted to see in, fear planted there by him; there was a yen to see Rainey afraid. Right on time, she came out the door with the little kid, they got in the car and drove away; in five minutes she was back home alone.

"I keep reading about the big party you're throwing," was

West's first attempt at finding out if Rainey knew about the letter, when they were sitting in the kitchen with the coffee she had served.

"I wouldn't call it a party. It's just something we're having. It's more like business than anything else."

"Free food, free drinks, big home. Big crowd. You're not afraid of having so many strangers in your house?"

"There won't be any strangers. They're all people who live in town."

"People, sure," West said, "no question . . . but there could be strangers sneaking in."

She looked surprised—and not too happy. "We're having it and I'm sure everything will turn out fine. Did you come here to irritate me? Why are we talking about this," Rainey said, getting up from the table and leaving West with the sense of something else going on, but was it fear?

"It must be nice, politics," was West's next attempt at finding out about Rainey and the letter, when she returned from staring out the window and sat down with him again. "It must be a very pleasant thing. Interesting—different. Exciting. I'm not saying what I mean . . . Not dangerous, no, no. Full of nice surprises."

Smart approach, almost dumb-sounding, except that he was having a conversation with himself, she sitting there stony and tight-lipped, looking down into her cup, maybe hiding something, maybe not, until West stopped talking because he was only making himself nervous.

"I got a funny letter in the mail the other day," was West's final, perilous attempt to see if Rainey knew about the letter. "A very funny letter, no name, how do they call it?"

"Anonymous," she said.

"Anonymous, that's right." West shook his head and laughed, "It was sure a funny letter. You could almost laugh about it. A few words about this, a few words about that. It's hard to describe."

"Yes—so?"

She didn't know about the letter. He was getting on her nerves, but he saw no hint that Rainey was afraid. Meanwhile, his own hide was sweating. He felt like a dope, especially when she started clearing the table and told him: "You're too strange for me, Alaman. I don't know why you rang my bell so early in the morning if all you wanted was to tell me trash like that."

No hint, no light, no fright, no peephole. West walked away fast—he had been crazy to take the risk. But he could be sure that Robinson hadn't told her about the letter. What else didn't Robinson tell her? Was keeping secrets normal? Did she have secrets too? Marriage was a mystery to him, what two people spoke about, how they acted all alone, how they shared their life, how they shared the bathroom, what they showed, what they hid. He would love to eavesdrop on their marriage. The experience would be worth the pain, if he could view the two of them all alone—just once visit where they slept. Couldn't he have a fine time at their party. He could walk in the front door and also be the stranger sneaking in.

His digging in Rainey excited him. So did the risk he had taken. So did idylls of marriage. West went out in the afternoon to stretch and look at his roost.

As he passed through the city hall park he spotted Jamie Robinson on his bicycle riding on Legion Avenue beyond the trees. The envy he once felt for Rainey's son had evolved into a painful kind of liking. Spoonfed and shy, he was his mother's favorite kid. Whenever he saw him, West felt his appeal and sensed the presence of Rainey. West tried to stay invisible but Jamie rode into the park and up to him and stopped a couple of feet away.

Shoot his father—have his mother. West felt a relation to Jamie so acute that it almost dried up speech.

"What did you do to your cheek?" West asked with the taste of the desert in his mouth.

"I fell off my bicycle."

"You must have been going fast."

Jamie nodded his head. "I was."

Jamie fidgeted in the seat, moved the handlebars around and asked, as though to keep the conservation moving, "Where are you going, to do some bookkeeping?"

"That's right."

"Do you like bookkeeping?"

West shrugged. Each was silent. Each stood there, sliding toward the other's age.

"I have to go home now." Jamie put his poundage down on

the pedal, wobbled, and pushed off. "So long," he called. "Careful," West called back.

Robinson was in the air. Trees in the park were hung with pictures of Robinson. On a table in front of the city hall steps were a Help Elect Robinson sign and a collection can. Nobody was around; it was on the honor system. West walked back to the can and dropped in a dime and a penny, a dime for death and a penny for mischief.

CHAPTER 35

ROBINSON'S WIDOWS were the first to arrive on the doorstep and peep their heads into Robinson's open house.

No sounding of the bell was necessary: in the spirit of the evening the front door stood open to all. Welcome Jericho, read the big letters on the banner that was stretched above the door-way—Elect Robinson, said a second, hanging by threads over the stairway in the lighted entry hall.

The perfect fall evening, moonlit and mild, entered into the house. Supper was spread on the dining room table, a come-serve-yourself supper with a free choice of cold drinks. Neighbors and friends, in couples and clusters, in a mood for a party, soon were crossing the threshold. The anxious braintrust was easy to spot, furrowed in a corner with drinks in their hands as the press of voters arrived.

The venerable Bob Millers of the Coast-to-Coast Store were timely arrivals at the open house. Not far behind them came:

Art and Ed from the grain elevator

Manager Hodges from the bank

Roy the depot man

And their freshly beautified wives.

Henry and Mary Ellen came straight from the Red Owl so as not to miss the supper, leaving trusty helper Joe to mop the floor and lock up.

Sam the barber and his wife were right on time for the advertised supper, along with two of their growing children, the only kids who were dragged to Robinson's open house.

Through the house they all came, into the Robinsons' dining room, folks with a lifetime of church supper and picnic lunch experience, old reliables like Eleanor Prain's husband Jim and Margaret Hanson's Bill, and the Jericho post office crew; but obscure, unlooked-for faces too, pressing in out of the night, retired men boarding at the Violet Hotel who had not recently been seen by anyone, young farmers and their wives who larked in from a from farms only technically in Jericho township.

Doc Sunderquist came by, though Doc didn't stay for supper, when he saw the complexion and felt the pulse of the crowd.

But the Jack Amundsons of the lumber yard, and John and wife of John's Saloon, with most of their customers imbibing here, they stayed and enjoyed a few drinks as they progressed toward the serving table.

The luminous evening sifted into the hall, the living room, the dining room, or, curling left, up the stairs toward the sleeping bedrooms of the house. Car doors slammed incessantly in the street; more people found the house and shouldered in, their curiosity an added appetizer since few had ever been inside the Robinson home. Platters of sliced ham and sausage sat in the middle of the supper table, flanked by dishes of baked beans and bean salad and a strawberry gelatin wheel that wobbled like an oldtime wagon wheel. Bottles of bourbon and soda stood on a separate table, well tended by a paid professional, but people helped themselves to the two big bowls of punch, both ruby red, the left one slightly jaded with a touch of rum. There were buckets of ice cubes. There were nuts and potato chips. There was a big frosted white cake, fruit bars if anyone cared, and coffee served from an army-sized coffeemaker borrowed from the Legion Club.

And every new face with food and drink in hand, looking for a place to stand and eat, joined not only the other feeding guests, but the people who had been in the Robinson house long before the evening began:

Margaret Hanson, in charge of the constant unwrapping and dispatching of food from the kitchen.

Eleanor Prain, mistress of the table in the dining room, keeping an eye out for needy platters and serving dishes while she cheerily filled rows of paper cups with steaming coffee.

Assistant hostesses all through the downstairs, the members of the Tuesday Club pitching in.

Hank—Hank had been there for hours, a perpetual guest but on duty, on the trail of the threatening letter, a gun under his suit jacket and vigilance in his eyes, a visitor from a different saga, moving from one room to another and back again while the pale moon outside moved its moon face from window to window.

Stephie Robinson, in her red velvet dress, sitting with a plateful of cake on her knees, looking down at the strange people coming into her house from her balcony halfway up the stairs. Higher on the stairs, Jamie Robinson, sitting hunched under his father's banner, wanting to move and come down but afraid of people asking him about the big red welt on his cheek.

Rainey Robinson, attired in black and white, hostess of her husband's open house while she privately entertained the thought of leaving him, circulating among the guests who filled her home, making the best of a bad night by outsparkling it with her hospitality, her liveliness and her eyes when other fires failed her.

The host, the candidate himself, a sure loser in the election but the lucky winner of a night with friends, sick at heart— convivial—giving them his campaign poster smile, wondering what to do with a mob of happy people who all seemed to think he could win.

Not a veteran drinker, to say the least—the last strong drink he had was the day he got a death threat—tonight his glass of bourbon never left Robinson's hand. He carried it through the festive crowd, lifting it to negotiate the denser feeding places, or greet some new well-wisher, or clink glasses and smiles with another, or drily salute Hank and his clandestine prowling on the other side of the room. He even drank from it sometimes, drawing little sips, not loving yet savoring the caustic whisky taste. And from time to time, when need be, he carried his glass to the hall and up the stairs, stepping over his children if need be, and into his bedroom where he shut the door, opened the closet, reached down, picked up a bottle and poured himself some more. For this was not the same bourbon whisky as the herd downstairs drank. This was choice stuff he poured, specially purchased for that deserving fellow, that prince of candidates, that lonesome campaigner and gallant, lonely loser, George Robinson.

Then down the stairs he came again, patting each child on the head, pausing on a lower step to survey his open house, bleeding to look at them all, eating his food, drinking his whisky, hitched to his star, or so they all believed. Give these folks the benefit of the doubt. They're not only here to eat, they think they'll have a pal in the State House. These wolves think I can win. Look at Hank—he thinks I rate an assassin. That makes him a real cop, growing muscle out of the fat. And what about the unknown letter-writer, was he here eating too—was the eagle in the wings in the house tonight? Hank was so sure that no one in Jericho had sent the death threat. So why was Hank hulking across his vision? Why didn't Hank stop looking and go home?

Look at my wife, Robinson thought: charming the electorate, winning over the already won, so pretty tonight in the perfect dress—black for me and white for her—so pretty. That wholesome face, those honey eyes, that smile—what a help she could have been if she had wanted, thought Robinson about the brown-haired woman with the lovely eyes who the more he stared at her, the more she seemed a stranger.

He left the stairs and walked into the noisy room, his uncertain state nourished by equal fingers of bourbon, blame, suspicion and a watery self-pity. Just inside the room he spotted an empty easy chair and on impulse boosted himself up and stood on it. Heads turned. Voices quieted to a hush all the way back to the punch bowls in the dining room. Robinson smiled down and a liquorish glow that was the essence of pumpkin lighted his cheeks and eyes. When all was quiet, he raised his glass and called down:

"You folks have been drinking to me. Now I want to drink to you folks. Welcome—here's to the hungriest damn bunch of voters any candidate ever had!

"Maybe some of you remember—oh yes, there's a speech too, folks—maybe some of you remember," Robinson went on, when the laughing and clapping died down, "how I paid a little visit to our State House a while back, back at the beginning of my campaign, if you can recall such ancient history. Don't worry, it's not a long story, folks. I had my look around the old State House offices, and an interesting chat with our lieutenant governor, touching on one thing and another, which I'm still not able to talk about—but the best time, the big thrill of my visit, as they say, came when I walked into the big State House chamber, under that big dome, you know, and seeing that nobody was around to arrest me, I sat down in the seat that I was hoping then and am still hoping tonight to occupy. When I sat down in that chair, under that dome, I can tell you, I felt small, and that might come as a surprise to some people who think they know me.

"But then," Robinson pushed on against a groundswell of dissident murmuring, "but then as I sat there I thought of all you people back home in Jericho who figured I was big enough to occupy that chair, and would do their damndest to put me there, and I'll tell you, I felt proud to be sitting there, even if the lights were out and it was only for a couple of minutes.

"It's not easy to win an election," Robinson said slowly, gazing above their faces at something shimmering in the air. "It's hard. You take my word for that. You can even say it's impossible—" He paused and took a long, slow, slit-eyed sip of bourbon—"Impossible," he got the mouse word out of his mouth again, "without a little good fortune and all the help and support in the world that a man can get.

"I feel sorry for the man who thinks he can win all alone," said Robinson. "I sincerely pity that unfortunate man," he told their wavy sea of faces, for he was drunk by now, though only partly on his bourbon, more drunk, falling-down drunk, on his sincerity, which he was swallowing in gulps before these people, telling them that the election was lost even if they didn't know that they were hearing it. "I can tell you how hard it is to win an election . . . even though I hear it's tougher to lose one." Robinson took his glass, sipped, and held his lips to it in a tender parting kiss. "Politics is people. That's our slogan."

That was all he could say. He could not say more—could not. The crowd saw his emotion and began to applaud. "Robinson for governor," a gruff voice called out, and they all cheered and clapped harder. Up on the chair, almost aloof, slightly swaying, his sight came back into Robinson's eyes. The prolonged out-pouring filled his veins—it brought him back and made him sober, if nirvana was sobriety. This was what he craved, this was all he had in mind. Why hide the tears? This crowd was his. Not wolves, these folks were lambs—they were his followers, his flock. He raised his arms to them, and as he did, the proposition dawned:

I'm not giving up. I'm running again. This is the beginning of next time.

"No more," he told them, with his arms still upraised. "No more," he kept smiling even after they quieted down. "No more—not now. I promise, you'll be hearing from me. I've talked enough tonight. You folks go and help yourselves to another cup of coffee. And try a piece of Rainey's cake. And thank you all for coming."

Their good wishes and handclasps met and enfolded Robinson as he made his way through the crowd, still holding his glass of private bourbon in his hand. By the time he came down from that chair he was a candidate running in a different election, though no one at the open house could have noticed the change. His pumpkin glow, his firm small smile, bespoke a man con-tented to be where he was. His grace of speech and tender manner touched even Rainey, who had listened to him speak from the recesses of the dining room, where she fled as soon as he climbed up on the chair. She smiled at his bittersweet story about the State House, feeling more affected by it rather than less for hav-ing heard it from the teller's lips long before. She alone, among everyone there, fathomed his words about losing, and running all alone, and she smarted to the point of feeling guilty, although she never blushed until he came to the part about the cake she really had never made. "Why weren't you like this more?" she asked him in her mind as she watched his dark-suited, somehow gallant, somewhere wounded silhouette moving among their guests. She was not ashamed of her marriage tonight; her house seemed not so much a domicile of fear, furnished with mistrust, and cooled or heated by anger. For this one night at least, with these good people here, she felt comfortable with her husband in their home. Her relief that her world felt safe to her made her sentimental. She felt an affection for these unassuming people, the old couple from the hardware store, the friendly postmaster, the Red Owl grocer, the mementos of her youth, with their predictable comments and homey, open countenances that reflected their admiration of her each time she passed like so many mirrors on the wall. Oh yes, she spied herself as queen, as lovelier than any of the women, as too much for any of the men—there was some of that too, assisting Rainey through the evening, as she circled in her black and white dress, any thoughts about leaving him more thickly veiled than ever, on this night of the open house.

"Goodnight," she said to people at the door while Robinson did the honors outside on the steps.

"Goodnight Mary Ellen, and you too Henry, so nice that both of you were able to come. Good night Roy, it was such a treat to see you. I must take the children down for a ride on the train."

The moonlit night sat back, shone down and looked mild. Cars slid out and carried the last guests homeward. The supporting cast of characters departed, the assistant hostesses and kitchen crew, the Bill Hansons, the Jim Prains, and Hank; the yellow-lit lantern in the front yard went out, then like a second thought came on again, Robinson appeared on the step and Big Red came bounding from out of nowhere and galloped toward him.

West had been around the block many times, circling to no end, returning always to the shrubs and shadows between two homes across the street from the open house. He watched them all come out, his boss Jack Amundson, his boss John of the saloon, Joe's boss at the Red Owl—the wives, dressed up and made up but not looking as appetizing as they did with their stray hair and everyday faces and not wearing their husbands. It was enjoyable being at the open house. No one saw him here; he came to the party so as not to be seen. He saw Doc Death come out early, but people were safe because he didn't have his doctor's bag. He almost didn't recognize his good friend Hank, half of the Jericho Police Department and looking like all of it in his big brown suit and tie.

He saw Robinson and the big dog hug in the moonlight and the dog jump away and go running down the street. Robinson took a step and gave a cough; to West not a cough brought on by any cold but by the dark, a feeler sent into the night, a cough addressed to the sender of the threatening letter.

Why not do it now, West asked himself. He might not see Robinson again until he had him in his sights at the big Event. Why not do it now. Before you get too scared. Take that Robinson sign where it's planted in the ground and stick it home. Hurry. While he's out here. Do it now.

The moon—the moon, what did he look to the moon to say— the moon and the upstairs window? No word came from that room where he imagined Rainey was, that room where shades were drawn, where by habit of dreams West stood and pictured her. He wondered if she was getting ready for bed, or maybe she was still downstairs in one of those lighted rooms, or back in the kitchen—or what? *Do it now. Then come up.* Is that what he expected Rainey and the moon to say?

The big red dog came trotting back to his master who was walking to meet him. The picture of a peaceful night, man and dog moved companionably down the street toward the corner streetlight. West came out from behind the shrub and began walking quietly, rapidly, in the other direction.

IN THE teeming small hours of the night of the open house, Robinson laid his plans for running next time:

Sweep Jericho this time around. Confirm his territory; overwhelmingly take the town. Don't stop campaigning and never talk defeat. Call for victory—keep the braintrust and their campaign-worker wives working and hoping.

Double, triple the publicity for the Event. Scrape up the money. More people from outside town would come and hear him that day than all the rest of his campaign combined. He had the chance to make a tremendous impression.

Make peace at home. Act nicer, be a better father to Jamie— win back Rainey. Kiss her, warm her, butter her, marry her all over again if need be. Next time was truth time and Rainey angry and cold was not a political plus.

Get rid of the bookkeeper. The worm by definition was a negative influence on Rainey. Make up a story, get rid of him and Rainey would have one less object draining her sympathy and time. He had already begun that process by telling Jack Amundson at the open house, "Your smart bookkeeper didn't show his face here tonight. There's a tawdry tale there that I'll be in to see you about."

As soon as he could, start putting away money for the next election. Divert some income, save a little at a time; in a couple of years it could amount to a healthy bundle. No bank account, no bank book, no telling tellers. Convert to cash and keep it in the safe.

Call off Hank before his snooping alerted Rainey. Don't let a town cop scare you. And cheer up: the death threat was a thing of the present. By the time the next campaign came around, the eagle in the wings would have flown off in another direction.

Take the town, win back Rainey, hold things together, save, pray and get ready for next time.

He had neglected to plant the kind of promise that might have challenged Armstead. It had to be something fresh, new and appealing. It didn't have to grow and bear fruit. It was enough to plant it on time. Plant it in the fall like winter wheat and by spring it might have frozen in the ground but the election would be history by then. By the time the next election rolled around, he would be ready with that promise.

CHAPTER 36

ROBINSON SET his sights on a future that was two years away; Rainey looked to the election next month and the demise of politics; Joe kept mopping the store and grinding the meat and tried not to see too far past the shelves; and West could count the future on the fingers of a hand, with one of them already lopped away.

Four days were left—four days. Little days, just daisies. Big days—as in a daze. In four days' time, the train could take him far from here. With four days left, he could catch pneumonia and be too sick to shoot. A boat could scram across the ocean in four fast days. Jesus Christ could die and rise in four days' time, with one full day left over to keep on going.

West went to Rainey's, biked there one last morning, rang and rang the doorbell, knocked and hit the door with the flat of his hand, all without an answer though her car was sitting in the driveway. She was in the backyard digging up plants for the winter and putting them in pots when he finally went around.

He followed her as she did her work, studying her sweatered back, the pitcher of cream of her neck, her hips as she knelt, her soft bottom where her heels dug in as she dug and pulled and filled in the ground. "You could come back this afternoon. Come for cake and coffee. Are you still there?" West brooded in silence behind her. She unwound from her knees and threw down her garden gloves. "I can't stand being followed around; it gives me goosebumps. Oh all right, I'll stop for a while," she said, wiping her perspiring face with her arm. "I really don't understand you."

She didn't understand him. And if she didn't understand him, he was of no use to her. He should be easy to understand, West reasoned bitterly as he followed her into the house, maybe giving her a few more goosebumps.

He stirred the coffee she poured for him and sat and played with the spoon, tap-tapping it on the kitchen table. He had nothing to say. It was exactly like his first visit here. He sat mute. Now that I'm here, what do I say to her? That I love her? That on Saturday I'll be waving from the Feed and Seed window? Will I ever be here again?

"Big day coming up Saturday," West said to the back of Rainey's head. She wasn't having coffee at the table, she was washing dishes at the sink, not wasting time on him. "That's true," she answered him.

He drummed with the spoon on the table. Talk to her. Find something to speak about—quick. Forget him and Saturday. "The kid, your little kid, how is she doing in school?"

"Excuse me a minute," Rainey said, going out of the kitchen, into the hall and with light quick footsteps up the stairs. Was she going to the bathroom, he wondered. Could she be taking down her panties and sitting peeing with him down here? Say she was; he looked at the ceiling. The dear act, the almost abysmally tender act, made him feel a little bit like crying. What a wreck he was. He really must be coming apart if he felt like crying over Rainey sitting on the pot.

Her purse was on a sideboard next to pictures of her kids. West went over, drawn to it, as though he could steal nearer to Rainey than if she were present in the room. He hesitated a second, afraid she might come back and see, then he opened the purse. Lipstick, a handkerchief, face powder, her billfold, keys, a little smudged mirror in which he saw her traces. From the purse came a mixed, sweet smell. He still remembered his mother's purse, where it always sat and what was in it. Half-listening for Rainey's footstep on the stairs, West closed his eyes. To live inside her purse. To be smothered in a woman . . . never to go. The smell of the purse was sweet, was too sweet, became sweeter, and unendurable.

"I'm going away," he told her when she came back into the room—with no clear idea why he said it. As she digested the news, showing no signs of heartbreak, he said with a smile:

"But don't worry. I'm coming back."

He was so afraid of never seeing her again. It was as though he was trying to plant love by picking a lovers' quarrel. Plant love any way he could. Grow it out of air. Hide love in his hand, pat it nice and small, and when she wasn't looking, sneak love in.

That was one side of it. On the other, he longed to wrap his arms around her and proclaim everything.

He asked her for another cup of coffee, and while he waited for it he drummed the spoon on the table so relentlessly that she told him please to stop. Finally, as she brought it to him and set it down—finally—she asked him gently if anything was wrong, to which he answered: "How could anything be wrong when everything is always the same?"

"As you say, Alaman. Be mysterious if you like. I don't have the energy today. I think you should go wherever it is you're going and come back some other day."

He swung his head with its broad smile and slowly got to his feet. End of visit, class dismissed. Smiling, he took a step, meaning to pass her. His face suddenly lowered—his lips kissed Rainey's neck.

She pushed out and leaped back.

"No," she whispered. "No no no."

All no's—all knives. Any more?

Sheer politeness itself. "Will you please go."

West smirked and rocked on the balls of his feet. Anything could have knocked him over. Rainey stood stiffly, her hands locked tight in front of her. She was looking in another direction and somebody had pasted Rainey's mouth on crooked.

He turned and walked himself out the door.

What a mistake! What a mistake! West couldn't believe he had done it. He was petrified—he had tasted the dark side of the moon. He was halfway down the street when he remembered his bicycle, rushed back and flew home to get out of the light of day, bolting then furiously kicking the rickety door.

She'd tell him. Would she? Would she tell Robinson?

Would Robinson tell Rainey about the letter and would Rainey tell him about the kiss?

THE KISS tormented West. He imagined it over and over, but as many times as he came past Rainey in his mind, each time the kiss was still the same, not a manly kiss, more an insect's kiss, its sneaky thievery burning him like a brand, being Alaman West's brand of love. He comes past Rainey, he ducks his head, his lips taste love—it never changed. Yet when he tried to turn this to his favor and see the harm, since it was such a little kiss, so quick, so innocent almost, and on the neck, the danger to himself seemed just as great as if he had thrown his arms around Rainey and pulled her close. His confession was written in that kiss. If Rainey spoke, Robinson would come banging on his door, abreast of Hank, abreast of Pete. The insect kiss imperiled all of his plans.

Should he really run away, say goodbye to Jericho, see Chicago again? Flop down in some room behind the railroad station, prowl those stare-back streets—shoot up the shooting galleries? Except this time he had no wad in hand, no army discharge pay to keep him going. Could anyone use a bookkeeper in Chicago? Should he take his lifetime kiss and get away while he could? West's rocking-chair rocked with a frail thing in it, a paling question mark, rocked with hardly a creak. Even Cat preferred the lap of the floor under the sink.

They were playing softball on the field beside the high school when West came by, the same field that presently would be iced over, with snowbanks and skaters and a warming house. It was close to dismissal time when West came walking by, paying no mind to the fresh-faced softball players. Yellow maples shed their leaves along the pathway turning in, a flag stirred atop the flagpole, through a tall window a blackboard carried the eye back into dim recesses, sights that had gone unattended by West passing by all these years; but his legs still remembered the steps, and his arm the weight of the door of the old red-brick building that felt airy and bright inside but in the same breath dense and unknown. Across from the entrance a boy and a girl sat behind a table with a sign saying Visitors. West cast a look down the corridor, but he

walked up to the table. "Mr. Whitehead around?" he said to neither
the boy nor the girl, who had watched him approach and who
seemed to West to respond in a chorus of two, telling him that Mr.
Whitehead was there, that visitors were welcome but school was
still in session, but he could ask for Mr. Whitehead in the office.

"Mr. Whitehead?" said a dark-haired woman sitting at the front
desk in the office, "He should be teaching in his room. Classes are
almost over, if you'd like to wait." "Mr. Whitehead was called away
this morning," said a white-haired woman seated at the desk in the
rear, "He won't be back in school until tomorrow." "No, no, he
came back later in the day," the dark-haired woman said, "I'm sure
I saw him here." "Whitehead's here," said a man who had entered
the office and was crossing to an inner room. "Wait until the bell
rings," the white-haired woman said without looking up at West.

He waited around a bend in the corridor, out of the view of the
office and the table with the honor society boy and girl, below a
metal stairway leading up. From the cafeteria, the school smell of
mop-pail and disinfectant squeezed tears from the back of West's
eyes. He had not been much of a student. Hadn't been interested.
Summer couldn't come fast enough, except that once. He carried a
book with him today, to hold in his hand, to make him feel more
comfortable. And it was true, he was a great reader.

The bell rang. The corridor suddenly filled with kids released for
the day. West moved against the darting stream, seeing no more of
their intent faces than they of his. As he neared the room, he saw
Mr. Whitehead come out and he called loudly, "Mr. Whitehead—
Alaman West. You taught me once," as if to push back the clock a
minute and have Mr. Whitehead back in his room, where desks and
blackboard, chalk and air sat preserved like summer flies in aspic
time. But even as he answered "Of course" and peered through his
glasses at West, Mr. Whitehead was locking his classroom door. He
was plainly in a hurry to leave. "Called away this morning"—West
remembered that obscure, algebraic notation of a private life. As he
turned, his arms full of schoolwork, however, Mr. Whitehead
stopped himself, forgetting his concerns for the minute and taking
the time to listen. This was how West remembered him, chalk dust
on his old blue suit, the white shirt with a bent collar that sort of
matched his beak nose. With his loping walk he resembled a great
bird, both motherly and fatherly. He had books and papers under

both arms but he managed to shake West's hand. "West—I can see you better now. How are you?"

"I'm keeping busy."

"I'm glad to hear it. What are you doing these days?"

"Books."

Mr. Whitehead's mouth was an oval of surprise.

"You write books?"

"None that you would know about," West murmured half under his breath.

"You're probably right. I'm stuck in these, the same old story," Mr. Whitehead sighed, though not unhappily. "So! What brings you back?"

"I'm thinking of making a big change."

"You are?"

"I'm thinking of giving up a certain plan of mine and maybe starting on a different plan."

"You should consider all the possibilities," said Mr. Whitehead.

"Like good old X and Y," West said with a smile.

Mr. Whitehead laughed. "That's right."

West jabbed the air, "Say X is the unknown. Say X is moving in one direction when he sees something coming from the opposite way. Say X could start in a different direction but he can see a big problem there too. Say X is in a bad position. He can't stand still but he can't seem to move straight either." West's eyes were pleading. "X is me, Mr. Whitehead. I need help fast. You knew me—do I belong here? Can I change? Can I be something different if I want to? What kind of a kid was I?"

"West . . ."

Mr. Whitehead shook his head, humane individual that he was, licensed teacher of high school mathematics, comfortable with his assortment of kids but not this X, who wore a different sign, whose infinite intensity and unknown power of trouble gleamed on the bones of his face. Mr. Whitehead blinked and shook his head so that his glasses slid unarrested down his nose. He raised his book-filled arms as much as he could: "Do you mind if we start walking?"

"Couldn't we go back to your room?"

Mr. Whitehead was edging down the corridor, not too fast, looking this way and that, looking for help himself, judged West, good old Mr. Whitehead, his soft breast and beak nose a treat in profile, the great mother and father bird, flustered wings flapping with papers and books. West touched his monster mask to see if it was still on straight; if the eyes were bulging bright, if the mouth still sagged enough. Mr. Whitehead was afraid of Alaman West. Good; West kept up with him if only out of spite. "I'm not going anywhere. I don't write books either." As they progressed, Mr. Whitehead kept apologizing for having to leave and hurry home. West almost felt sorry for him, or would have, if he weren't so disgusted and angry. But Mr. Whitehead didn't notice the anger and that was how West remembered him too.

A school bus was parked outside, an old and mudstained orange bus, its motor running. Kids were passing through the school's wide-open portals into daylight. Mr. Whitehead stopped inside the entrance for a parting word:

"You're a bright boy, West. Don't be discouraged. Follow your plan. You'll succeed—I'm sure you will. Remember me to your folks."

West gazed skyward and slammed his book down viciously against his hand. Kids turned at the explosive sound but the perpetrator was out and gone, down the steps, head down, book in hand, walking fast, lest more feeling catch up with him, a wind blow more ground from under his heels. He had no past; that kid had never lived—that was how it felt. Going back, he was no better off than before. Call it worse.

But there was worse still waiting for him on Legion Avenue. Craving a face, thinking to look in on Joe, he approached the Red Owl Store and saw a big sign pasted in the window. The sign hit West in the eyes like a side of beef, like a stampede:

JOE'S FRESH
GROUND BEEF
SPECIAL PRICE
59¢ LB
BEST GROUND BEEF AROUND

All in the big-lettered, big-headed moron printing of the letter.

CHAPTER 37

JOE'S PRINTING—big as death in the window. West's heart was thumping so hard he wrapped his arms around his chest. He saw Henry the store owner up front at the register and then Joe clad in an apron in the back and all West's confusion, fear and rage flowed to Joe in an apron. Betrayed. Buried with the sun out. Up and down the avenue, over in the park, on the steps of city hall, there were no eyes looking, no one near. The trap he jumped from was Sam's barber pole turning around and around.

His instinct was to hide. He dumped his book in a trash can and blindly carved his way—brilliant sun to the sudden shaded room, order and walls made deep by books and dimness. There was no one in the library except for Alpha Davis seated behind her librarian's desk. West pulled the door shut and plunged into the room, Alpha peering at him with suspicion and a glittering distaste over the rims of her glasses.

"This is a library, not a racetrack, Mr. West."

No answer—no common decency. He was back, groaned Alpha, after weeks, and she had already thanked God he was gone. But he didn't slouch himself over to the bookshelves or come and smirk by her desk. Instead he hung by the door, pretending that he wasn't here—for what? There was always that twist to him, that twist she would love to twist even more by the neck. Now she saw his arm jerk strangely, and his lips part nastily and curl up in a snarl. And Alpha spoke up again in a louder if slightly quavery voice: "I can only guess what you're up to, but don't think you frighten me for a minute, young Mr. West."

"Fucking prick—I'll cut off his balls!"

Alpha's coloring turned pink, like a chemical in a beaker. It was not from shock alone; it was Alpha's blood pressure, chief mischief of her twilight years, that set her cheeks aglow. A pressure pot was bubbling inside Alpha, a forecast of dizziness and worse, warning her to calm herself and take deep breaths and not try to run to the tiny back room that had no lock on the door anyway.

"*Shithead*" split her ears. "*Asshole! Scum!*"

Alpha's hand sought a sharp-pointed pencil from her container on the desk. Her other hand was a pearly-white choker about her neck, as if she was too afraid of him to let a cry escape her lips. Never mind doing it with soap, was Alpha's quivering idea—she wished she had a shotgun to wash his mouth out with. His vile babble never stopped for air, but gushed and frothed and raised a lava of spit around the edges of his mouth. He must know that she was here. Why was he doing this to her? What or who was he slashing with his arm? Now she was starting to feel dizzy; sweat was beading all over her, the bubbling pot was coming to a boil. Alpha's fingers crept down her throat and held her heart. Treat him like an animal, don't speak, don't move, don't attract attention—don't meet his eyes. Her eyes were kaleidoscopes of fear. She saw snarling teeth on mad-dog legs, and arms like malevolent streamers of the sun, arms that would attend to Alpha soon, arms that would pull all the books from the shelves—yank her false teeth out of her mouth—bare her gums. Hit her. Ah God, there it was: her heart was palpitating. She sucked in air. So did he.

"*The son-of-a-bitch—I'll kill him!*"

And she saw him clap his hand over his mouth. He looked at her, as dazed as she was, and fled.

WHAT WAS he doing? Why was he wrecking everything? He had to be quiet. Sit on himself. Everything could still go as planned and still come out all right. No, there wasn't a chance.

When West saw Joe's sign hanging in the Red Owl Store window, he knew he would never see Rainey again. They would make a chain, and at the end of that chain would be West. Rainey would see him dead or running for his life, dead if his luck ran true.

All thanks to Joe. Safe at home, free if caged, West paced his kitchen fulminating at Joe—Joe who only existed because of the plan, who would never have set foot in his house otherwise. Scrap his life because of Joe, who was too dumb to remember printing the letter when he started printing the sign? Since he was that dumb, don't start educating Joe now, don't say a word, or he'd be too scared to go through with the plan. Who looked at those Red Owl signs anyway? Not Robinson. Not Hank or Pete. Rainey—but she hadn't seen the letter or he was in trouble anyhow. If he thought of a good excuse, he could have Joe take the sign out of the window when Henry's back was turned, but there was no such innocent excuse. He could break the window himself at night, vandalize the place, rip down all the signs and tear them up, incidentally stealing Joe's. That seemed too risky; it could blow up in his face. There was too little time. Leave it as it is.

Leave it as it is. After all the frenzy, he had come around to that . . . was satisfied with that. His flunked visit with Rainey, Mr. Whitehead at the high school, Joe's sign in the window, everything seemed to be moving him toward the appointed end. It was as though he had always known just how things would turn out, had even intended them to, so that at the end he would stand alone. He knew he would never marry Rainey. The love line was gone. Only the original line, the Robinson line, the good reason line remained. Remove Robinson. Pure and simple, simple and pure.

But shoot from the Red Owl Store apartment, not the Feed and Seed window, the old Red Owl Store apartment where he lived with Annie West, that place of doom. West felt an appetite to be alone and desperate that even in the offing soothed like a hunger satisfied. This was the night he was to tell Joe that the plan was changed and the real roost was the Feed and Seed. But the real roost was the Red Owl Store apartment after all; Joe had it right all along. The place of doom was also the best and snuggest place, according to good pal Joe. Which squarely fit the case. He was doomed. But doom was home.

He sat down in his chair and waited for Joe.

ALL WEEK long the proprietor of the Red Owl Store had been in a sanguine mood, a selling mood, a storekeeper-of-the-week kind of mood. Not only was business decent, with the nice fall weather bringing folks downtown, but this event of Robinson's on Saturday promised to be a goldmine, with the city hall park just across the street and so many people with money in their pockets coming from other towns. "This is America, he should run for election more often," Henry chuckled more than once to Mary Ellen as he savored the gravy of his deal for the sixty turkeys for Saturday's barbecue, all freshly delivered and nestled in his freezer; if he had been the type to whistle, like his good helper Joe, he would have filled his meat locker with song. Now he had Joe bring those boxes of red, white and blue dinner napkins up from the cellar where they were collecting cobwebs and stack them in the window. He had real hopes of getting rid of them on Saturday and without being the big giveaway they were the last time he dug them up for display.

Just as his red-striped awning shaded his sidewalk, Henry's horizon was the near-term future, a future made of perishables, of sweet cream down two cents this week and ham and pork chops up, of perennial bargains like his day-old bread and special little seasons inside seasons; change, as in small change, was the law of life in Henry's world. Under his awning on Saturday would go a sidewalk sale of crabapples, pumpkin, squash, garden carrots, all his sidewalk could hold of the fast disappearing autumn. He had been up Legion Avenue keeping his eye on what the other merchants were doing. Most of them had Robinson's election poster hanging in the window. At the Coast-to-Coast, they had their Great Firecrackers sign, their Fourth of July bunting, and a clearance sale on garden tools and lawn chairs. At the Dakota Store there was a big banner saying Picnic in the Park on Saturday, Rain or Shine, and they had the umbrellas out on the sidewalk again, though they knew, and everyone on the street knew, that no one could sell umbrellas for a profit on the prairie.

But a thing like a napkin might go. It was worth a little extra time and trouble. He had Joe crawling in and out of the window trying different combinations of boxes before he decided on a pyramid, with Robinson's poster hanging over it with a napkin spread under his chin and a sign saying: Get Your George Robinson Barbecue Napkins, Only Sold Here. Seeing his old stock dressed up like that in the window, Henry was almost glad he still had them, though even if they all sold out tomorrow he would never put another nickel into a fancy dinner napkin again.

Joe was a good worker. He did everything he was asked to do and he never complained; it was hard to believe, thinking back to first impressions, that he would be working here a whole year pretty soon. Henry felt mellow as he observed Joe in the back of the store later in the morning, toiling in his apron, pounding a mallet over a piece of meat. What kind of a life can he have, Henry asked himself as he looked at the tender menial figure of Joe. And a little lightbulb lit up in Henry's mind, nothing big, a little twenty-five or fifteen watt bulb, nothing important, but a nice way of rewarding Joe and without it costing anything, just in case Joe was thinking about asking for a raise. So Henry strolled to the back of the store, put his arms up on the meat counter and told Joe: "It's getting to look like your department, Joe. Okay. Go ahead and make your own sign for the ground beef special this week and from now on."

But Joe, as he came through Jericho that night, on his way to his last meeting with West before the Day, Joe wasn't thinking about any sign in a window. He was too jumpy; too gloomy. If Joe happened to let himself remember the ground beef sign and Henry's words about the meat department, it was only to think how he would have been whistling through town tonight if it wasn't for what was happening on Saturday. Not happening, Joe couldn't swallow it yet—sleeping and dreaming in West's head.

Joe carried a bag of firecrackers he had bought that afternoon, which he put down the minute he was inside West's, as far from himself and from supper as possible. As he made the meal, and they sat and ate, Joe's head was a jumble of worries—that Saturday would go crazy and succeed—that it wouldn't succeed, because the one link that broke and failed West was Joe. He wouldn't look at West. He glanced furtively into kitchen corners but he didn't see West's gun or the boxes of bullets. There was nothing about this meeting tonight that seemed different from any other night. West ate fast and silently but that was normal for West. Joe began to think that he had made a mistake and maybe he was the one who was dreaming, when West stood up, wiping his mouth with his napkin. "Let's take a look at the firecrackers."

Joe brought the bag to the table and took them all out, a dozen strings with six small firecrackers to a string, West handling each of them and counting under his breath. Then West smiled at Joe. "Anything changed about the Red Owl Store apartment?"

Joe shook his head.

West's smile broadened. "Safe and snug. All as planned . . . Your buddy Henry say you can go hear the speech?"

"It's okay—you're okay."

"Don't look up at the window. Light the first firecrackers when he's just standing there. Light more firecrackers the minute he opens his mouth. Keep doing it until he falls. You bring the matches?"

Joe reached in his pocket and took out a little box of wooden matches.

"Do it," said West. Joe took a match and ignited it with his thumbnail, something he had practiced so he could hold a firecracker string in his other hand and light it quickly. The match flared; Joe watched it burn down toward his fingers, almost reach them, then blew it out. He put the matches in his pocket and the firecrackers back in the bag.

"I'm going home now," Joe said.

West dangled then offered a hand. "See you Sunday morning for breakfast."

Joe looked at the hand and turned away. "Yeah, breakfast."

CHAPTER 38

WHEN JOE had gone, West cleared the table, did the dishes, tidied up the kitchen. An imaginary West, in the meantime, departed from the house, navigated the bike, and climbed the stairs leading to the Red Owl Store apartment. They worked together smoothly, the ever-moving West on the stairs with the gun and the West at the sudsy kitchen sink, they functioned with a quiet hum, the day being Thursday, the plan calling for West to stay in his house until the small hours Saturday, to rest up and get himself ready.

He went to sleep early, the methodical West in pajamas, but the stair-climber soon woke him up and lugged him out of bed. West peeked at the immense night behind the window shade. Not the cool, sound sleeper envisioned in the plan, he sat in his rocker and tried to read, a spray of his boyhood thrillers in his lap, the same thrillers he always meant to throw away; but he couldn't lose himself in the pages of those books. Their mustiness spoke to the yarn inside West, these companions of a lonely boy, bent, old, toilet-worn, immortal, their pages smelling of life inside the Red Owl Store apartment. Putting them down, fainter-hearted than before, he crept back into bed. To make sleep come, he pulled down his pajamas and masturbated, blankly and quickly, as though drinking a glass of warm milk; but sleep came not at all and daybreak found him staring from his pillow at the coldly dawning certainty of Friday.

He stayed in pajamas all day, knowing he would need to lie down and sleep, so why get dressed? Or was he shying from the dawn around the bend—hoping to be stopped before he ever got started? Was he waiting for Alpha Davis to send the police—for the police to see Joe's sign—for Rainey to tell Robinson about the kiss? If he was, no one came, nothing stopped him, he was doomed and charmed. Only Cat scratched at his door to come in. When Cat was around, West talked to him. "I'll get dressed," he promised Cat, who was often curled up and asleep. "Don't worry, I'll be ready." And Cat's ears would twitch in his sleep. "I'll be there, count on it," nodded West.

In the afternoon he wheeled his bicycle into the house and parked it in the middle of the kitchen. His window shades were all drawn. Putting on his kid gloves, he slid the rifle and a paper bag out from under the bed, carefully tied the rifle across the handlebars with rope, put the bag containing the extra clip and his last box of bullets into the bicycle basket. Then he laid out his clothes on the floor: his old army boots, warm pants, clean shirt, a sweater, the gloves. He needed these small narrow things to do. He needed the minutes they took, the concentration, the build-up. There were times when he was scared, not just of being caught, but seeing Robinson alive one minute and dead the next, up then down, seeing him double and fall. But if there were many steps, and he took one step at a time, then it wouldn't be so high to the next step.

When he thought of Rainey, he saw her in the center of her family, like a bright sun that only shone on them, its warmth reserved for the Robinsons. It wounded him to realize this, but he bore no bitterness, only surprise that he had ever presumed differently. The fault was his. He had made a mistake to trust her. Already she was slipping back into the sights of memory where she belonged, becoming what she was in the beginning, the woman he used to see in the distance who was the girl he once admired from afar, back in a time when her fate seemed the image of his own, to be left all alone in this place.

His eye followed the time: the Red Owl Store apartment was

barely twelve hours away; the day of the calendar was over, now it came down to the clock. Joe had filled up the icebox but he had no appetite for food. He went and lay down in bed again but he couldn't fall asleep. Time to shave, but West didn't shave. All lathered, he stood before the bathroom mirror, mesmerized by the shaky hand in the mirror holding the razor. More than a bloody face, he feared seeing that unraveled hand attempt to shave, seeing his jitters. "No one will see me—I'll shave afterward," he announced to Cat, emerging from the bathroom, his face washed and his hair all combed, but still unwilling to part with his pajamas.

He had nightmares. His nightmares proved he slept. In one, he was running for his life, yet not running, not even able to lift his slab legs. In another, or maybe it was the sequel, something horrible was happening to him. At the same time, his mother sewed and watched. He woke up moaning, his sweat-wet pajamas clinging to him, swaddled in fear, hugging his own dear self. "Get up—just get up." West stumbled into the kitchen where a fantastic bicycle armed with a rifle was standing in the middle of the floor like his ride into one more dream.

After dark he heard firecrackers popping. In the long ago that was only last night, he had heard a scattering of them, but tonight there were more, popping like kids talking to each other across town. No one was allowed to light firecrackers before Saturday, the police chief warned in the *Pioneer*. But kids could never wait. Kids were automatically opposed to peace and quiet—kids were wonderful. His kinship with kids brought maudlin tears to West's eyes. No matter how old he got to be, and it could end tomorrow, he would always side with kids.

Two A.M. West tied up the loose ends. He burned Accounts Receivable, burned the sketch of the assassination scene, the *Pioneer* article on Robinson, his private map of Jericho, burned them page by page in the kitchen sink and ran the ashes down the drain.

Then he saw the tip of Cat's tail in the bathtub, flicking. Cat was just awake and washing himself.

If he never came back, who would love Cat, feed him, take care of him? Not Joe. He'd never give Cat over to Joe. He didn't want any part of himself left for Joe or anyone else.

Trembling, West lifted Cat up and turned on the faucets. Cat squirmed against his arm and meowed at the sound of the water running. It was such a big tub, getting enough in it even for Cat seemed to take so long. West kept testing the water with his hand. Don't make it hard, don't make the water too cold for Cat.

But when he swung Cat over the tub he couldn't part with him. He couldn't harm a hair on Cat, much less drown him. He stood hugging Cat, the tears running down his cheeks, hugging him close and crying until Cat jumped free of his arms. Cat would live.

He peeled and ate the hardboiled eggs that Joe had left in the icebox; then West put on his clothes, lacing up the army boots tightly. The boots would serve him if something happened to his bicycle afterward and he had to walk any distance. Besides, laced high and tight they gave him support and solidity against the feeling that the slightest hitch in the plan could sweep him away.

He put the kid gloves on and maneuvered the bicycle with its jutting rifle out of the house. He set Cat loose and locked his door. If he came back, Cat would be around.

CHAPTER 39

DAWN'S LIGHT rose behind Jericho's water tower, mottled the sky, and came through the white lace curtain of an upstairs window, making a black lace pattern on the sill. Dawn, Saturday; the cold cheek of the sun came up for a kiss.

He knew the town from this window, the big dark hulk of the city hall, the big dark ocean of the park, the gray white-frame houses that in obscurity fooled your eyes into believing they stretched on forever and didn't end just a few streets away, the next street being the plains. He used to sit in this window while his mother was still asleep on the sofa against the wall behind him. It used to be just as quiet then. So maybe the future was a dream and she was still asleep on the sofa. West didn't turn around to look. He had yet to see the old place in the light and couldn't say he wanted to, even if he always figured he would find himself back here one day. It was easy to climb the stairs without a flashlight, find the door and feel his way through, much simpler without a light to see by, that could have been caught by someone passing in the street below. There seemed to be nothing in the place, not a stick of the furniture he left behind or anyone else's since. The old sour cooking smell that the past breathed into his nostrils was the only thing he bumped into in the dark.

He parted the lace curtain with the tip of the barrel of the gun.

270

Below, Legion Avenue was creeping back on the map in the pale coming of daylight, not as different from how it looked seven years ago as only the day before yesterday. Streamers and banners were strung overhead for as far as West could see, and likely over the whole downtown, all three blocks of it. He saw flags in darkened store windows, banners over doorways and bunting wrapped around telephone poles. Above the door of the city hall was a banner he could read easily, it was so big: Politics is People, Elect George Robinson. In the park, with daylight seeping through the trees, he made out picnic tables and benches, and on the park's far side a barricade of cement blocks facing his window that he couldn't explain, until he remembered and relaxed: it was the pit for the big turkey barbecue.

He had been standing at the window waiting for daylight ever since he came in. Now West sat down on the floor, shook the extra clip and bullets out of the paper bag, loaded the clip and then in the lengthening daylight loaded the rifle that lay across his lap. With one bullet he had purposely left in the chamber, he had five shots ready in the rifle. He made sure the safety was on and lay the rifle beneath the window, to the right of it the loaded clip, and beside that his reserve of a dozen bullets. He kept his kid gloves on; it was cold, his fingers kept warm besides not leaving prints. Still sitting, he picked up the rifle, nudged the curtain open and lined up the sights on the city hall steps just under Robinson's sign. Ping, West said softly, so as not to wake his mother up, the dead.

But his kid-gloved assurance slid off West's skin when he put the rifle down and climbed to his feet and stood killing time at the window, and time died in both directions. His mother curled up on the sofa behind him, old walls all around him, the dead alive in him yet, so that West's heart jumped like a clutch of wings panicking, feeling her eyes on the back of his neck, his neck squeezed tight like the rest of him, a man in a small boy's skin. Here lived Annie West and her boy Alaman, two strangers in town whom the four winds had thrown together. Here they lived, the contented little son and his wonderful mother. No father, no dad, lived here with them. Each night, little West would sit on no-dad's knee and run and fetch his slippers for him. Every Sunday, the three of them went fishing: there was no such thing as a fishing season where no-dad was concerned. And when no dad went to work, Annie stayed at home, acting like no waitress, no, but just for West, and read him fairy tales, good as this one, and made him pies and smothered him with kisses, just an ordinary day in the life of Annie and her boy Alaman.

West crossed the room and sat down against the sofa wall and pressed his back against it to make it know it was only an empty wall. He closed his eyes. To climb up here in darkness meant he had time to waste. He let himself doze . . . to catch some sleep, also milk the sadness out. It wasn't so bad to nap here on the floor like Cat and picture him curled up. West dozed and woke and dozed, and when he opened his eyes a second time he didn't know where he was, dazed in sunlight with white curtains in an empty room. Then West remembered and sat up straight. What was happening outside?

He rushed toward the window and dropped to the floor—a man on a ladder was outside the window. West stretched himself flat and by degrees looked up. The man, working several yards away, was fastening something to the corner streetlight; he yelled to someone on the ground then disappeared down the ladder. West finally crawled to the window and raised his eyes above the sill. No ladder, no man, but there was something strung from the streetlight to a tree across the way, a long banner that the angle made difficult to read but which he figured out to say: Jericho Welcomes You.

West smiled his appreciation. That must be for the strange kid living here. They want him to know that the whole town welcomes him, that's why they woke him up early—so he won't miss anything.

A couple of crows flew off one telephone wire and settled on another. A couple of dogs started barking on different sides of town. A couple of cars drove past about fifteen minutes apart, early birds going to work, he guessed, down to the post office or depot.

Pete came out of the city hall with a folded flag tucked under his arm. He swept it open, fixed it to the chain on the pole, sent it aloft, and went back into the city hall. And only West was watching.

Storekeepers came and unlocked their doors, Henry down below with a loud clank of a padlock. Two guys from Amundson's lumber yard then a guy from the grain elevator straggled into the café for their morning cup of coffee. Here's Joe coming to work, crossing Legion Avenue, looking both ways, walking toward the Red Owl Store like any ordinary morning, except for his little bag of fireworks in his hand.

The storekeepers swept the night's dust off their sidewalks. The Coast-to-Coast husband-and-wife started bringing lawn furniture outside for the big sidewalk sale. Soon others were hauling their stuff out too, up and down the street, Jericho turning itself inside out for Robinson Day. Except for Joe, nobody looked real. They all looked like doll people down there, putting their doll town together. Some in high school band uniforms began putting up folding chairs and music stands under the trees near the city hall steps. On the other side of the park, strings of smoke rose from the fires they were starting for the turkey barbecue. The city hall was alive with them doing things, carrying out loudspeakers to put on either side of the steps, placing wooden police barriers around the bottom of the steps. Meanwhile, small ones in scout uniforms on bicycles, and pickup trucks decorated as floats, moved down the avenue in the direction of the depot. The band dolls finished their work and they also headed toward the depot. Hank, a cop doll, with blue folded arms, stood in front of the city hall looking all around him before he got in his car and drove in the same direction toward the depot.

Cars were parking and people collecting on the sidewalk on both sides of Legion Avenue. Behind the lace curtain, West waited too, time running on, time running out, one way or the other. West jumped at a childhood sound, a close harsh grating sound, the awning of the Red Owl Store unrolling underneath him. When it stopped, he was listening to distant music, marching trumpets and drums, coming from the depot. It was time to open his window.

ROBINSON CALLED down the stairs:

"Don't start my breakfast yet. I'm dressing."

He closed the bedroom door behind him, opened his closet door, took a package down from the shelf and carried it to the

bed. Quickly he pulled off string and wrapping and held his pur-
chase at arm's length in front of him: his first pair of Long Johns.
Let it blow cold as hell on the city hall steps this morning, they'll
never know it looking at George Robinson, braving it without a
coat on, the youth and vigor candidate. If fitness was the question, Long Johns were the answer. He shed his pajamas and
climbed into them, legs first and then his arms, and looked in
the full-length mirror. Off him they were stringy and ghostly but
on him was a different story. They looked complete, which was
nothing compared to how they felt, warm and snug in every bend
and hollow. No wonder farmers wore them. You felt them on
you and you thought: "Us—to hell with the rest of the world."
The button-front was dignified, likewise the trap-door seat. He
had been wise to buy them in Malden where he was comparatively unknown. Shirt buttoned and socks pulled up high and
not a soul would guess—not even Rainey knew. The only catch
was getting caught in them by surprise, like if your pants fell
down, or came off on Doc Sunderquist's emergency room table.

That wasn't funny. He almost stopped dressing, that was how
sorry he was he had thought of it, damned sorry, as he pulled on
the other leg of his dark suit trousers. Long underwear wouldn't
stop cold lead, and outdoors was a big cold place. Hank was still
against all this, with his stalking assassin theory. Hank argued
that any crowd was dangerous. But Hank and Pete would be
armed and watching from the minute the parade began. He
would never back out now, this was the beginning of his campaign for next time; he couldn't throw away his hope for that
election of the future. And he had been out in public a thousand
times since he got the letter. The eagle in the wings had flown
on. There was no assassin anymore.

At the breakfast table, Rainey there on the run to nibble some
toast and serve him, his children hushed into chewing silence in
their pajamas, the candidate braced himself with poached eggs,
warm sweetrolls and fresh hot coffee, and one last time delivered
his speech in his head. If he was no longer afraid of a death threat,
or a threat of rain, and his speech sounded flawless to him, he
worried about the microphone, the space for parking, the food
for the barbecue, the length of the parade. Like a sensitive bride-
groom he fretted over every detail that had been left in other

hands, he wished he was out there directing all of it himself; but like the bride he couldn't be seen by anyone too soon. What kind of impression would he make? Would people really remember? How long would they remember? How many people would there be? Going in circles, craving reassurance, with only his Long Johns to hug him, he sat alone in the kitchen until he could sit no longer and went into the living room and roamed the big front window until he abandoned that too and went to the foot of the stairs.

"The car for the parade is picking us up in ten minutes," he yelled upstairs to Rainey who appeared at the top of the staircase with her hairbrush in her hand.

"All of us ride in the same car?"

"In the back seat. Stephie sits on your lap—we're a family. That's fifteen minutes at the very most."

Unhurriedly brushing her hair, observing her husband's back as he turned and walked away, with his self-important little swagger, like a drum major in a parade, Rainey remembered Alaman West's kiss that was now a few days old and seemed not so fresh anymore, in one way and another. Lazily brushing her sun-filled hair, she wondered how important George's little parade would be to him if he knew she had been kissed by another man, even if the man was something of a boy and it was no Romeo-oh-Romeo of a kiss. What would he say if he knew, Rainey wondered, smiling at her thoughts, brushing out her hair. Would he have a fit? Would he just say it was stupid and laugh? Poor George, he knew he was going to lose the election, so which was more stupid, Alaman West's kiss or George Robinson's parade?

Collecting her purse and her gloves, calling "Jamie and Stephie, we're going," Rainey descended the stairs to where Robinson waited in the hall. Behind her came Stephie, hat and coat on, gripping the bannister and carrying her little purse. But there was something ghastly-looking about Stephie. Her mouth was a gash of red. Her cheek wore a big red smear. Rainey screamed "Oh no!" and grabbed her when she reached the bottom of the stairs. She had been at Rainey's lipstick. There was lipstick on her hands, her coat, her neck, on the front of her dress. Rainey screamed again. And Jamie yelled from the window: "The car's here!"

"Bring her!" Robinson shouted. "It's a closed car."

Rainey gasped, "Go with Jamie. We'll come later."

"But you'll miss the parade!"

"Just go. You're going out like that? You'll freeze to death!"

"Rainey—we're leading the parade!"

Rainey had a sudden thought and ran to the door and looked out, but Jamie had his coat on. She turned around and snatched Stephie as she was making for the door.

"Wonderful start. Come as soon as you can. Look for me on the city hall steps," said Robinson grimly. "That's where I'll be."

Rainey pulled off Stephie's coat and hat and then her dress, up over her head. She dragged her to the bathroom and with a washcloth scrubbed the lipstick off her mouth, her cheek, her neck, her pried-open hands. Maybe she scrubbed harder than she needed to. Stephie howled, bawled *parade,* had a tantrum, stamped her feet and lost her breath. Rainey screamed back. Stephie ran after her into the living room, a hysterical child pursuing a screaming mother who was that to her own despising. She sat and waited with Stephie, punishing her by staying in the house, pleasing herself by staying in the house, never having wanted to go in the first place, while Stephie sat on the floor in her panties and undershirt, glowering and panting with red, wet cheeks.

HE'S UP there, Joe told himself. He's up there, so don't look up, look normal, keep sweeping the sidewalk, keep your mind on the broom, do your job.

Joe hadn't slept much last night, lying awake wishing today would never come. When he saw the sun shining and heard the birds singing, he swore he wouldn't get up; then he wouldn't get dressed or anyway leave the hotel, and then he promised, okay, but he wouldn't go to the store. So here he was at the store, scared stiff, without sleep, and there was a lot of work to do this morning. When he finished sweeping the front, he helped Henry carry pumpkins and boxes of produce out for the sidewalk sale. Then there were the cuts of meat to put on the trays, and he had to grind up the beef, more today than usual. But wherever he was, he never forgot for a second that West was overhead. Joe kept straining his ears but he didn't hear a sound. Maybe he's not there, Joe thought with a miserable lack of belief in such good fortune. Then Joe had an idea. He went to the back and opened the door and stepped out by the trash cans. Joe was sorry he looked. There up the alley, leaning against the fence, was West's bicycle. Joe came back inside feeling as sad as he had ever felt in his life. He kept working, but now he began checking the big clock on the wall every other minute and glancing out the front window at the city hall across the street. Finally when the store was open for business he went to remind Henry, outside unrolling the awning, that in a little while he was leaving to hear the man's speech—he didn't say whose speech, which man's, he couldn't speak the name. West's plan said act excited. Maybe scared and nervous was better than excited, because Henry said, "Sure, Joe. Go watch the parade too, if you want—go right now."

So Joe was out of the store, out on the street, out of the nest, and in a different Jericho. Strangers' faces passed by hurriedly, bunches of people stood on the sidewalk, a band was playing and people were shouting. The parade was coming down the street. Joe heard it but he didn't look. After weeks with West's plan he knew it was coming. Holding the bag of firecrackers he dodged the crowd and ran toward the city hall park. There was plenty of time, he didn't have to run, but Joe ran to his spot at the edge of the grass. Some people were standing there whom Joe didn't know, farm people probably, with dark sunburned faces. They looked like nice people. They had no Plan; they were just here to see a parade—good people, average people, with cute kids. They could be one big family, going to the turkey barbecue. On a different kind of day Joe could imagine himself inviting them to come visit the store and see the bargains—on a different kind of day. But not today.

Joe wondered if West was watching him from the window. How he ached to look up at the window, if only for a second. But he wasn't going to make any mistakes—don't get blamed. *Don't look up at the window. Watch the city hall steps. Light the first firecrackers when he's just standing there. Light more firecrackers the minute he opens his mouth. Keep doing it until he falls.*

Joe heard the parade getting louder and nearer. The family all surged toward the street to watch it come. He clutched the bag of firecrackers in one hand, the thumbnail of his other hand, the match-igniting thumbnail, tingling. Joe could read the future like a postcard, and it told him, Don't worry—it's OK—West won't shoot. But the same postcard had a PS—*If you don't help me, I'm gone, I'm dead.*

CHAPTER 40

AND THE parade came in sight, the leader car—no, first a lookout car, all by itself, the police cruiser, Hank at the wheel, the chassis polished but not the top, the top a blind-eye dull to West's second-story eyes—and then the real leader, a bigger car, the Robinson car, "Robinson" plastered in white across it, Pete driving, the back seat hard to see in, a hand in a dark sleeve waving from the back seat window.

Next came two American flags on poles carried by men walking in soldiers' uniforms, and behind them a clump of men dressed in no particular way but with American Legion caps on their heads. And then came the boy scouts with the smallest ones last and sure enough the girl scouts likewise—it was the Fourth of July parade all over again, with the town firetruck coming up now, the volunteer firemen sitting on top of it or hanging to the sides by an arm and waving to the crowd with their firemen's hats just like they did every July. Now the Robinson car was passing underneath the window. The police cruiser in front of it was slowly turning left, setting the same funereal pace. The thumping band didn't sound far away. Dressed-up pickup trucks that he had seen going toward the depot now were moving past in the parade, as the Robinson car also began to turn at the corner. Men dressed like clowns on the Lions Club truck threw free candy to kids on the sidewalk and the salesladies on the Dakota Store float held hands in their Indian-girl suits, as the Robinson car slowly turned and left the parade, West's eyes following it as it followed the police cruiser leftward around the park, bound for the back of the city hall and no future. Here was the band—three drum-majorettes, all spinning batons, white legs, cold legs, like frozen turkey drumsticks—and then the high school marching band, in Jericho blue-and-gold, fancy braided jackets and high peaked hats to match, all halting at the corner and marching in place to the drums. The rest of the parade kept going straight down the avenue, past no more stores or sidewalk, marching out of sight, all except the band, led by the drum-majorettes, that now turned left, turned like a well-oiled wheel, the big drums rotating in place and the rest of the wheel, flutes, trumpets, small drums, quick-stepping to catch up, then the whole band marching toward the park, the people who were caught by surprise scattering out of the way. There was Joe— West saw Joe, true to the plan, standing with his little bag of fireworks right by the edge of the grass.

Cars with people watching from them stood nose to nose at the curbstone facing the city hall. Warmly dressed people were standing in the park; others stood in front of the loudspeakers on each side of the city hall and along the wooden barrier around the city hall steps, and people who had watched the parade from the sidewalk were flocking over from Legion Avenue. The band sat down in their chairs under the trees. The flag Pete had raised flapped in the breeze, in the blue. West's open window let in the lull after the music, the whole scene taking a breath. Joe was standing stark and still, like a statue with people around him. Hank and Pete had come out of the city hall and were surveying the crowd from the steps. It couldn't be the cold legs of the drum-majorettes that sent his great big shiver through West. He had imagined all this for so long, it was as though he had dreamed it all up. It was all his doing. The crowd, the sky, the steps, Joe, everything emanated from him kneeling at the window with his gunbarrel resting on the sill. These people all thought they were here because they wanted to be here, but they were here because of him.

The band began to play, sitting in their chairs, led by the teacher-bandmaster in gold-braid uniform, bareheaded, with a conductor's baton. It was the advertised band concert, beginning with a medley of college fight songs, fast and rousing. The city hall door opened and Robinson came out; he stood on the wide top step where a microphone was standing, under his big Robinson banner, turning and looking this way and that, bobbing in and out of the gunsights. Jamie was with him—where was Rainey, somewhere down in the crowd? West never figured on seeing her—he didn't want to see her. Say goodbye for me, his lips whispered to Jamie. Now Robinson went down the steps and had a conversation with Hank and Pete, who then came around the wooden barrier, pistols sticking out of their holsters, and took different directions through the crowd. The accomplished band had gone to softer music, roaming, rambling melodies, selected themes from western movies, sweet nostalgia without a name. And then, in a little drama of suspense, with each solo performer standing up, from sprightly flute to dramatic drumroll to trumpet fanfare, they launched into their full finale of patriotic music for today, the figure of Robinson at stiff attention on the chilly steps, hand plunged into his jacket pockets, through the final trumpet blast and drum crescendo that had the whole band finishing on their feet. There was applause from every corner of the crowd, led by an animated Robinson moving in the direction of the microphone. The bandmaster bowed; the band sat down again. West's eye caught Joe taking a step away from the crowd, a string of firecrackers in one hand, his other hand raised with a match.

Gunbarrel slid out further on the sill. Trigger-finger curled around the trigger. West was sweating. His sweat burned his eyes; he wiped them. It was a cold day—nobody down there was sweating. He wiped them again. Still spying, his trepidation told him—still only watching. His eyes couldn't focus. The man on the steps was a man and a half. The heart—sight the heart.

Joe's first string of firecrackers went off, exploding as if they were in West's pocket. Robinson standing at the microphone glanced quickly toward the sound. "Welcome to Jericho, friends,

I'm George Robinson"—the loudspeaker voice reverberating, "Welcome to Jericho, friends, I'm George Robinson." Joe's second round of firecrackers went off, one sharp crack after the other, Robinson's voice following with a rasping geniality: "All right, folks, I know you're as anxious as I am for our big day to begin, after that wonderful music by our Jericho High School band, and they'll be playing for us again a little later. But right now, folks, let's just wait a few minutes so that all of our friends who are still on their way here can join us. Just a few more minutes, folks. Thank you."

Silence on the steps—Robinson walked away from the microphone. Silence that rushed to the window—West almost ducked his head. The quiet threw everything off. It was as though Robinson was always his better, always knew something he didn't, always started ahead. Six loud cracks broke the quiet—firecrackers—it was Joe. Was Joe crazy? Robinson wasn't speaking, he wasn't even standing still. But West saw Joe light yet another string of firecrackers, throw them on the ground and jump away. Their noise was swallowed up, but in its wake West felt an undertow pulling him to shoot. All of life ebbing pulled on him to shoot. He didn't know what Robinson might do next—how much time he had left—if he would ever be ready again.

He shot the gun. Robinson was still standing. Quiet fell, the same as before, then came the lonely answer from below, Joe's stuttering firecrackers and the tug on West to shoot. He pulled the trigger. Robinson was still standing. He couldn't bring down Robinson. He shot and shot again, like a man frantic for something.

Down came Jamie. West saw him take a small leap back, then sprawl on the step behind Robinson. Robinson's eyes were scanning the street. The crowd stood shifting and waiting or sat back in their parked cars. No one was looking at Jamie. He fell behind his father while no one noticed, or while absently they saw a boy tripping on a step and falling.

West stood up in the window, the rifle in his hands forgotten, not believing what he had done—believing and beyond believing, all finished, Alaman home at last, entwined in the curtain and in the twisting horror and deep repose going through him.

"You up there—you up there—you up there—"

Pete down in the street was shouting up at him, shouting and waving his pistol. In fright West dropped to the floor. And then over the loudspeakers from Robinson's open microphone on the steps came the informed, amplified groan: "Oh my God."

And then they all looked and they saw.

CHAPTER 41

WEST DASHED out of the apartment and ran down the stairs. He flung open the back door—Pete was rounding the corner into view. West slammed the door and ran up the stairs, back up the same winding space, the clamor of his boots walloping his ears. He locked the apartment door and stood behind it, breathless. There was no sound on the stairs. Pete was waiting down in the alley. West flew to the window. Outside, everything was happening at once. People were running away from the city hall. There were scattered men running toward the steps to Jamie and Robinson. At the same time, people far from the steps were standing still and looking around.

Open the window wide. Jump. If he jumped he would hit the Red Owl awning and drop from there to the sidewalk. Do it— never mind if people saw. Leave the gun, jump and go with the crowd. His one chance was to jump from the window. Wait and he was done for.

Now came a shriek, a shriek—the fire whistle—not stopping, long blasts of it, over and over, terrifying West, like a giant spotlight searching him out—like a blast from a firehose forcing him back into the confines of the room.

It was Hank who had the fire whistle sounded. Not far away when he saw Pete shouting up at the window, Hank followed him around to the alley where Pete told about the armed man in the Red Owl apartment and quickly Hank improvised a plan. Leaving Pete to guard the door, he used the Feed and Seed phone to call the firehouse and have the whistle blown, then he raced his big chugging frame through the crowd in the street across to the city hall. On the steps, two men were lifting Jamie Robinson to take him to Doc Sunderquist's office. Hank winced at the oozing blood of the chest wound; he stopped and squeezed the arm of the drawn and shaken Robinson. Volunteer firemen ran up to him. Most had remained in the vicinity after the parade; they were alerted but confused by the still-blowing fire whistle. Hank gathered them round and gave instructions: Get people out of the area fast, empty the park and this end of Legion Avenue, have the people in cars drive the hell away, clear the buildings—if people won't go home get them inside stores farther down the avenue, out of the line of gunfire. As he reeled off orders, Hank kept an eye on the windows above the Red Owl Store, only himself here to do it, praying he and Pete could hold things for a while, as always one cop short. The firemen fanning out to do their job, Hank hurried into the city hall to police headquarters where he called the state police. Attempted murder, he told them, dangerous man armed with a rifle in a second floor apartment, could be others with him, no telling, a child seriously wounded. Hank loaded two high-powered rifles from the gun cabinet. He walked and ran back to Pete and handed him one and had Pete, the better marksman, go around in front and take the windows while he stayed in the alley with his rifle trained on the door, brutally confirmed in his suspicions as he waited for the state police and watched for the still-unidentified assassin to show his face.

The men carried Jamie to a car and laid him on the back seat with his head in Robinson's lap, and one of them drove the car a block and a half and across the street to Doc Sunderquist's office. Doc had office hours on Saturday morning. He was inside with a patient when Robinson burst into the waiting room, hollering for Doc with Jamie limp in his arms. Doc came out, as did the patient, a pregnant farm wife who watched and listened aghast to Robinson raving about somebody shooting Jamie on the city hall steps. Doc had Robinson carry Jamie into the examining room and lay him down on the table. Quickly Doc opened his coat and unpeeled the bloody shirt and undershirt, baring a bullethole. He turned Jamie over on his stomach, exposing a bigger, bloodier hole that almost made Robinson faint. Doc took Jamie's wrist to check the pulse. He grabbed a slender flashlight and shone the light in Jamie's eye. And Doc's face had a look of surprise, as though Robinson's frantic urgency had fooled him, as he slowly turned Jamie over on his back again.

"George . . . he's dead."

By this time, Eleanor and Jim Prain had reached the office, and Margaret and Bill Hanson. The white room gyrating around him, Robinson glimpsed their faces crowding in at the door. He gripped the edge of the table to steady himself. Then, Jamie's blood on his jacket, his pants, his shoes, he walked to Margaret, he approached a moment he had dreaded ever since he knew that yes there was an assassin in Jericho, and he had shot at his target and missed. "Go bring Rainey," he whispered to Margaret. "Please."

Jamie had been covered with a sheet; still Robinson couldn't look. Doc slid a chair beside the table. "Sit down, George." Robinson obeyed. Rainey here would complete the devastation of the day, a devastation in which a fleeing crowd and ruined campaign was a loss so small, so insignificant in comparison, that to feel it now was to add one more guilty secret to his list, and yet feel it he did, as he sat here hiding his face in his hands and asking himself what he could ever say to Rainey.

GLORY BE—it's a boy, Annie West.

It was quiet like dawn; they were all gone, the steps bare, the park deserted, the street still, the banners flapping, the whole scene empty, all except for Pete, crouching down there behind the police cruiser that he had brought around and parked just across the street. Pete had a rifle. He popped out and showed himself every now and then, maybe inviting West to stand in the window and take a shot and then take his turn as the target. It wasn't a complicated game. There were only three pieces, him up here, Pete down there, and Hank who would be down in the alley guarding the door. Old friend Hank he knew over time to nod to. Pete was newer; he had the look of a loner, a loner on the opposite side. Fair is fair. All alone he had watched Pete raise the flag, and now Pete was watching him.

He killed Jamie, Alaman West did, shot him dead. Killed? How could he be sure? Oh, he was sure. Jamie was dead, dead, dead. "Nip it in the bud," was West's thought for the father, all the way back in the beginning. He missed the father and got the son. Missed, mystery, there it was, the little bud was nipped. "How's the swimming?" West asked him that time he came running in the house, fresh from the pool, still wet. A shiver. *"Cold."* A tremor, West's. How Rainey hugged him, hugged him, hugged her Jamie. *Jump for joy—it's a boy, Annie West.*

Oblivion the lullaby, West rocked inside himself, rocked and closed his eyes. He had no age, no aim, no past, no future, like the second you wake up in the morning and you could be a kid, a man or maybe an old man—at first you don't know. Then the truth sinks in:

It's me. And I'm going to die.

Playing peek-a-boo, Pete popped out from behind the cruiser, raised his rifle, then ducked behind the hood again. Old Hank must be getting weary of waiting around in back in the alley. Joe was long gone. Robinson was nowhere. Jamie was dead and Rainey had never been. The town had flown; but they left their sign behind them, Jericho Welcomes You.

West froze his fists against the sides of his head.

What now? The door or the window, Hank or Pete, heads or tails?

The door. More sure. But promise: don't mind Hank when he yells to stop. Just keep on going, keep on walking till it comes. Promise.

Hallelujah—it's a boy, Annie West.

West picked up the rifle and pretty slowly walked down the stairs. At the bottom he kicked the door open and he stepped outside, aiming for the sky.

DOWN LEGION Avenue in bright sunshine, out of the line of gun-fire, a group of people herded inside a store had edged out into the open, encouraged by the presence of two volunteer firemen there on the sidewalk with them.

Some were from Jericho, most were visitors from other towns. From here they could see Pete where he crouched behind the police cruiser or at moments stood clear of it with his rifle aimed upward and across the street.

"He's up in the Red Owl apartment," one of the firemen said. "It's lucky no one lives there—he's dangerous."

"Who is he?" a man asked.

"Nobody knows. Some maniac."

The other fireman said: "Hank—the police chief—thinks there could be more than one, that's why they're waiting . . . I saw Robinson's kid back there. He looked real bad. There's the mother," he said pointing across the street and they all saw a woman running from a car into the doctor's office.

Then they heard a shot and all heads turned, and then a second shot. They saw Pete race across the street and disappear behind the Red Owl. A minute later, Pete came running back and took his position behind the cruiser. "Hank's in the back alley," one fireman said; the other agreed, "He must be." But no one could say what had happened. Presently they heard sirens and saw the arrival of a state police car, an ambulance and a black van out of which came a swarm of troopers carrying rifles. Pete ran to meet them and the troopers marched around to the back of the Red Owl. The crowd tensed, waiting for more shots. Then a trooper appeared in an upstairs window calling below and waving his arm. Hank, a rifle drooping from his hand, came walking very slowly from around the back of the building and wrapped his arm around Pete's shoulder and the two of them stood together silently, while a pair of troopers bearing a stretcher went around to the back and in a minute they and the stretcher with a covered heap on it swerved into view.

Some in the crowd looked queasy and hurriedly left. Those who remained stood hushed. One of them was Joe; he huddled among them, scared, but not able to go away, keeping his head low, wearing his black woolen hat and his short thick jacket, the clothes in which he had landed in Jericho. When he heard that first shot, Joe froze, and with the second, his heart started pounding. Once he heard those shots, all the police in the world couldn't scare him from this spot, and now his bright eyes watched the covered thing on the stretcher, there under a blanket, no face, his friend, carried by the men without hurry, swung and bump-slid (Oh West!) into the ambulance in a way that told Joe that nothing could harm it or help it anymore.

CHAPTER 42

ALPHA DAVIS fainted at Jamie Robinson's funeral.

People were seated; the service was beginning. The church organ played softly, with understanding, played sweetly. Alpha felt herself starting to go as the casket came down the aisle in the grip of the pallbearers. Her breath failed her, her eyes swam—she swayed. As the casket was set down before the altar, she slumped against the shoulder of the person sitting next to her. The church pews were jam-packed, the warm air weepy; no one was surprised when an old woman swooned. Doc Sunderquist was roused from his seat behind the Robinson family pew, and he helped Alpha down to the church basement where he determined she was all right and left her sitting with the minister's wife, whom Alpha politely released to return upstairs. But Alpha never went back. She hoped they forgot about her. As it was, she could never again face Rainey or even him, when not calling the police that day West terrified her in the library had as good as put their little boy into that coffin. *I'll kill him! I'll kill him!* Alpha still cringed in daydreams at her brush with the killer West. Why didn't she call the police? Why? But what if they hadn't believed her, what then? Even if they believed, they would think she was too old, she was feeble, she couldn't manage. Hungering for aspirin, her head aching and her frail shoulders cold,

Alpha sat alone in the darkened church basement. It was better not to draw attention to herself. They would shake their heads. They would think she was senile. There was no telling what might enter their minds if they started paying attention.

Upstairs, the Robinson family was seated prominently up front, George and Rainey Robinson with Stephie between them, and Robinson's mother and father. The minister read from the Bible, the choir sang, the minister offered a remembrance, the organist played once again, people filed past the open casket with Jamie in suit, starched collar and tie, his mortal wound clothed, his only mark the bruise from his father's hand that turned out to be a scar for life. Then, the organ music climbing for the journey, the four pallbearers carried the casket back up the aisle and out to the waiting hearse to lead the processional drive of the few miles to Cemetery Hill. Once there, the inseparable pallbearers unloaded the casket, carried it to the grave and set it down. Those grieving the most were sick of the pallbearers' faces.

Brown leaves clung to the trees and the thin wind shook them to mordant life as the mourners, a fair portion of those who had been at the church, left their cars ringed below and climbed past other graves to the large raised stone with the carved Spencer name, the two headstones for Rainey's mother and father and the new, open grave. Lorraine Robinson, all in black, leaned heavily on Robinson's arm. Her friend Margaret Hanson and Robinson's parents beside him completed the small circle of the bereaved, Stephie having been left behind with a neighbor and spared the sight of the unforgettable.

The polished walnut casket rested on straps that would lower and ease it into the ground. The minister glanced around him at the silent crowd in place, and then at the Robinson family. "Loved ones of Jamie, friends . . . Just as some of our brethren have planted their winter wheat, so we are now gathered to plant the body of this small boy. He is the good seed of his mother and father, destined not to grow on this earth, never to be seen by our eyes, but to lie forever warm and blessed under the eternal snow. To bloom in heaven, the spirit, the hope and the resurrection."

The minister took up a handful of dirt. At the last instant

Rainey reached out—she touched the casket with her hand as though it was velvet. Robinson sobbed and covered his eyes. The minister opened his hand and sprinkled the dirt on the casket.

"James Spencer Robinson, our little brother—"

At the complete, completed name of Jamie, Rainey cried out with such force that her cry dented the crowd near her. She sagged against Robinson, her mouth made hideous by her grief. Robinson strengthened his hold and held her tight.

On the stumbling walk down, in the back seat of the car driving them away, neither looked back at the hill that would be crisscrossed with sled tracks when the snow came.

People came to the house all week to show their sympathy, bringing homemade cakes, bread and hot dishes to be fed to other people who came offering sympathy. Flowers from the funeral sat in borrowed vases through the house. The white roses on the mantle were from Rainey's sister in the East; Robinson had not encouraged her to come, not so much because the sisters were cool to each other as that their reunion might rekindle memories of their parents dying and overwhelm Rainey all the more. He saw how helpless, how listless, she was with Stephie, and so Stephie had a suitcase packed and went to Margaret's for a while. Even Robinson's parents seemed to hurt her with their presence; he sent them out on errands or drives in the country and sat and held her limp hand. He was very protective of her—with the nights turning cold, he made comfortable fires in the fireplace, taking care the flames did not leap up to startle her. He took these pains to show his loving, tender side, a man desperate to make up for the recklessness he had shown in ignoring the threatening letter. But there was an inside to Robinson's tender side: he still faced the job of telling her about the letter. Hank had spilled its contents to the state police, then he himself cravenly removed it from the safe and handed it over. He should have burned the damned letter. She was bound to find out—better that the awful news came from him. Confess, and cry along with her. But Robinson couldn't bring himself to do it, even though preparing her for this shock about himself was part of every kindness he enacted every day. How could he tell her that if he had been careful, Jamie would be alive?

He made himself enter Jamie's room. Like an intruder in a

paradise he had scorned, he forced himself to cross the threshold. Jamie's things were there untouched, his toys, his shelf of books, his brush and comb, his clothes, the still unreturned school books. As Robinson gazed almost furtively around him, the most damning thing, now that Jamie was gone, was how much of this was new to him. Here were the little possessions of a child that Will Carpenter had wept about. Here was the age-old lament of the living: he should have been a better father while he could.

When he thought of the instant that changed their lives, the murderous act itself, Robinson was still flabbergasted. He saw it with a kind of detached wonder. West the bookkeeper, the cyclist, Rainey's friend, was West the assassin, the killer. The odd sock and the eagle in the wings were one and the same. How? Why? What was the motive? Hate? Spite? Sport? Lunacy? Was there a political purpose to it? Was he a fan of Armstead? Outrageous idea, but what part of it wasn't outrageous? Those visits by West to their house—that always rankled him. He should have listened to his instincts. The visits must have suited West's plan, allaying suspicion, ingratiating him with Rainey, though there could have been something more to it than that. Then a death threat from nowhere, from someone hidden in the wings, that other brain in Jericho, seething, stewing, festering. So was he in love with her? Was he? Was that dank stew love? Robinson recoiled from imagining more—there was nothing to imagine. He trusted Rainey, that was a first principle, and he knew better than to take her hand and try prying the lid off the subject of the man who killed her Jamie.

Robinson's parents departed. They would be back for Christmas—just like last Christmas, with one difference. He said goodbye to them at the airport, the mournful grandparents, his bewildered mother and father; they had seldom heard Rainey speak a word. A hired woman came in to do the housework. Robinson walked Big Red at night and took care of the shopping, glad of any excuse to escape from those walls. In the drugstore he was waited on by none other than Will Carpenter. On opposite sides of the counter, as of almost everything else, the two men concentrated on the little list of items, the father of Dixie uncharacteristically holding his tongue, the father of Jamie sighing to himself that Will's definition of a child gone was Dixie getting fucked. As he was paying at the cash register, he said to Will: "How's that little girl of yours? Still the apple of your eye?"

Will darted a look to see if Robinson was baiting him. Will mumbled, "I'm sorry about your boy . . ." He rang up the sale and handed Robinson his change. "But I still don't like you."

"Thank you, Will."

Attentive to Rainey, at home to everyone who came knocking at the door to offer sympathy, still absent from his law office, Robinson felt estranged from the world, living in a universe of flowers, murmurs, timeless cups of coffee and sitting and sitting. Hardly a week had passed since Jamie's burial. He sat beneath an avalanche of mail, mail from Grafton, Malden, the other towns, other regions of the state: condolence cards, handwritten notes, long letters, the letters often from people who had lost a child too, or suffered other great family misfortunes. Eleanor Prain collected them all at the post office, opened them, wept over them and brought them to the house. Sitting in his living room, Robinson was amazed at how the story had carried. As a remorseful father and confessed self-centered man, this outpouring by complete strangers overwhelmed him. He even got a phone call from Miss Brown at the State House, late one evening. She expressed her sorrow, and she extended condolences from the lieutenant governor and the shocked governor himself. Her tone was of a friend. She told Robinson she had been speaking with some interested people she knew, and Robinson was stirring up a lot of positive feeling in the district. Then came Miss Brown's soft question: Was he still in the campaign for the State Assembly?

Robinson, for a second, didn't know what to answer.

CHAPTER 43

WEST'S BODY returned to Jericho in a plain pine coffin to be buried beside his mother on Cemetery Hill. A special town fund for the indigent paid for the gravedigging and headstone. A prison chaplain accompanied the body and performed his brief ceremony while a state trooper and a gravedigger stood by and the driver waited at the wheel of the mortician's van. This took place a few days after West's death. Days later, after much procrastinating, Doc Sunderquist drove out to the hill and parked his car down by the gate. He had a bunch of geraniums he had cut from plants he was moving inside for the winter, one more job he was late in doing. Talk about procrastination, thought Doc as he surveyed the lone hill, covered with frost; he had been putting this off for seven years.

He made sure to pick a time when no one was apt to be around, early in the morning before he drove to his office. Not that he was ashamed of being here, but it might be hard to explain if anyone saw him. As he climbed the slope, looking at graves, Doc was conscious of the other side of Cemetery Hill and Jamie Robinson's grave beside Rainey's mother and father, killed in that other terrible tragedy years ago, and his heart went out to Rainey. Doc was a solid tough man, not notably sensitive, known to some as a fairly cold fish, but the women made him swallow hard sometimes because of the pain they took and held in, soaking it up like a sponge. Men gave back the pain one way or another, but not the women—they caught their breath and held it in, the Rainey Robinsons, the Molly Carpenters, the Annie Wests.

Annie West, her grave, a small flat stone that he had never seen. Doc felt a chill, seeing the son's headstone beside it, despite knowing it would be here. The two stones had the bare names and the dates. Doc leaned down and laid the geraniums on her grave, mumbling something like "Annie, may she rest in peace." He always liked Annie, someone who had a hard enough life but kept her troubles to herself, raised a kid all alone, lived in her own little shell. She was a pretty little women, and he flirted with her the way you could with a waitress without anyone thinking anything of it. The cemetery was where doctors buried their mistakes, the old wisecrack went. Annie, may she feel no pain, was one of the mistakes.

You couldn't stay guilty forever. At least he couldn't. Mostly, he felt pity for Annie, curled up on a sofa, small hands holding on—some pictures never faded—and disgust for the doctor who skimped on his examination, hurried through it, was on his way someplace else, called an inflamed appendix stomach flu, didn't take the right precautions, ill-served Annie West—it was hard to remember after seven years, especially when you were anxious to forget. But it went something like that. And the son guessed.

The son knew. The son never accused him, but he let Doc know he knew. The hate, the despising, in the son's eyes—that trick of baiting Doc whenever he saw him, starting to say hello, getting Doc to start, then just walking away—he never got tired of that. As long as the son walked the streets, Doc couldn't be allowed to forget. But when he saw what happened to the Robinsons, Doc knew he had gotten off cheap.

The son was a mystery that no one ever solved. Doc remembered him from all the way back, when Annie was waiting tables in the old Eagle Hotel. He remembered the son being there inside the kitchen when the swinging door swung open, or you would see him out in front as you came up the walk, waiting for his mother, playing some game by himself under the old hotel sign. Now here he was beside her, dead beyond recognition, a bullet-hole in the back of his head and most of his face obliterated.

Begrudgingly, for Annie, Doc bent down and took one of her geraniums and tossed it on the other grave.

Doc finally called it quits with the West family.

THE STATE police had the rifle from the slain assassin and the bullet that passed through his victim, gouged a city hall brick and came to rest on the grass. They had shell casings from the same rifle, found in the Red Owl Store apartment. They had the threatening letter from Robinson's safe. The fingerprints on the letter and envelope, made by Robinson, Eleanor Prain, Hank, a post office clerk, led to nothing. They studied the message, the wording, the printing and the paper. They ransacked West's house. Still, they could find nothing to implicate Joe. They wanted Joe for questioning because of his known association with West: neighbors, Hank himself had seen him visiting West's house. There was no proof of anything against him. But Joe had disappeared.

A detective came to question Henry at the Red Owl Store. Luckily, it was the noon hour and no customers were in the store, because Henry had no private office, only a crammed little storeroom and the meat locker. The detective said it would only take a few minutes of his time, but Henry was feeling unhappy, uneasy, especially with the state police car parked prominently out front with another detective sitting in it. He had already talked to Hank about Joe going out before the parade and never coming back. Between customers, neighbors and the police, it seemed to Henry that he had been answering questions about Joe all week.

"Yes," he had to say when the detective demanded to know if Joe had gone outside that morning to hear Robinson's speech, the detective taking note of that fact in a little notebook.

"He specifically asked if he could go hear that speech?"

"Yes."

"Did he seem different to you that morning, was he impatient? Nervous?"

Henry's eyes flitted to the detective in the parked car who seemed to have nothing better to do than sit and stare back at him through the plate-glass window. "Not a bit," he told the questioning detective.

"Did Alaman West come into the store that morning?"

"No."

"Did you ever see him speak with Alaman West?"

"No."

"Did you ever hear him talk about George Robinson?"

"Never."

"Did he ever express any strong political beliefs, unusual ideas or violent opinions?"

"Not once."

"What do you know about his life before he came here—the type of work he did—where he lived?"

Henry saw the other detective, not content to sit outside, getting out of the car and walking toward the store, squinting in the window.

"Repeat. What do you know about his life before he came here, what did he tell you about himself?"

"Nothing—nothing. He just did his work."

The detective took a folded sheet of paper out of his inside breast pocket.

"Did he write letters to anyone in town, so far as you know?"

"Letters? God, no."

"Would you recognize his handwriting if you saw it?"

Now the other detective, who had been standing in front of the store, staring at the window, came into the store—very fast. He yelled as he put a foot up on the window ledge: "The ground beef sign!" In his enthusiasm he knocked over a stack of boxes, pulled down Joe's sign and leaped down with it. "He wrote it! He's in it!"

Henry's mouth stood wide open.

So now they had their proof that Joe was one of the assassins.

CHAPTER 44

THE WAY the candidate saw it, nothing had changed, it was merely a different way of looking at things, seeing the same substance in a different light, in that sense a kind of illumination. The public sympathy, the stream of neighbors knocking at the door, the strangers coming up to him on the street—the mountainous mail—all that aftermath that began to seem so much of a burden, necessary, healing even, and yet a burden, now was really seen to be opportunity in disguise, the challenge, almost the obligation to hear what all those people were saying and make the run for the State Assembly. Miss Brown's viewpoint helped, of course, helped a lot, considering her savvy and station and the opinions of the people she knew. Yet Robinson leaned to the notion that sooner or later he would have stepped from the shadows into this new light all by himself.

Which was not to say that he didn't consider the other way of seeing it, that in personal terms this was not the best of times to make his challenge. When he sat with Rainey, held her hand, and read her brimming eyes, he all but melted into this other point of view. Wait, it said to him, don't run now. Be patient. Ride the sympathetic wave into the next election, a mere two years from now. Run as planned—run next time. No, he decided sadly; better run now. People forget.

Like a ghostly volunteer, stuffing envelopes and ringing doorbells, reaping votes along the way, the spirit of sympathy, which insists that nothing that is wholly bad should ever be, moved across the farms and towns of State Assembly District Five, bringing hope to Robinson. In Malden, where he went to test the waters, people came up to him to shake his hand, shake their heads and vow support. Farmhouse living rooms filled up quickly at his new informal gatherings. Back in the dim beginning, people had been curious to see the man who was running against Armstead. Now they came to meet the man who had been targeted for death and whose little son had been murdered, and they came with a different intensity. Whether they had been in Jericho themselves on that terrible morning, or they heard about the tragedy from others, what made the profoundest impression on people were those three words that Robinson had uttered over the loudspeaker: "Oh my God." People remembered those few words as though they expressed the agony, the humanity, the character of the young political candidate.

People thought: "He's lost so much." Once they thought that, it was easy to think: "Maybe it's time for a change. Give the younger man a chance."

As steady as ever, Dwayne Armstead stuck to his timetable. He dealt with the challenge like the solid veteran he was, campaigning on experience and his record, appearing at a homemakers' luncheon here, a businessmen's banquet there, always finding a loyal audience, like a lion only seen feeding, never hunting. He had all the funds he needed. Beyond his Grafton stronghold, he had every advantage of the incumbent: his reputation with voters, his vaunted Assembly power, the sheer horsepower of habit. On the other side was the youthful challenger and his tragic story, a sensational story for the normally tranquil district, right in their own front yard: a bookkeeper turned killer—an attempt on the life of the young candidate—the brutal murder of his little son and in turn the death of the killer—the child's mother in a state of collapse. There were further twists to the violent story, reports of an actual death threat, a letter, and the fact that a second man was being sought, a grocer's helper, a drifter-strongman-laborer dubbed "Joe the butcher." The young candidate, who was barely acquainted with his child's killer, and had never even spoken to the second man, had no idea why there should be a political conspiracy against him; evidently there were people who feared his election. As for the existence of a written death threat, he would neither confirm nor deny. With remarkable control he told the *Daily Herald*: "As an attorney, it would not be appropriate. The case is in the hands of the police."

Now Robinson went up to police headquarters and had a long chat with Hank. At the end of it, Hank put on his badge and police chief's hat, and went and paid a visit to Rainey. After once again expressing his sorrow, Hank told Rainey that a while back a letter had come to George, that it mentioned some kind of a warning, some kind of possible harm, that it probably came from West. It was a crazy letter, Hank told her, like a note from a kid—from a crank. Hank shook his head ruefully. That short, crazy letter. Nobody could have guessed. He could tell her as a police chief that individuals in the public eye got that type of letter all the time. They had no cause for alarm. Nothing could have been done. There was no way to protect people from all the people who wrote those insane letters. Here, Hank stopped babbling. She was sitting right there in front of him, and yet he couldn't tell from her face if she was even listening to him. He put on his chief's hat, excused himself and went back to police headquarters where Robinson was waiting. "I never thought that lying could be tougher than killing," Hank told him. As a reward for his visit, Hank got Robinson's profound gratitude, plus the promise of the third cop he always wanted, a promise that Robinson as the celebrated grieving father was in a position to move the town to deliver.

Always deferent to his secluded wife and to the memory of their child, the candidate made no public reference to their sorrow, preferring to take on the larger issues posed. His message was clear—his old banner, Politics is People, pressed into new life and service. He was running to affirm the American free election process. "We will never give in to the forces of terror in our midst," he told his attentive audiences. "We will show our mettle, pass our test and press forward . . . whatever may have happened," his firm voice told their empathetic faces. "Ours is a wonderful community," he reminded them. "We were lucky to be born here, in these neighborly towns, on these fertile farms.

When we say to ourselves, go forward, we don't reject the past. We are like a family. We respect our fathers and grandfathers. But times change, yes, even for a family. New challenges arise, calling for fresh ideas and brave determination. All I ask for is the chance to prove myself. No one can predict the future—and my friends, no one knows this better than do you and I of the Fifth Assembly District, though we are only a tiny dot on the map of this great country. But when you leave this room today and go outside, take a look around you—that dot extends as far as our eyes can see. Isn't it time we took a fresh look at what is nearest and dearest? With all due respect, isn't it time for a change?"

The *Herald* played a hunch and took a survey. Its results produced a headline and left the challenger not quite ecstatic: he was only pulling even with one of the established powers in the state. But the news shook the calm of Armstead, even as he was disputing it with an overnight survey of his own. Now pursuing their grassroots sensation, the *Herald* launched a running account of the suddenly wide-open horse race surrounding Grafton and Jericho. Smoke signals floated from the Grafton camp. Word was passed that Armstead had been campaigning less than wholeheartedly in view of Robinson's family tragedy, and would understand if his bereaved opponent asked for an end to all further efforts for the remainder of the campaign. That was one tactic. Next, with the back of his hand, Armstead saluted his opponent for being able to wage a full-scale political campaign in the wake of a tragedy that would have silenced most men. Finally—announcing that he was stepping up his own efforts—Armstead demanded that the rest of the campaign be fought on the real issues, hinting that if he saw signs of an honest attempt, he might be willing to meet the challenger in a face-to-face debate.

Robinson refrained from comment on his opponent's maneuvering. To press and public he spoke in platitudes of modest hope and cautious optimism—he was the underdog in an uphill race just doing his best. Privately, he reveled in Armstead's daily wrestle with thin air. Armstead couldn't find his way out of his overalls—Armstead was an old hand trying to hold on to his seat. Thus the candidate exulted in his wilder moments, but wild optimism could turn to nervous hope and then to still more gnawing dread. Now that he could win, he had it all to lose. Was Armstead trapping him, should he rein in his campaign? Instead of sounding high-principled, should he be attacking Armstead more? Did he want to meet Armstead in a debate? They pressed each other on the smallest questions. An enormous bear-hug, not friendly, locked the two antagonists together. Each day added more weight to every move made by Robinson and Armstead.

Then one of them stumbled, made an understandable, emotional mistake, reflecting the stakes and tension of the final week before the election. Knowing that time was now against him, Armstead insinuated to a reporter that Robinson was exploiting the murder of his own child to win an election. For three key days, the Fifth District race commanded front page headlines in the *Herald*. From all sides charges and insults flew like knees rebutting elbows. At grave cost, under pressure from public officials, church ministers, statewide editorials and outraged voters, Armstead was forced to claim that he had been misquoted and misunderstood. So now, when the incumbent openly called for an eleventh-hour debate, Robinson could declare, with equal measures of anger and acumen, that he would never stand on the same platform with a man who had so lied, so vilified and slandered him.

On the Saturday night before election day, a Rally for Robinson was held in the American Legion hall in Jericho.

By eight o'clock, the enthusiastic crowd had spilled over from the main hall into the Buffalo Lounge, directly across the corridor, where, to only scattered grumbling, no drinks were to be served during Robinson's speech. In Legion Hall itself, all the folding chairs had to be taken up and removed by the beaming braintrust—several hundred places were not nearly enough. The hometown crowd stood from the stage edge to the rear door and shoulder to shoulder.

Robinson strode to the podium to a burst of applause. In the fully lighted hall, as quiet fell, the stage looked small and bare: a flag on a stand, a podium, a glass of water on it. Robinson thanked them for giving up their Saturday night "to come hear a speech by a candidate frankly asking for your vote . . . From the beginning, this has been a hard and all too eventful campaign.

By now, you must know how I feel on every subject worth mentioning. Except for one small matter, there isn't a lot to be said that hasn't been said. First and foremost, we will never yield to the forces of darkness that threaten us, whatever they may be, no matter how close to home." With that, he moved into his vintage themes, and for his audience he was not unlike the itinerant poet of old, retelling what his listeners already knew, if not a tale still a dauntless epic, a politician's stump election speech, giving them a few new lines to go with the old refrains, their hearts responding to what they knew by heart, their hero not simply invoked, but in the flesh—on the stage. After one of numerous times when they broke in with applause, at a natural breathing place, Robinson took a sip from the glass, stared down at his hands somberly, then came around the podium to the edge of the stage.

"My good friends, when I chose as my campaign slogan, Politics is People, I didn't realize what a good crystal ball I had. These last few days many people, a whole host of people, have spoken up for me, not only elected officials and church ministers, but many of you folks, so-called ordinary people. For that, I humbly thank you. But now I think it's time I spoke out for myself.

"My opponent . . . my opponent has accused me of using my own boy's death in order to win this election. Well, I won't repeat to you the first words that crossed my mind when I saw that vile accusation, or the lengths I've gone to just to keep it from soiling the eyes of Mrs. Robinson. And yet, folks, it may be that in his own cruel way, without knowing it, my opponent has hit on an important truth about this election. If he means that one senseless, violent act has made us see how precious our system is, and how careful we must be about where we place our trust, then maybe he's right that I've been helped. If he means that one family's sorrow has brought out the true colors of a powerful man who was once thought to be honorable . . . then again he may be right and I've been helped.

"Oh, you could accuse me of making this election my memorial to my son, if you like. It wouldn't be so far from the bitter truth. I don't mind admitting that I'd like to have something besides memories and snapshots, something noble, with which to remember Jamie. I don't mind admitting that when I went into my dead boy's room . . . wishing I could hold him just once more, as a wiser man . . . I couldn't see the room for my tears. I don't have to tell any of you folks about children. A dear friend of mine—he has his own share of grief—once said to me, 'They had their little toys, their little toys, and they played. We still remember their toys. We knew every word they knew.'

"So call this election my memorial to Jamie. It won't do the world any harm, even if it won't bring him back. Call any future I may have in public life a memorial to my son . . . I won't complain.

"Thank you and bless you."

They weren't content merely to applaud him—and they were already standing so they couldn't give him a standing ovation—so they started to chant his name. It began in the back of the hall where people felt boldest and soon all of Legion Hall was chanting it. He raised his arms and they responded with a surge:

"Robinson! Robinson!"

Someone had thrown open a window. It was an exceptional birth of November night. King Winter was holding his breath—withholding his blow. To Robinson's sweetened, boy-tender face, the very mildness was heady. His name was on their lips, he was their choice, victory was in the air. What lay ahead of him? Would he succeed in the capital? Would he gain power? How far would he go? What did it matter tonight—

"Robinson! Robinson! Robinson!"

THE PRINCE came.

It materialized as though by magic in the living room, above the ashes of the fireplace, on the mantle. No act of witchcraft put it there; Alpha Davis in her remorseful state had rush-ordered it for Robinson and brought it to the house herself, where Margaret Hanson, or the woman who cleaned, or someone, had set it upright on the mantle near some other books. There it stood, staring into space, waiting to be seen by Rainey when she wandered through the room. She had long forgotten what Robinson once told her it was about. Merely the title of it pierced her stillness, where it touched some still unbroken string and made her cry so despairingly that Robinson shoved it in a drawer and took it to his office in the morning, cursing Alpha Davis and the book that had been such a damned nuisance to him from beginning to end.

CHAPTER 45

SHE LIVED in a medium other than clear air—moved along a surface that was less than firm ground; fishes in a tank could have recognized her silent glass-walled little haven. Flowers, visitors, conversations, all passed before her unfocused, on purpose indistinct. That passivity that had attended Rainey the time before, when her mother and father died, had returned like an old nurse in white, to take over and care for her, get her out of bed in the morning, slowly brush her hair and dress her, and sit her in a chair. Unlike the girl of a dozen years ago, the woman bathed, so as to skirt indecency. A conventional shame was her only social sense. For that, she came downstairs to face the condolence-bearers, when what she wanted was to stay upstairs and be alone with her emptiness, so swollen she could hold it with her hands. Because speaking shared the space she felt inside her, she sat among these people in withdrawn silence. She scarcely touched the generous food they brought, as though by fasting she nurtured the lifelike emptiness.

She dressed herself all in black—even her underthings had to be black, desperate purchases made by Margaret Hanson to satisfy the craving for black against her skin. Her figure when she disrobed startled Robinson, so pale, apathetic and erotic in flimsy black; untouchable too, and as unwholesome as his lust. At Robinson's insistence she allowed Doc Sunderquist to examine her, provided it was here in the house. Doc came, found nothing dreadful, and prescribed good food and fresh air. But nothing he said overcame her first sight of him: seeing Doc she saw his examining room table. She saw her baby lying on the table with a sheet pulled up to his chin. His hair was combed, his pretty face asleep. This was her primal agony, that if only she had gotten there in time, while he was alive, the all-powerful mother, the mother tiger, the mother wren, she could have saved him.

Crying won't bring him back, crying won't bring him back, Rainey wept, knowing this but still imploring. Have mercy, start all over, send the bullet back. How many times in her mind had she retold the story of these last few weeks, and each time he and she left Robinson, left Jericho, left their future behind them; each time but the one time that mattered. Why didn't she have the courage to leave while they had the chance? Like a mouse on the doormat, a spider by the door, a frail thing that would hold back a schoolgirl, her old fear of leaving Robinson seemed to Rainey now.

Her hate for him at times overwhelmed her. It seemed to reach further and further back, nearly always to have been there, like a first hate, puppy-hate, the bitter hate reserved for broken trust. He never loved Jamie. That was the original betrayal. Signs she refused to see, not glorying in his little boy, almost the opposite, should have told her the truth, that Jamie's own father didn't love him. Then the politics, for which he forgot his son's birth-day, and that he cared so much more about that he hit him in the face, and if not for her was likely warming up to do again. And then, to find out about a letter, a warning, that somebody meant to shoot a gun—to kill. Knowing what he knew about the letter, Jamie's father, who didn't love him, who slighted him, and walloped him, took him out that morning to his death.

But as much as the letter was proof of his infamy, Rainey knew that something else, not the shock of the letter, made her freeze and hold her breath. When the police chief rang and stood in the doorway, she was sure he had come to ask her about Alaman West. Every minute he sat here talking about the letter, she was terrified he was going to ask her about West's visits, why West came there, what kept him coming back to their house? She kept waiting for that question—she had a freshly minted lie on her lips, that West seemed anxious to know all about George. The question never came; she never had to speak. The law withdrew and left her to herself. Her own small hands were none too clean. The memory of a kiss whispered to her that she had something to do with the matter too, that some of the blame was hers, by inviting West into their lives, befriending him, and maybe a little bit more, allowing him to think whatever it was he thought in those visits—to hope whatever he hoped. The wound that cut out her heart was caused by her. Whether West was crazed or not, whether the bullet went wrong or right, she was the cause. She was the reason she was draped in black—it was she.

Now her child—yesterday her mother and father. Why? What had she done? What was there about her? She grew like any other girl. She was pretty. She was sweet enough. Why was she on such easy terms with death?

And her debasement of herself would lead her by the hand back toward Robinson, as though because of it she blamed him less, or had no stamina for hate, or there might be one tug left on her bedraggled daisy love. Two children born, one gone, and she was still half-bound by the promises of her girlish past, when she and Margaret sat in backyards by the hour, painting their fingernails and having and naming their babies. She couldn't say that George Robinson just happened to come along, any more than it was possible to say that she had come along by accident for him. If not heaven, something played a part. She couldn't just call it a mistake and end it. How could she leave him now, when he was all of Jamie she had left?

Margaret came often, though never with Jimmy. She made them tea and some lunch and sat in the living room with Rainey, a woman bigger in size, in every way like a big sister. Rainey would take note that Jimmy was absent; it was the first thing she always saw about Margaret. She would sit at her end of the sofa, draped in her thoughts, saying nothing . . . *Jamie was the real boy. Jimmys could be made a thousand times over. Why wasn't it Jimmy who was dead?* . . . Rainey sipped the tea and said nothing. But now a wall slid in place between Rainey and Margaret, and Rainey was never sorry to see her go. Margaret would tell people in town that Rainey was feeling better, but her eyes must have told her that the real truth was blacker, because she began pressing Rainey for permission to ask the minister to visit. And finally Rainey nodded her head.

She had never been a great churchgoer; she hadn't seen the minister since the morning of the burial. On the day he was to come, though she had agreed to it indifferently, she waited for him with passion and dread, for the marking of death was his stock-in-trade. But the minute she saw his familiar, decent face, and heard his humane, consoling voice, she knew she was in the presence of an amateur in death, and her passion turned to coldness and contempt. There was no sorrow over his leaving the house either. No one was welcome. Jamie was welcome. To others she turned the face of her monumental passivity. She was an object in the middle of the room around which Robinson and all the others had to go. She was a stone who knew she was a stone and wanted to be a stone and got satisfaction out of being a stone and having the world take infinite pains to let her be.

Though in time she took Stephie by the hand, and shopped in stores and walked in town, she had a vague way of greeting people, talking, smiling, and yet holding something back, that spoke of her affairs being in a still unsettled state. Whenever the time came, she could leave Jericho without regret. Leaving no longer frightened her. It had become her wish. She never thought about Alaman West. It was as though she had completely forgotten him. It was as though no such person had ever known them, had ever grown to be a man, had ever spoken, drawn a breath or been born.

As FOR Joe—when he saw with his own eyes that West was dead—he fled Jericho.

As he stood watching the police swarm around the Red Owl Store that morning, Joe saw well enough that he could never go back. He knew they would find out he was West's friend and arrest him for helping in the crime, murder if the little boy was dead. Once they had him, he would break down and confess; he had never been hauled in by the police for anything, but he had heard enough stories from men who had. It was finished here. West was dead. Because of a little kid. It was a terrible thing, and he could slam West for being up there and shooting the gun. But West never wanted to shoot a little kid.

Slipping out of the crowd of people on Legion Avenue, Joe made for a sidestreet and walked hurriedly to the Violet Hotel. He went up the steps to the front porch expecting faces to turn, but it was too chilly for the old farmers to be sitting out and the chairs were empty. Joe started to open the front door, but caught his breath first and slowed down, tiptoeing in, though not a soul was in the little lobby, there was no one on the stairs, or on any of the floors, and the whole hotel seemed fast asleep. With a good headstart, he didn't think they would be after him yet, but his fear and sense of aloneness launched Joe on his new way of life. As fast as he could, he threw his possessions together and squeezed himself and his suitcase through the window in the hall and crept down the fire-escape. As he dropped past the kitchen window and hit the ground, he thought one of the old sisters fixing dinner looked up. Joe didn't look back.

He ran for the tracks with his suitcase, ran from the town and disappeared, some think by lying low all day and night and catching the sunrise freight that rolls westward across this country, a strapping, grieving man of unknown age and no known destination. They are looking for him.